she needs therapy

A CHAOS & CHEMISTRY ROMANTIC COMEDY

BOOK 1

V. BRANDY

Published by: Emerald Lion Press, LLC.

23901 Calabasas Rd., Ste 2088, Calabasas, CA 91302.
emeraldlionpress@gmail.com

ISBN: 978-1-964161-98-3

Editing provided by Sharon Lennon-Mehlschau.

Printed in the United States of America.

Visit the author's website at: www.valeriebrandy.com

Formatted with Vellum

contents

one

RODRIGO

MY NAME IS RODRIGO, *and my girlfriend is crazy.*

Before you cancel me— please, hear me out. I *know* most men who say things like this are actually the problem, or the ones *making* their girlfriend crazy. But I am a good man, and my situation is different. I'll prove it to you.

Right now, I'm standing outside a meat-packing warehouse on the outskirts of Chicago, listening to my girlfriend create what the Police will later call "a crime scene." It's snowing tonight. The air cuts through my jacket, rivers of frost lining the edges of my sleeves. I moved to Chicago from *mi bella ciudad*— my beautiful city, Barcelona— a few months ago, and my body still hasn't acclimated to the cold.

From within the warehouse— a loud banging sound. A man screaming. I open up one of the sliding metal doors, daring to look inside. Carcasses of meat hang from the ceiling on hooks. Two men stand among the swinging bodies, their arms crossed. Tattoos run up and down their arms— they're much tougher than me, but not tougher than Alana (my girlfriend, who, if you have not figured it out by now, is a huge problem).

"No enfades a esta. Tiene el corazón más frío," one of the tattooed men says, crossing his arms. He speaks Castilian Spanish, my native language. He's probably part of the cartel Alana was working with when we met just six months ago in my city of Barcelona. I didn't know it at the time, but that was the worst day of my life so far. "Do not anger this one," he repeats in English. "She shows no mercy."

I lean closer into the hole in the doorway, trying to get a better view. Just then, the dead animals overhead start moving. "Shh," the man whispers to his friend. "She's coming back. *La diabla*."

And then— Alana appears. She's gorgeous. Stunning. Dressed from head to toe in her favorite color... pink. She's wearing a puffer jacket to defend against the cold, and a beanie cap with a pink pom-pom on top. Ever since we met, I've thought she looks like a Barbie doll come to life. Her big blue eyes are a special shade of pale steel with dark centers around the irises— probably hinting at the darkness within her soul. Her long blonde hair swings all the way down to that perfect, tiny waist that's made me make some of the worst decisions of my life. God, I hate her. But she is undeniably *hermosa*. Beautiful.

I fell in love with Alana because I am a man, and she is irresistible, and I was thinking with the wrong part of my anatomy. I tend to jump into romantic encounters without thinking them through. Before you judge me for it, please understand— I am fully reaping the consequences of this decision.

"Marco wants a ten percent boost," Alana says, nodding at a man across from her, who's appeared next to the lackeys. He has a big beard and a thick neck, and he looks like an arms dealer. Most of the men Alana deals with trade in weapons, drugs, or both.

"Marco can have whatever he wants, as long as we get the uranium," the man nods.

Uranium, I think to myself. Looks like it's weapons. *Nuclear* weapons.

There's a long pause as everyone waits to see if Alana will agree to the deal, and then— she giggles. A high-pitched girlish laugh. The one that will haunt my nightmares.

"Well, like, small confession," she says, her voice a sing-songy, valley-girl timbre. "It's not Marco who wants the extra ten percent. It's *me*. But like, clothes are so expensive, and I have to buy designer. What else am I gonna do? Shop at Target and call it Tar*gét*? Way too basic."

The lackeys look at each other. The youngest man laughs. "¿Paga dinero para parecer un bastoncillo de algodón?" he says, nodding at the pink pom-pom on her beanie. *Does she pay money to look like a cotton swab?*

I cringe, leaning further back in the doorway. Unfortunately, I know something this man doesn't know: Alana speaks perfect Spanish.

Alana steps forward, a big smile on her face. Then, her leg is in the air, and one of her high-heeled feet is delivering a perfect kick to his face. His head snaps back— a knockout shot. He falls to the ground. The other lackeys stare.

"Ug, now I feel bad," Alana says, reaching down to touch her high-heeled shoe. "Not about him," she clarifies, nodding at the lackey. "Just about my shoes. He got blood on them. What a waste. Anyway, should we like, totally close this deal up?"

The lackeys move at lightning speed. Within minutes,

they hand Alana a silver suitcase full of cash. She says her goodbyes and waltzes out of the place as if she owns it. She smiles at me as she slips out of the warehouse door, pulling me toward her for a kiss. She bites my bottom lip before setting me free.

"How's my favorite getaway driver?" She says as we cross the snow toward the parking lot, where my car awaits.

"Not sure I love that term," I joke. "Getaway driver implies criminal involvement. I'm just a boyfriend giving his *novia* a ride home."

"Here we go again," she rolls her eyes and clucks her tongue. "You're so judgmental about my line of work! Honestly, what would Benny think about your attitude?"

Benny is my degenerate cousin, and he is also a criminal. He's the reason I met Alana. But we'll get into that later.

"If I didn't know any better I'd think you weren't being supportive of my career," Alana says. I open the passenger side door for her, trying not to be distracted by her gorgeous eyes. *She's a murderer,* I remind myself. *And you've got to find a way to break up with her.*

In case you're wondering, I *do* plan to break up with Alana. I just have to find the perfect time to do it. A perfect time when I'm not afraid she'll take a hit out on me, or have my cousin Benny murdered for introducing us. Benny is a loveable idiot, and I'd hate to see him murdered. And yes, maybe the perfect time would also mean a moment when I'm willing to admit I leapt into this relationship too quickly, again, like I always do. I don't want to face my own terrible patterns, and just when I'm about to leave— I make excuses for her. I tell myself that she can change. That all she needs is a different job, or maybe to go to therapy. I project the perfect woman– the kind, deep, emotionally-aware one I'd *like* to be with– onto her. But every time I think we might be able to work it out, she proves me wrong.

Keep your mind clear, Rodrigo, I think to myself as I walk back around the car to the driver's side. *Think with the right part of your body.* I've promised myself I'm going to get out of this relationship— I'm just not quite sure how, yet. We've only been together six months, but Alana has decided we're soul mates. Lucky me.

As I start the engine, Alana reaches into her purse and pulls out a folded piece of paper. "I made a new one," she says, smiling at me with an angelic grin.

Dios mío. It's another vision board. Alana's been making vision boards without ceasing since she saw them featured on an episode of Oprah. She talks constantly about manifesting.

"Now that I've manifested my perfect love," she says, pinching my cheek. "I want to manifest the perfect best friend!"

I stare at the collaged work of art. It features pictures of female best friends, ripped from magazines. Women laughing in the park. Women going to yoga together. If I didn't know Alana, I'd say it was charming. Wholesome, even. But I *do* know Alana, and therefore the collage is ominous. Like a serial killer's note left behind.

"Wha—" I stammer, horrified at the idea of some unsuspecting woman being lured into a friendship with Alana. "Why do you need *friends?*"

"Somebody's jealous," Alana scoffs, folding the vision board backup. "I need friends because it's part of my perfect life plan! Also, *somebody* has to be my maid of honor at our wedding." She grabs my thigh and I try to keep my eyes straight ahead on the road, resisting the urge to throw myself from the vehicle. "You *do* see us getting married one day, don't you?"

I glance over at her. Dots of blood from the man she face-kicked are sprinkled in her pale, blonde hair.

"A man will be ready when he's ready," I shrug, praying she'll drop the subject. "Besides, you have to find a friend first, right? To be a maid of honor?"

The truth is, I never want to marry Alana. I want to get out of this relationship as quickly as possible. But— to keep from dying— I have to play along in the short term. Still, the dream of another woman clings to me like a thirst I can't quench. *She is out there, somewhere,* I tell myself, thinking about the woman I might love. *She's just not sitting in this car.*

"You just don't get what women want," Alana says, frustrated. She leans back in her seat and turns the radio up, which is my cue not to speak anymore. Good.

I shudder, thinking about the unlucky woman Alana will choose to be her best friend. Whoever she is... she better have *sangre fría*— "cold blood," as we say in Spain. Or what you Americans call "nerves of steel."

two

BILLIE

"YOU'RE the wrong woman for the job, Billie. You just don't have nerves of steel," my boss— Mr. Franklin— says, staring at me with his watery, brown eyes. They narrow as he looks at me, as if it's physically painful for him to be exposed to my pathetic presence. Mr. Franklin is in his late sixties, and he's tough. Old school. He always tells it like it is— which is bad news for me right now. He shakes his head, then says the worst thing I've ever heard in this office:

"I can't give you this promotion."

I shift in my chair, clutching its structured arms with a confidence I don't feel. Behind Mr. Franklin, a set of windows overlooks Lake Michigan, towering floor-to-ceiling glamour screaming, "Billie, this place is too fancy for you." The whole office is like that, actually— all clean angles, marble surfaces, and high-end finishings. Everything in Franklin Luxury Developments is designed to suggest that compromise is for other people.

"You're not the kind of woman who can stand up to difficult buyers and sellers," Mr. Franklin continues. "This is Chicago, and we're dealing with multi-million-dollar real estate deals. There are sharks out there, and you're not one of them."

"But I *am* a shark! I *do* have nerves of steel! My nerves are so steely I'm practically a hardware store," I say, hating the way my voice rises in pitch. *Try to be a killer, Billie,* I think to myself. I've been preparing this argument for weeks, even sticking post-it notes to my mirror with affirmations. *You are a badass. Boss Queen.* "I handle every issue this company throws at me," I say, executing my rehearsed arguments with precision. "Scheduling, last minute appointments, proper-paperwork filing. I understand our clients, I can position our unique properties... I may only be an assistant, but I'm the *definition* of nerves of steel."

"Then why are you crying right now?" Mr. Franklin sighs.

Oh no. He's noticed the tears streaming down my cheeks before I've even clocked their presence. I resist the urge to wipe them away and try to wear them proudly instead.

"This isn't crying. I have allergies," I say. "I'm just very, very allergic to... bad news." I take a deep breath, swallowing hard.

"And you think someone who is allergic to bad news should be our head negotiator?" Mr. Franklin asks. "I'm sorry, Billie, but we're going to fill this role externally. Maybe if it had been a more introductory job listing—"

"Excellent point!" I agree heartily, attempting to seize my moment. "So maybe instead of promoting me from assistant to head negotiator, we could take a step back and just make room for me as a *regular* negotiator. Like I've been asking for the past *seven years.* Then you could give me a chance to show you what I can do."

"No," he says.

The silence sits.

"Oh," I manage to choke the word out. "I guess— okay then— I'll just go back to my desk," I grab my purse and get ready to leave, but Mr. Franklin holds up a hand, stopping me. I sink back into my chair.

"See, this is what I'm talking about," Mr. Franklin says, taking the seat across from me and folding his hands across his lap. "Right there. You gave up so easily. You're *right* when you say you do everything I need from you and more. You're *valuable*, Billie. That means you have leverage. But you don't recognize your own worth, which means you never *use* your leverage. I can't have someone out there making deals on behalf of Franklin Luxury Developments unless they understand value, and what it means to fight to the death for things that matter." He raises a hearty fist in the air as if he's cheering me on, when he's really just ruining my life. "If you can't do that for yourself, how can I expect you to do it for us? I mean, I just told you you're not getting promoted, and you didn't even threaten to quit—"

"I can threaten to quit!" I say, standing up and leaping to my feet. I catch a glimpse of myself in a gold-framed mirror hovering above Mr. Franklin's desk. There I am: caramel brown hair. Freckles. I'm in my thirties but I've always had a baby-face, and the blazer I'm wearing is just a little too big for me. I can't help but think I look like a kid playing dress up in her Mom's work clothes. Still, I stand up straighter and turn back to Mr. Franklin. "I will walk out of this office *right now!*" I say, pointing my finger at him. I let the moment rest, then— when the silence becomes too much to bear— I add helpfully, "After I file the next proposal. And answer all my emails. After all of that, I can leave."

"So, you're threatening to leave... *after* all the work is

done?" Mr. Franklin confirms before adding, "... Chilling." He lets his head rest in his hand for a second, then looks at me again— really looks at me, taking me in like I'm his disappointing niece, or a free-loading grandchild. "I see something you in, Billie," he says. "But before I can promote you, you need to see it in yourself."

The tears fall again, even though I beg them not to. I can feel my nose turning red, and a sniffle escapes my lips. *Why am I like this?* I want nothing more than to stop crying, but no matter how hard I try to pull it together, I just keep thinking about one terrible truth I've known my entire life:

I'm just... not enough.

Mr. Franklin seems to notice that I'm spiraling. He clears his throat and grabs a card off his desk.

"See, this is why we have a company therapist on site. For difficult moments like this."

I take the card, looking at the name on the front. *Dr. Rhonda. Corporate Wellness. Suite 4B.* There's a small lotus flower printed in the corner. Our company therapist. I haven't been to see her yet, but I've watched people leave her office crying. Perfect. I'll fit right in.

"Don't we also have a company therapist so you don't get sued?"

Mr. Franklin waves a hand in the air. "Details," he shrugs before adding. "Today is archetype day. Everyone who takes her personality test gets a badge to wear around the office. Go see her. I think you'll get a lot out of it."

"But I don't want to—"

"That was an order, Billie." He taps a tag on his blazer which reads, *The Commander,* then says. "The Commander. That's my archetype. Fun, isn't it?"

With that, I'm dismissed, and I start the long walk toward Dr. Rhonda's office.

* * *

Rhonda's office looks like someone asked an algorithm to design a room that makes people feel better. Everything in it is soft— soft lighting, soft colors, soft abstract art prints on the walls. There are plants everywhere. Too many plants. *How does Dr. Rhonda have time to care for all these plants?* I think to myself, pushing away the wayward leaf of a particularly aggressive fern swinging over my head. *I'm too busy trying to keep my job to keep any plants alive.*

A sound machine in the corner whirs. A small chalkboard sign on the table next to me reads: *Good Things Are Coming.*

"Archetypes can really help a person be seen," Dr. Rhonda says. She's seated across from me, a clipboard in her lap. She's warm, and earthy— pulled completely together in a way that makes the rest of us look like we got dressed in the dark, which, to be fair, I did, because I leave for work at five in the morning. She has braids pinned back from her face, glasses, and she's wearing a forest green blazer. She matches the plants.

"Everyone who chooses to partake in our exercise today will be assigned their personality archetype, and then—" she reaches to her side and produces a small stack of nametags, fanning them out like a hand of cards, "—they'll wear their nametag for the rest of the day."

"I didn't really get to choose..." I start to say, but Dr. Rhonda waves a hand in the air as if this news isn't relevant.

She opens a small bag of trail mix on the side table next to her, helping herself to a handful. "Don't worry, you'll love it," she says, tossing the trail mix into her mouth.

"Before we get to the assessment, let's just chat. How are you feeling today, coming in here?"

And here is the thing about me, about my particular curse: I am constitutionally honest. I can't help it. Give me an open-ended question and a person who seems like they might actually listen, and I will tell you things I haven't told anyone. My ex-boyfriend said I don't know when to stop talking. But he also cheated on me with a girl he met on a ski trip, so I don't give too much weight to his opinions.

"I feel like I've been invisible for years," I say. "Especially when it comes to this job. I think Mr. Franklin only sees me as an assistant because I have character, and care about other people. People confuse me being nice with me being a pushover. But they're not the same thing. I'm nice because I care about people, but that doesn't mean I can't really accomplish things! My dream is to be a negotiator. Not just an assistant. I'm meant to be *more* than an assistant. I know it. I just can't seem to get anyone else to know it, too."

Rhonda nods slowly. She eats another piece of trail mix.

"Isn't it great, though," she says, "that the company offers this benefit? Access to a therapist right here in the building?"

I look at her. "It would be better if Mr. Franklin were just nice to us in the first place, so we didn't need therapy."

There's a beat. Rhonda tilts her head slightly, like a bird processing new information. Then she writes something on her clipboard. *Oops,* I think. *I already made the clipboard.*

"Tell me more about why you feel invisible," she says.

So I do. I tell her about the first boyfriend who cheated on me— nineteen years old, six months in, and I still apologized to him afterward for "making him feel trapped." I tell her about my dad, who left when I was eight and sent a birthday card every year with a twenty dollar bill inside until I was seventeen, like the twenty dollars was doing the emotional work he couldn't. I tell her about my current boyfriend, Tyler, and how I met him right after the first one and that we've settled into a rhythm that's too comfortable to feel rewarding. And then I share the heaviest truth: that I've spent most of my life trying to prove that I am worthy — to employers, to men, to friends, to a universe that seems basically indifferent to my efforts. I confess that I'm thirty-five years old and I still can't ask for what I want without first checking if the other person is comfortable with me wanting it. I'm aware this is my problem. I just don't know how to fix it.

I say all of this in about four minutes. Rhonda eats trail mix.

"It sounds," she says, when I'm finished, "like you've been trying to be enough for everyone else. But maybe the person you most need to be enough for is *yourself*."

I sit with that for a moment. It's a good line. Annoyingly good, actually. "That's a very therapist thing to say," I tell her.

"I am a therapist," she points out.

She sets down the trail mix and lifts the clipboard again, clicking her pen back into action. "Okay. Let's do the assessment. Think of it like—" she pauses, searching for the right frame. "It's like finding a Hogwarts House, but for your *soul*."

"My soul," I repeat.

"Your soul," she confirms. "This test is a scientific window into who you are. You might have some hidden talents, Billie. And today, we're going to find them."

And for the first time in awhile, I feel a little hopeful.

The assessment takes twelve minutes. I answer questions about how I handle conflict (carefully, thoughtfully, and while composing an apology in my head), what energizes me at work (helping people succeed), what I want my legacy to be (I write: for people to know I tried really hard, which I immediately suspect is a wrong answer). When Rhonda looks at the results, she goes very still for just a moment.

"So," she begins.

"*So*," I echo, starting to imagine what kind of archetype I must receive. I couldn't help but glance at the pile of nametags in the corner. Roles like *explorer* and *magician* jumped out at me. *Maybe I'm something cool!*

"The archetype system is incredibly nuanced," she says. "And every archetype carries tremendous value within the ecosystem of—"

Oh no. My heart starts to race. I decide to cut to the chase. "What did I get?"

Rhonda turns the clipboard toward me. At the top of the page, in a font that is trying very hard to seem empowering, it reads:

THE ASSISTANT.

I stare at it. "I got... The Assistant?!" I shout. "When I literally just told you that all I want in life right now is not to be an assistant anymore?"

"The Assistant archetype is a helper," Rhonda reads, in the tone of a person reading a diagnosis at a low-key volume. "This is a person who *enjoys* aiding others in their quests. Kind, thoughtful, and empathetic, the assistant can anticipate the needs of others." She glances up at me over her gold-framed glasses. Checks my face. Continues. "Look, it's not all bad. Let's scroll down to the best roles within the company. The Assistant archetype is best suited for roles like..."

I wait. I watch her scroll.

"What?" I say.

Rhonda looks up at me. Her expression is the picture of professional neutrality, which somehow makes it worse. "Assisting," she says, glumly, and places the nametag in my hand.

I look down at it. White background. Black text. Clean, simple font.

THE ASSISTANT.

I peel off the backing. I think about my bathroom mirror post-it notes, and thirty-five years of trying to be enough. I think about Mr. Franklin and his floor-to-ceiling windows and his nerves of steel.

I press the nametag to my chest. "I'm going to wear this," I say angrily, staring at Dr. Rhonda, "But only so I can show my friend in marketing that everything I've been telling her about me *not* needing therapy is true."

"Fair enough," Dr. Rhonda agrees, looking like she wants to disappear.

I storm out of the room, glancing down at the nametag one last time. At least it's accurate— which is the worst part.

three

BILLIE

OUR OFFICE BREAK room is all clean countertops and motivational wall art. A canvas print above the coffee station reads *Collaborate. Elevate. Innovate.* The refrigerator hums. The lighting is a shade of fluorescent that makes everyone look like they've recently received bad news, which, in my case, is accurate.

I'm sitting at the small table in the corner with a bowl of cereal. It's the good kind— the kind with the little marshmallows— and I bought it specifically for moments like this, moments when the universe decides to take a running start before kicking me directly in the chest. I leave it in the pantry of the breakroom, because being kicked in the chest happens a lot here.

The nametag is still on my chest.

THE ASSISTANT.

I try not to look at it. I focus on the marshmallows.

"Oh my God," says a voice from the doorway, and then Melissa, my best friend who I call my "work wife" is there

— all eight months of her, magnificent, relentless, and very pregnant. She's wearing a floral wrap dress that somehow accommodates the full architecture of her pregnancy. Her own nametag reads:

THE INNOVATOR.

The words on her nametag are in the same clean, black font as my own, but the meaning is so very different. She points at my chest. "Is that what I think it is?"

"It's a nametag," I say, pulling my bowl closer to me.

"It's a *verdict*," she counters, collapsing into the chair across from me. One of my favorite things about Melissa is that I never have to fight to get her on my side. She's already there without me saying a word. She puts both hands on the table and leans forward. "Spill. Tell me everything."

So I do. I tell her about Mr. Franklin's office, and *nerves of steel* and *sharks* and *you gave up too easily*. I tell her about Dr. Rhonda and the trail mix and the twelve-minute personality assessment that concluded, after all of its scientific rigor, that I am best suited for *assisting*.

Melissa listens. She eats a granola bar she's pulled from somewhere on her person. When I finish, she's blunt:

"You need to quit," she says.

"I'm not going to quit."

"Then you need to march back into that office and tell Franklin that if he doesn't give you a real title and a real salary, you will walk out of this building and take every single piece of institutional knowledge you have with you, because you know where everything is and how everything works and this place would fall apart in a week without you."

"It wouldn't fall *apart*," I say, poking at my cereal.

"It would absolutely fall apart. Billie. You are the only person in this office who knows the password to the old filing system."

That's true. I don't tell her that. I eat a marshmallow.

"You owe this to yourself," Melissa says, putting her granola bar down. Then, she pulls out the big guns and says: "Not just to yourself... You owe this to my unborn child."

I look up, gasping. "How *dare* you bring my perfect future niece into this," then add, "Besides, I don't owe her anything. I haven't even met her yet."

Melissa points at me. "Exactly," she says. "You haven't even met her, and you're already setting the shittiest example possible."

I open my mouth, but for a moment, can't find the words to defend myself. Then, I say, "She's not going to remember this..."

"She will *sense* it," Melissa says, placing one hand over her stomach in a gesture that is both maternal and prosecutorial. "Babies can sense things. I read it in a book."

"What book?"

"I don't remember. I read a lot of books." She sweeps a hand toward her nametag. "I'm an innovator."

And here is the thing about Melissa's ***THE INNOVATOR*** tag— it doesn't seem like satire. It seems exactly right. Melissa has been the most creative problem-solver I've ever known since the day we met. She's the kind of person who figures out a better way to do something before she's even been told what the original way is. The tag fits her like it was made for her, which makes it worse, because mine fits me the same way.

"It's different for you," I say, and I know how it sounds

even as I'm saying it. "You got 'The Innovator.' That's a label that opens doors. Mine just confirms what I already am."

"Billie—"

"I'm not saying it to be pathetic," I say, holding up a hand in the air. That's one thing about me— you might think I'm being pathetic, but I'm actually just being factual. I take a deep breath and add, "I'm saying it because it's *true*. When you walk into Franklin's office, he takes you seriously. I walk in, and he looks at me like I'm a misprint." I stir my cereal. "It's hard to fight for yourself when you've been spending your whole career trying to convince everyone else that you deserve to be in the room."

Melissa looks at me for a long moment. Then she says, "I *am* super creative."

"I know—"

"Which is why," she continues, leaning forward on her elbows, "I can think of a million ways for you to quit this job and find a better one. I have imagined at least four different versions of your better life just since I sat down. If I can see it— if *I* can imagine you with a life where you're actually valued— why can't you?"

I don't have an answer for that. The question sits there between us, a little inconvenient, like furniture arranged wrong in a room.

"The cereal's good," I say instead.

Melissa looks at the cereal. Then she looks at me. "Is this the only thing making you happy right now?"

"Yes," I say. It's true. I love this cereal. Always have. Always will.

She reaches across the table and takes the bowl.

"Melissa—"

She takes a huge bite of the cereal, letting some milk

dribble across her chin. "I was just really hungry," she says, mouth full. "Pregnancy cravings. You get it."

"Oh," I say, thoroughly disgusted and trying not to show it. "That's fine then. You can have it. I wasn't really that hungry anyway."

Melissa sighs, then stands up— which takes a moment and involves a sound effect— and walks to the trash can. I watch, in real time, as she holds my bowl over the bin.

"Melissa, those are the marshmallow ones, don't waste—"

She drops it. Bowl and all.

I stare at the trash can. Then I stare at her. She walks back to the table and sits down like she has just made a very important point and would like me to acknowledge it. When I don't, she explains:

"You just let me *have* the cereal! And it was the only thing making you happy today!"

"But you're pregnant—" I start to say, but she waves a hand in the air.

"Doesn't matter," Melissa sighs. "I know you were trying to be kind, but Billie— you just let me steal the only thing bringing you joy in a tough moment. You assumed my problems meant more than yours. You saw me walk to the trash. You had time to get up, to grab it back, to say *no, that's mine and I want it.* But you didn't."

I look at the trash can. "I was hoping you'd stop," I say, in a very small voice.

"You were hoping someone else would make a better decision on your behalf," she says. "Billie. That's what you do. In this office."

The break room hums around us. I look at the trash can one more time. There's something quietly awful about the cereal being in there. It's not just cereal, and I know it, and I think that's what makes it land.

"I'm eight months pregnant," Melissa says, after a moment. "My back has been hurting since Tuesday. I can't sleep on my stomach, I can't sleep on my back, I can't eat anything acidic, and last week someone on the train offered me their seat and I cried in front of a full train car because I didn't know how to accept a simple kindness." She pauses. "And even in this state, even today, when Franklin sent around that memo about the new scheduling system that makes everyone's lives harder, I walked into his office and told him it was a bad idea and that I wouldn't be implementing it."

I look at my hands. The nametag presses lightly against my chest.

"You're so afraid of losing things that you don't take a chance," Melissa says. "You do it with Mr. Franklin. You do it with—" she stops, and then continues, gentler— "with a *lot* of things."

I know what she's talking about. She doesn't have to say it. My boyfriend, Tyler, is on Melissa's list of "people that need to be destroyed," and she doesn't try to hide it.

"I know Tyler's the reason you won't quit the job..."

"He can't afford our apartment all alone!" I counter. The truth is, I pay half our bills, and I'm afraid that might be the only thing keeping our relationship together.

"Yes, he can," Melissa rolls her eyes. "You told me a few months ago he could cover everything, but he's worried he won't be able to max out his 401K. Tell me, Billie, when was the last time *you* were able to put money away for the future?"

I dodge the question, because the answer is— never.

"We split equally," I say defensively.

"And the dishes?" Melissa counters. "Is he still leaving you those?"

"... I don't like the sink full."

Melissa walks to the fridge and roots through the top shelf, pulling out a can of coca-cola and cracking it open like it's the cold beer she really wishes she could have right now. She takes a few gulps then wipes her mouth. "I really wish you would take my suggestion and get into therapy. It's really helped me and Steve become the best versions of ourselves."

"Thanks," I say, pointing at my nametag. "But I've had enough of therapy for awhile."

Melissa doesn't try to rebut my point. Instead, she pauses for a moment, then adds helpfully, "Have you tried vision boarding? I have a new friend who saw it on Oprah and she says it's a game-changer."

"You have a new friend?" I ask, surprised. "Since when?!" Melissa and I tell each other everything. I'm alarmed at this new development.

Melissa chugs some more of her coke. "It's super new. I just met her a couple weeks ago at a yoga class, and she *insisted* we grab a coffee. Her name is Alana, but she was joking with me that everyone at her work calls her *La Diabla,* the devil, because she's such a go-getter." Melissa talks with the bright, cheery attitude of a kid who's found a new toy to play with. *Great,* I think to myself, *Just what I need right now. Competition for my best friend.* Melissa looks at me like she's reading my mind. She sits down and puts an arm around me. "You'll like her, Billie. She's coming to the baby shower," she adds, chewing on the inside of her cheek as if she's just remembered something. "She kind of invited herself, to be honest and I didn't want to be rude... anyway, you should get to know her. Ask her about the vision boards. It's supposed to help you manifest things," she says, completely straight-faced. "You cut out pictures of what you want your life to look like, and you—"

"I get it, I get it," I agree. "That sounds really fun. Thanks, Mel."

I stand and head back to my desk, ripping **THE ASSISTANT** nametag off my shirt and dropping it in the trash as I go.

"Think about the vision board!" Melissa calls after me.

I don't dignify that with a response. But I do think, on my way down the hall, that if vision boards actually worked, I would have glued my promotion to a piece of cardboard six years ago and called it a day.

RODRIGO

THIS APARTMENT IS SO EXPENSIVE, its mere existence should be offensive to anyone who's not a multi-millionaire.

Alana pays for it, obviously. It is her taste, not mine—the glass-and-steel high-rise overlooking the Chicago skyline, the Italian espresso machine, the white linen sofa I'm not allowed to sit on with my work boots. The view alone is the kind of thing people put on screensavers. Lake Michigan stretches out beyond the floor-to-ceiling windows like it's trying to impress someone.

I glance at my work boots, which sit unbothered by the front door. I work in construction, and before I left Barcelona, I was helping to design buildings. Alana says it's the one thing about me she doesn't like— she wishes I had a more glamorous career. Perhaps one like hers, which involves murder and bloodshed. I've never told her, but when I was a child, I wanted to be a painter. But that's something I've kept to myself— she knows I paint as a hobby, but not that I once dreamed of making it a career.

That is information too fragile to be trusted in Alana's hands.

Speaking of art: I'm sitting on a kitchen stool, watching Alana do the thing she calls "vision-boarding."

She has covered an entire wall of the apartment in butcher paper. The entire wall. It's the wall directly across from the windows, the one that catches the afternoon light, and it is now a full installation piece. There are printed photographs, magazine cutouts, paint swatches, ticket stubs, what I think is a grocery receipt, and at least six photographs of Alana herself— Alana at a dinner party, Alana on a yacht, Alana holding a very small dog that I have never met and hope I never will. She's dressed for the project in a coral-pink tracksuit that has never once been anywhere near a gym, her nails— long, squared, the color of a sports car— tapping against a glue stick as she assesses where to put a photo of Santorini.

"Do you think Santorini goes next to the Maldives, or like, more toward the Paris cluster?" she asks without turning around.

I have never been asked about a Paris cluster before. "The Maldives," I say, because it sounds like the less consequential answer.

She tilts her head, considering. Then she nods— decisive, Napoleonic— and pastes Santorini firmly beside the Maldives.

The television is on behind me, set to some British period drama. I haven't been watching it, not really, but I've absorbed enough to know there's a man at its center who does an enormous amount of staring into the middle distance. It's a look that suggests he has recently suffered a great tragedy and would like everyone in the room to acknowledge it— or, maybe, that he's recently had a stroke.

"Oh my god." Alana's voice goes up half an octave. She spins around, glue stick in hand, pointing at the screen with one pink-manicured finger. "That's Reggie."

I look at the TV. The man in question is standing in what appears to be a very tasteful drawing room, jaw set, eyes full of manufactured sorrow.

"Reggie," I repeat, wondering if I'm supposed to know him.

"Reginald Ashcroft." She says as if it is obvious. "He's a famous actor."

"Never heard of him."

"He's also a friend of mine. Like, a real one. We've actually hung out. Oh! I should add him to the board." She turns back to the wall, opens her laptop on the little step stool she's using as a worktable, and begins searching for a photo of Reginald Ashcroft.

I look at the television again. Reginald Ashcroft has now clasped his hands behind his back and turned to gaze out a window. He does this with the full weight of someone who has decided that window-gazing is his life's highest art.

"*That* man," I say, gesturing at the screen. "Is your friend? You know him?"

"Of course I do," she clucks. "We've been to some bars together. Made out a couple times. Like, don't be jealous though because toxic masculinity is not a good look."

"I don't actually care—." I start to say, but she cuts me off.

"Don't be weird about it." She doesn't look up from the laptop. "I'm only telling you because I don't want you to, like, be jealous or whatever. When I put him on the board." A beat. "Which I'm going to do. Just as a friend, obviously."

There's a kind of silence that lives between what someone says and what they mean, and I have spent enough time around Alana to be fluent in it. She is absolutely not telling me about Reginald Ashcroft to prevent my jealousy. She is telling me about Reginald Ashcroft because she wants me to feel, in the most targeted way, the discomfort of knowing she has a beautiful, famous friend I cannot compete with, and then— crucially— she wants to watch me decide not to say anything about it.

She finds the photo. Prints it. The little wireless printer on the kitchen counter hums to life.

I watch Reginald Ashcroft on the television deliver a line I can't quite hear— something with "honor" in it, probably, or "sacrifice"— and he does it with a fake sort of gravity that suggests he rehearsed it in the shower and was very proud of himself afterward.

Alana retrieves the printout, holds it at arm's length, approving of something. Then she pastes Reginald Ashcroft to the vision board, directly beside one of the Alana-at-a-dinner-party photos, which makes them look, from across the room, as if they are at the same dinner party together.

"There," she says, satisfied. She takes a step back, hands on her hips, surveying the full wall the way a general surveys a map.

I survey it with her. It's an overwhelming document of a life— her life, specifically, projected forward in the boldest, most unapologetic terms possible. Everywhere she wants to go. Everything she wants to own. Everyone she wants beside her. The photographs of herself outnumber everyone else, which seems, in some way, the most honest thing about it. I am featured on the board as well, wearing a tuxedo. Alana is pictured next to me in a wedding dress. *Dios Mío.* Horrifying.

On the television, Reginald Ashcroft stares out yet another window.

"He's a good actor," Alana says generously, like she is doing him a favor by acknowledging it.

I nod. I look at the wall. I look at the view of Chicago and the white sofa I'm not allowed to sit on.

The apartment is beautiful. The light is perfect at this hour, going gold where it hits the butcher paper, warming the photographs into something that looks, from a distance, like a life. It should feel like something, being here. The city laid out below as an offering, the skyline doing its level best. But somehow it feels less like a life and more like a waiting room I wandered into and cannot find the exit for.

But the espresso machine, I will say, makes an excellent cortado.

"I'm going to take a walk," I say.

* * *

The hallway outside our apartment greets me with a blast of fresh air, none of it shared with Alana. Marble floors, recessed lighting, a console table with fresh flowers that no one ordered— this building is like a hotel. Perfect, but not personable. That's why Alana likes it. I stand next to the flowers and check the time on my phone. It's just past four in Chicago, which means it's past eleven in Barcelona. Late enough that my degenerate cousin— Benny— will be awake.

He picks up on the second ring.

"Primo!" His voice comes through the speaker, a warm collision. I can hear the faint sound of what might be football commentary in the background and also might be an argument between neighbors— in Benny's apartment these are difficult to distinguish. "You called! I was thinking about you today. I saw a new action movie, there was a guy in it who—"

"Benny." I keep my voice low. The hallway has good acoustics, which is beautiful and also inconvenient. "I need to talk to you."

For once in his life, Benny goes quite. Benny is loud and ridiculous and has memorized the script of every action movie made between 1980 and 2005, and I love him more than almost anyone else on earth. He knows when I need his full attention.

"Ah," he says.

"¿Qué coño me has metido?" I press the phone closer to my ear, lean against the wall, close my eyes. *What the hell did you get me into*? I say it in Spanish because there's no version of that sentence in English that carries the full weight of what I'm feeling right now. "Benny. She vision-boarded a wall."

"A what?"

"The whole wall. She covered the entire wall of the apartment in paper and photographs. There's a photo of me in a tuxedo at the wedding she's planning for us! And another of a famous British actor she claims is her friend."

Silence. Then: "Which actor?"

"Benny, that is not— that is not the point."

"No, no, I know, I just—" Benny pauses, then adds, "I didn't know, cousin, when I introduced you that she was the actual *La Diabla*. I thought she merely worked for the woman, not that she was the woman herself. An unfortunate misunderstanding."

"That's an understatement," I agree.

"Has she killed anyone lately?"

"She head-kicked a man in a warehouse. I'm not sure if he made it. But trust me— the vision board is worse."

"¡Sí! ¡Es una gran noticia!" Benny exclaims helpfully. "She's in a good mood then! She could have shot him on the spot. Instead, she only kicked his face."

"I have to break up with her," I say, and then it's out there, in the hallway, between the marble floor and the fresh flowers, and it feels both obvious and terrifying at once.

"Hold on, not so fast now," Benny says, his voice trembling a little. "Let's think this through..."

"I'm only telling you because you introduced us, and she may send a hitman after you as a 'thank you' for ruining her life by bringing me into it," I say, knowing that Benny is enough of an idiot that he won't take cover on his own. "You might want to disappear for a while."

"No, no," Benny answers, and I imagine him shaking his head on the other end of the line. "*Por favor,* wait a minute cousin, now is not a good time. I am scheduled for a job this week, driving for the Twin Ledger. Let me cash out and finish the one big fish before you anger *La Diabla*—"

"There's always a new fish for you, Benny—"

"Come now," Benny sighs at me. "I can't be the only reason you stayed with her this long, no? I know you love your only cousin, but surely there is more than my safety."

I pause, letting the silence rest for a second. Benny may be an idiot, but he can be surprisingly perceptive.

"I kept thinking— I kept telling myself it would get better, or that I was misreading things, or that she wasn't —." I stop. Exhale. "She was great the first few months, Benny. She was bright, and *alive*, and fascinating. Or..." I pause, letting the truth settle. "I think maybe I projected all of that onto her because I want that woman in my head to be real so badly..."

"You're a romantic, primo," Benny offers.

"But then I got to know the *real* her, and Benny— she's a monster."

Benny is quiet for a moment, which is rare. When Benny is quiet, you pay attention.

"I want what is best for you, cousin," he says, and his careful tone tells me he is about to ask for something very difficult. "But you can't break up with her yet."

"What—"

"I'm still in Barcelona." His voice goes slightly higher. "I'm still here, primo. I have not yet left. When this job is done I will have enough money to live off of for two years, at least."

"That's a big job, Benny," I say darkly. Benny is just a driver, but he's well-compensated for transporting the most dangerous cargo.

"We will leave Spain and go to the family country house in Italy," he continues. "And you will meet me there. We will disappear together, lay low for awhile. Drink wine and meet women. But *La Diabla* always gets her revenge. She will not let go of this quietly. Do not think I'm the only one in danger. She will command a price for your head as well."

He's not wrong. It's occured to me that Alana will be so angry when I break up with her that she'll hire someone to kill me— and that's assuming she doesn't do it herself.

I rub my face with my free hand. I look at the console table. The flowers are white, very elegant, completely useless. I have never once been comforted by a flower.

"How many days?" I ask.

"Four. Five at most. I have a few things to— there are some logistics I need to—"

"Benny."

"Four days," he says quickly. "Four days, I am on a train to Tuscany, I am sitting in the old house, I am unreachable and invisible and you will meet me there, and we will be free men, together. I will owe you for this forever, primo. Forever. I will name my firstborn after you."

"Let's be honest with each other, Benny. You're never having kids."

"A dog. I will get a dog."

"Four days," I say. "Not a week. Not five. You have four days to get yourself out of Barcelona and into the countryside, and then I am ending this relationship."

"Understood," Benny says, with a genuine solemnity that says he understands he has just been granted a small but significant mercy. "I love you. You're my favorite cousin."

"I'm your only cousin."

"Still true."

I hang up. I stand in the hallway for a moment longer, letting the silence settle. The flowers smell faintly of something I can't identify, something clean and expensive, the way everything in Alana's orbit smells. I tuck the phone into my back pocket. I tell myself four days is nothing. I am a man. I can handle anything life demands of me. Four days is the length of a bad week, stretched out just slightly. I've survived worse. Probably.

I turn around.

Alana is standing in the hallway.

She's wearing a painting tarp— the kind that comes in a roll, heavy canvas-cloth, slightly translucent where it folds— wrapped around her body in a way that suggests there is absolutely nothing underneath it. She is barefoot on the marble floor. She has a paintbrush in one hand, held loosely, the bristles just barely touching her hip. Her nails are still coral. Her eyelashes are still approximately three times the length of any naturally occurring eyelash.

Her hair is down, slightly tousled, falling over one shoulder.

I freeze. *Is it possible she heard me?*

Then, she tilts her head toward the apartment door.

That's it. That's the whole communication. The tilt of a head, the faint suggestion of a smile, the paintbrush swinging gently at her side like it's perfectly casual to be standing in a luxury apartment hallway wrapped in a canvas tarp at four in the afternoon.

She didn't hear me. She's inviting me to bed.

There's nothing to say. Alana still leaves me speechless.

She turns and walks back toward the door, which is standing open the way she left it, the apartment warm and golden behind her, the vision-board wall visible from here — all those dreams, all that ambition, Reginald Ashcroft smiling from the paper in his tasteful drawing-room setting.

I follow her.

This is the part I can never fully explain to myself afterward— not the wanting to leave, which is clear and reasonable and present. Not even the staying, exactly. But the ease of the following. I think it is because I imagine Alana as someone she is not– as the woman who only exists in my dreams. Someone kind, and deep, who has eyes like caverns and can make a man feel understood.

But Alana is not a dream– she is a nightmare. I can't wait to get away from her, but I might as well make the most of the moment, no?

She is a monster.

But she does look extraordinary in a painting tarp.

BILLIE

MY BOYFRIEND– Tyler– is on the couch when I get home. He's always on the couch. I used to find this comforting— after a long day, there's something to be said for someone who is always reliably where you left them. Now, I'm not so sure that reliability and stagnation aren't the same thing wearing different outfits.

He's in his usual configuration: baseball cap backward, legs stretched across the length of the sofa, a controller in his hands, feet resting on the coffee table beside a chip bowl and an empty glass. The TV screen is full of explosions. He's twenty-nine in spirit, even though he is technically thirty-two and capable of, according to his own words, "crushing it at budgeting apps." He looks up when I come in.

"Hey," he says, with a big, easy grin. Tyler has a nice smile. I want to be clear about that. He's always had a nice smile. "How was the— thing— you were worried about?"

"The meeting with Franklin," I set my bag down on the kitchen chair. "Not great," I say. I shrug out of my coat. "

"Aw, Billz," Tyler says. He pauses his game. I want to note that for the record— he pauses his game, which is the sort of small kindness that has tricked me into staying for years. He turns to look at me, his face soft with genuine sympathy. “Come here.”

I go to the couch and sit next to him, tucking my feet up under me, and he puts an arm around my shoulder in a way that should feel good and mostly communicates care, but also carries a faint hollowness tonight.

“It’s fine,” I say. “I mean, it’s not fine. But *I'm* fine.”

“You’re the best person at that office,” Tyler says. “Franklin doesn't deserve you.”

With that, he restarts the game— and the rest of our conversation happens over the sound of explosions and limited eye contact.

“He said I didn’t have nerves of steel,” I offer.

“That’s insane,” Tyler says, punching keys on his controller. “You’re great under pressure. You handle all our bills, planning trips... You’re so good at handling everything.”

“That's what I said! But he meant it differently. He said I’m too—“ I pause, trying to locate the right word. “Accommodating. That I don't fight for things.”

“His loss,” Tyler says, and a sound from the game makes me aware that he’s just exploded a building. “You’re great. You just— you know what people *need*.”

I sit with that for a moment. He’s describing something true about me. But somehow it still doesn’t feel like what I was hoping to hear.

“If I quit,” I say, watching his face, “what would you do?”

Tyler looks at me. He pauses the game again. From his headset, I hear a series of dismayed groans from whatever invisible person he’s playing with. “What do you mean... quit?”

"I mean, if I left Franklin's. If I just— left. Took some time to figure out what I actually want." I look at him. "Could you pay the rent while I do that?"

Tyler is quiet for a second, like he's doing quick math without a calculator. "Right now it's pretty tight, and you know I'm trying to FIRE–"

Yes. I do know this. Tyler is part of a movement called FIRE, which stands for: "Financial Independence, Retire Early." He hates his job as a data analyst, and puts away extra money every month in the hopes he can quit working by fifty-five. I love that he's financially responsible. I do.

"And that works with us splitting everything equally, but if I had to do it alone I couldn't save as much. That would really impact my future, you know?"

His future. Not *our* future.

Tyler continues: "... I guess if you had something lined up, you know?"

"I wouldn't have something lined up right away," I say. "That's sort of the point."

"Right, no, totally." He nods. He picks up the remote. Starts the game again. "I just think— you know— we both have to support each other here. It takes two."

I don't say anything. I want Tyler to be happy– to retire early– and I don't want to stand in the way of that. Splitting the rent is cheaper for both of us. But I wish he'd think about me with the kind of burning passion men show for women in romance novels– women they'd fight for, die for, live for– take a *bullet* for. That's not the kind of love we have. I look at the coffee table. At the empty glass and the chip bowl and a fork that I don't remember being there this morning.

There's another exploding sound, and Tyler cheers this time. He's not worried that I'll quit my job— he knows I won't. He's not worried that I'll quit this relationship, either. Because I never do, even when I know I should.

From the couch, I can see the kitchen. I can see the pile that was already in the sink. Dirty dishes— ten plates and a dozen mugs and a spatula from this morning that I told myself I'd get to later. I've been leaving them all in the sink intentionally, waiting to see how long it would take for Tyler to get to them if I didn't do them.

The answer is: never. He'll never do them.

I think about what Melissa said in the break room. That I wait for someone else to make a better decision on my behalf.

Tyler laughs at something on the screen. It's a good laugh— warm, genuine.

I look at him and try to imagine the version of me who is not afraid, and is not the one with a big heart. Not the one who splits everything equally and answers all the emails and does the dishes before she goes to bed. I try to imagine what this apartment would look like without that version of me in it. Would Tyler still be happy? I don't know.

But honestly? I think the dishes would be a real problem.

I stand up. I tell him I'm tired. He says *sleep well, Billz,* without looking away from the screen. And I walk to the bathroom to get ready for bed, carrying something I can't quite name— not anger, not sadness. Something quieter than both. Something that has been sitting in the sink for a long time, waiting for someone to deal with it.

* * *

There's a special kind of awake that happens at midnight when the person you live with is asleep. It's not insomnia exactly. It's more like the day hasn't finished with you yet, and you have to lie there in the dark and wait for it to let go.

Tyler's breathing is even and deep beside me. He fell asleep immediately after getting into bed, in the same easy, untroubled way he does everything else. His baseball cap is on the nightstand. The room is dark except for the greenish glow of the cable box in the corner. I turn on the TV and play a television show in the background: it's some period piece with that handsome actor— Reginald Ashcroft— reciting a monologue.

I stare at the ceiling and think about nerves of steel and Mr. Franklin's watery eyes and a nametag in a trash can and a bowl of cereal going in after it.

I pick up my phone.

I tell myself I'm just checking the time. Then I'm scrolling. I do this sometimes— a midnight audit of other people's lives, which always makes me feel terrible and which I cannot seem to stop.

There's a text from Melissa, sent at eleven-fifteen. It reads:

MELISSA

Baby shower is Saturday, don't forget, Steve already tried to reschedule it with his family golf thing and I almost divorced him, so please just be there.

Then, below that:

Also Alana's coming. Be nice. She's great.

Then, below that, a single firework emoji, which I think

is supposed to be celebratory but with Melissa I can never quite tell.

I type back: *I'll be there.* Then I put a heart. Then I click out of the text and, almost against my will, open Instagram and pull up Melissa's profile.

Melissa's last story is still up. Posted three hours ago. It says *Namaste new friends!* in a font that has little stars around it, and features two women in a yoga studio. The studio has exposed beams and good natural light, which in Chicago means someone is paying for the aesthetic. One of them is Melissa, large and magnificent and wearing workout gear that I recognize because I was with her when she bought it. The other woman is a complete stranger and also one of the most beautiful people I have ever seen in my life.

She must be Alana.

She's tall, and blonde, and even in a yoga pose— some kind of impossible hip-open thing that I would have to be sedated to attempt— she looks like she belongs on the cover of a magazine. Her hair falls in a perfect wave over one shoulder. She's in a pale pink workout set, naturally. She's smiling at the camera with an ease that says she hasn't once questioned whether she should be in the room.

I tap to the next story. Then the next. Alana has clearly tagged herself, and Instagram, being the pusher it is, serves me her profile immediately.

I click on it.

I scroll through Alana's grid and I'll be honest with you — it's a lot. It's a very glamorous kind of a lot. She's in a series of pink outfits in various European cities. She's laughing on a terrace somewhere that looks like Croatia. She's holding a cocktail in front of an ornate, stone building, and the location tag says she's in Monaco.

I look at her for a long time in the blue glow of my phone.

Why can't I have a life like that?

It's not even a real thought, more of a reflex— the late-night brain doing its least helpful work.

Maybe *she* has thousands of dishes in her sink, I tell myself. Maybe she's a disaster. Maybe she's terrible.

Her most recent post is a selfie captioned: *living my best life and yes these lashes are real.*

She seems fine.

I keep scrolling, and that's when I see him. A man that is exactly *my type*– and I didn't even know I had a type. He might be the most handsome man I've ever seen.

He appears in the background of one of her photos first— just an edge of a person, standing behind her on what looks like a balcony somewhere warm. Dark hair. Strong jaw. A jacket pushed up at the sleeves. I don't pay much attention to him until I scroll a few more pictures and he appears again, more clearly this time. He's at a construction site in this one. He's wearing a hard hat pushed back on his head in a way that looks accidental and perfect at once, a pencil tucked behind one ear, some kind of architectural plan rolled under his arm. He has the kind of build that comes from actual physical work rather than a gym— broad through the shoulders, solid, a presence that seems to take up exactly the right amount of space. He's not looking at the camera. He's looking at something on the plans, one hand braced against a scaffolding pole, and the light is catching him at an angle that is honestly unfair.

I click on his profile.

His name is Rodrigo, according to the tag. His bio just says: *building things / painting things.* That's it. No hashtags.

No inspirational quotes. Just those two lines, like he knows what he is and doesn't feel the need to prove it.

His grid is half construction projects— buildings going up, beams being set, that kind of thing— and half paintings. The captions tell me these are things he's painted himself. The paintings are good. They're really, actually good. They're full of color and weight and feeling, crafted to make viewers feel the person who made it was paying full attention to the world. One of them is just hands— a pair of large, paint-stained hands, rendered in a sort of warm ochre light. I stare at it for longer than I should.

I look over at Tyler.

Tyler is sleeping with one arm thrown over his eyes and his mouth slightly open. He went to work today at a job he doesn't care about and he came home and played a video game and went to sleep in four minutes and tomorrow he will do the same thing. He's not a bad person. I need to be clear about that. He's a *fine* person. He has a nice smile and he pauses his game when you're upset, at least for a few minutes.

But he has never made a painting of hands.

I put my phone face-down on the nightstand and lie in the dark for another few minutes. Then I get up.

The kitchen is just as I left it. The dishes are in the sink — Tyler's bowl from earlier added to the stack from before. I stand in front of them in the yellow light of the overhead fixture, the one that hums a little because we've been meaning to replace the bulb for three months.

I think about Alana on that terrace in Croatia, laughing, her hair perfect. I think about a man looking at architectural plans with a pencil behind his ear. I think about Melissa's baby shower on Saturday, about meeting this new person who apparently manifests her best life like it's a hobby.

Why can't I have a life like that?

I turn on the tap.

I do the dishes because I always do the dishes, because the alternative is going back to bed with a sink full of dirty things and I won't be able to sleep knowing they're there. That's the thing about me— I know it's a problem. I know what it means. I watch myself do it anyway.

The water runs warm over my hands, and I think about the baby shower, and Alana, and her unreal lashes, and the small, creeping terror of meeting someone whose life looks like everything you've been trying to manifest without actually getting around to making the vision board.

I am nervous, I realize. I am nervous about meeting a stranger at a baby shower.

I scrub a bowl clean and put it in the rack, thinking all the while that Alana's life is probably perfect, and she never feels the rage toward Rodrigo that I am starting to feel toward my own boyfriend. The two of them probably get along perfectly.

six

RODRIGO

THERE IS a philosophy I have developed, living with Alana, about the relationship between beauty and danger. The most beautiful things in the world, I have found, are almost always the most dangerous ones. A coral reef. A live wire. A wolf in a snowfield. Alana, in a silk robe the color of a flamingo, currently winding up for her third plate.

I should explain. But first, I need to duck this flying object.

I side-step just in time: slam! The plate hits the wall and breaks into a hundred pieces, broken shards collecting next to another, similar pile.

"*¡Cálmate!*" I shout, momentarily forgetting there's nothing an angry woman loves more than being told to calm down.

"You said you don't think I'm worth marrying, and you want *me* to calm down?!" Alana shouts, this time grabbing a mug off a shelf on the back kitchen wall. It zips past my ear and shatters.

What I said, to be precise, was: "I've been thinking that maybe we should slow things down a little." I thought this was a gentle approach. I thought this was the compassionate entry point into a larger conversation that would eventually, over time, allow me to extricate myself from this situation with my family members still alive. I was wrong.

Alana grabs another mug and shoots it toward me with the speed of a professional baseball pitcher. This one I manage to catch somehow, snatching it from the air by pure reflex. My palm burns with the force of the thing. I set it carefully on the counter. Alana looks at me with an expression that says she is not impressed.

"Slow. Things. *Down*?" she repeats, in her particular sing-songy cadence. Her voice carries the same warm, airy sweetness it always does. She holds the lapels of her robe together and tilts her head. "That is so funny that you said that. It's actually hilarious. Because, like, what does that even mean?"

"It means—" I begin.

"Because we are soul mates," she continues, over me, "and soul mates do not slow things down. That's actually the whole point of them, Rodrigo. That's the definition."

"Alana—"

"I've been thinking," she says, walking around the kitchen island with careful steps, "about our future." She reaches the vision board. She taps it with one long, perfectly-manicured nail that's painting toward a photoshopped image of us as bride and groom. "I have manifested this. This is our life. We are going to get married and we are going to have friends and I am going to find my *best friend*— my maid of honor— and none of that," she turns to look at me, her pale steel eyes doing the thing they do where the dark centers expand slightly, like a cat preparing to pounce, "is going to be slowed down."

I take a breath. I think about what I'm going to say.

"I just think," I say carefully, "that marriage is a serious commitment, and—"

"Is Benny a serious commitment?" Alana asks.

I stop. There it is. The name I knew was coming, delivered in exactly the sweet, mild tone I dread. She picks up an apple from the fruit bowl and bites into it.

"Because Benny introduced us," she continues, "which means Benny is part of our love story. And I would hate for anything to happen to Benny." A pause. "He's *such* a good driver."

This is what I get for letting my degenerate cousin meddle in my love life. I cannot let Alana kill Benny because I couldn't handle one difficult conversation.

"Benny is great," I say, very carefully.

"He *is* great," Alana agrees, smiling. "So. We are staying together. And you are coming with me today."

I look at her, searching. Then, I remember: "The baby shower."

"Oh my goodness," Alana softens, her face opening with gentle realization. "That's what this is about, isn't it? That I'm taking you to Melissa's baby shower! You got cold feet because the shower made you think about commitment, and love, and children—"

"That's not—"

"Shhh," she puts a finger to my lips, stopping me mid-sentence. "It's normal for men to get cold feet at a serious event like this. I like, totally understand now." She smiles, her blistering white teeth shining at me. "This was never about how you feel about *me*! Because like, I'm totally amazing so how could you have any doubts?"

"Right..."

"Look, honey," she says, her voice sweet again. "I made a friend, Rodrigo. A real one. And today I get to be there for her, and I get to meet her *other* friends, because Melissa says there's one in particular I might really hit it off with–"

"I thought Melissa was your new friend–"

Alana rolls her eyes like I'm stupid. "She *is* a new friend but she's about to be very busy with a baby, and so I'm going to use my connection with her to meet someone that better suits my needs. *Got it?* And you are going to come with me because that is what supportive partners do." She takes another bite of her apple. "Besides," she adds, her voice dropping back into its lower register, "if you don't, I'll be very sad. And who knows what I'll do when I'm sad."

I look at the remaining plates on the shelf.

"Okay," I say. "I'll go."

She smiles. Radiant. Devastating. She crosses the kitchen, stands on her toes, and kisses my cheek in the way she does that makes me forget, for exactly three seconds, every single reason I have for wanting to leave. Then she turns and disappears into the bedroom to get ready, and I hear the sound of her humming to herself— something bright, something cheerful, as if the plates never happened.

I stand in the kitchen for a moment. I look at the vision board on the refrigerator. All those magazine women with their magazine friendships, laughing in the park, walking along cobblestone streets in each other's company. I think about Melissa, and this other friend Alana keeps mentioning— the one she hasn't met yet, the one she's saving that maid of honor slot for, the one who is going to be at this shower today.

I look at the vision board for a long time.

Whoever she is, I think, pressing my palms flat against the cold of the counter, she has no idea what's coming.

I go to find my jacket.

* * *

Melissa's house has a banner across the front that reads IT'S A GIRL in letters large enough to be read from a moving vehicle. There are pink balloons tied to the mailbox. There is a wreath on the door that appears to be made entirely of pastel ribbon. Standing on the sidewalk looking at all of this, I feel overwhelmed.

Next to me, Alana is practically vibrating.

She's changed into a dress the color of a peony— fitted, feminine, immaculate— with a pair of heeled shoes that are so pointed they abuse the sidewalk. Her hair is perfect. Her nails are perfect. She's holding a gift bag wrapped in coordinating tissue paper and topped with a bow that took her fifteen minutes to tie correctly. In the car, she rehearsed what she was going to say to Melissa when she saw her. She rehearsed it three times. I didn't interrupt.

She rings the doorbell. The door swings open.

The woman in the doorway is eight months pregnant and moving through the world as if this is something she has decided is not going to slow her down, not even slightly. She's in a floral wrap dress, hair pulled back, and her face is so open and kind. She sees Alana and lights up.

"Oh my God," Melissa says, and then she's wrapping Alana in a hug.

Alana beams in her embrace.

Dios mío, I think. Alana really does want a best friend.

Melissa steps back, one hand on her enormous belly, and looks at me.

"You must be Rodrigo," she says.

"That's me," I confirm.

She looks at Alana. "He's hot," she says flatly, as if

reporting a fact. Then she looks back at me. “Come in, come in.”

The inside of the house is warm in the way only lived-in homes are warm. Everything is slightly too much— too many flowers, too many balloons, too many small sandwiches arranged on tiered trays in the kitchen. The light is low and yellow. There are a handful of women scattered through the main room, balancing small plates. Soft music comes from somewhere. I stand near the kitchen island and accept a cup of something pink.

Melissa introduces us to her husband Steve, who shakes my hand and says, “Hey, big man.” Then he winks at me in a way that says we share a secret. I wink back, but I have no idea what secret he’s referencing.

Melissa introduces us to the remaining guests, then adds, “Remind me to introduce you to Billie when she gets here!”

“Oooh, yes!” Alana squeals, clutching Melissa’s arm in her hand. “She sounds so amazing. Can’t wait to meet your best friend.”

A new victim, I think to myself.

Melissa disappears into the kitchen, then reemerges with a stack of printed papers in one hand, fanning them out.

“Okay, so,” she announces, and immediately everyone pays attention, because she is the kind of woman who commands a room without trying, “we are doing the baby photo game. I have printed out everyone’s baby pictures— yes, everyone’s, including yours, yes you know who you are — and you each get a sheet. You write your guesses as to which baby picture belongs to which person. Whoever gets the most right wins, and you’re gonna want this prize. The prize is big. Steve can tell you.”

Steve waves a hand in the air.

There's a round of laughter. She hands out the sheets. I take one. The page is a grid of small photos— babies in onesies, babies in hats, babies making faces at cameras.

I scan the sheet. *I don't know these people. How am I supposed to guess?*

I pause at a photo of a dark-haired baby sitting in what appears to be a garden in Spain. He is wearing a tiny knitted cap and making a face of extraordinary concentration, as if he is solving a very small problem. He looks like someone I know very well.

"Is that me?" I ask.

Alana nods, her mouth full with snacks. "I called your Mom." She shrugs. "Can you guess which one is me?"

The job requires no analysis. Baby photo number seven is, impossibly, the most beautiful infant I have ever seen in my life. Perfect features. A luminous, absurd, kind of beauty that looks too old for a child approximately six months old. The effect is so creepy and jarring and strange– I'm almost certain Alana edited this photo. "Did you use a filter on your baby picture?" I ask Alana.

She slaps my arm and laughs but offers no confirmation or denial.

We mingle around the room, getting to know different guests as we begin the baby-game. During a break in chit-chat, when the group we were taking to begins to disperse, Alana leans over and whispers in my ear, "When that Billie girl gets here, make sure you don't ruin it for me. I think she might be my future best friend."

"I thought she was Melissa's best friend?" I pause, confused. "And I thought *Melissa* was your intended target."

Alana clucks her tongue. "In case you haven't noticed,

Melissa is very pregnant and will be too busy to be my maid of honor one day. No, no. If this Billie girl is nice, she'll be perfect. Melissa told me so much about her. We're going to be *super* close. She just doesn't know it yet."

I take a sip of my pink sparkling non-coffee and look at the front door. Somewhere out there, a woman named Billie is on her way to a baby shower. She thinks she is going to a party for her best friend. She thinks today is going to be normal— a little awkward, maybe, the way events with new people always are, but fundamentally unremarkable. She has no way of knowing that there is a vision board on a refrigerator in our apartment with a carefully cut-out place reserved specifically for her. She has no way of knowing any of it.

It will be too late when she finds out, and she'll be trapped, just like me.

I look at Alana. Her beautiful face, bright with anticipation, is completely sincere.

I look at the front door.

I really, genuinely wish I could warn this woman– Billie– to run away.

seven

BILLIE

I AM twenty minutes late to Melissa's baby shower, which I tell myself is basically on time in baby shower terms. I stand on Melissa's front porch for one extra second, looking at the banner— IT'S A GIRL, huge and pink and absolutely committed to the mission— and I take a breath, knowing I'm stuck here for the next two hours. Just as I'm building up the courage to knock, the door opens. Melissa stands on the other side, a knowing look in her eyes.

"Tyler bailed," Melissa says, by way of greeting.

I open my mouth, searching for a response. Melissa crosses her arms. She's in a floral wrap dress that accommodates her spectacular pregnancy.

"Tyler did *not* bail," I say, stepping inside. "He had a—"

"He bailed."

"He had a previously scheduled thing—"

"A bail," Melissa confirms, nodding, holding the door wide.

I step into the warmth of her house, which smells like vanilla and those little sandwiches that only exist at events like this. Everything is just a little too much— balloons, flowers, a stack of pastel-wrapped gifts on a side table—but in that warm, abundant way that makes a house feel like a house.

"He forgot he had a video game event," I say, keeping my voice carefully neutral. "With a friend. He's been planning it for a while."

"He forgot he had a *video game event,*" Melissa repeats back to me, in a tone that says she is storing evidence for an impending trial.

"It's fine," I say.

"Billie."

"Today isn't about me," I say, waving a hand in the air. "You can hate on Tyler later, but not today, when it's all about you and the baby." I hand her the gift I've been carrying– a bag wrapped in pale yellow tissue paper. "Here. I got the one from the registry, and also a back-up because I wasn't sure if someone else might get the same one, and also a card, and I brought the cake stand you asked me to hold at my place and I can set it up right now—"

"Billie." She takes both my hands with one of hers. The other rests against her belly. "You are at a party. You are a guest. You are not here to work."

"I was just going to—"

"No tasks," she says, steering me firmly toward the main room, where a handful of other guests are scattered with pink drinks and small plates. "No helping. No organizing. I want you to just be a person and not be helpful for two hours"

"That sounds very difficult," I say.

She ignores me. "We're playing a game," she says, plucking a sheet of paper from the stack on the side table and pressing it into my hands. It's a grid of baby photos—tiny faces, all ears and eyes and extraordinary concentration. "Baby Picture Bingo. Everyone's photos are on there. You match the baby to the guest. Whoever gets the most right wins."

"What's the prize?"

She cups her hand around my ear. "It's huge," she whispers, low and conspiratorial. "And I want you to win."

I look at her. "*Me?*"

"Yes, you, because I love you and you had a bad week. Now," she says, already pivoting. Her eyes scan the room. "You have to meet Alana." She raises a hand in the air, making a small summoning gesture across the room.

Not the woman from instagram, I think, cringing at my own blatant spying last night. I feel like such a creeper that I already know everything about her— the perfectly filtered photos in European cities, the yoga studio, and the eyelashes. I brace myself. Meeting someone so fabulous is going to hurt, especially now, when my boyfriend is being useless, my best friend is pregnant, and my boss doesn't think I'm worth a promotion. *Oh well,* I think. *Pick your tits up, Billie, be an adult about it.* Let's rip this off like a bandaid. I put on my best smile.

And then Alana is there.

She is, in person, somehow more than her Instagram, which I would have said was not possible. She's in a pink dress that's fitted, radiant, and completely without effort. Her lashes are, as advertised, real, or if they're not real, they're the best fakes I've ever seen. She descends on me with both arms open like we are old friends reuniting at an airport, and before I have fully processed that this is happening, I am being hugged by this woman.

"Billie!" she says, beaming, stepping back to look at me with a warm, assessing expression. "Oh my God, you are so cute. You look exactly like someone I'd want to be friends with. I can just tell."

I have no response to this. She wants to be friends... with *me*?

Melissa, from somewhere behind me, gives my shoulder a small, encouraging pat. Then she is gone— absorbed back into the party now that she's completed her mission— and I'm alone with Alana and a sheet of baby photos.

"I already have half of these," Alana says, nodding at my sheet and pulling out her own. She leans close. "See her?" She nods toward a woman across the room, red wine in hand, laughing at something her neighbor said. She has short, blunt-cut brown hair and the kind of laugh that involves her whole face. "Baby photo number four," Alana says, completely certain, without hesitation. "Dimple, right cheek. Same laugh."

I look at photo four. The infant in it is laughing— impossibly, with its whole face, just like the woman— and there, just visible in the crease of its cheek: a dimple.

"How did you—"

"I'm good at reading people," Alana says "Also, I may have paid her ten bucks to tell me which photo is her." She winks at me. "We should help each other. We're going to win this."

"Oh," I say, feeling a little awkward. Then, I add, "Well, Melissa said she want me to win, and I think that meant working alone—"

"She told me that too," Alana says, without even blinking. "How dare she!"

The idea makes me deflate, a little. Was Melissa kidding when she said she wanted me to win? We stare at each other. Then Alana laughs first— a bright, unself-conscious sound— and I follow, and just like that, I am disarmed. Now I'm not sure if she was joking or not.

We scan our sheets together. We talk. It's easy— easier than it should be, really, with a stranger. She asks about Melissa, and I tell her about how we met.

And then she asks: "So what do you do?"

I open my mouth. I feel the word sitting there, waiting to come out— the word I've been answering this question with for seven years, the word printed in black font on a white nametag that I left in a break room trash can: *Assistant.* I think about last night and Tyler on the couch and the dishes in the sink. And I stare at Alana, who is radiant and reads people like they're open books.

And then, for the first time in my life, I tell a *really* big lie:

"I'm a negotiator," I hear myself say. "At a luxury real estate firm. Commercial deals, mostly. Large-scale. It's—" I manage a small, confident shrug, "—a lot of pressure, but I'm good at it."

There is a pause. Half a second, maybe. Then Alana's eyes light up with an energized, recalibrated interest— the kind of look that says: *oh, okay, you're someone.*

"Oh my God," she says. "That's so impressive." She tilts her head. "I knew it. I could just tell you were smart. You have that thing, you know? That X Factor. I bet you're really good at your job."

I *am* good at my job. I hold the warmth of that a little longer than I should.

"Thanks," I say, and my voice comes out steadier than I expect. "I love being a negotiator!"

The lie comes out in a tumble– again. But for exactly this moment, standing in Melissa's warm, too-pink living room, matching baby photos and being seen— actually seen— by the most magnetic person I have ever met, I can almost believe the lie a truth.

And if I concentrate hard enough on that feeling, I can almost not hear the small, correct, extremely inconvenient part of my brain that says: *that was a really stupid thing to do, Billie.*

"I just got back from Montenegro," Alana says, switching the subject as she takes a delicate sip from her pink sparkling drink. "Before that, Budapest. Before that, Croatia. It's like— sometimes I think I travel more than I'm home, you know? Which is crazy, because I have such a good life here in Chicago."

"What do you do?" I ask, because it's only fair, after she's asked me.

She waves a hand in the air, an airy, dismissive gesture. "I guess you could say I'm in sales. Imports and exports," she says. "Very boring. Not nearly as impressive as what you do. The best part about my job though is that it led me to Rodrigo."

"Rodrigo?" I repeat, pretending not to know who the man is even though I've already stalked his Instagram.

"My boyfriend," she sighs, like she's describing a luxury item that she is also a little tired of. "He is— okay, how do I put this? He is *so* devoted. Like, intensely devoted. It's sweet, really, but I had to literally shoo him away so I could come meet you properly, because he just— he wants to be wherever I am, all the time. He's so obsessed with me it's almost annoying." A pause. "Almost. I'm thinking about marrying him. He's brought it up a few times and I think eventually I'll have to say yes. Foreign men are just so romantic, you know?

"Oh boy, do I know!" I agree, even though I have absolutely no idea what foreign men are like.

I am constructing a mental picture of Rodrigo's personality. I'm imagining that he trails after Alana like a very beautiful shadow. Maybe he does the dishes without being asked and carries her bags through European airports.

"Let me see where he wandered off to," Alana says, scanning the room with her blue eyes. "There," she says, and nods.

I follow her gaze across the room.

I want to say that I saw him coming, because I'd already seen photos of him, and should have been prepared. I want to say I had some warning, some preparatory moment where my brain did the sensible thing and noted: the attractive man you saw online is now across the room. Catalog this information and proceed with your normal, functional personality. I *want* to say that.

What actually happens is this: I look across Melissa's living room, and I see him, and I lose approximately four seconds of time.

He's over near the kitchen doorway, holding a pink paper cup that looks like it was designed for someone else and which he is accepting anyway with a kind of quiet dignity. He's in a dark jacket and dark jeans, and he has the kind of build that comes from actual work— broad through the shoulders, genuinely, specifically physical— and his hair is dark and his jaw is— I mean. His jaw is a *situation.* Carved like a statue. I know immediately, with the full-body recognition of someone who spent twenty minutes on an Instagram profile at midnight, that this is the man from the construction photo.

He is so much more handsome than his photos– exponentially more alarming in person.

Alana lifts a hand and waves at him. He sees her. He crosses the room.

"Rodrigo, this is Billie," Alana says, with the bright, proprietary warmth of someone introducing two things they own. "Billie is Melissa's best friend. She's a head negotiator at a luxury real estate firm. Isn't that incredible?"

Rodrigo looks at me. His eyes are dark and steady and give absolutely nothing away. He nods. "Hey," he says.

That's it. That's the whole thing. *Hey.*

"Hi," I say. I smile. I am aware that I am smiling slightly too much, which is something I do when I'm nervous.

"Rodrigo's in construction," Alana offers, looking at him with affectionate, performative exasperation. "He builds things. He also— tell her about the painting, Rodrigo."

"It's just a hobby," he says.

"He's incredible," Alana says to me. "He paints these gorgeous—"

"It's just a hobby," he says again. Firmly, but not unkindly. He's looking at a point slightly to the left of me, like he has been brought to a party against his will and is processing his options.

There's a beat.

"I love that," I say, because I always try to fill the silence when the other person won't. "The combination of building and painting. Like— making things in different ways. You must be a creative person."

He looks at me. For exactly one second, something shifts in his expression— a small, genuine thing, quick as a blink, like a light catching briefly in a window. Then it's gone.

"Whatever you say," he says.

Alana links her arm through mine as if it's something she's done a hundred times. "I'm going to drag Billie to a yoga class with me," Alana says the words as if she's making a decision.

"I've never done yoga but I'd love to try it–" I start to say, but Alana interrupts me and continues filling Rodrigo in on a plan she's made entirely without me.

"I'm going to take Billie to that yoga place I like in the West Loop, which is so close to us."

"Sounds fun," I say, hoping I'll be able to keep up.

"We should all go," Alana says, looking at Rodrigo.

"I don't do yoga," Rodrigo says.

"He doesn't do yoga," Alana confirms to me, as if this settles something. "But Billie and I can go, right? Like, a girls' thing."

"Totally," I agree. "Although I've never done yoga so I might end up in Rodrigo's camp and decide I don't like it if I'm terrible at it."

Rodrigo looks at me properly for the first time. I think for a moment that something is going to happen— that we're going to have an actual conversation. Then: "Maybe you shouldn't go to yoga. Especially if you know you won't be any good at it. *No te vayas.*"

I blink. "I— what?"

"I think you might be too busy," Rodrigo says. "With work."You said you're the head negotiator. Commercial deals. That is many hours, sí?

"I can make time for—"

"You'd probably be better off," he says, quietly, not unkindly but certainly conclusively, "sticking to your own friends and not making new ones."

There's a silence. It's not a long silence, but it has weight in it.

Alana doesn't seem to notice how uncomfortable things have gotten. She's already spotted something across the room— Melissa opening gifts— and she squeezes my arm. "Oooh I have to explain something about my gift to

Melissa! It's a baby rattle from France— I'll be back— Don't go anywhere. We have to finish our baby sheets." And then she's gone, and I am standing next to Rodrigo, and neither of us says anything for a moment.

He takes a sip from his pink paper cup.

"Did you hear what I said?" he says, in a tone that is polite and absolute.

I blink, trying hard to believe this is actually happening.

"You told me... not to make new friends?" I ask helpfully.

Rodrigo nods. "Good," he confirms. The silence settles between us.

"You're a real talker, aren't you?" I say, shaking my head at him. I put my hand in the air in a "stop" signal. "Hey now, don't say so much all at one time! I can barely keep up."

He makes a pained expression at me, then says, coldly:

"Perhaps you should go back to your game."

He's so cold. Almost... angry. Did I do something to make him mad before I'd even met him? *What a jerk,* I think.

I look down at my baby sheet. I look at photo five— the dark-eyed, serious infant with a mop of brown hair on his head. Begrudgingly, I write "Rodrigo (rude man)" next to it. I flip the paper over and show it to him.

"Were you this unhappy when you were a baby, or did it develop over time?"

He stares at me. I don't know what's come over me. It's been a rough week, and maybe being treated like I'm garbage by this insanely attractive man is my breaking point? Who can say. All I know is: Rodrigo is rude.

And I can't stand him.

RODRIGO

I'M REELING. The room is spinning. The air has left my lungs.

I should tell you that I was not affected. This is important to me. I *want* to tell you that I looked at that woman— Billie— across Melissa's baby shower and registered nothing. That I filed her away as another guest, another name, another woman holding a pink paper cup. I *want* to say that. I cannot say that, because it would be a lie, and whatever else I am, I am not a liar.

So here is the truth:

Billie is beautiful.

Not in the way Alana is beautiful, which is a dangerous, weaponized kind of beauty— the kind that hits you between the eyes before you've had time to raise a defense. No. Billie is beautiful like water in a desert. Softer. Unguarded. She has this face that is— I am going to sound ridiculous, and I accept the consequences— she has the face of someone you want to tell the truth to. Big, dark eyes with these gold flecks in them, genuinely harmless and deeply perceptive. She reminds me, immediately and entirely against my will, of a baby deer. A bambi. It's not an insult. I mean it as a compliment. There is something about this woman– Billie– that makes me want to keep her safe— but then— she has a strength in her.

She doesn't know she has it. I can tell she doesn't know, which is somehow the most alarming part of all. It's there in the way she straightens her shoulders when she's uncomfortable, and in the way she makes statements into questions. But she's funny and ironic, and all of this—

All of this is a problem.

Because I know exactly what Alana wants from her. I have seen the vision board. I have spent the last three months watching Alana construct her perfect life like a military operation. And I cannot stop what Alana wants. No one can stop what Alana wants. But I can make myself useful in the one small, stupid way that is available to me right now.

I can make Billie Harper dislike me, and by proxy, perhaps, dislike Alana.

This is what I tell myself as Billie looks at me with those bambi eyes and asks, "I mean, I'm seriously asking, have you *always* been this rude, or is it just to me?"

My eyes blink open and shut. *She believes I am being rude,* I realize. My plan is working. She does not understand what I am saving her from.

"I cannot explain—" I start to say, but she cuts me off.

"I mean, I'm a total stranger to you and you're acting like I'm some horrible person!" She stands, her cheeks turning red. "Did I do something to *offend* you, or do you just not want your girlfriend to make new friends?" She crosses her arms, and I know immediately I am in enormous trouble. Excellent. "Maybe you're the controlling type?"

Oh no, I think. This woman— Billie— is most worried about Alana's safety when in fact she should be considering her own. But there's no way for me to tell her the truth without putting her in more danger. Instead, because I cannot think of anything else to do, I reach out and take her hand in mine. I want her to understand. I wish I could explain all of it to her, but instead— I take her hand. She freezes, then melts a little. She is so close to me I can feel her chest moving up and down as her breath quickens. I lean toward her and whisper as gently as I can, "Be careful. That's all."

Time slows down. I am so close to Billie. Her perfume smells like vanilla and oranges. There is something electric in the air, and I could stay here for days. Her hair falls gently over her cheek as we separate, but my hand is still on hers and I do not want to let go.

From across the room, I feel Alana's gaze land on us. I don't look over.

I shouldn't have done that, I think, aware once again that I am standing too close— to Billie.

I let go of Billie's hand and keep my posture neutral. I take a measured sip from my cup.

Billie clears her throat. "Alana mentioned you paint," she says, her voice suddenly very formal. "What kinds of things do you—"

"It's just a hobby," I say. It isn't safe to let Billie know me more. If she knows why I paint she might like me, and I am determined that she should hate me, and thus stay away from Alana.

"No, it's not," Billie says with so much intensity I'm taken off guard. "People don't paint just for something to do."

"Why do *you* think people paint, then?" I say, keeping my voice even as if I don't care what the answer is.

"I think people paint because they want to imagine a world that's beautiful." She looks at me in such a way that I swear she is seeing straight through me. "Because they want to make the world better, or more bearable. I think painting is a way to take what you see in front of you and realize what's wrong with it, then use all the pieces to create something better. Something that only exists in your imagination that you can finally bring to others. Painting is wish fulfillment."

My mouth opens, but no words come out– I'm speechless. I'm struck by the desire to pull this woman close to me again. *She is wise, and gentle,* and just as I'm thinking of all the ways I would want to be near her, if I weren't currently dating—

This is the moment Alana materializes beside me, linking her arm through mine with the easy, claiming precision of a woman who has done an inventory of the room and is now collecting her assets.

"Okay, so I have a strategy for you," she says to Billie, as if she's been thinking about this for some time. "You need to just ask people outright which baby picture is theirs."

That's right, I think. *The baby pictures.* I had forgotten all about the game.

"Walk up to someone, point at the sheet, and go— 'Hi, which one is you?'" Alana continues. "Everyone thinks they're the kind of person who'd recognize themselves. They love the chance to confirm it."

Billie shakes her head. "That's— isn't that cheating?"

"Completely," Alana says, absolutely delighted. "That's why it works. People never expect dishonesty at a party."

I watch Billie consider this. I watch the small, genuine

smile settle on her face. She excuses herself— graceful about it, warm, like she doesn't want to be rude even when she's walking away— and crosses the room toward a woman with short hair and a stern face.

Alana squeezes my arm and tilts her head up toward me with a private, proprietary smile.

"I love her," she says, watching Billie go. "Don't you love her?"

I watch Billie approach the disgruntled woman, pull out her sheet, and— I can see it from here— simply ask. The woman lights up. Points to her photo. They both laugh. Billie's smile is breathtaking.

I think I might love her, I want to say jokingly, but I work hard to keep the smirk off my face, which is the face of a scoundrel. Billie is gorgeous. And she needs to stay far away from me.

"She seems fine," I say.

Alana narrows her eyes at me, reading something in my voice. Then she lets it go— stores it somewhere, files it under: deal with this later— and turns back toward the room.

I look at the baby game sheet in my hand. I don't look at Billie Harper again. This requires more effort than it should.

* * *

Later, Melissa announces the game results from the center of the room. Everyone stops what they're doing. The room adjusts to her.

"Okay," she says, sweeping the stack of submitted sheets. "I've tabulated the results." A pause. "It wasn't close," she adds.

The winner, of course, is Alana.

Alana does not look surprised. She holds one hand to her chest and makes a small, delighted sound, as if the universe has done something considerate. I've seen this performance before. Alana is always surprised by exactly the things she engineered.

"She absolutely cheated," mutters the woman with the dimple, though she's laughing when she says it.

"I used strategy," Alana corrects, with absolute serenity.

Across the room, I catch a small, startled smile on Billie's face. She is, I notice, also holding a game sheet with significantly more correct answers than she walked in with — a fact she seems to be quietly deciding to keep to herself. Good for her. She doesn't want to win through cheating. I bet she tried Alana's way and felt too guilty to submit her paper. My heart swells with understanding— I, too, have done things Alana's way, only to feel regret later.

"And the prize," Melissa announces, a tone of pride in her voice, "is courtesy of Steve's company."

Steve materializes from the back of the house, and I will say this for Steve: he commits fully to the moment. He is beaming, and I can tell he's been waiting to do this for two hours. Behind him, the hallway contains something large, wheeled, and decorated with an enormous pink bow.

It is an electric scooter.

It is not a small one.

"We just launched the Mark IV," Steve says to the room. "Goes up to twenty miles an hour, self-balancing technology, app-controlled speed limiter—" a meaningful look at his wife— "though I've already disabled that." He winks.

There is a beat in the room. Then a sound that I can only describe as the collective processing of twenty people realizing the prize they've missed out on is much nicer than a scented candle.

Alana claps her hands together once. She looks absolutely delighted. "I'm like, going to go so fast!" she says to no one in particular.

I think about Alana on an electric scooter moving at twenty miles an hour through Chicago. She will, no doubt, run over a few small children and forcibly remove car side mirrors. The idea is horrifying. I decide not to think about it further.

From the other side of the room, Billie turns to Melissa. I am near enough to hear it. She keeps her voice low, but not so low that it doesn't carry a little, and she says, with a flat, honest delivery: "Just how rich *are* you guys?"

Melissa looks at her. "We're treading into 'it's starting to get embarrassing' territory," she says, narrowing her eyes.

"You got an electric scooter at your baby shower," Billie says.

"Wait until you see the one Steven is building for the baby," Melissa answers.

Something about this— the precise, baffled economy of that exchange between them— makes me laugh. Billie isn't just beautiful— she's funny. I press my palm against the kitchen counter, reminding myself my goal is to make sure this woman stays away from me.

The party begins to wind down in the comfortable, slow way of parties that were good. People retrieve coats, trade numbers, give their departing comments: this was so fun, you're going to be such a wonderful mother, call me if you need anything. The room gives up its warmth gradually, guest by guest, until there are only a few of us left standing in the yellow light.

Alana finds Billie.

I watch her do it from across the room, and I want you

to understand: watching Alana befriend someone is one of the more alarming things I have ever witnessed. It looks so effortless. It looks so genuine. And I know what Billie's thinking, because Alana did this to *me* once. Billie doesn't know she is a target in the crosshairs— and neither did I.

Alana crosses to Billie and descends on her with both arms open, and Billie— Billie goes right into it, because of course she does, because who could help it— and they are hugging for a long moment while Alana says something low and warm into her ear that I cannot hear from here. Then she steps back, holding Billie at arm's length, beaming. "Yoga," she says. "Tomorrow morning. West Loop, right? What time works for you?"

"Eight o'clock?" Billie asks.

My heart sinks. *I have failed.* They're becoming friends.

"Perfect. I'll meet you there." Alana squeezes her hands. "I'm so glad Melissa has you," she says, and she means it, I think, which is the most complicated part of all of this. Alana means everything she says in the moment she says it. That's what makes her so dangerous. "I feel like I've been *waiting* to meet you."

Billie's face does something I am not equipped to look at directly. It softens— fully, without defense. There is something in her expression that says she is not used to being told she was waited for.

I look away.

Near the door, Melissa is watching all of this. She has one hand resting on her belly, and she is smiling— because Melissa is generous enough to smile— but it is a slightly smaller smile than the one she's had all evening. It's the smile of someone who has just watched their best friend be recruited by someone new, and who is choosing— because she loves her best friend— to be glad about it instead of whatever the other thing would be. I wonder if Melissa knew this would happen. Maybe she hoped for it, in a way — that these two would hit it off. She's eight months pregnant. Her life is changing. Her best friend is making plans with someone else for tomorrow morning, and nobody invited her.

I understand this, I think. More than I'd like to. Alana made me feel this feeling often when we first started dating — that I am only lucky to be in her orbit.

When Alana comes back to collect me, she takes my arm and steers me toward the door, pausing to say goodbye to Melissa with another enormous hug, and I shake Steve's hand, and then we are at Billie, and I nod. That's it. Just a nod— the most minimal possible gesture of leave-taking.

Billie looks at me. There's that question again, the one she keeps deciding not to ask. It sits in her eyes for exactly a second, then she looks away and says something warm to Alana, and that's the last I see of her face as we step out the front door.

The cold hits me like a hand. Alana is already talking. We make our way to my car— wheeling Alana's new scooter behind us— and I'm so lost in thought that I'm only catching every other word. By the time I've adjusted the mirrors and fastened my seatbelt, Alana is already deep into what I can only describe as a keynote address. She has not, as far as I can tell, taken a breath since we left Melissa's porch. The electric scooter is in the back of the car, partly disassembled, wearing its pink bow at a defeated angle. I ease us out onto the street.

"—and Billie just has this quality, you know?" Alana is saying. She's got her legs folded under her in the passenger seat. "Like she's so warm. She's just such a nice person. But not in a boring way. In a way where you actually *feel* something when she's nice to you."

"Mm," I say, which is my contribution.

"And smart," Alana continues. "I mean, a head negotiator. She's not just pretty, she's substantial. That's the thing. I need a friend who's substantial. Someone who gets it. She matches my vision board perfectly. That's the kind of friend I deserve." She pauses, and I take this as an invitation to respond, but before I can, she adds, "And her eyes, Rodrigo. Did you see her eyes?"

This is a trap, I think. *Do not fall into the trap.* But of course I noticed Billie's eyes. They're impossible to miss. They are dark, like the night sky, with flecks of hold patterned throughout, an infinite fractal around her irises.

I keep my gaze on the road. Straight ahead. The light at the intersection turns yellow. I brake early.

"I wasn't paying attention," I say.

Alana makes a sound that says she does not believe me. She doesn't pursue it. She goes back to her keynote. "I think Billie is exactly what I've been manifesting for a maid of honor. Like, exactly. She'll look so cute standing next to me, but also won't overshadow me. Perfect balance. Did I show you the vision board section for best friend energy?"

"It takes up our entire *wall,*" I say, shocked that she has no sense of scale. "How could I miss it?"

"Well, Billie is in it. There's a model who looks like her in one of the pictures, almost exactly. She fits my plans just right."

I think about where Alana's plans tend to lead.

I have been in warehouses in Barcelona and a parking garage in Zurich that I am not going to describe here because the statute of limitations may not have run out yet. I have watched Alana make decisions about people, and I know as someone who has been along for too much of this that the world Alana moves through is not safe for a woman whose face is like a baby deer.

Billie Harper's face is open, and kind. I could see this within approximately two minutes of meeting her. She has the kind of face that belongs on a person who tells the truth at inconvenient times and believes, still, against all available evidence, that things will work out if you are simply good enough to people for long enough– even when they don't deserve it.

This is not the face you bring to uranium warehouses.

"We're planning yoga tomorrow," Alana says, "and then next weekend I want to take her to dinner. Somewhere nice. And then I want to bring her to Budapest."

"No," I say, my heart racing.

Alana looks at me. "You haven't even—"

"Budapest?" I say. "Where you're going to be for *work?* No. Billie doesn't belong in that world. Don't you dare."

She studies me for a moment.

"We'll see," she says, which is not the same as agreeing with me. We both know this.

I think about Billie. I think about what I could do. What would a warning even look like? I play it out. I imagine pulling Billie aside somewhere— maybe calling the number I don't have and wouldn't know how to get— and I imagine saying: that woman who wants to be your best friend? She sells weapons to people you don't want to think about. She kicked a man in the face in a meat-packing warehouse last week for making a joke about her hat. She has a vision board on our wall with a spot cut out specifically for you. She will use you for her own selfish purposes, then throw you away the minute you need her most.

I imagine the way Billie would look at me if I told her.

Those eyes. The gold flecks. She'd probably ask me to repeat myself.

And then— and this is the part that gets me— I think she might actually believe me. There is something in her that doesn't flinch from truth. I sensed it in the twelve minutes we spoke at that party, in the way she kept her voice level when I was cold to her, in the way she watched me with that patient, considering look that said: I see you doing a thing and I am choosing not to name it yet. She'd probably believe me, and then she'd have a whole new set of problems— problems that involve knowing things about criminals, and knowing them about Alana specifically, which is its own category of dangerous.

So either Billie *doesn't* believe me, and I look like a lunatic, and Alana has me handled within the week. Or Billie *does* believe me, and I've handed her a problem worse than the one I was trying to save her from. Both roads go somewhere bad.

I drive.

Alana finishes her summary of Billie's virtues, cycling naturally into a new topic— something about whether the electric scooter will fit in our storage unit.

Chicago moves past the windows in its winter way— a grey and amber blur of storefronts and streetlights.

I think about a woman named Billie Harper driving home right now— to wherever she lives, to whatever apartment, to whatever version of her life she came from tonight. She went to her best friend's baby shower. She played a baby picture game. She made a new friend who hugged her like she meant it and told her she'd been waiting to meet her, and she went home smiling, probably, from an evening that turned out better than expected. She has no idea what she's mixed up in.

And I can’t tell her.

nine

BILLIE

THE YOGA STUDIO Alana's invited me to is exactly the kind of place I'd expect her to choose. It's beautiful, obviously— exposed wooden beams, enormous windows, and a succulent at the front desk that's thriving to such a degree it looks fake at first glance.

I'm carrying my yoga mat I overnighted from Amazon in a rolled bundle under one arm. I'm wearing my only pair of leggings, and I've just discovered a hole in the right leg.

Then Alana walks in, and I get a glimpse of what "athleisure" looks like when done right.

Her mat is a deep blush pink and has a matching carrying case that's monogrammed and zipped. Her workout set— coordinated from crop top to high-waist leggings— features a repeating pattern of moons and stars. She has a small gold ring on her right hand. She's radiant.

"You look great," she says when she sees me. She says it with full conviction, no performance— I almost believe her.

"Your mat has a monogram," I say dumbly.

"*Everything* should have a monogram," she answers with a wink.

I offer to pay at the counter, but Alana waves me away. "This one's on me," she tells me. Then, she turns to the woman behind the counter, "You can just charge both our reservations to my account." The woman winks at Alana as if she does this often for her.

She's treating me to free yoga? I think. She must... really like me.

We collect our spots near the middle of the room and unroll our mats.

"I started coming here because of Oprah," Alana tells me, settling cross-legged on her mat and reaching her arms up into a stretch with the casual ease. Her body does what she asks it to, and I wonder what that feels like. "Oprah does yoga. Did you know that? So, obviously."

"Obviously," I say, not even sure what I'm agreeing to.

"However," Alana continues, pressing one hand flat to the floor and tilting her torso sideways in a stretch that extends her whole ribcage, "her down dog is a little shameful. Like, I was behind her in a class in Los Angeles once, and I was shocked." Alana takes a beat to stretch her other arm then adds. "This yoga studio is actually where I met Melissa. A few weeks ago, but it feels like years! She was doing this exact class and we just started talking and she's incredible, right?"

"She's my favorite person," I say.

"She's one of mine too," Alana says, simply. She draws one knee across her body and holds the stretch, then looks at me again. "Which is actually why I wanted to bring you here. I think we could be really great friends, you and me. I felt it yesterday." She releases the stretch. "And also— I'm going to be honest with you, because I feel like you're someone who actually appreciates that— once Melissa has this baby..." She opens her hands in the gesture of someone presenting an obvious but unavoidable truth. "She's not going to have time for either *one* of us the way she does now. You know?"

A tight feeling grips my chest, and I want to shout "*Of course I freaking know*!" My first reaction when Melissa told me she was pregnant was "oh my gosh, I'm so happy for her and I can't wait to meet this child" But as the months went on, I started to realize: I'm going to see less of my friend. And she'll make new "Mom friends" who have babies of their own. It would be a lie to say I haven't wondered if there will still be room for me in all of that. It's a selfish question, but I've been asking it just the same.

"She'll still be around," I say, which is what I say to the part of me that is afraid.

"Of course," Alana agrees, easily. "But it'll be *different*. That's all I mean. So we should be each *other's* people too." She looks at me across our two yoga mats— hers monogrammed, mine the cheapest one I could find— and her expression is open and genuine. "Just because, like, Melissa has found her happiness. We're allowed to find our own. Like, everybody has to do what's right for them, you know?"

The instructor arrives before I figure out what to say to that. The room settles.

For the first twenty minutes, I hold my own. I know a few of these poses. My warrior two is acceptable. My tree pose wobbles.

Then I look over at Alana.

She is in a backbend so complete that her hands are flat on the floor behind her head and she is simply— hovering there, suspended, chest open to the ceiling, without any apparent effort. Her expression is serene. The instructor passes her and makes a small sound of appreciation. Alana is not showing off. She is just *doing* this, like she's an acrobat or a cirque du soleil performer.

Somewhere around the advanced flow sequence, she transitions from the backbend through a movement that is — there is no other word for it— a back*flip*. A single, controlled, unhesitating backflip, smooth as a breath, landing without sound. Two people nearby actually stop to look. The instructor tilts his head in a gesture that says he is deciding how to feel about this.

I am still in a forward fold. I have been in a forward fold for some time because I am trying to touch my toes, and the distance between my fingertips and the floor is the distance between California and Alaska. *Why don't I find time to stretch at night?* I ask myself, cursing the hours spent watching reality tv shows after work instead of getting more limber.

When the instructor calls us back to center for the final resting pose, Alana drops immediately into savasana, arms loose at her sides, eyes closed. She appears to have achieved the kind of complete bodily peace that I have been chasing since I was twenty-two.

I stare at the ceiling. Soft snores echo beside me. Alana is so relaxed she's fallen asleep. *She's so relaxed about this class she's taking a nap.*

Class ends. Alana's mat goes back into its monogrammed case. We walk out into the grey November morning together, and Alana is laughing at something before we've even hit the sidewalk— some small observation she makes about the man who fell out of his tree pose directly into the person next to him— and I am laughing too, easily, genuinely, before I've decided to.

I think: *I like her enormously.* Maybe it's okay that I can't do a backflip. Maybe this is what it looks like to finally find someone who thinks you're worth showing up for at eight in the morning. Plus, Melissa is going to be busy with the baby soon, and— like Alana pointed out— I need to find my happiness, too. And if it's as simple as having a friend to do yoga with early in the morning, so be it.

I don't think anything past that. I *should* probably think past that.

But I don't.

* * *

Later, we get burned hash browns and eggs at a trendy diner down the street with black and white checked floors. It's way too expensive for what they're offering, but the chandelier is made of gold leaf, and there's a neon sign on the wall that says "*People are the best thing that can happen to anyone,*" so I figure we're paying an ambiance tax.

We have a small corner table. There are two mugs of coffee. We are, I realize, having a very good time.

Alana's talking about Rodrigo, and I'm embarrassed that hearing his name makes my heart beat a little harder for a second. *You're not allowed to be attracted to your new friend's boyfriend,* I remind myself. I shake the feeling off immediately. He's taken by someone I'm starting to consider a friend, and also— he's an asshole. My heart shouldn't flutter for him at all. Besides, it sounds like he's driving Alana a little crazy, and I don't need that kind of drama in my life anyway, even if it comes with a sculpted jawline.

"Oh, and he leaves his paintbrushes in the sink in this little coffee mug," Alana says, taking another bite of her omelette. "Rodrigo's like, crunchy on the outside and soft on the inside. He looks all tough because of the construction stuff, but his personality is all mush. I seriously don't know what he'd do without me." She pauses. "He annoys me though. Like now he keeps talking about he might have to go home for a construction job for a little bit. Like, some work thing. Which would be totally fine!" She puts her arms up in the air defensively. "But it's like... he's *so* needy and then just tries to get my attention with stuff like this. Sometimes I honestly think I could just kill him." She laughs as if the idea is preposterous.

"You're lucky you have someone who likes you so much," I say, staring into the abyss of my coffee.

"Like, yeah, I guess," Alana shrugs. "But he keeps talking about this construction job in Spain in a way that's just driving me nuts," she continues, shaking her head. "Back in Barcelona, apparently. He keeps mentioning it like it's just this thing he *might* do— like it's nothing— when I'm over here trying to plan our wedding. It's neglectful honestly."

I look up from my glass. "You guys are engaged?" My heart almost stops, and I mentally remind myself to breathe. I'm not supposed to care. He's practically a stranger. But for some reason— I *do* care.

She makes a face. Not an offended face, but one that looks like it's considering a proposal. "Not yet," she says. "But I know it's coming. He talks about our future constantly. Marriage, the whole thing. He's basically desperate for it. It's very sweet." She tilts her head. "But then in the same breath he's talking about going back to Spain for a job! Which would mean he's away for months. Right when I need him present for all the planning," She exhales, the exhale of a project manager whose contractor has gone off-grid. "Men," she adds, as a conclusion.

I absorb this. I nod. There is something in the spinning

of this story— the man who talks about marriage constantly, who is also obliviously planning an extended absence during the wedding planning— that I can't quite square with the Rodrigo I met yesterday. But then again, I've been wrong about people before. I have been wrong about people in ways that have cost me considerably.

"What about you?" Alana asks, and the way she asks it is direct and gentle at once, the way a person asks who actually wants to know. "You mentioned your boyfriend Tony—"

"Tyler," I correct her.

"Sure whatever, like, Tyler. You mentioned him yesterday. How long have you been together?"

The words pour out of me because my heart has been breaking lately, and— in an effort not to overwhelm people close to me, like Melissa— I've been trying to keep the whole picture to myself. But I tell her everything. I keep the facts about work vague— I keep up the lie and say only that I'm head negotiator and it looks like I'm not getting promoted— but I tell her I don't feel like I'm where I'm supposed to be in life. I tell her about the dishes. About Tyler's video games. About how I've never been more lonely.

"It's not that he's cruel," I say, which is the truest and most frustrating thing. "He's not. He's kind. He's just— kind in the way that—"

"Prioritizes him?" Alana laughs. She taps my arm. "Honey, like, he's just playing the game. You don't even have your piece on the board."

What game? I want to ask. *What board?*

"It's okay," Alana says, nodding at me. She has been listening with her full face, and her expression has gone very still and quiet. "I see you," she says.

That's all. Just that. And I didn't know how much I needed to be seen until she said it.

I look at my coffee mug. My eyes do the thing they do.

"Don't you dare," Alana says, with a warning look that is also warm.

"I'm not," I say. "I have allergies."

Then, *her* eyes start watering, and for some reason we're both tearing up. And then, in the same breath, we both start laughing at how ridiculous we are.

"You are so funny," Alana says, which is something people tell me sometimes, but usually in the way they tell a child they're funny. "Okay," she says, and sits up a little straighter, like she's made a decision. "I want to ask you something, and I want you to know there's absolutely no pressure. I mean it. It's so far off that it's basically hypothetical right now."

I wait.

"When the wedding eventually does happen," she says, "Will you think about being my maid of honor?"

I do the math: we've known each other for less than forty-eight hours. I don't say this out loud because I don't want to be rude, but... why would a woman this glamorous, this *together*, not have any better options? Maybe this is the universe telling me that no one has it totally together. I should embrace it.... right?

"It would only be if we're still close by then," she says. "Obviously. And if you want to. No pressure whatsoever. I just—" she looks at me, perfectly direct— "I travel so much that I don't have many friends because I'm not usually in one place long enough to meet anyone. But now I've put roots down in Chicago and– I don't meet amazing people that often, and Melissa speaks so highly of you. I feel like we get each other. I just think... I'd want it to be someone like you."

For a moment, the image of Rodrigo in a suit, getting married, flashes across my eyes, but I push it away. He's not mine. It's weird I can't stop thinking about him. *Be normal, Billie,* I tell myself.

"Okay," I say. "Yeah. I'd like that."

She raises her coffee mug. I raise mine. We toast over hashbrowns.

Just then, the waiter brings our check. He leaves just as Alana grabs it.

"It's on me!"

"But you paid for yoga—" I object.

"Oh, hush, you have to let me pay," Alana says, then gets to investigating the charges. "Oh my gosh, like, he charged us for three omelettes and we only got two." She rolls her eyes. "I'll be right back."

She takes the receipt to the counter and waits for the server, but while she's waiting, starts chatting with a man sitting on a stool. He's in his late thirties— broad— and, judging by his empty plate, he's been here awhile. Alana touches his arm, and says something. I can't hear them because I'm too far away. The man laughs. So does Alana. The man looks charmed.

Then Alana's hand shifts from his arm to his forearm, and she holds it there—not gently, in the way you touch someone's arm at a party. More precisely than that. Her fingers wrap, and something in the angle of her grip looks less like an invitation and more like a question he's already answered. He's nodding. He's nodding vigorously. Wow, now he's nodding... a *lot.*

She hands him the paper receipt and comes back, beaming.

"That nice man paid for our check," she smiles at me. I look back at the man, who's already got his credit card out.

"He... did?" I ask, stumped. "Why?"

"He knows my boss," Alana says, shrugging. "Plus, I can be pretty charming when I want to be. Stick with me, Billie," Alana winks at me. "You'll learn how to get what you want. A little flirting never hurt anyone. And if that doesn't work..." she leans in like she's about to tell me a secret. "You can always threaten to have him tossed into the river, right?!" Alana cackles at her joke, and I can't help but laugh along with her. "Seriously though," Alana says, her voice lowering. "I can teach you this stuff. You need to learn how to grab life by the balls. You'd be unstoppable. You might even get that promotion you want from negotiator to something... bigger." She waves her hand vaguely in the air.

Hot, sticky guilt runs through my veins. I can't believe I lied to Alana when I first met her— and now, I'm sort of trapped in the story that I'm a negotiator. I hope Melissa doesn't tell her I'm really just an assistant before I get the chance to set things right. I *should* tell her the truth right now, but we've had such a good time, and I'm enjoying the way my new friend sees me— as someone successful, and worth knowing. *Oh, Billie, this is so lame.* I promise myself I'll tell Alana the truth some day. Preferably soon. Before she finds out from Melissa and I'm caught in the lie.

As we pack up, I think about what it would feel like to be a woman who walks into a room and takes what she needs without apologizing for needing it. Someone like Alana.

Maybe this friendship is going to be good for me.

ten

RODRIGO

WE'RE FIGHTING (AGAIN), and making pasta.

The pasta water is not boiling. This is, in the larger context of my evening, not the most alarming thing happening in this kitchen, but I keep returning to it— the pot sitting cold on the burner, untouched since Alana filled it twelve minutes ago and then got distracted by having extensive feelings about my character— because I think the pasta water is a metaphor, and I think I am the pasta water, and the thing I am waiting for is going to be very, very hot when it arrives.

"The thing that I really, like, cannot understand," Alana is saying, waving the wooden spoon in the air like a weapon, "is why you keep bringing up this job in Spain thing. Like, every single day. Spain, Spain, Spain. What is Spain?"

"Spain is my home," I say, from my position against the far wall, which I have selected for its defensibility. I have been tracking her hands since she opened the utensil drawer. The garlic press is not dangerous. The wooden spoon is not dangerous, but *could* present a problem in

Alana's very capable hands. The knife block, which she has been standing mere feet away from for the better part of this conversation, is very dangerous. "I grew up there. My family is there. And now there might be a job for me. My work is—"

"Your work is here," she says. "Your life is *here.* I am here!" She gestures at herself with the wooden spoon. "Do you see me? Like, hello! Am I not reason enough to stay?"

She is wearing a robe and no shoes, and her hair is loose, and she is, as always, the most beautiful person in any room she occupies. But I know now, her beauty is a trap, and I only hope I can leave this relationship safely. *Don't make her mad*, I remind myself. *La diabla does not like to be angered.*

"You are reason enough for many things," I say carefully, which is the diplomatic version.

"Then why are we even—" she puts the garlic press down, thank God, and opens her hands— "talking about this? I want to stay in Chicago. You have a life here. You have me. You have a beautiful apartment. You are, I want to say this gently, much better-looking than most of the other men out there, and the bar is genuinely low, so that's saying something."

"Gracias," I say.

"You're welcome," she says, and picks the garlic press back up. Then she puts it back down and opens the refrigerator, and I watch her stare into it for a moment— and I take the opportunity to breathe.

I knew this was going to happen. I have been preparing for this conversation like it's an impending surgery— not looking forward to it, but clear on the fact that the alternative is worse. I have been floating the idea of a job in Spain for three days. Small mentions, casual references— I left a job listing up on my laptop. I told Benny about it in a phone call I made sure Alana could overhear. I have been building a paper trail of my own exit because I know Alana, and I know that a man who disappears suddenly is a different problem than a man who has been publicly considering another option. One is a betrayal. The other could be a negotiation followed by a slow separation, if I approach it gently.

Benny is done with *his* job now, which is the other thing. His part in the whole Twin Ledger situation is finished, and he's already at the family house in the countryside of Tuscany, probably eating the very best food and pretending to be someone who has never been within three hundred kilometers of an illegal arms deal. There is no one for Alana to threaten, is the point. Benny is safe. I am the only person left in this apartment with a stake in this conversation, and I have decided that tonight is the night.

I think, briefly and entirely against my will, about Melissa's baby shower and the woman I met there. Billie. The woman with baby pictures and gold-flecked eyes that looked like they had recently been used to see something very clearly. I know that I can't ever be with *her*, in particular— but if I go back to Spain, maybe life will bless me with someone *like* her. Someone warm where Alana is cold, and soft where Alana is all sharp edges.

"I think," I say, when Alana closes the refrigerator, "that I should go to Spain for the job."

She turns and looks at me. The wooden spoon is still in her hand. Something in her expression goes very still.

"And I think," I continue, because I have rehearsed this, "that maybe this is a natural point for us to— take some space. Re-evaluate. Give *you* the chance to explore all the incredible options you have." I clear my throat. "Separate."

The word sits there. A very short word for a very large thing.

Alana doesn't move for a moment. Her robe flows softly around her, but she stays frozen like a statue. Her loose hair seems to sway even in our windless apartment, medusa's tendrils portending danger. The wooden spoon, held at her side now, not gesturing, not waving, seems heavier. I have seen her face do this before— go quiet, go internally somewhere— and I know from experience that the quiet is never actually quiet.

"Separate," she repeats.

"Sí," I say.

"You want to break up with me." She says it the way you state a mathematical equation. Neutral. Confirmational.

"Well," I say, "the exact term is not— things are not so black and white— but we *do* want different things— you should think of it more as a chance to explore–"

"*No one* breaks up with me," she says.

Her voice has not changed. It is still the voice she uses to talk about yoga and Oprah and vision boards and getting drinks at the bar. Sweet. Airy. That makes this moment all the more terrifying.

"Alana—"

"I'm going to make us dinner," she says, pivoting back to the counter. "And then we're going to talk about this properly. Okay? Because I think you're just— stressed, or whatever. The job. Everything. You're overwhelmed and you're catastrophizing." She opens the cabinet above the counter and pulls out a box of pasta. "You know what? I should have cooked for us weeks ago. I just— I'm not, like, a traditional home-type person, you know? That's not my identity. But I can cook pasta. I can absolutely do that."

She opens the box. She turns the burner on— finally,

the pasta water is on the agenda— and she tears the pasta open and then, because there is no other explanation, dumps the entire box into the cold water immediately. Before it's boiling. As a lover of food, I must admit— this might be the most horrifying thing I have watched Alana do. And that is saying something, because I have watched her kill a man. More than once.

"I have been thinking," I say, carefully, "about what I want my life to look like. And I think—"

"Everyone thinks pasta is hard, right?" Alana says, poking at the cold water with the wooden spoon, seeming satisfied with this activity. "But it's like, it's literally just water and pasta. There's nothing to it. I saw this video where the guy said you can put it in cold water from the start and it's even better. Something about even cooking."

"That's not—" I begin.

"I'm trying to take care of you," she says, and turns to look at me, and her face is so genuine that for exactly two seconds I think that maybe I've been overreacting. Then she adds, "And you are going to appreciate it," and the moment is over.

I realize there's nothing I can do, now. There's no way for me to get out of this safely. But at least I know Benny is in the clear. If my own death arrives as a result of this choice, I am alright with that. I look *La diabla* straight in the eyes and tell her the facts:

"I am breaking up with you," I say.

The wooden spoon stops.

The kitchen is very quiet, except for the burner. The cold pasta sits in the cold water.

"No," Alana says.

"Sí," I say.

"This doesn't fit my vision board," she says, looking as if I've slapped her.

"That's unfortunate," I agree. "But it is what's happening."

"Rodrigo." She sets the wooden spoon down on the marble counter, very precisely. "I understand that you are feeling some kind of— episode— right now. I actually have a lot of compassion for that."

That's funny, I think, *because you have not once asked me why I'm unhappy in this relationship.*

"But what you need to understand is that you and I are going to get married," she continues, "and we are going to have a wonderful life, and the only thing that is going to happen tonight is that you are going to eat some pasta and tell me how pretty I look in my new robe."

I watch her hand close around a handle.

She pulls a knife from the butcher's block.

It is a chef's knife. A large one.

"You can kill me, Alana," I say, looking at the knife as if it's nothing. "But I will still have broken up with you, and the result will be the same."

To my surprise, I'm not afraid. I know she will try to kill me, yes, but a man must live his life on his own terms, and this relationship has made me less afraid of death and more afraid of a life lived without love.

She looks at the knife for a moment, then at me, and her expression is the same warm, slightly exasperated expression she uses when I've done something she considers mildly inconvenient. She points the knife at me, then says, "I have been planning our future—" she gestures with the knife to indicate the future, which is apparently located somewhere to my left "—since April. April. Do you know what I gave up in April for this relationship?"

"Alana—"

"A trip to Monaco, Rodrigo. I had a whole thing in Monaco and I stayed here because I was committed to travelling less, and wanted to put down roots in Chicago *with you*—"

"I'm still breaking up with you."

She throws the knife.

In Alana's defense, it is not— I want to be clear here— thrown *at* me. It is thrown past me, close enough that I feel the air from it before I hear the sound of the blade embedding in the cabinet behind me with a very definitive thunk. I have, in a single reflex, moved sideways against the counter. My heart is doing something unpleasant. I look at the knife. I look at her. She is looking at her nails.

"I missed on purpose," she says. "You're welcome." A pause. "You don't even thank me for the most basic things."

She's telling the truth. I've seen Alana throw a knife with such accuracy she pinned a fruit fly to the wall. If she wanted to hit me, she would have.

The pasta water has begun, distantly, to heat.

"I'm going," I say. "To Spain. And we are not together anymore. I need you to understand that. No one has to know that this didn't work out. You can tell everyone *you* broke up with me."

"And Benny?" Alana's voice hardens, and for the first time, I hear *La Diabla* in her tone. There's the woman I know. The one who can turn on a dime.

"Benny is somewhere you can't touch him," I shrug. "He's retired from the Twin Ledger. Maybe you should do the same."

Alana does not lunge. She does not pick up another knife. She does not produce anything from the utensil drawer, which is, now that I think about it, more alarming than if she had. Instead, she turns and looks at me for a long, level moment— those pale steel eyes going somewhere dark where I can't follow— and then she picks up her phone from the counter.

I watch her do it. I watch her hand close around the phone, and I understand immediately that this is worse than the knife. The knife was a feeling. The phone is a *plan*.

"Where are you going?" I say.

She picks up her purse from the hook by the door. She slips her feet into the shoes she left there— silk mules that match nothing she's wearing, which tells me she is, in fact, *very* upset— and she opens the front door.

The hallway light makes a halo of her hair.

"Who are you calling?" I ask.

She turns and looks at me one last time, and she smiles — a full, luminous, unhesitating smile, the one that has cost me six months— and she says: "You'll regret this."

And then the door closes. I hear her feet padding toward the elevator, followed by the ding of a button, and then– silence. She's gone.

I stand in the kitchen. The pasta water is finally beginning to boil, because the universe has a sense of irony. The knife is still lodged in the cabinet door. The vision board still covers our wall— the magazine women, the magazine lives, the carefully curated spot for a best friend who does not yet know she's been selected. Alana has not told me whether or not she's befriended the woman from the baby shower yet— Billie. I want to stick around to find out, only to warn her, but this is my one chance to leave. My continued presence will only make Alana angrier— which is good for absolutely no one.

Maybe if I leave this city, Alana will also leave Chicago and start over somewhere new. That's been her pattern for many years. If I give her nothing to stay here for, perhaps she'll finally go and terrorize some other trendy hot spot, like Milan or New York. Then, Billie will be safe, and I'll be able to start again. For a moment, I think about what might have happened if I'd been single and able to get to know a woman like Billie— but I push the thoughts away as quickly as they came. My attraction to the woman is one thing, but the truth is, I don't know her. I tend to rush into relationships, and it's a mistake I'm not going to make again. *Think with the right part of your body, which is your brain*, I remind myself. If my experience with Alana has taught me nothing, it's that. I was wildly attracted to her, too, in the beginning, and look how that turned out— with knives in cabinets and my degenerate cousin in hiding.

I move to the closet and pull out my bags, which I've pre-packed. One duffel and a suitcase. That's all my life needs.

I open the front door and peek into the hallway. Alana is gone. I run for the stairwell like a thief in the night, taking the emergency exit to avoid running into Alana in the building's lobby. As I run down three flights of stairs, my suitcase plodding behind me, Alana's last words to me echo in my mind:

You'll regret this.

And the thing is— I believe her.

eleven

BILLIE

OUR WASHING MACHINE is in the hallway, which is a design choice I have never once made peace with. Our apartment has many qualities that the listing described as "cozy" and "unique layout" but that really means "cheap." I'm standing in front of it now, sorting laundry from the basket— my least favorite chore. Three of the shirts in this pile are white and are Tyler's, and they got in the colored load here because Tyler doesn't sort his laundry, no matter how much I beg. I am so tired.

From the living room, the sound of a video game reaches me in waves: an explosion, a reload click, a burst of music from what sounds like a cutscene Tyler has already seen sixteen times. The apartment smells like the fabric softener I buy in bulk and the remains of the takeout we had last night. I shake out a dark shirt and fold it. I pick up another. I fold that one too.

"Have you seen the— no, never mind, got it," Tyler calls from the couch.

"Great," I call back, which requires no actual information about what he was looking for.

From the living room: another explosion, another reload.

In moments like this, I remind myself why I stay. What are the things I like about Tyler? He brings me coffee (sometimes) in the morning, appearing in the doorway of the bathroom with a mug before I've asked, which is a small thing but a genuine one. He says sleep well, Billz, every night, and he means it. I *do* love him like an old friend. But I'm not sure I can love him and myself at the same time. We met a long time ago after my first boyfriend cheated on me, and I thought Tyler seemed like someone I could trust. We were young. I've grown, but he hasn't. I don't know what to do about it— or maybe I *do* know, but it's too hard and I can't face it.

My phone buzzes on the top of the dryer, screen-up. It's Alana.

Alana texts the way she talks— in a brightly-paced cadence that communicates exactly what she wants. She uses way too many words, probably because she's so confident everyone wants to hear what she has to say. The first text reads:

ALANA

Okay so I need to tell you something about Rodrigo...

I answer with a simple:

ME

?!

ALANA

He is driving me crazy with talk about this job in Spain! He is so, so needy and went on tonight about how he can't live without me but also has cold feet about getting married. And then I made him pasta and he was SO ungrateful. I need to get out for a bit. Like I love him I truly do but also I need space to breathe, you know??

I read this. I think, briefly and without meaning to, about the Rodrigo I met at Melissa's shower— he was so cold, and so distant, it's hard to imagine him as needy as she describes. But maybe the men who seem coldest in rooms full of strangers are the ones who are neediest. Maybe.

I file this away under: not my business. I read the next text:

ALANA

ANYWAY. I am at Tilly's Bar. I ordered you a drink already. Yes I know you haven't said yes yet but you are going to say yes because you deserve a girl's night and also honestly? Forget Tyler. I mean that in the most loving possible way.

I think about not going but then the next text arrives:

ALANA

You've been doing laundry, haven't you?

I look at the washing machine. I look at the basket, and at the pile of Tyler's shirts on top of the dryer. They're folded, stacked, and waiting to be returned to Tyler, who is one room away doing nothing at all. I type back:

ME

I'll be there in twenty minutes.

And before I have fully processed the decision, I'm already reaching for the laundry basket lid to push the remaining pile inside and sliding my feet into the boots I left by the hallway wall this morning, and pulling my coat off the hook by the door.

From the living room, the game makes a triumphant sound.

I grab my keys.

"Hey," Tyler calls from the couch, not urgently, "What do you want to do for dinner? Are we ordering, or—"

"I'm going out," I say, over my shoulder. I turn the handle. The cold air meets me.

"Oh—" Tyler starts, and I can hear him shifting on the couch, can hear the creak of it, can hear the beginning of a follow-up question. I pause with the door open and wait for him to ask where I'm going. To care about what I'm up to. But instead, he disappoints me. He goes back to the game. I can hear him cheering as he makes another kill. *That's it, then,* I think, somehow a little surprised even though I shouldn't be.

The door closes. And I'm on my way to Tilly's.

twelve

RODRIGO

I DID IT. I've escaped. I'm on a plane— 33,000 feet up— and Alana can't get me here.

The seat is a plastic sardine can in coach, and it is the most beautiful seat I have ever occupied in my entire life. Aisle. Exit row.

The woman to my left is already asleep, her head tipped toward the porthole glass. The man across the aisle is reading something thick and joyless about finance. The flight attendant is three rows ahead with the drink cart, moving toward me at the glorious speed of imminent rescue. Outside the window, Chicago recedes into the grey — a smear of amber and cold light going soft behind a wall of cloud— and our plane is high above it all, taking me, Rodrigo Esperanza, alive and unbroken, back home.

I sigh. So this is what safety feels like.

The drink cart arrives. I accept a sparkling water and then, because I feel I've earned it, I add: "And a whiskey. Gracias." The flight attendant moves on. I settle back against the headrest. The engine hum surrounds me— the sound of the universe being reasonable for once. I think about our family home in the Spanish countryside, where Benny will have already stocked the fridge. When all of this is remedied, I can go back to my old life. I can work construction, and paint on the weekends— I'll be able to sit in front of a canvas without worrying for my life.

In a moment of peace, without thinking, I reach for my phone.

I open Instagram. The feed delivers its familiar freight: a sunset from someone from a job site in Seville, a restaurant meal, a dog in a hat, a painting by an artist I've followed for years.

And then: Alana.

My thumb slows before my brain gives it permission. I can't help it. Her account shows a new post: forty minutes ago. My chest does the thing it does when I see her name now— not longing, but fear. The body's memory of danger.

I look at the photo.

She is at a bar, wearing something pink, because she's always in something pink, and her hair is perfect, and she is laughing her full-luminous laugh.

And next to her, laughing too— with a real laugh, the unguarded kind— is Billie Harper. The woman from the baby shower.

I sit with this information, a cold chill running through my veins.

Billie, I think, *how can I tell you that you must get away?* My heart breaks for her, but I try to shake the feeling away.

I remind myself I don't really *know* Billie. She is beautiful in the particular way of someone who doesn't know they're beautiful, which is the most disarming kind. She has enormous dark eyes with gold in them. And from what I could tell, she is kind and she is smart. *She could be a monster,* I remind myself, *just like Alana.* But then I concede that— even if Billie is a person with flaws and not the idealistic woman of my imagination— almost no one on the planet deserves what Alana is likely to put them through.

Billie is at a bar. With Alana.

Laughing.

And then: DING.

A text notification, from Alana. Of course. She couldn't just let me go without getting the last word.

I open it.

The first thing is a photo: same bar, same amber light, same two women, drinks raised this time. Billie's smile is aimed at the camera with an open, trusting quality that tells me this is best evening she's had in a while– she doesn't know enough to be afraid. Alana's smile is radiant. It is always radiant. That's the problem with Alana's smile — it means nothing at all.

Then the text:

ALANA

Having a great time without you 💕 My vision board is still working. Better watch out when you land, though, babe. Wouldn't want you to get HIT at the airport. The fun will continue if we don't get back together by Thursday. XOXO

Then, below that, a small pink heart emoji.

I stare at the message for a moment. Then I put the whiskey down, because it seems like a bad time to be enjoying anything.

Alana has taken out a hit on me. She has gone to the Twin Ledger and put a price on my head. This means my photo has been sent to hundreds of assassins, all of whom will get a cash prize if they take me out and send a photo of my remains to the Twin Ledger. Alana has put a contract on me and communicated this via text message with a pink heart at the end, while sitting next to Billie, who does not know that any of this is happening.

Billie is drinking with a murderer, and I'm going to get taken out at the airport as soon as I land, before I can even warn her. We are both in real trouble.

Then, it hits me: why didn't Alana kill me herself? Perhaps because— even though she is *La Diabla*— there is some real feeling there. She cannot kill me herself, because there is a piece of her— an icy, tiny little piece— that is attached to me. And perhaps I can use that fact to stop anyone from getting hurt.

My hands are moving before I've fully committed to the decision. This is what happens in situations like this— you don't decide so much as you start moving and let the decision catch up. I open the conversation with Alana. I type:

ME

Coming back. Please don't do anything crazy.

Send.

The lie lands in my chest with a dull, boring weight. I am not coming back. But I am buying time.

She responds immediately:

ALANA

💕💕💕 Don't worry babe. You don't have to come back.

Then, a long pause before the next message:

Because I'm coming to YOU.

I put the phone face-down on the tray table. I look

out the window. The clouds are solid white below me, a clean, complete erasure of everything. I breathe for a moment. Maybe Alana will believe my lie enough to cancel the hit? But now she plans to come to me herself. That, too, will inevitably end in murder when she realizes I have no intention of getting back together with her. But perhaps it will give me a chance to do what I should have done at that baby shower and get a message to Billie, an innocent woman, warning her to stay away from her new friend.

I think about Billie's gentle smile, and her Bambi eyes. I cannot be the reason this woman suffers.

I pick the phone back up.

Melissa.

Melissa was at the shower. Melissa is Billie's best friend — the real one, the actual one.

Alana made me add Melissa as a Facebook friend after the shower, because she claimed we'd be doing "couple's stuff" with her and Steve. I open up facebook and scroll through my friends— thankfully, Melissa has accepted the request. There's an option in the Messenger app to video call her. I hit the call icon, and wait as it rings.

It rings twice. Three times. I look out the window at the white. I think about Billie raising a glass in the amber light of Tilly's and not knowing to put it down.

On the fourth ring: the line connects.

"Hello?" Melissa appears on the screen of my phone, her face arranged in a confused expression. She's probably wondering why a near-stranger is video-calling her late night from an airplane.

"I know you don't know me well," I say, speaking as quickly as I can. "But this is Rodrigo, Alana's boyfriend? And she's not who you think she is." I pause, trying to find the right words. “Your friend Billie is in danger. We don’t have much time.”

thirteen

BILLIE

WE'VE IMPROVISED a dance floor at the back of Tilly's pub. I feel young— like I'm going to live forever. My hair whips around my shoulders. I'm moving in a way I haven't moved since college. Alana is next to me, dancing like she's been cast as the lead in a music video, and I swear she's so good at dancing it's making *me* look better.

Alana spins, catches herself, laughs at her own laughter. She has her phone in her hand— she keeps picking it up, typing something, then putting it face-down on the table when we take breaks from the music.

"He keeps texting," she shouts over the music, holding the phone up briefly so I can see the notification before she dismisses it with one swipe of a perfect nail.

"Rodrigo?" I ask.

"He's literally saying he's going back to Spain," she says, mildly exasperated. "Work thing. Very sudden. But he is just—" she makes a gesture with both hands— "texting me every twenty minutes like he has not just gone to another country but to the actual moon. He misses me *so much* it's honestly almost inconvenient how much."

"The curse of being adored," I say.

"Exactly," she says. "You'll get it when someone adores you properly. It's a lot."

I decide not to think too hard about what she means by that. I take a sip of my own drink.

Then, my phone rings, and for a moment I think it might be Tyler, actually realizing I've been gone way too long and worrying about me for once. Instead, Melissa's name appears on the screen.

"Hey, Mel—"

"Are you with her right now?" Melissa's voice is the voice she uses for serious things. "Alana. Are you with Alana?"

Something in her tone moves up my spine. "Yeah, we're at—"

"Go outside," she says. "Don't make it weird, don't say anything. Just go outside and take this call."

I look at Alana. Alana is checking her phone again, thumbs moving, smile doing its full-wattage thing. She doesn't look up.

"Just give me two seconds," I say to her, pitching my voice casual. "I have to take this." I hold up my phone, the universal signal for nothing interesting, just a call. Alana waves a hand— of course, go— and turns back toward the bar.

I push through the door.

The cold hits me the way only a Chicago winter can. Behind me, through the glass, the warm amber blur of Tilly's continues. In front of me, the street is dark and quiet under the streetlights. I put the phone back to my ear.

"Okay," I say. "I'm outside. What's going on?"

There's a tense pause.

"Rodrigo called me," Melissa says. "He called me tonight, from the plane."

"Oh yeah, Alana said he went back to Spain for a work thing—"

Melissa cuts me off. "He said he doesn't have much time, and I know that sounds weird, but Billie— I need you to listen to me." Her voice is steady. "Alana is *not* who she says she is. Rodrigo said she's been— she's involved in *things*."

My mind whirls. "Things? What things?

"Dangerous things. He said international crime. He said arms dealing. He said—" a breath— "he said she has a record of pulling people in who she likes and keeping them there in ways that are not—" she pauses, selecting the word— "safe."

I stand on the sidewalk outside Tilly's and look at the streetlight.

"Mel," I say, carefully. "You're eight months pregnant. You're not sleeping well, you've been under a lot of stress—"

"Billie. I'm pregnant not—"

"—and Rodrigo only met me for a few minutes at a baby shower, during which his biggest communication was a single nod and a rude comment. Why would he care what I'm doing? Alana says he's super intense. He's probably insecure and totally in love with her and just wants to know where she—"

"Billie." Her voice is quiet. "Look at your email."

I pull the phone from my ear. I navigate to my email with cold-stiff fingers. There is a message from Melissa, sent eleven minutes ago, containing a forwarded bank statement. I zoom in.

There it is. A charge from the West Loop yoga studio for $75. Yesterday morning's eight o'clock class, times two. *The class Alana and I went to together.* I check the name on the statement— this is Melissa's card.

"You paid for our yoga class yesterday?" I say, trying to make sense of what's happening. "That was nice of you Mel, but you really didn't have to—"

"She used my account!" Melissa shouts, her tone communicating that I am the world's biggest idiot. "Without my permission. She's been using it since I met her three weeks ago and I didn't notice because I go there all the time, too. Apparently she told the woman at the front desk I was treating her because I owed her for saving my life, and in exchange, I gave her perpetual yoga classes. She made up some insane story and she's been going to yoga for free ever since. She's a grifter! A con artist! And if Rodrigo is to be believed, maybe even a murderer."

I stand in the cold and look at the amber blur through the glass. Alana. Is. ... a murderer?

"Alana," I repeat. "Who wears the pink beanie caps. Is a murderer?"

"Correct," Melissa says.

"And... Rodrigo called you," I say again, slower. "He called you specifically. To warn me."

My heart pounds in my chest, and I'm not sure if it's because I'm afraid of Alana, or excited that Rodrigo thought to try and help me. I think about Rodrigo's face at the baby shower— that chiseled jaw, the deep, brown eyes that— upon further reflection— seem warm, now, when interpreted in a different light. *Come on, Billie, wake up.* I shake myself out of my musings.

"Rodrigo saw the photo Alana posted of the two of you. On Instagram. He knew you were together and he—"

Melissa pauses— "he left her, Billie. He broke up with her. They're done. He got on a plane to get away from her."

Something happens in my chest. Something I have not given permission to happen.

"Wait," I say.

"Billie—"

"Does that mean," I say, very carefully, "that Rodrigo is *single* right now?"

The silence that follows is long. And I can tell that Melissa— who is eight months pregnant and has just delivered a comprehensive international criminal warning— is using this silence to judge me. Heavily, as only best friends can.

"*That*," Melissa says, in a voice of extraordinary restraint, "is what you took away from everything I just said. That Rodrigo is single?"

"It's just, he's really kind of handsome and— I mean, like you *saw* him, he's—"

"Billie!" Melissa says with a tone that's attempting to snap me back into reality. "Get away from Alana or you are going to *die*! She is an international arms dealer who will kill you if you make her mad. Dating her ex-boyfriend seems like a bad idea, right? Wake up!"

Right, I think. I've got more pressing issues than Rodrigo's amazing biceps, which were super-toned, by the way. *Pull it together, Billie.*

"I'll tell her my stomach hurts," I say, reaching for the lamest possible excuse. "I'll say I got food poisoning."

"Just get out of there without tipping her off," Melissa whispers. "Rodrigo said you can't let her know that you're aware of who she really is. He says he thinks Alana took a hit out on him—"

"Like, to have him killed?" I say, shocked at the idea. I

still can't reconcile the blonde Barbie doll I've come to know with a dangerous criminal. "Or maybe just a firm talking to?"

"Yes, to have him killed, Billie."

My skin prickles, and it's not the cold. A sticky sense of dread washes over me. Rodrigo can't get hurt. It's not fair.

"We have to help him—" I start to say, but Melissa cuts me off.

"Trust me, I'm on it. And Rodrigo's a grown man. He can take care of himself. Right now, we need to get you out of there. Go back inside and act completely normal, then make some excuse and escape. Call me as soon as you get home."

"I will," I promise. "Going back inside now."

"Be careful," she says, and it is the simplest, most urgent thing she has said all night.

* * *

When I go back inside, the bar looks the same. Tilly's is exactly as I left it, amber and warm and people who came here on purpose. It should feel like relief. Instead, It feels like a stage set— and I'm about to give the best performance of my life.

Alana is already turned toward me. She has two fresh drinks on the small table, and she looks so hopeful that I almost feel bad for what I'm thinking right now, which is: *I've got to get the hell out of here.* As she moves toward me, she looks different— changed, somehow. For the first time, I notice that her incisors are a little too pointy, almost as if they belong on a dog. Her eyes— which I thought were a cheerful, cool blue— have turned cold, and there are dark circles around her irises I never really noticed before.

"Everything okay?" she asks when I reach her. Her voice carries exactly the right amount of gentle concern. It's the warmth I fell for in the first place. It hasn't changed, but suddenly I notice it isn't just concern. There's a sense of accountability in her tone— as if I'm not living up to a standard she's set.

"Fine," I say. "Melissa. Baby stuff." I wave a hand in a vague direction.

"She's okay?"

"She's great. She's just—" I shrug— "close to the end. Everything feels like an emergency when you're that close to the end."

Alana nods. She does not push. She doesn't ask the follow-up I'm half-braced for. Instead, she sets the two drinks— light beers— down in front of us and leans in.

And then Alana says: "Okay, I need to tell you something."

Her voice has shifted— not dangerously, just privately.

"Oh sure," I say, trying to act as if I really care. "But before you do that, I should warn you my stomach is really upset and I think I might have to head out soon and head home because—"

"Sure, sounds good," she interrupts me, apparently not having heard a single word I've said. She leans forward on both forearms. "So," she says, "It's about Rodrigo. And the Spain thing. I have to admit, I kind of invited you here tonight under false pretenses."

"You did?" I gulp, my heart pounding in my chest.

"I didn't just need a night out," she smiles at me again. "I'm going to Spain. I'm going to surprise him." She says it as if going to Spain is like heading for the deli three blocks away. "I'm going to fly to Barcelona and just— show up. He'll love it. He *loves* when I do things like this."

I have a very alarming thought, which is: Rodrigo is running away from her, and she is chasing him. *Run, Rodrigo,* I mentally cheer him on. It's becoming clearer by the second that Alana's story doesn't match reality.

"That's uh, very— spontaneous," I say.

"That's me," she agrees, the way you agree with something you've always been proud of. "And maybe... you, too?" Then, she reaches into the cream canvas bag on the back of her chair. She puts two airline tickets on the table between us. They're printed, and folded once.

I look at them.

"I have one for you," she repeats as if I didn't understand the first time. "A plane ticket."

I just stare at her.

"Before you say anything," she says, both palms up— "hear me out. It's eight hours. The flight leaves at—" she checks her phone— "two in the morning. We go, we stay a few days, we see Barcelona, we eat the food Rodrigo keeps going on about—" she looks at me with that recalibrated smile— "and then we come home. Easy. Fun. The kind of trip you tell people about forever. Plus, Tyler will get the chance to miss you!"

I notice, for the first time, that Alana is an excellent salesperson. If Melissa hadn't called me, I'd be seriously considering saying yes to this. Alana would have found me angry at Tyler, embarrassed by my life, and looking for a change. The perfect victim. *Thank God, for Melissa and Rodrigo,* I think.

"I can't go," I say. "I have work." A pause. "And Tyler. I can't just leave so suddenly."

Something crosses her face. It's fast— faster than a blink, really, more like the shadow of a cloud that has already passed by the time you think to look up. It is there, and then it is gone, replaced so swiftly by warmth that I almost tell myself I imagined it. Almost. But I caught it: the stillness, the microsecond of— not anger, exactly. Not disappointment in the ordinary sense. Something colder than that. Something about not getting her way.

Then she laughs, easy and fond. "Tyler," she says, as if he is a problem to be addressed at another date. "Right." She picks up her glass. "Well. I tried."

"I tried with you," I confirm. I pick up mine.

She tilts her glass toward me. "To friendship," she says, with full conviction. "Wherever it takes us."

"Wherever it takes us," I say.

Then, a terrible, insane thought occurs to me. *What if she drugged my drink?* I shake off the idea. Why would she do that? There's nothing to be gained. What's her plan... to knock me out and steal my wallet? Still, I know better than to accept an open drink from anyone I don't trust, even if that person is a woman. But Alana is staring at me, waiting for me to drink our toast— she still hasn't sipped her own beer.

"Oh my gosh!" I exclaim, pointing behind her to create a distraction. "That woman is wearing the same heels as you!"

"Where?!" Alana gasps, like I knew she would. She looks over her shoulder and sets down her drink at the same time, and I use the moment to switch our glasses, accidentally spilling on the table in the process. I hope Alana is too tipsy to notice.

Luck is on my side. When she looks back at me, she's laughing. "Billie," she rolls her eyes. "You are so basic, it's honestly cute. Her shoes are knock-offs. Mine are the real thing, obviously."

She raises her glass— the glass that used to be mine— in the air and says, “Where were we? Cheers.”

We clink the glasses together, and I take a sip, knowing that I was probably overly cautious. But hey, when you’re dealing with international criminals, you’ve got to be careful. Alana watches me drink, delaying her own sip by just a couple of seconds—

But that’s all it takes.

The first thing I notice is that the warmth comes too fast. That’s not the right way to describe it— it’s not the warmth of alcohol, which I’ve been drinking all evening and know the feeling of. It’s something else— a warmth that spreads from the center of my chest outward and goes immediately to the backs of my eyes, and I blink. I set the glass down.

The table is there. I can see it. I can see Alana across it, smiling with her full face— but something is wrong with the number of times her face appears. I grab the table edge. The grain of the wood is sharp under my fingers, very real, as everything else is beginning to go soft.

Did that bitch drug me? I think, or maybe say out loud. I’m not sure, because I can’t feel my tongue.

I look at the glass on the table. I look at Alana, who has not moved. She is watching me with her hands folded and her face perfectly, beautifully composed.

I think, ridiculously: *Rodrigo is single.*

An image of his face— warm and unforgettable— floats before me like a painting.

Then the amber light goes flat and the table edge stops being an anchor and Tilly’s, blurry and full and entirely indifferent to what is happening in a small corner between two repurposed tables, continues humming.

Alana is beside me— unhurried, efficient, her hand at

my arm and her voice saying something to the room around us, something plausible and concerned, in the tone of a woman whose friend has had a little too much to drink and needs a moment. Her face, when I look up at it last, is the same face it always is. Radiant. Present. Perfectly, completely sincere.

I go down.

fourteen

RODRIGO

BARCELONA EL PRAT airport has a smell to it I'd forgotten about— jet fuel and industrial cleaner and, underneath both, something warm and Mediterranean. I try to enjoy my homecoming for just a moment, but Melissa's voice on the other end of my cell phone brings me back to reality.

"Billie believed me, but I told her to call me when she got home and she hasn't! I've called Tyler but of *course* he's not answering his phone. He probably fell asleep in front of a video game—"

"Tyler?" I ask, trying to keep up.

"Billie's boyfriend," Melissa says, her tone implying this is obvious.

I stop walking for just a moment. *Billie has a boyfriend.* I should not care about this information, but for some reason, I feel— disappointed? Of course, it is my fault for daydreaming— for jumping ahead, thinking silly thoughts about a woman I just met. A woman I don't even *really* know.

"I think I should call the police but I don't know what to

tell them— and I need to send them to Alana's apartment and—" Melissa is talking a million miles a minute. It's hard to follow her train of thought.

"No police," I whisper, shaking my head. My duffel is slung over one shoulder and my suitcase wheels behind me with a sound that echoes off the tile, and around me the arrivals hall is bustling— families reuniting in front of the sliding doors, a man in a black uniform holding a handwritten sign, a woman running because she is late for something. I navigate through all of it with my phone pressed to my ear. "Police will only make this worse unless absolutely necessary. You don't want Alana to *know* that you know... *¿entiendes?* You understand? We are trying to avoid making her take the darkest path..."

"I've been calling Billie for three hours and she hasn't picked up once."

I do the math without wanting to. Three hours is a long time. It is long enough for a great many things to happen.

"Maybe everything's fine," I say. "Maybe she couldn't get away from Alana without making her aware. You *told* her not to tip her off, yes?"

"I did."

"Alana is volatile, but she's not—" I pause, rethinking this sentence. "She's not looking to hurt anyone without cause. Maybe she has forced Billie into going on some wild adventure with her in Chicago, bar-hopping until the bars close, just to take instagram videos with men to make me jealous," I say instead. "She is very good at that. Making a point. Sending a message. She has done this before."

"Has she?" Melissa asks. Her tone says wants very much for me to be right.

"Yes," I say. "I've told Alana I'm coming back. That I'm coming home."

"And what did she say?" Melissa asks.

I pause. "She said *she* would come to me."

I watch a family of four walk past me, the youngest asleep across her father's shoulder, one shoe off. I think about Alana's text. The pink heart at the end of it.

"And the hit?" Melissa asks.

"Maybe it was a threat," I say. "To scare me. Not a real—"

"Rodrigo," Melissa says my name like we are both too smart to believe such a thing.

I let out a heavy sigh. "If it was real, she'll cancel it if she believes I will go back to her, which I've told her I will. And if she does not cancel it, well, it's been a good life and a pleasure knowing you." I smile dryly to myself— Alana has pushed me to the point where I no longer care, completely, if I live or die.

"I'm going to keep trying to call Billie," she says. "I'll give it two more hours and then I'm going to the Police."

"Sí," I agree.

"I'll give you her number too," Melissa adds. "In case you manage to get through to her when I don't. Send Billie a text. See if she answers."

I hear the ping of a message arriving. Melissa has sent me a contact card. One name: Billie Harper, followed by a phone number with a Chicago area code. This isn't how I imagined getting Billie's number, but I'm glad to have it anyway.

"I've got it," I say.

"Good." A beat. "Call me if you hear anything— from either one of them." And then she is gone.

I stand for a moment in the middle of the arrivals hall and look at my phone. Around me, the airport continues its indifferent business. Someone is being paged over the intercom.

I look at Billie Harper's phone number.

What am I supposed to say to her? *Alana sells weapons to people you don't want to think about and may have put you in danger by being your friend?*

I think about what to say.

I type:

ME

We don't know each other well but I was trying to warn you at the baby shower. — Rodrigo

I read it back. It is, by any reasonable measure, a bad opening. It is the kind of text that a person receives and immediately shows to a friend with a concerned expression. It is also, unfortunately, the truth, and the truth is the only thing I have at the moment.

I send it.

Outside, the Barcelona afternoon is grey and cool and smells like sea-salt.

I request an Uber. The wait time says four minutes. I stand at the curb with my duffel over my shoulder and my suitcase at my feet and watch the traffic, waiting for something— a response from Billie, a call from Melissa, a sign from the universe that I have done enough of the right things today to earn a quiet life.

The car arrives. A black sedan. The driver is a compact man in his late forties, a Barcelona FC scarf on the hook behind his seat, the radio playing something quiet. He confirms my name. I settle into the back seat and close the door. The airport recedes behind us.

I look down at my phone. Billie has not responded. I write the beginning of a follow-up:

ME

I know this sounds strange, but please call me. It's about Alana.

— and hold my thumb over send. Then I look up, because we have pulled briefly to a stop, and I want to see the city, my city, after months away.

The driver's eyes are in the mirror.

He is looking at me.

My phone is still in my hand. The unsent text sits there — *I know this sounds strange, but please call me. It's about Alana.*— and I am aware that my thumb has stopped moving. We've pulled over into an alley— one I don't recognize, but then again, it's been a long time since I've been home. We're out of sight, invisible to other vehicles, cradled by old stones that keep the buildings on either side aloft, in the company of only battered garbage cans.

I'm about to say we've taken a wrong turn, but then—

The driver whips around.

In retrospect, a rope is a strange choice. I say this not as a critique— I understand there are professional considerations— but simply as an observation made in the two-thirds of a second between seeing it and having it around my throat. It is a short length of nylon cord, the kind sold in hardware stores, and the man is very fast with it. He probably chose a rope because it's quieter than a gun. I register all of this with the clarity that arrives when the brain understands its owner is in trouble.

"*Lo siento, amigo*," the driver says. The rope is around my throat, so I can't answer. He is applying genuine pressure, and his tone is apologetic, as if he wants me to understand this isn't personal. "Your girlfriend." He says it with the resigned shrug of a plumber explaining a burst pipe. He can't help it. It's just the job. "La Diabla— whatever she wants, she gets." I pull at the rope as best I can, but the man has me at the perfect angle. He has more leverage than me. A horrible choking sound fills the car, and I realize, quickly, that it's my own voice.

This man is from the Twin Ledger.

So the hit was real. Alana wasn't just trying to scare me. And, apparently, she hasn't cancelled it.

The rope is at my windpipe and the man outweighs me by perhaps twenty kilograms. This is the thing I know from construction work and maybe also from painting: when you fight the constraint directly, you lose. You go with it first. You find a different angle. My left hand drops. My right hand finds the seatbelt buckle. Click.

The driver takes this as surrender and leans further in, which is what I need— because the extra inch of his movement over the center console changes the geometry. I twist, hard and fast, dropping my left shoulder and driving my right elbow up and backward in the space between his forearms. It is not elegant. It is not the kind of thing you would film. It connects with the side of his jaw. He takes the full brunt of my rage. I've spent six months being afraid and am, at this moment, done with it.

The driver makes a sound. His grip breaks.

The rope falls.

I have an opening, if not a brief one.

I grab my duffel bag from the seat beside me— it has my documents in it, my phone charger, the painting I was working on in the apartment that I folded carefully between two shirts because I couldn't bear to leave it. Then, I find the door handle. The sedan is still parked in the alley

— unnoticed by all— and the door opens against a garbage can with a scrape of metal.

I go through it anyway.

The pavement comes up fast. My shoulder takes the landing. I roll— not well, not like someone who has trained for this, but adequately. My duffel hits the cobblestones beside me. I grab it and get up.

The driver is already moving— I can hear the car door on his side— and I run.

Barcelona, when you are running through it in a state of genuine emergency, is not the city from the photographs. It is narrower. The streets are uneven. The afternoon light, which looked golden and welcoming from the arrivals hall, is now just light— present, indifferent, illuminating nothing except the next corner and the one after that. My lungs burn: they are not happy with me. My duffel swings and slams against my hip with every stride. I try to disappear into the city. I turn a corner and then another and then I am in a small square— a plaza, café tables, a fountain, pigeons— and I am not being followed. Not yet. I press myself into the alcove of a doorway and breathe.

I look at my hands. They are steady. I find this annoying, because it means some part of me expected this, no matter how much I hoped the alleged hit was fake. Alana has calibrated me to her world, and I hate it.

My phone is still in my hand. I look at it.

The text to Billie is still there. Still unsent— the follow-up one.

I think about what just happened, and the fact that Alana deployed all of this within the span of a single flight, because she could, because she has the infrastructure for it, because that is the world she moves through and the one she was building Billie Harper into, one yoga class at a time.

Billie. Who has very likely been with Alana tonight. Who hasn't responded to my text. Who, at last report from Melissa, wasn't answering calls.

I am very still in the doorway. A pigeon walks past me without concern.

I hit send on the second text:

ME

I know this sounds strange, but please call me. It's about Alana.

Then I write a third:

ME

I'm in Barcelona. I need you to tell me you're okay. My heart will not rest until I know. Please.

These texts are oddly personal, coming from a man she has met only once. I do not care. I have to know she is safe.

It strikes me that I've left my suitcase in the sedan, and all I have left to my name is the simple duffel bag slung over my shoulder.

There's a strange liberation in the feeling. Yes, I'm starting over— but without fear. Alana may have taken out a hit on me— but I will, I must— make all of this right. Not just for me. But for others like me— others like Billie, whose golden-brown eyes will haunt me if I cannot make sure she's safe.

BILLIE

THE FIRST THING I'm aware of is that I am extremely comfortable, which is wrong. The second thing I'm aware of is the hum— a pressurized, thirty-thousand-feet-in-the-air kind of sound— and my brain, which is still not fully online, serves me the information before the rest of me is ready for it: I am on a plane.

I open my eyes.

How did I get here?

The ceiling above me is cream-colored and curved. The lighting is soft and warm. I'm wrapped in a blanket that is so soft, I almost think I *can't* be on a plane, because I'm too comfortable. The seat beneath me reclines in a way that suggests it could go flat, like a bed. Okay, now I'm *sure* this can't be a plane, because people like me aren't allowed that much luxury. Then, I realize:

I'm in first class.

I've *never* been in first class. I'm a coach person, all the way. Shove me in a corner and yell at me— that's my general travel experience.

"Wha—" I say loudly, grabbing at the space around me.

"How did I get here? This can't be— first class?— no," I clutch my head, which is throbbing, and let out a massive groan.

A woman in the seat across the aisle is watching me with an expression that says she has paid for a certain level of quiet and feels I am undermining it. She has reading glasses on the end of her nose and a glass of red wine that she is now gripping with both hands, as if it needs protecting. From me, apparently.

"Sorry," says a familiar voice to my left, warm and airy and absolutely unruffled. "She's used to coach. Totally feral."

I turn my head. Alana is in the seat next to mine, reclined exactly the correct amount, wearing a pale rose cashmere set— top and matching pants— with a silk eye mask pushed up on her head like a headband. She has a small dish of warm nuts on her tray table. She looks like a picture from a magazine about first class travellers. She looks at me with fond exasperation.

"Hi, babe," she says.

"Am I— I'm on a plane," I say.

"Girls' trip!" she says. She claps her hands together once, delicately, the way you'd applaud a very small recital. "I know. I know! I'm so excited too."

The woman across the aisle takes a pointed sip of her wine.

I look at my hands. I look at the blanket. I look at the small, illuminated screen in front of me, which is showing a route map: a tiny plane icon hovering over what appears to be the Atlantic Ocean, angled toward the Iberian Peninsula.

"How," I say, very slowly, "did I *get* on this plane?"

"Okay, so," Alana says, turning slightly in her seat to face me with enthusiasm. She's been waiting to tell this story. “You know how you fainted at the bar? Which was so scary, by the way, you’re okay though, good news.” She pats my hand. “Well, you were knocked out cold— can’t hold your liquor very well, can you?— so I just drove us to the airport and put you in a wheelchair and sent you right through security. I told the TSA agent that you have a seizure condition, and I’m your sister, and you’d just had an episode. They were so sweet. They have a whole thing. Nobody asks very much. They’re way more focused on finding contraband, honestly.”

I stare at her.

“Turns out the TSA is way more interested in finding illegal weapons than in human trafficking,” she adds, sounding as if she’s learned something very useful.

“Glad to know my tax dollars are hard at work,” I say, which comes out flatter than I intend because I still can't entirely feel my face.

“They really are,” she agrees.

A beat.

“Wait,” I say. “Trafficking.” I look at her. “Am I being trafficked?”

Alana tips her head, considering a technicality. “Trafficking is defined as forcing someone across international lines,” she says, reaching for a warm nut. “And we’re already in Europe, so— yes!” She smiles. “Technically.”

“How many—“

“International borders?” she asks, then shrugs. “I don’t know. Probably like, three by now. Check your little map thing on the screen.” She eats the nut.

I try to remember things. I try to sequence events. Tilly’s. The warm amber light. The drink I switched. The drink I *thought* I’d switched.

“The glasses,” I say.

"Honey," she says, not unkindly. "I saw you switch them." A pause. "I had already put something in mine, too. Just in case."

There it is. There is the thing that confirms what I am dealing with. I had a backup plan, and she had a backup plan for my backup plan, and this is the gap between us as human beings. I put my passport in my purse in case of emergencies. She puts drugs in both glasses in case of emergencies. These are both contingency plans. Hers was better.

"My passport," I say. "You used my passport."

"I know, I really lucked out on that one." She sounds genuinely delighted by this. "You literally had it in your purse. Who does that?"

"I keep it with me at all times in case of an emergency," I say. "Which, in retrospect, is incredibly ironic, considering it enabled you to kidnap me and take me across an international border—"

"Three," she says again, calmly.

I look around the cabin. There are maybe a dozen other passengers in first class, all in various states of expensive sleep or expensive reading. No one is looking at me. The flight attendant is at the far end, and I consider, seriously, what happens if I stand up and announce the situation.

Find the air marshal right now, Billie, I tell myself.

I start to do it. I actually shift forward in my seat, and Alana's hand lands on my wrist. Not hard. Just— there.

"Tyler," she says, very quietly.

I stop.

"And Melissa," she continues, still in that same warm, level voice. "Who is eight months pregnant. And Steve. They're good people. I'd really hate for anything to happen to them." She releases my wrist and picks up her water glass. "I'm not saying that to be dramatic. I just want you to have the full picture."

I sit back.

"I still don't feel like I have the full picture," I say calmly, as if we're talking about getting lunch. I know from negotiation classes I took at the local community college— an effort to get Mr. Franklin to believe in me— that I need to de-escalate the situation, and try to get as much information as I can out of her.

"My job," Alana says, setting the glass down with a small clink. "I should tell you properly. I deal in things that are difficult to move. Uranium, mostly. Some weapons. Occasionally information. I work under a larger organization. They're called the Twin Ledger." She says it as if the job is no different than being an accountant. "I've been doing it for a long time."

"The Twin Ledger," I repeat.

"They're very powerful," she confirms. "And here's the thing." She turns to face me more fully now, and her expression has shifted— still warm, but now also direct. "I got upset about Rodrigo. He tried to break up with me."

"I thought you said he was obsessed with you and never leaves you alone?"

Alana clucks her tongue at me. "Two things can be true at once, Billie. Anyway, he clearly has commitment issues and he panicked and tried to break things off. And I may have— in the heat of the moment— placed a call. To some people." She presses her lips together briefly. "And those people have been asked to— take care of him."

I feel the blanket around me: a thing I did not choose, that I cannot get out of.

"You took out a hit on him," I say.

"I was emotional," she confirms. "And I've regretted it

since. As soon as I did it I thought, I've got to get out of this. And then I thought— who could help me? And I was like... Billie, obviously! Which is why we're going to Spain!" She fixes me with a look that suggests this is excellent news. "And you get a free trip out of it. You're so totally welcome."

"Wait..." I say, once again rubbing my throbbing head. "Why do we have to go to Spain? Can't you just call them and say you want to cancel the hit?"

"Well," Alana looks away, tapping her perfectly manicured fingers on the arm-rest. "I *did* try to call and they sort of laughed at me. They said once something like this is in motion there's no cancelling it. Seems as if they've already broadcast the hit to all assassins in the area for a bounty, and they think it would look bad to cancel it." Alana sighs. "They also don't take me seriously, probably because I'm a woman. It's a very sexist industry, Bille."

The world spins, and I try to make sense of what Alana wants from me. "So... why me? Why am *I* being dragged to Spain?"

"You're a negotiator. A head negotiator. The Twin Ledger doesn't exactly have a refund policy, but if we come in person, with the right approach, and frame the request in a way that—" she opens her hands— "makes them see why they have to cancel the hit, then there we go! Rodrigo won't be killed." A pause. "I'm bringing you to negotiate. Because you're a negotiator and you're like, the best at it. Right?"

My stomach turns. I have made a terrible mistake, and now I'm being punished. *This is what you get for lying, Billie,* I think to myself. I've told one big lie in my tiny, little life, and this is how it ends?

I pick up the in-flight airsickness bag from the seat pocket in front of me and get up, moving to the bathroom at a pace somewhere between running and walking. The door clicks shut behind me, and I get sick in the very elegant first-class toilet for a while.

Alana's knock comes before I've finished.

"I'm fine," I say.

"Open the door, babe."

I open the door. She comes in, which is possible in first-class bathrooms in a way it is absolutely not in coach, and she stands with her arms crossed and looks at me with genuine concern that I am somehow still kind of believe.

"I have to tell you something," I say, to the mirror.

"Okay."

"I lied." I meet my own eyes first, then hers. "At the baby shower. I'm not a head negotiator. I'm an assistant. I've been an assistant for seven years. I answer emails and I order lunch and I once spent four hours trying to book a grooming appointment for my boss's purebred poodle. That's my full skill set. So you can let me go, when we land. I'm not useful to you. I just– want to go home."

Alana is quiet for a moment.

"Billie," she says, and her voice is very even. "I have to be honest with you. I'm really disappointed." She shakes her head. "Lying is wrong. That's no way to start a friendship."

I turn and look at her. I look at her for a long moment.

"You *trafficked* me," I say.

"That's—"

"Across three international borders." I hold up three fingers. "While unconscious. You drugged me! And failed to mention you're an international arms dealer—"

"That's a completely different thing," she says with the conviction of a woman who truly believes this.

"Is it?"

"Yes. Because I told you I was in imports and exports. I

was honest and you just didn't ask questions. What *you* did was outright deception." She says it simply, as if these are two points on entirely separate spectrums. Then, without pause: "I'm not letting you go when we land. You still have to help me."

"Alana—"

"Rodrigo will die," she says. "That is the actual thing that happens if we don't fix this. I know you don't like him — I could tell at the shower."

I think of his face. The jaw. The warm ochre painting of hands on his Instagram. And the way he whispered, "be careful" into the air between us like it cost him something. He was so handsome and so rude that the combination of both made me angry.

But still– I don't want him to die. He didn't do anything to deserve this treatment from Alana. And neither did I.

"I don't *dislike* him," I say.

"Then you'll help," she says. "Obviously." She brightens. "And when we land— you can buy the drinks. As an apology to me. For lying." She reaches out and squeezes my hand. Her grip is warm and certain. "We're still besties. Obviously. This is actually really good for our friendship, if you think about it. Girls' trips are like therapy— we can heal our wounds and like, eat, pray, love or whatever."

She turns and goes back to her seat.

I stand in the first-class bathroom of a plane I didn't board willingly, over the Atlantic Ocean, and look at myself in a mirror that is lit better than any mirror I own at home, and I think: maybe I can really help save Rodrigo. If Alana is telling the truth, we may not have a lot of time before someone finds him. And as angry as I am, this is kind of... exciting? Alana believes in me enough that she really thinks I could help her negotiate with international arms dealers.

Mr. Franklin won't even let me negotiate a deal for a luxury condo.

My eyes widen at myself in the mirror. Did I really just think that? Am I so overlooked at work and so bored with Tyler that being drugged and kidnapped feels like it's... at least some attention?

Is this the beginning of Stockholm syndrome?!

Snap out of it, Billie, I think, horrified at myself. *You've got to get out of this.* I need to get away from Alana and call for help as soon as I can. I'm obviously having a massive trauma response, and am going to need therapy after if I'm lucky enough to survive this experience.

Then I think: I am going to die in Spain.

And I suddenly wish I had paid closer attention in my high school Spanish classes.

* * *

Barcelona's *El Prat* airport smells like coffee and jet fuel and, underneath both of those things, something warmer — bread, maybe, or stone that's been in the sun. I know this because I am standing in it against my will.

Alana has her carry-on— monogrammed, obviously— and is walking with an easy stride. My feet follow her because they don't know what else to do yet. I know I will only get one shot at signaling for help, and I can't mess it up. My brain, which is finally fully online after being drugged to sleep, is running a parallel process: looking for exits, looking for uniforms, looking for a person in a position of institutional authority.

There. By the far corridor. A security guard, broad-shouldered, in a dark jacket with an official lanyard. I make eye contact with him. I hold it. I do the thing where you try to communicate via sustained eye contact that you have recently been trafficked across three international borders and would very much like assistance.

He looks back at me.

I take a breath. I start to move toward him.

"Oh my goodness, there you are!" Alana says, suddenly beside me. Her tone makes it sound as if she just now realizing something she should have caught sooner. She turns to the security guard with her hand pressed to her chest and an expression of gentle, embarrassed concern. "I'm so sorry. She doesn't travel well. It's a medication thing. We just got off a very long flight." A small, conspiratorial pause — an apology between two reasonable people, conducted over the top of an unreasonable situation. "She sometimes gets a little— you know." Alana makes a small, circular gesture near her temple. "We're almost to the car."

The security guard looks at me.

I have, I realize, been standing very still with very wide eyes making sustained unblinking eye contact with a stranger, which is not the behavior of someone who is fine.

"Can I—" I start.

"She's great," Alana tells him warmly, already steering me gently by the elbow. "She just needs air and maybe a juice box. Thank you so much for your patience." She smiles at him, and the full wattage of it is, I will say, extraordinary even now. He nods. He steps back.

Outside, the November air is cool and bright. The Uber is already at the curb. Alana gets in first, gives the address in Spanish, and I get in because the alternative— running, in an unfamiliar city, with no local currency and no phone signal yet— is a calculation I haven't finished making.

The car pulls into traffic. Through the window, Barcelona opens up.

Alana is talking. She has been talking since approximately the moment we landed, the way she always talks—bright, fluid, filling the available air. She is talking about Rodrigo. She says he doesn't understand what she's built, what she's committed to. She says he has never appreciated the vision. She says she loved him— *loves* him— but there is a difference between loving someone and letting them dismantle your life plan, and she thinks he confuses the two. She says this with genuine feeling, and I do not doubt she means every word, which is the most complicated part of listening to Alana explain anything.

I am looking at my phone.

It's been off since Tilly's. Alana had it at some point during the flight— I assume she went through it— but it's in my jacket pocket now, returned without comment during our layover because her hands were full with her own powder-pink bags. I ease it out and press the power button, angling the screen away from her.

The loading screen. Then the lock screen. Then, the notifications arrive.

Melissa: forty-one missed calls. A string of texts that begin with BILLIE PICK UP and end with something entirely in caps that I can't read in full before I'm scanning past it. Fourteen voicemails. The most recent message is from a couple hours ago and says only: I'm coming. Don't die.

Tyler: two texts. Both sent last night. The first says:

TYLER

hey, you coming home?

The second, sent thirty minutes later, says:

k. Going to sleep.

The trail ends there. *How inspiring,* I think. *I wonder why I don't want to fold his socks for the rest of my life?*

I look at those two messages for a moment. I think about what I would have felt two months ago, reading them— how I would have hoped for more from Tyler. Now there's no desire in me. Not for him. Not for his love. What we had just hangs there, like a sentence someone else started and never bothered to complete.

I scroll. And then I see another name:

Rodrigo. Three messages. All checking on me, making sure I'm alright. The last one makes my breath catch in my throat:

RODRIGO

I'm in Barcelona. I need you to tell me you're okay. My heart will not rest until I know. Please.

I stare at it.

My heart will not rest until I know.

I have never in my life received a message like that. Not from Tyler. Not from anyone. It is the most plainly, unself-consciously honest thing a person has sent me in years, and it arrives via a man I met for twelve minutes at a baby shower, who told me not to make new friends and also whispered be careful into the space between us like it was something he had to give.

My heart will not rest until I know.

Alana is still talking. I am not listening to a single word.

I want to reply to him. The impulse to type something

back— I'm here, I'm okay, I'm in a car on a coastal road outside of Barcelona— is so strong that I actually start to do it, my thumb moving toward the keyboard, and then I hear my name.

"Billie?" She's looking at me.

I lock the screen. I put the phone in my lap with my hand over it. "Sorry," I say. "Just checking the time."

She gives me a look that says she is deciding whether to believe this, and then she looks back out the window and continues.

The road narrows. On the left, the coast opens up— wide and grey-blue and completely indifferent to me— and on the right, the land rises into low hills scattered with white buildings. A village. Small, compact, real. A cluster of narrow streets and the particular density of people living their ordinary lives in the same square kilometer they've always occupied.

The car slows.

There's a bend in the road— tight, the kind that requires the driver to brake properly, to actually reduce speed— and as we come into it I look at the door handle and I look at the village and I look at the door handle again and I think: *I'm going to do this.*

I don't decide, exactly. I just sort of— act.

The door opens and the air hits me like a wall and then I am out, rolling onto the side of the road with more noise than I'd planned and considerably more gravel than I'd hoped, and then I am on my feet, and I am running.

Behind me: the car brakes. Hard. I hear Alana's voice— not frantic, just precise and crisp, cutting through the engine noise. I don't look back. I run toward the village. My legs are doing something I didn't know they could do, which is move fast when a real reason presents itself. The pavement narrows into a cobblestone alley and I take it at full speed, and my shoulder scrapes a white wall, and I don't stop.

It's only when I reach the far end of the alley and flatten myself against a wall to breathe that I understand.

My hand is empty. *Where did my phone go?* I just had it!

I reach into my jacket pocket. I press both hands against my jeans. I have no phone. It was in my lap— and it's gone. And I know, before I even finish the thought, that Alana already has it. I know because I know Alana, and that she sees things coming before they arrive. She already had one hand on that phone before the car door opened, while I was too busy fleeing to feel it.

I press my back against the warm Spanish stone and listen to my own breathing.

Rodrigo is somewhere in this city. Melissa is coming. I have no phone, no money, and no idea what street I'm on.

I look at the alley, and the village opening up in front of me, its narrow paths and morning light coated in the sound of someone's radio coming through an open window somewhere above me.

I have never been less prepared for anything in my life.

I start running again.

sixteen

BILLIE

THE BARN STINKS, and is too small. As a woman from Chicago, I am not equipped to deal with living, breathing animals in a farm setting, but here I am, crouched behind a cow. The cow has turned her enormous head towards me, and is looking at me with a resigned expression that says she can't wait to turn me in at the first opportunity.

I was able to run for about two more minutes before my legs started to burn. I think I heard on one of the survival tv shows Tyler watches that if you can't run away from danger, you should hide instead. That's how I ended up in the barn.

Besides the cow I'm currently bunking with, there's four others arranged in stalls, and they're tan-colored rather than black-and-white. The floor is straw and packed earth.

My breathing is loud. Too loud. I am trying to make it quiet, which only makes it louder.

I hear the barn door.

Not a creak— it was already open. Just a shift of light at

my back, the way a shadow changes when someone steps into it. I go very still. The cow in front of me continues being a cow. I'm learning that cows are incredibly unhelpful.

"There you are," says Alana.

She's standing in the middle of the barn, her hair still immaculate, as if she has been for a stroll and not pursuing a fugitive through rural Spain. There is a smear of what might be dust on her left shoe. This appears to be the full extent of the inconvenience I've caused her. Meanwhile, I'm covered in dirt, out of breath, with straw poking out of my hair. I am sure she sees me, because the stalls have no coverings, and she is staring right at me.

I do the only thing that makes any sense in this moment. I try to blend in.

"Moo?" I say.

It comes out smaller than I intended. The cow nearest to me turns its head again and regards us both with disgust.

Alana looks at me.

She looks at the cow.

She looks back at me.

"Really, Billie?" she says.

I glance at the cow with disdain. "Couldn't have helped me out there, could you?"

Alana's hand moves to her waistband. She produces a gun and holds it at her side, not pointed at anything in particular, just present. Just a gun, existing in a barn in Spain next to unhelpful cows.

"Are you done?" she asks.

I stand up slowly. Straw falls off me. Dignity does not return. "I was going to say yes," I say, "but then I thought about it and I think the honest answer is I'm about sixty percent done."

"You ran out of a moving car," she says.

"It wasn't that fast."

"It was going thirty kilometers an hour."

"Which is very slow, actually, when you consider—"

"You hid in a barn," she says.

"It was available."

"Behind a cow."

"She's a new friend," I say defensively. "And I felt we had an understanding. Shockingly, she has not drugged and kidnapped me yet, which means she's the best new friend I've managed to make, recently."

Alana is not laughing. She is doing something more like a giggle, which is worse. "You said moo," she says. "To me. As a strategy." I think she's making fun of me for a second, but then she grabs my hand and pulls me out of the hay, patting me on the back. "You're amazing, Billie. You're such an innovator. You're going to do great negotiating with the Twin Ledger."

"Really?" I look at her sideways.

"I mean it," she nods. "You have a sense of humor even in times of danger. And you're creative. An innovator! I mean, the courage it took to look at me—" she points at herself like she's the President of the world— "*La Diabla,* holding a gun, and to say ... moo?" Alana cackles again. "Grown men have cried in this situation and you just made a hilarious joke instead. You've got courage, Billie."

I pause, trying to take all this in. "*La Diabla,*" I repeat.

Alana waves the gun in the air as if this is small information. "Oh, that's just my nickname. It means she-devil. We'll have to get you a nickname, too! Oh my gosh!" She jumps up in the air and grabs my arm. "Twinsies, am I right?!"

I think about my job. I think about seven years of

answering emails and sourcing marble tile and being good while no one is watching. *Maybe I should have gone into arms dealing instead of real estate.*

"Come on, let's go," Alana nods at the exit to the barn. "The Uber driver is still waiting for us. I told him you have sudden psychotic breaks where you think you see an old lover from many years ago and chase him across the road."

"Can you make the next story about me less tragic, please?" I roll my eyes. "Also, wait." I stand my ground, holding a hand in the air. "If you really want me to do this for you— if you want me to negotiate on your behalf in an incredibly dangerous environment— I am going to need my phone back."

The air seems to thicken. Alana looks at me— gun still in her hand— and crosses her arms, blinking slowly so that her long eyelashes flutter. "Go on..." she says.

She's asking me to make my case. I clear my throat. "We don't have anything if we can't trust each other," I try.

"I don't trust anyone," Alana interjects.

"Sure—" I nod. "You don't trust anyone with *everything.* But you have to trust *some* people with *some* things. And right now, you want me to do a big job for you. I need that phone to brush up on—" I pause, inventing— "negotiation strategies. If you want me to do a good job for you, you have to give me the tools."

Alana chews on the inside of lip as if considering, then smiles.

"You *are* a good negotiator, Billie" she says. She puts the gun back. Just like that. Back in her waistband, disappeared, as if it was never there. "I need you, Billie. Not as a hostage. As someone who can get this done."

Then she reaches into the canvas bag and produces my phone.

I actually reach for it before I've processed what's happened. She lets me take it, which is its own kind of test. I unlock the screen— my background, my apps, my whole portable life— and I feel, for exactly three seconds, something like rescue.

Then I try to call Melissa.

No signal. I try to pull up the map. Greyed out. Messages— I can open the app, but the send button doesn't function. I scroll through what remains: a weather app that still loads. A flashlight. An app that makes your phone sound like a lightsaber, which I downloaded as a joke two years ago and never deleted because I am who I am. A meditation app I have opened exactly once. The camera.

Alana has left me the camera.

I hold the phone. I hold all its warm uselessness. "You stripped it," I say.

Alana pats me on the back. "Like you said, Billie: I don't trust anyone with everything. Now, let's get you some new clothes. You can't negotiate looking like that."

"Where are we—" I start to ask, but Alana cuts me off.

"We're going shopping."

seventeen

RODRIGO

I MADE sure I wasn't followed.

The hotel I've found is called the Hotel Mirador, which means "lookout point," and the only thing it has a view of is a dumpster and the back of a pharmacy. This seems correct for where my life is at the moment.

The lobby is small— undecorated. There's a man behind the desk who does not ask me anything, but takes the cash I slide across the counter. He gives me a key attached to a metal circle. Room seven. Top floor. The elevator is occupied by a bicycle, so I take the stairs.

The room has a bed, a window, and a lamp that works on the third try. Old, amber wallpaper lines the entire room like a present wrapped in reverse. The window, when I push it open, gives me a direct line of sight to the pharmacy's service entrance.

I set my duffel on the chair— the only chair— and sit on the edge of the bed. The mattress makes a sound. I give it a moment. This place may be cheap, but I believe— for the moment— I am safe.

My fingers shake a little as I pull open the zipper on my

duffel and tear at the lining— there, I've sewn emergency euros into the pack. I count them. Three hundred euros, folded flat. It won't last long in this city, but it will last long enough to get me to the Tuscan countryside. I put it on the bed beside me and look at my phone.

No response from Billie.

I dial my degenerate cousin, Benny.

He picks up on the second ring, which means he was already holding the phone, waiting for my call.

"Primo!" he says, his voice warm and surprised. "You are alive! Fantastic news. I had this feeling, you know? I lit a candle for you. At the church here in Tuscany. The little one near the olive trees. I told the priest my cousin might be murdered, possibly with a rope, very suddenly, and he said—"

"Benny."

"—he said he would pray, which I thought was nice. I knew about the rope because an old contact called me and I begged him to intervene but of course he would not. I tried to call you but you did not pick up and thank God you are alive—"

"Benny."

"Alive!" he says again, as if confirming it a second time settles something for him. "Good. Good. Because I felt responsible—"

"Benny," I say, for the fourth time. "I need to get to the house."

"Yes," he says, immediately serious. "Yes. Of course. But you can't come direct. The Twin Ledger has people watching the road from the north, I think. I haven't confirmed this, but I have a feeling, and my feelings have been very accurate since I stopped drinking so much. The doctor says the two things are related but I don't see how. The hit *La Diabla* took out on you was broadcast to everyone, amigo. Every assassin in Europe. The Twin Ledger has put quite a high price on your head—"

"What's the plan?"

He thinks for a moment. I can hear him thinking, which sounds like the scrape of a chair and then a low, tuneless humming. "I send someone," he says finally. "Someone I trust. He can be there tomorrow. He'll take you through the back roads— through Ávila, the long way, but safer. He knows the ground."

"Who?"

There is a pause. The kind of pause that has something in it.

"A friend," Benny says.

"Benny."

"A very trustworthy friend?" he adds, helpfully.

"How trustworthy?"

"Very. Almost completely." A brief silence. "He has a small— a very minor— connection to the Twin Ledger. Only driving, like me. He drives for them sometimes. *Did* drive. Past tense. He's mostly retired now."

"You're sending me a Twin Ledger driver," I say flatly, "to help me escape the Twin Ledger."

"He only drives!" Benny says, with genuine offense. "He's not a— he doesn't do the other things. He just drives. He's the best driver I know. He drove for the Spanish national rally team for two years before the— the incident — which was not his fault, by the way, it was the co-driver's fault, everyone knows this—"

"Fine," I say.

There is a beat. I fill the silence with the question I can't escape.

"Benny, do you know where Alana is? Have you heard the name 'Billie' mentioned in connection with her?"

Benny clucks his tongue. "No, no no no. Benny has not heard of a man named Billie— is this Alana's new Rodrigo? Has she moved on so quickly? Good news for you if that is the case—"

"No," I say, sighing. "Billie is an American woman." *A very beautiful one,* I want to add, but I don't, because I know Benny would only tease me for it. "Alana has befriended her and, well, we have not heard from her since."

"Oh, this is very bad news for Billie then, yes? Last I heard, Alana was in Chicago. There has been no mention of *La Diabla* being on the move, but word travels at first very slow, and then very fast—"

"I'll wait for your driver—" I interrupt. Benny can opine on many subjects for hours. Time I do not have. "Tomorrow."

"Primo," he says, and his voice raises to the timber he used when we were twelve and playing football in the grass, "I'm glad you're not dead. I mean that sincerely. You are my favorite cousin and also the only one who has never asked to borrow money."

"That's because I know you don't have any."

"This is true," he agrees. "Rest. I'll send you his number. Don't tell him about your paintings. He'll try to sell them."

"Noted," I say.

We hang up.

I set the phone on the nightstand and look at the wallpaper for a while. I try not to worry. It's impossible.

Alana is not the type to disappear. So many hours and not a word from her. *What has she done with Billie?* My stomach seems to flip in place. Is it possible Alana noticed the way I looked at Billie, and has chosen to eliminate her?

The idea that my attraction to Billie might have gotten her killed is something I cannot live with.

I check my phone. Still no response from Billie.

I think about what I know: Alana posted a photo— at Tilly's, the two of them laughing, drinks raised. Alana sent me that photo on purpose, to show me the vision board was still working. Billie was there. Billie was smiling. Billie did not know, in that photograph, what was standing next to her.

I think about Billie's face at Melissa's shower. The enormous dark eyes with the gold in them— I keep returning to the gold, which annoys me, because it is a very specific detail to have retained about a woman I met only once. I think about the way she stood her ground when I was cold to her, the way she absorbed it and came back sideways with humor instead of resentment. Her joke about the baby picture game sheet. *Were you this unhappy when you were a baby, or did it develop over time?* I think about her saying that, showing me the sheet, and how it was genuinely funny, and that I almost laughed, and that I spent the rest of the shower reminding myself not to.

She has a boyfriend. I remember this now. Melissa said it on the phone at the airport— Tyler, she called him, with a tone that did not suggest high regard. Tyler, who texted twice and went to sleep. I file this information away in the section of my brain labeled: not relevant, and then I notice that the section labeled not relevant has gotten very crowded lately and most of it is about the same woman.

I look at my sent messages. The last one reads: *I'm in Barcelona. I need you to tell me you're okay. My heart will not rest until I know. Please.*

I read it back. It is, by reasonable measure, too emotional. It is the kind of thing that a man says when he has stopped pretending that what he feels is ordinary concern. I decide that I am not embarrassed by it, because there is no room left in me for embarrassment on top of everything else.

My phone buzzes.

I read the message faster than I intend to, because the name on the screen is one I cannot stop thinking about: Billie Harper.

She's answered me.

I sit up straight. I breathe. I open the message.

BILLIE

Alana is my best friend and you barely know me. Stop texting me. Stay away from both of us.

I read it once. I read it again. I set the phone face-down on the bed, and look at the water stain on the ceiling.

I pick the phone back up and read it a third time, because I am a man who likes to be thorough, and also because some part of me is hoping the meaning changes on the third pass. It does not. The message is exactly what it appears to be: short, cold, final. A door closing.

I notice that it stings. I am mildly annoyed that it stings, given that I have spent a more-than-average amount of tonight evading a murder attempt, and this— a brief text from a woman I've met once— is the thing that lands with the dull weight of something *truly* unfortunate. I put the phone down again.

I lay down on my back— the bed's firm coils digging into my shoulders— and stare up at the pockmarked ceiling. *This is what you get for thinking with the wrong part of your body, Rodrigo.*

I don't know Billie, this is true. And I am nothing if not a romantic— a prisoner of love. Am I doing it again? Am I projecting a personality onto someone I do not really *know*? And yet– I sit up on the bed, as I realize:

I do not believe Billie wrote that message.

Billie Harper— the doe-like creature I met— is someone who *cannot* tell a lie with ease. It is in her face. It is in the way she talks.

That woman did not write this text.

I am as certain of this as I am of anything. The cadence is wrong. The register is wrong.

And, perhaps, I do not truly know Billie— yet— but I *do* know Alana. Alana, who writes in short, conclusive sentences when she is being strategic— I have received enough of them to recognize the pattern. *Stop texting me.* That phrase. It *sounds* like Alana in that it lacks tact, or gentleness.

Billie would write something that was trying to be firm but had some apology built into it. The directness— the coldness—

Alana wrote this from Billie's phone.

Which means Alana *has* Billie's phone.

Which means Alana... has Billie.

I open Instagram before I have finished thinking this through. Alana's stories. The first is from earlier tonight— Tilly's, the photo I already know, the drinks raised, the amber light. The second was posted ten minutes ago: Alana and Billie, together in a place I don't recognize immediately. White walls, good lighting, designer outfits hanging on racks. It looks like a luxury women's clothing store.

Did Alana kidnap Billie... to go shopping?

I expand the photo.

Alana is holding something against herself— a jacket,

silk or something very close— and her expression is its usual radiance.

Beside her stands... Billie.

She is wearing— or has been put into— some kind of structured blazer. Fancy. High-gloss. The sort of garment that belongs on an executive who walks into rooms and makes decisions. Billie is raising a hand toward the phone as if she does not wish to be photographed.

Her eyes are not smiling.

She is not fine. She is along for the ride. Appeasing Alana until she can get away. I am familiar with this.

Then, I notice a sign in the back. It reads: *Exclusivo en tienda*, meaning "in-store exclusive." The sign is in Spanish. The store interior is upscale and glamorous, like many I've visited in Barcelona's premier shopping strip, *Las Ramblas.* Is it possible...

Alana and Billie are not in Chicago?

The idea lands on me, making me press myself back into the mattress.

Alana said *she* would come to me. And she knew I was headed to Spain. And now, she has brought Billie with her. Which means Billie is here, in Barcelona, possibly against her will.

I look at the photo for another moment. Then I close the app.

I find Melissa in my recent calls and press call. The phone rings.

Outside the window, the pharmacy's delivery alley is dark and quiet. The lamp flickers slightly when a truck passes on the street below.

The phone rings a second time.

I am not leaving Barcelona until I know Billie is safe.

Finally, the line connects: "She's here," I say, before

Melissa can even say hello. "Alana brought Billie here, to Barcelona."

I explain the text message I received from Billie— telling me to stay away— and that the store pictured on Instagram is somewhere on *Las Ramblas.*

I do not say the other thing I noticed about the photograph— Billie's eyes, her open lips, her perfect features. How beautiful she looks, even when protesting having her photograph taken.

"Well, that makes sense, because I finally heard from Billie," Melissa says, and her tone makes me imagine that her eyes are rolling.

"And?"

"She sent me a message saying we couldn't be friends anymore," Melissa continues, annoyed. "And it said—" she pauses, and I hear the sound of her unlocking her phone— "'Hey so like, this has been fun but I think we're honestly just at different places in our lives. Like I'm sure you're great but this whole baby thing is kind of a lot and I'm just not, like, feeling it. Totally not sorry, bye.'"

There is a long silence between us.

"Totally not sorry, bye," she repeats. "I'm supposed to believe that Billie Harper, who made me a card when my cat died that was four pages long and had a dried flower pressed into it, sent me 'totally not sorry, bye' to permanently end our friendship."

"Alana wrote both messages," I say.

"Obviously Alana wrote both of us," Melissa says. "I got a call from Tyler, too. He's freaking out. Apparently Alana texted him from Billie's phone and broke up with him. Something about him being a selfish asshole who she never wants to talk to again, which is true, but— is Alana trying to overhaul Billie's life?"

Alana is not that selfless, I want to say, but I get to more important things instead.

"Billie's boyfriend is so bad you see this as an improvement?" I ask, trying not to let too much curiosity into my voice.

There's a long silence, and I almost feel like I can hear Melissa smiling on the other end of the line if only briefly. Then, she gets straight to business.

"We called the police, but they said there's nothing they can do internationally. And Billie's in Spain, so— so we're coming," Melissa says. "We're already on our way to the airport."

I pause. "We?"

"Steve and I."

"Melissa," I say.

"Don't."

"You are very pregn—"

"She's my best friend and she is in Spain with an international arms dealer, and she doesn't have anyone else."

"What about Tyler?" I try not to let a sarcastic edge enter my voice. Tyler does not sound like a winner, so far.

"Tyler is and always has been— useless," Melissa admits. "He's having a meltdown right now because he genuinely believes she's dumped him. Every time I try to explain what really happened he freaks out, says I'm lying, and hangs up. I'm going to try to get him on a plane too," Melissa continues, with the weary determination of a woman who is managing a great many people at once. "If he can get over himself long enough to understand what's actually happening and that his girlfriend has literally been kidnapped."

"Good luck with that," I say, and mean it. "But are you sure you should fly when you're pregnant and—"

"The baby is coming in four weeks whether I am sitting in my living room or on a plane, and if the baby comes early then Steve will handle it, because he is a grown man who has been to Lamaze class, and we will figure it out, and my baby will have a cool story about being born in Spain. But I am not sitting in Chicago doing nothing."

I consider arguing further. I decide this would be the same as arguing with a wall that has decided to move and has the full structural advantage.

"Fine," I say. "I can call Interpol. I know I said no Police, but at this point Alana is aware that Billie knows what she is."

"You can do that?" she asks. "Just— call Interpol?"

I have been, for the last six months, adjacent to a world that operates alongside institutions like Interpol in the way that a drainage ditch operates alongside a river— parallel, aware of each other, occasionally exchanging information under conditions of mutual benefit. I know a name. I know a number. I know a man who has, in the past, found it useful to be owed a favor by someone who knows where certain cargo goes and who moves it. I have never called in this kind of favor before. I had hoped, genuinely, never to need to.

"I can try," I say. "I have a contact. He's motivated, I think, by the prospect of a Twin Ledger connection. It's not nothing, what I can offer."

"Then do it," Melissa says. "As soon as we hang up."

"Sí," I say.

"And Rodrigo—" she pauses, and her voice shifts slightly, "Billie is okay. I think she's okay. Alana likes her. She's not going to hurt someone she likes."

I think about Billie's eyes, and what she told me about painting, and that electric single moment I have not been able to forget. She *has* to be okay.

There is a knock at the door.

"—the flight is at six-fifteen," Melissa is saying in my ear. "Steve found two seats, business class, which he insists on—"

"One moment," I say.

"Rodrigo?"

The knock comes again. Housekeeping, almost certainly.

"Hold on," I say, to Melissa, and then louder, toward the door: "*No, gracias*. Tomorrow, please. *Mañana*."

Silence from the hallway.

"Anyway," Melissa says, "Steve found the seats, and we—"

The door flies open. The sound of the lock breaking shocks me into action. The frame splinters in a cascade of shards, making me avert my eyes. I hear the thud of the door hitting the wall, and the wallpaper behind it accepting the impact.

The man who stands there is large. Larger than I am. He has, in his right hand, a gun. Not a rope. No rope this time — the Ledger has apparently decided to upgrade.

The lamp flickers when he steps in.

I look at the gun and then at the man. His expression says he has done this before and found it uncomplicated.

"Melissa," I say into the phone, and my voice is— I am going to say this with some amount of private pride— extremely calm.

"What's happening," she says immediately.

"I'll have to call you back."

I put the phone in my pocket, and prepare to fight.

eighteen

BILLIE

THIS STORE— like all others lining *Las Ramblas*— looks like a postcard sent from a life you didn't know you wanted. It's immaculate, the decor all gentle creams and blistering whites. Clothes aren't just displayed on racks, but curated and color-coordinated like items in a museum.

I'm walking three feet behind Alana, who is in her element here, heading toward the fitting room.

"Don't we have to look through the clothes before trying things on?" I say, trying to keep up.

"Of course not silly," Alana giggles and rolls her eyes. "This isn't Macy's. Here you get a personal shopper who stocks the room for you."

"Who's paying for this?" I ask darkly.

Alana opens her canvas bag and produces a credit card. She holds it up between two fingers, and the gold-flecked light in the boutique catches it. I recognize it well.

It is *my* credit card.

My name is on it. Billie Harper.

"That's my card," I say.

"Mm," she says, her tone communicating she is aware of this. "You left your purse unattended while you were sleeping on the plane. Really irresponsible of you, Billie."

"I wasn't sleeping, I was *drugged*— and I don't need new clothes just to—"

Alana stops in her tracks and turns me toward a mirror on a nearby wall. Seeing us side by side, it's not difficult to understand her wordless point. She looks effortlessly glamorous. I am covered in dirt and hay.

"Why can't you dress for who you want to be?" Alana says, and she leans over so her toothy smile reflected in the mirror looks like a devil on my shoulder. "You're so willing to spend time and energy on everyone else. Who's spending time on *you?*" She pats my shoulder gently. "Besides, if you show up to the Twin Ledger and don't look the part, Marco and Mateo— my bosses— will shoot you in the face. So let's make it good."

"You've talked me into it," I say, following her again. "But my clothes wouldn't be that bad if they weren't covered in hay—"

"It's not the hay," Alana says.

We reach the fitting rooms and Alana pushes me into the biggest one, then perches herself on a perfect white-cushioned couch outside.

The saleswoman returns with an armful of things in dark, structural colors— charcoal, black, one deep plum— and passes them to me through the door. As it closes behind her, I spot the gun still lingering on Alana's waistband, and am suddenly reminded there's nowhere to run. Trying on clothes— in my ordinary life— is already stressful. Pants that are too tight. Stomach bulge. Itchy fabrics. Now, I have to do it at gunpoint.

The fitting room is large and features flattering lighting. I look at the pile of garments on the small bench. I pick up the first thing— a blazer, charcoal, clean-lined— and put it on.

I look in the mirror.

I look in the mirror for a *long* time.

Who the heck is that?

The woman in the mirror looks like me— if I were the sexy CEO of a glamorous social media company. I'm wearing a blazer that fits— not approximately, not with the small adjustments and compromises of something that was made for someone else's body and accepted by mine, but that actually *fits*. The shoulders are exactly where they should be. The fabric lies flat. The woman in the mirror stands like she has somewhere to be and is deciding whether the people there have earned her presence yet.

I don't recognize her.

"Well?" Alana calls.

I come out.

Alana looks at me and something happens in her face— not surprise, but satisfaction in being right. "Yes," she says immediately. "That. Exactly that."

"It's expensive," I say.

"Billie, we have your credit card! Don't worry about it! It's on me."

"With *my* credit card," I remind her— a fact she conveniently ignores.

She tilts her head. "You want to know why this works? It's because of what it says before you open your mouth. Before you sit down, before you speak, before you do a single thing— people have already made a decision about who you are." She gestures at me, at the blazer, at the general fact of my reflection. "Right now you look like someone who won't accept a bad deal. That's the whole negotiation. Half of it. More than half." She pauses. "Do you know what you looked like before?"

"Don't," I say.

"Like someone who raises alpacas," she says. "Sweetly. From a small farm." Then, she adds generously. "You looked like someone who is very good at it."

She's not wrong. I've been wearing bohemian blouses and cut-off capris for years, mainly because I haven't had time to evolve any type of new fashionable perspective. I've been too busy getting Mr. Franklin coffee, and making his dinner reservations, and managing his calendar.

"People treat you like the assistant because you dress like you've already accepted it," Alana says, not unkindly. "Dress like the thing you want to be instead, and watch what changes." She reaches out and adjusts my collar a half-inch. "The world is extremely shallow, and this is like, totally good news for people like you. Because shallow things are easy to change."

Alana produces her phone. "Okay, stay right there," she says, already moving to stand beside me. She extends her arm. "For Instagram. We're on a girls' trip. Obviously."

"No, I'd really prefer you didn't—" I hold my hand up to decline but... click. I'm too late. She takes the photo. My face is contorted in awkward protest. Alana is radiant.

Alana looks at the photo with genuine pleasure. "Perfect," she says. "We look incredible. Also, this way if you decide to double-cross me and go to the police later, I can show that you were totally on board with taking this trip." She posts it before I can think about what that means, or who will see it, or what it will look like to a man named

Rodrigo who is somewhere in this city, waiting to find out if I'm okay.

I feel guilty thinking about Rodrigo. *You have a boyfriend*, I remind myself, thinking of Tyler. I wonder if he's panicking. Maybe he's sent an entire search party after me. Even as I think about the idea, I know it's unlikely.

"Oh my gosh!" Alana says, reversing her phone so I can see her feed. "Tyler posted a picture of his latest video game score on instagram! Looks like he's really winning."

My heart sinks. *He doesn't even care that I'm missing.* Then, suddenly, I'm filled with rage. "He— he doesn't even care that I'm gone," I say, feeling my cheeks flush.

"Billie," Alana shakes her head. "You can do so much better than him." There's a long pause. "Also..." She hesitates.

"What?" I ask.

"... he might be posting as if it's no big deal you're gone because I used your phone to text him and break up with him, on your behalf."

"You did *what*—"

She holds up a hand. "You can thank me later. But seriously, Tyler was dragging you down. I just figured you could use a fresh start, you know? With someone who really appreciates you."

At first, I want to shout at her. But then, I think about the piles of laundry Tyler leaves for me. The dishes in the sink. And how I always feel like he doesn't see the real me—who I could be, if someone just... cared about me.

Alana grabs my shoulders and spins me back toward the mirror. "I mean, like, would *this* woman really put up with Tyler?"

No, I think to myself. *She wouldn't. She would go after*

what she wants. I shudder, thinking about how terrible it would be if Alana knew that what I really want is a man like Rodrigo.

I look at my reflection one more time.

The alpaca farmer is still in there somewhere, I think. But she's wearing better clothes now.

nineteen

RODRIGO

I'VE HUNG up the phone and placed it in my pocket, and now, my only concern is finding a weakness in the man standing in the doorway of my hotel room.

He's tall— very tall— and he knows it. The gun is already out, already level. He moves like someone who has done this before, which means I need to be faster than someone who has done this before. The overhead bulb flickers on when the door opens because it's on a sensor, and for half a second we are both blinking at each other under its terrible yellow light.

I grab the lamp.

It's a bedside lamp– small and ceramic and shaped like a pineapple, which is a detail I will think about later and possibly laugh at. Right now, it is a weapon, and I bring it around in a wide arc and catch the man across the side of the head before he can fully correct his aim. It makes a sound I don't love. He staggers. The gun swings wide. I don't wait— I close the distance between us immediately, because in a small room with a man that size, distance is not my friend.

His hand comes back up. The gun comes back up. The barrel is level with my chest.

There are moments that slow down. This is one of them. I can hear the radiator ticking. I can see his trigger finger, which has not moved yet. I'm surprised he hasn't taken a shot. Maybe he doesn't want to draw attention by risking a missed shot— he needs a clean, quick kill.

I go sideways instead of backward, which surprises him, and I get both hands on his gun arm and fold it against the natural direction of the joint. He makes a sound. The gun doesn't go off. He actually seems surprised I'm fighting back. Maybe his other targets generally choose to flee. I use this to my advantage and elbow him in the face. He jerks back and throws a left hook that lands in my shoulder and sends me flying against the wall, but that's okay because the gun is in my hand now.

We're both a little surprised at this fact.

The man comes at me and swings. He is very large and the swing has real intention behind it. I level the gun at him.

He stops.

"*Siéntate,*" I say, which is not something I practiced for this particular situation, but seemed appropriate. Sit down.

He looks at me. He looks at the gun. He looks at the lamp, which is on the floor, the pineapple broken neatly at the stem. He does what I've asked and sits on the bed.

I back toward the duffel bag, which is where I left it— on the chair by the window, still packed. This is a good habit, the not-unpacking. I've learned it gradually, over months of situations that required rapid exits.

I get the bag onto my shoulder without taking my eyes off him. He is watching me with a look that says he's recalibrating his options, and I have maybe forty-five seconds before he decides his options have improved. I go to the window.

It opens outward, which is not ideal, but I've made worse exits. One story down, there's a narrow ledge that juts out. Below that, a fire escape and a five foot drop to the street. Doable. There's a cat meowing in front of the pharmacy, but otherwise, no witnesses.

I go out feet-first, grab the sill, and let myself down until my boots find the stone ledge. I grab onto the fire escape and climb to the bottom. It holds. I take a breath, let go, and drop.

The landing is hard. My knees absorb it, my shoulder takes a small complaint from the duffel, and I am standing in an empty Barcelona street.

Above me, the window is still open. I don't look up to see if he's there.

I start running.

* * *

Many blocks later, I decide I'm far enough away that the man will not find me. I find a doorway on a side and stop to catch my breath. The gun goes into the duffel bag. The duffel bag goes back on my shoulder. I take out my phone and call Melissa.

She picks up on the first ring, which tells me she's been waiting.

"Rodrigo—" she starts.

"New plan," I say.

A pause. "Why? The old plan was pretty good."

"Things just got... more urgent," I look back down the street in the direction I came from. Nothing moving. Not yet. "I had a visitor with a gun come to see me at the hotel."

Melissa gasps. “Are you—”

“I’m fine.” I say it before she can finish asking. “Listen to me. I need you to do something.”

She listens. She is good at that when she needs to be, which is not always obvious about her until the moment you need it. “I’m going to go straight to Alana and give her what she wants, which is me.”

“You’re going to use yourself as bait.”

“*Sí.* Maybe I can convince her to let Billie go and cancel the hit she took out on me.”

“That’s insane,” she says.

“Probably,” I agree.

“You could just— wait. You could go to the Interpol contact and let them—“

“There’s no time for waiting.” I say it quietly. The street is narrow and old, the kind of Barcelona architecture that’s been here for three hundred years and doesn’t particularly care what's happening on the street level. Laundry lines the buildings. “I need to find Billie before Alana decides she’s no longer useful. You understand?”

Another silence. “Yes,” Melissa says.

“I’m sending you and Steve a contact. His name is—” I check the name on my phone. I give it to her. “He knows a woman high up at Interpol. My cousin Benny has worked with him. You tell him everything. Everything, Melissa. Don’t decide what he needs to know. I’m going to set my phone so you can find my location. Once I link up with Alana and Billie, send Interpol after us. Don’t wait.”

“Okay. Rodrigo?” she pauses. “Good luck.”

I stay in the doorway another moment after I hang up. The Barcelona night has the kind of quiet that isn’t ever completely silent. Faint music echoes from somewhere, the distant murmur of traffic; I go into my phone settings and enable location sharing. Melissa will now be able to see where I am at all times.

I think about Billie. I think about that unique steadiness in her eyes that she probably doesn't know she has, the same quality that made me think, when I first saw her, of something small but unbreakable. There's a Spanish phrase I've heard my whole life: *resistencia silenciosa*. Silent resistance. The kind of strength you carry before you know you have it. She has it. She just hasn't been told yet.

I'm going to make sure someone tells her.

I open a new message to Alana.

I type: *I know you're in Barcelona. Where can I meet you?* Then, painfully, I add a heart emoji at the end.

I send it before I think too carefully about whether it's wise.

The reply comes in less than one minute.

She's sent a pin with our meeting spot, along with the time she wants to meet—just two hours from now.

I Google the pin's location. It's a compound, according to the satellite view. The images online show a concrete building set back from the road; a property that was intentionally built to be hard to approach.

And I'm going there with a stolen gun, a duffel bag, and hope.

I push off from the doorway and start moving.

A cat appears on the street, and I notice he looks just like the one that stood outside the pharmacy near my hotel. I wonder if he followed me here? If he was able to follow me, maybe the man who attacked me did the same. I move faster, waving at the cat as I go.

Buena suerte, I think. Good luck. The cat disappears.

The night swallows me up, and I walk toward it.

twenty

BILLIE

I'M STANDING outside a criminal compound, about to negotiate with international arms dealers.

We're on the outskirts of Barcelona, and The Twin Ledger compound is an imposing concrete building that's all angles. Grey walls, no windows on the lower floors, a fence that means business, a gate that means even more business. There are guards. Multiple. The surrounding landscape is flat and scrubby and thoroughly unimpressed by everything around it, which I find relatable.

I'm wearing the blazer. I'm standing up straight and doing my absolute best to look like I've been sent to this sort of place before.

"You look great," Alana says, reading me like a book.

"I feel like I'm going to be sick," I say.

"If you throw up, just don't get it on my shoes," she says helpfully.

"Can we go in yet, or—" I've been asking this question for the last fifteen minutes.

"Not yet," Alana says, checking her Cartier watch. "We're waiting for a special guest."

She's mentioned this special guest multiple times but won't tell me who it is. I'm afraid. I've learned that surprises are never good if they're coming from Alana.

Then, a car turns off the main road. A black sedan, plain — the kind that wants not to be noticed— and it slows as it approaches and my heart does a small, preparatory thing in my chest for no reason I can identify yet. The car pulls to a stop at the edge of the access road. A door opens. A man gets out.

Everything goes quiet.

It's Rodrigo.

He's wearing a dark jacket and his jaw looks exactly like it did at Melissa's baby shower, which is to say it looks like it was carved from stone by someone who took their time. Moonlight strikes a path through the dark night, and Rodrigo walks it, his boots crunching over the brush. When he gets closer his eyes find me. They're warm, those eyes. Warm and dark, and I have been refusing to fully admit that I remembered them perfectly since the baby shower, and the refusal has been doing me no good because here we are and here they are.

My heart is pounding. I tell my heart to keep it together.

"You're okay," he says, when he reaches us. At first I think he's talking to Alana, but then I realize he's looking at... *me.*

Alana must have thought the same, because she leaps into his arms, wrapping herself around him. "Of course I'm okay, you silly duck," Alana purrs. Rodrigo lets her embrace him, but he's looking at me the entire time. "But you've really put me through hell. And now I have to go to all this trouble to cancel the hit I took out on you, and get my best friend all wrapped up in it, which is like, totally unfair. And all because you had cold feet!"

Alana releases him and Rodrigo is still looking at me. "Billie," he says, and hearing him say my name makes me feel like we've known each other forever. "Are you okay?"

"I'm okay," I say.

"You're sure?"

"I'm sure." I hesitate, and then I say, because I want him to know that I know: "I understand now. What you meant. At the baby shower." I look at him. "I didn't listen, and I should have."

Something moves through his expression— not surprise, exactly. More like relief. It's as if he's been carrying a weight and has been given permission to set it down briefly. "It wasn't your fault," he says. "You didn't know."

"What's going on here?" Alana says, throwing her hands up in the air. "Like, Rodrigo, you don't even seem happy to see me!"

The warmth leaves Rodrigo's face. "Maybe that's because I've spent the last two days dodging assassins you sent my way."

"It's fine!" Alana waves a hand in the air as if this is nothing. "Billie's going to help me cancel the hit."

She tells him. All of it. The hit, the Twin Ledger's refusal to cancel. She tells him that Marco and Mateo run this particular compound, and that the Twin Ledger operates on momentum, and that momentum, once started, has to be interrupted by something compelling enough to warrant the disruption.

"And that," she says, gesturing at me with the full authority of someone presenting evidence, "is Billie. Who is the best head negotiator in the city of Chicago. Or really, like an assistant, but whatever, her career is on the rise!" She pauses. "The three of us go in. Together. Billie makes the case. You are a human being with value, which is a concept these men struggle with, but which Billie can communicate in a way that makes them feel it's in their interest. We get them to drop it. We leave." She spreads her hands. "Easy."

Rodrigo is very still.

Then: "No," he says. He says it quietly, which is worse. "No. I'm not bringing her into this compound. Billie didn't ask for any of this. I will handle it myself—"

"You'll handle it yourself," Alana says, with the tone of someone who has heard this sentence before, "by doing what, exactly? Dying?"

"If necessary," Rodrigo shrugs. He turns to me and presses his car keys into my hands. Then, he adds seriously, "Billie, take the car. Go right now. Drive as far away as you can." He pulls me close to him into a tight hug, pressing himself against me. Then, he whispers in my ear. "Call Melissa. She'll get Interpol. You'll be safe." He releases me, and I can smell his cologne still hovering nearby, the scent of sea salt making me imagine summers that we'll never have.

I could take the keys. I could go.

But then I look at Rodrigo and I know— I just *know*— if I let him walk in there with Alana, he won't come out alive.

He turns. Alana follows. The two of them start to walk toward the compound together, but stop when I call out—

"Rodrigo!"

He turns.

I have no idea what I'm doing. My hands are entirely steady, which surprises me. "I want to do this."

Silence. Rodrigo stares at me. Even Alana looks a little surprised.

"I'm not standing outside while you go in there by yourself because you think you're protecting me." I take a breath. "I know I lied about being a negotiator. I know I'm technically an assistant who orders lunch and books appointments for a poodle named Bernard. I know that." I pause. "But I have spent years watching what actual negotiators do. I've been in every meeting. I've read every file. I've made more coffee than any human being should be allowed to make, and I've used that time to learn everything there is to know about how to walk into a room and make someone feel the value of what you're asking for." I look at him. "Let me help you. Please."

A long moment. The compound waits behind us, grey and still.

"Please," I say, again. Quieter this time. "What are you going to do otherwise? Spend your whole life running?"

Because if that's the case, there's no way for us to be together, I want to add. But it's an insane thought. I barely know this man. Sure, I might be imagining running off to the Mediterranean countryside with him. But he doesn't know that. *Also, Billie, you have a boyfriend,* I remind myself.

Rodrigo looks at me for a moment that stretches long in the afternoon light. Then, almost imperceptibly, something in him settles. His shoulders drop a half-inch. "Fine," he says, but I can see the worry etched in his eyes.

Alana, beside me, makes a sound of quiet satisfaction.

The three of us turn to face the compound.

I look at the gate. The gate looks back.

I straighten my blazer, and we start walking.

* * *

Walking toward a criminal compound with an arms dealer and a man whose life is currently listed as a bounty item is not, it turns out, what it looks like in the movies. In the movies there is music. In the movies everyone's hair is doing something intentional. In real life, there is the sound of gravel under my shoes and the feeling of the blazer across my shoulders.

Alana walks like she owns the place, which is, I have learned, simply how Alana walks everywhere. Rodrigo is on my left and he keeps looking over at me like he's trying to memorize my face. I attempt to project serenity even though my internal organs are twisting around.

"Okay," Alana says, still walking, voice low and practical. "Before we go in. There are things you need to know."

"I'm listening," I say.

"No empathy," she says. "None. You walk in there and you are the most important person in the room. Not them. You. You don't apologize, you don't hesitate, you don't make a face when someone says something alarming—" she pauses— "and above all, you do not show weakness. Not for a second. Not even a small one." She glances at me sidelong. "Because if you so much as stutter, they're going to rip out our fallopian tubes and tie them around our necks like scarves."

I miss a step.

"Is that— is that a metaphor?" I ask.

"No," she says.

"Right."

"It's happened before."

"Of course it has," I say, trying to act like this information doesn't bother me at all.

Alana stops walking. Just briefly— and she turns to face me with the full seriousness of someone who has forgotten something very important.

"Oh my gosh, I didn't tell you about the rings," she says.

"Could you have waited any longer to inform Billie of everything she needs to know?" Rodrigo hisses at her.

Alana rolls her eyes. I wait.

"Marco and Mateo each wear a ring." She says it carefully. "They're not jewelry. They're keys. Together they unlock a vault— the Ledger's vault, everything they own, billions in assets, weapons, gold, accounts. The whole empire." Her voice drops further. "They are obsessive about them. Paranoid. If you look at the rings, even *glance* at them, they will notice. They will clock it and they will decide you are a threat." She holds my gaze. "Do *not* look at the rings. Don't let your eyes drift toward their hands. Don't acknowledge them. They do not exist. Understood?"

"Understood," I say.

"Say it back," she says.

"The rings do not exist," I say.

She nods. She turns back to the compound and resumes walking.

I straighten my spine. I think about the woman in the mirror in the boutique fitting room— the one who looked like she was deciding whether the people in the room had earned her presence. I think: be her. *Just be her.* She has better posture and she isn't afraid of anything.

Billie, why are you here? I ask myself. I don't have to do this. I could still turn away. But then I think about Rodrigo, and how he didn't ask for any of this either.

The ground shifts under my left foot. A loose stone, half-buried in the path— the compound's access road is old and uneven, the kind of surface that doesn't care about your intentions. My ankle twists. I go forward in a lurch that is entirely at odds with the composed professional image I have been constructing. I catch myself, barely, three stumbling steps before I find my footing again and stand upright.

There is a pause.

Rodrigo does not comment, but gently helps me stand a little taller by grabbing my hand, then sliding an arm around my waist to help set me right. Alana does not comment. This is, I think, the most generous thing either of them has ever done for me.

I straighten the blazer and keep walking.

The gate is tall, iron, and guarded by two men. They look at us as we approach. The larger of the two reaches for something on his belt.

And then we're inside the perimeter— I'm not entirely sure how, except that Alana said something in rapid, authoritative Spanish that I didn't catch, and someone made a call on a radio, and the gate opened, and then we were surrounded.

There are four of them, suddenly— guards, materializing from the sides of the entrance like they stepped out of the concrete itself. They are armed and not friendly, and my heart is doing something I would describe as "a lot." Someone says something I don't understand, directed at Alana, and Alana responds in a tone that says she finds the question irritating.

Then, a fifth figure appears from the far side of the entrance.

He is bald. Wide. His expression belongs on a monument to the concept of disapproval. He looks at Alana. Alana looks at him.

"Ivan!" she says, in the warm, bright, completely disingenuous tone of a woman greeting a neighbor she has always found deeply unremarkable. She switches to Croatian with a smile that never touches her eyes: "Izgledaš umorno, Ivan. Malo odmora bi ti dobro došlo." She pratters on and then looks at me conspiratorially and says, under her breath: "I told him he looks tired and could use a rest, and that his bald head looks like the dark side of the moon. He loves it when I tease him," Then, back to him, in English: "Long week?"

Ivan stares at her. His jaw works. He says something back, quiet and sharp, and Alana simply waves her hand at him the way you wave off a small and irritating insect.

"He'll let us through," she says, to me. "He hates me, but he's also afraid of me." She turns back to Ivan and smiles again. It is an absolutely spectacular smile. "Hvala, Ivan," she says, all sweetness.

Ivan steps aside. He does not look happy about it.

We move forward, into the compound proper.

It is everything the outside promised. Concrete walls. Low ceilings in the corridor we enter. The smell of metal and something chemical underneath it. There are weapons visible— mounted, holstered, racked in neat rows through a half-open door we pass. The whole place hums.

Two guards flank us immediately, falling into step behind.

And then Rodrigo's arm comes up— just slightly, just enough— and he steps fractionally forward and to my left, positioning himself between me and the nearest guard. It is not dramatic. He does not announce it. It is the most ordinary thing in the world if you don't know to look for it, and I am looking, and I see it completely.

He is putting his body between me and the thing that could hurt me.

Something sits very still in my chest. Something I don't examine too closely, because we are in a criminal compound and this is not the time.

I look forward. The corridor narrows toward a set of heavy doors at the far end, and behind those doors, somewhere, are two men with matching rings and a price on a life I've been asked to argue for.

I am an assistant who orders poodle grooming appointments... but I'm wearing a blazer that fits.

I keep walking.

twenty-one

RODRIGO

WE'RE STANDING in front of the leaders of the world's most dangerous criminal organization, and all I can think about is the scent of Billie Harper's perfume.

She is beautiful. *Hermosa.* I shouldn't have let her come to this place. But she would not take the keys to my rental car. She would not leave. And I worried— because I can see it in her doe-like eyes— that if I had made her go, she would have thought it was because I did not believe in her.

Billie *needs* to be believed in. If only she knew; I don't just believe in her. I would cross countries for her. She has the kind of beauty that makes a man commend his life into her hands without care.

And that's what I've done.

We're in a concrete room— a killbox, if you care to look at it that way— and Marco and Mateo Ledger are standing across a table from me.

Alana is to my right, drumming her nails against the table. And to my left is Billie, who I'm trying very hard not to stare at. Still, I risk a peek. Her shoulders squared. There's a small crease between her brows. Her eyes are fixed on the twins with an expression I can only describe as fearless. These men are dangerous, but Billie Harper looks like she might, at any moment, ask to see their manager. I find this extraordinary.

"You thought this request warranted an in-person visit, Alana?" Marco says, his long, dark hair hanging heavy over his face. His hair is greasy and shoulder-length, and both he and his twin are dressed in Europe's finest: bomber jackets in ugly prints. Gold chains swing around their necks.

"Okay, so." Alana steps forward, and the temperature in the room changes. She is wearing a shade of pink that has no business existing in a building like this. She gestures at Billie and me with the casual authority of someone presenting a school project. "I brought my representative. This is Billie. She negotiates. She's like, honestly? So much meaner than me." She pauses to let that land. "And this—" she gestures at me, "—is Rodrigo. He's the one with the contract on his head. See?" She tilts her head at Marco with great sincerity.

"The contract *you* took out," Marco reminds her.

"Right, but you cannot kill him. Look at him."

I hear Billie exhale very quietly beside me. I think it might be the only laugh she can afford right now.

Marco, across the table, does not look like a man who takes direction from anyone, let alone a woman in a bubbly pink dress describing me as visually compelling. His brother Mateo, beside him, is identical in structure— same jaw, same cold precision in the eyes. He looks at me the way a collector looks at something he's decided to acquire.

"Once a contract is issued, it cannot be reversed," Marco says, shaking his head. "Alana— you of all people know this to be true. The contract is already distributed. Hundreds of freelancers. They have spent their time. Their resources."

He opens one hand. "We pull back now— what does that say? That the Ledger changes its mind?" He says this like the concept is mildly offensive. "That we waste the time of the people who work for us?"

Mateo nods. "Assassins are not patient people," he adds, almost pleasantly. "And nobody wants to make an assassin feel disrespected. That is, as you might say, a bad investment."

I look at the window on the far wall. It's open. About two meters from where Billie stands.

I lean close to her. Her hair smells like something warm — honey, maybe— and I make a note not to think about that right now either. "If this goes wrong," I say quietly, barely moving my mouth, "you run. That window." I tilt my head toward it slightly. "Don't think about it. Just go."

She turns to look at me, and for a moment those Bambi eyes are aimed directly at me and I nearly forget what I was saying. "What about you?" she whispers.

"I'll be behind you." I know this is a lie. I'll be dead before she makes it out the window.

She holds my gaze for just a second too long, and then nods once, very seriously, like we've agreed to something binding. Without planning it, I take her hand. Just briefly. My thumb against her knuckles, her fingers small in mine. She doesn't pull away. Then the moment closes, and Alana is talking again, and Billie steps forward.

"Boys," Billie says. Her voice only wavers once, on that first syllable, and then it doesn't waver again. "Thank you for meeting with us."

Marco says nothing. Mateo spreads his hands— go ahead.

And something happens. I watch it happen. Billie Harper, who came in looking like someone's very earnest assistant, straightens to her full five feet and three inches and begins to speak like she's spent years studying what makes people say yes.

She doesn't threaten them. Not directly. She is too smart for that, and I suspect she understands, the way good negotiators do, that the most dangerous thing in a room like this is a person who isn't afraid to walk away from the table. "You may think pulling the contract is a logistical nightmare. You have vendors— assassins— to whom you've promised payment. You may think it makes you look weak to reverse direction on an order. But have you considered you'd be exhibiting strength? Picture this..." she puts her hands in the air, painting a picture for them. "The Twin Ledger is an organization that can not only issue a hit— they can stop it mid-contract. Cancelling a contract tells the world that *you* control the game. You dominate this hemisphere. Furthermore," she leans in, motioning at Alana. "Alana's knowledge of your operation runs deep—"

"Well, I wouldn't say that," Alana answers, looking nervous.

"What does it tell your contractors if you won't cancel even for one of your own employees who's worked for you for years? What thanks can they be assured if you won't stop a hit? There is power in ceasing just as there is power in commencing. Don't you want to show your power... today? Perhaps Alana could repay this favor by doing the next three jobs for free."

"... I'm actually really busy right now," Alana starts to say, but Billie shushes her.

Marco and Mateo consider this. They look at each other and then— they nod.

"Your negotiator is good," Mateo says to Alana. "But we cannot cancel a hit. The wheels are already in motion."

My heart pounds in my chest. Is this the part where they shoot me?

"But we won't kill him today," Marco says. "You made this mess, Alana. You will clean it up. We will let the contract run its course so one of the assassins can collect. And—" he pauses, "as a personal favor, we will ask our most aggressive assassins to ignore the order. You will have to deal with the rest. "

"Good luck to you," Mateo adds. He looks at me once— brief, like a notation. "Today. This room. You walk out." He looks back at Billie. "But the contract stays. It is no longer ours to pull. We gave our word."

Alana, Billie and I look at each other. The air chills. The meeting is over. There's nothing we can do but turn to leave.

Then, Marco says— almost as an afterthought, in Spanish, to his brother— "Just like a woman, isn't it, to change her mind. Emotional, aren't they?"

The brothers laugh.

I think: *oh, no.*

I look at Alana first. She has gone quiet, which is always bad news. Billie stares at her, and I forget that she doesn't speak Spanish. I lean over and translate the comment into her ear. Billie's hand flies to her mouth and she looks at Alana— she knows as well as I do that this will anger *La Diabla.*

"Okay," Alana says, and her voice is still very sweet. It's always sweetest right before. "So I'm sorry— did you just say something about *women* being emotional?"

"It is simply an observation," Mateo says, gesturing with one hand in a way that means he doesn't consider the subject worth his full attention. "Women. Very emotional. Very— changeable."

"Marco," Alana says. "I once saw you shoot a man in the face because he brought you the wrong lunch order. And you think *women* are emotional."

"Excuse me," Billie repeats. "But Alana works really hard for you and sure, she made a bad decision, but you both kill people every day! She's trying to change! That's growth, not being emotional..."

And then they are both talking.

I would describe what follows as a duet, in the sense that two people are performing it and there is a structure of sorts.

"I've run dozens of operations for you and never *once* asked to change the objectives, which change on *me* minute to minute!" Alana says, flipping her hair over one shoulder. "It is like, so unbelievable that you don't think the two of you are emotional—"

"Right?" Billie says, and suddenly I'm worried the blazer has given her a little too much confidence. "When men get angry in the workplace, it's viewed as constructive but women can't even have one feeling without being labeled—"

I should, at this point, be steering us toward the exit. I know this. I can see the window from where I'm standing, and I have a very clear sense that this room has a limited quantity of goodwill left in it, and we are spending it faster than we can afford. I know all of this.

But I'm watching Billie Harper hold the floor in a room full of the most dangerous people I have ever stood in front of, and I find that I cannot make myself interrupt her. She is so determined, so strong, so beautiful.

"Sì, sì," Mateo says finally, doing the worst possible thing and laughing at both of them. He gestures at Alana's side, where her gun sits in its holster. "If the women are so capable, then— "He makes a small, contemptuous motion. Go ahead.

He points over his shoulder at a table filled with food. There's an apple sitting on top of a pile of fruit. "Hit the apple."

It is, clearly, a taunt.

I know it's a taunt. Alana knows it's a taunt. The walls of this concrete room know it's a taunt.

Alana can hit the apple all day, every day. She doesn't need to prove herself. But the taunt wasn't for her: it was for Billie.

I watch Billie's jaw set. The brothers look at each other and laugh.

"Billie—" I start.

She reaches across and takes Alana's gun from its holster.

Later, I will think about this moment and try to identify the exact second when I should have stopped it. I will run the sequence back many times. But in real time, everything happens in the space of a breath.

Billie raises the gun and holds up in the air. She says loudly, "... as if I can't shoot an apple anytime I want!" And then, she raises it. She's about to point it at the apple but her wrist adjusts.

The trigger catches. She doesn't *mean* for the gun to go off. These black-market arms don't always function properly. But Billie doesn't know that.

The gun fires.

The sound in a concrete room is not like the sound in the open air. It fills every corner. It has nowhere to go, so it bounces— off the walls, off the floor, off the inside of my skull.

Billie jerks backward from the recoil.

Mateo makes one sound. It is not words.

I'm surprised. Billie is surprised. But no one is more surprised than Mateo, who looks down at the gaping wound in his chest.

Then, he falls down behind the table, and the room is still, and I understand what has happened before I can fully process that it has happened.

Mateo Ledger is dead.

Marco stands, looking at the place where his brother was standing. He doesn't move for three full seconds. He doesn't make a sound.

And then, very slowly, he looks at Billie. Alana gasps. She knows just as well as I do— we're in huge trouble.

My body is already moving. I don't decide to do it. I step in front of Billie— put my back to Marco and my arm out behind me, finding her, my hand closing around her upper arm and pulling her close. She makes a small, stunned sound against my shoulder. The gun is still in her hand. I can feel her shaking.

"Window," I say, very quietly. "Billie. The window. Right now."

Marco hasn't moved. There is something in his stillness that is worse than anything I have seen from him today, and I have seen enough. He lets out a sound like an animal crying in the night. Then, his eyes turn cold. Grief, when it belongs to a man like Marco Ledger, doesn't look like grief. It looks like the moment before a decision.

"Billie," I say, holding her arm in my hand. "We're going to have to run now."

twenty-two

BILLIE

THE THING about accidentally shooting a man is that no one prepares you for it. They don't cover it in corporate onboarding. There's no pamphlet. No HR module titled "What To Do If You Kill Someone At Work, Part One: Managing Your Response." I'm looking at Mateo on the floor and the gun still warm in my hand and I can't quite figure out how to reconcile those two things into a coherent thought, so instead I just say it out loud, to no one in particular:

"I'm a murderer. I just killed a man. Murder. That's something I do now, I guess."

Nobody answers me. Probably because the room has exploded.

Marco is on his knees next to his brother. That's the part that freezes me in place for exactly one second longer than is strategically advisable. His hands are on Mateo's chest. His face is doing something between fury and grief so deep it looks like the ground opening up beneath a person. He's speaking in Spanish, low and fast, and I don't understand a single word of it, but still; I understand all of it.

Then he looks up.

His eyes find mine across the room and I am genuinely certain, in a way I have never been certain of anything in my thirty-five years of professionally underestimating myself, that I am going to die here. Alana takes a step back, and there's a click-clacking of heels as she disappears, but my vision has gone blurry, and I can't tell where.

"Get down—" Rodrigo says, pulling me across the room and removing the gun from my hand.

Rodrigo gets a hand on a heavy metal table and flips it with a force that shouldn't be possible for one person, and then his other hand closes around my wrist and he pulls—hard, fast—and I am behind the table before I've consciously decided to move. The first round hits the table while I'm still folding to the floor. Then another. Then several more in quick succession, and the sound is enormous, filling the room from every direction, and I press my back against the table and pull my knees to my chest and try to remember if I've always been this small or if I've somehow gotten smaller.

"Are you hit?" Rodrigo says. His voice is calm. He's checking my arms, my sides, his hands moving quickly.

"I don't— I don't think so." I do a fast mental survey of my body. Everything reports in. "No. No, I'm okay."

He exhales once. Short and controlled. His hand stays on my shoulder.

"Good," he says. "Stay close."

"How did the gun go off?" I murmur. "I didn't even pull the trigger–"

"Black market weapons," Rodrigo says as another bullet hits the metal table. He peeks over it and returns fire using the very same gun that just betrayed me. "They're unreliable..."

And then, because the universe has a special sense of humor about me and my life, I hear the click of heels again.

I peek around the side of the table just long enough to see her:

Across the room, Alana is crouched next to Mateo's body. No one seems to notice her in the chaos; Marco has already abandoned his brother's body and is yelling at the guards in the corner.

Alana is alone with Mateo's form and her pink blazer is immaculate. Her nails—I can see her nails from here, pale pink with tiny crystals—are moving with delicate precision as she slides a ring off Mateo's finger. She does it the way you'd unclasp a bracelet you found on the sidewalk. Practical. Unhurried. She examines it for one brief second, then tucks it into her blazer pocket and runs toward us, sliding behind the table to join us as if she's making a home run and shooting all the way, keeping our enemies at bay.

"Really," I say. "The ring? That's what you're thinking about right now?"

She looks at me the way a very patient teacher looks at a child who has just asked why the sky is blue for the fourth time.

"You're bad at taking opportunities, Billie," she says. A round hits the wall six inches from her head. She doesn't flinch. "This is why you're behind in life."

More bullets fly from behind us, heading toward Marco and his men. It takes me a second to realize that the guards behind us are... *helping* us. We're in the middle of a full shootout between Marco's loyalists at the far end of the room and the guards who allowed us entry at the front doors. I turn to Alana. "Why are they protecting us?"

Alana shrugs. "Not everyone likes Marco, Billie. He's a bad boss. Unlike you, and very much like me, they probably see an opportunity now that you assassinated his brother." She calls out over her shoulder to Ivan, whose bald head is visible above the crowd that's giving us cover. "Keep it going, Ivan! *La Diabla* thanks you!" She winks at me. "I'm very popular."

I genuinely don't know if she's the most terrifying person I've ever met or the most instructive one, and I don't have time to figure it out because she's already standing fully upright— in the middle of an active firefight, in heels — and she's raising her gun.

What happens next is not something I can describe in real time because time stops existing when Alana goes to work. It's more like a series of still photographs. One guard in the doorway. Then not. He collapses. Another coming around the side of the room, weapon raised. Then not— she takes him out. A third one I hadn't even clocked yet, near the far window. Then not. She moves through the room with the kind of unhurried efficiency that I have, until tonight, only seen applied to things like very good espresso service. The dissonance is so complete that some part of my brain just refuses to fully process it as real.

She pauses. She checks her nails. One is chipped.

"Unfortunate," she says, to herself.

"Alana," Rodrigo calls out, a warning in his voice. "Get us out of here! ¡Rápido!"

"Yes, yes." She drops her hand. "I know."

She's cleared most of the path to the far window, but the room is still active, still loud, still full of men who want us dead for a variety of reasons that have escalated dramatically in the last four minutes. Rodrigo keeps his body between me and the remaining line of fire, which is something I notice and immediately file under "things I'm going to think about later." He's been doing that since the moment everything went sideways. Putting himself between me and whatever's coming next, like he's thought about this before— like this is a decision he made quietly, somewhere in the chaos, and didn't mention.

I duck when a guard comes around the edge of the table at a low angle, faster than the others, getting past Rodrigo's line of sight. His hand closes around my throat before I can get my voice working, and the world tips sideways— and then there's a sound, one shot, close, and the grip disappears.

The guard goes down.

I stumble back. My hand goes to my throat. I'm breathing.

Rodrigo is standing on the other side of where the guard used to be, a gun in his hand. He shot the man to save my life. I look up at him, and he looks down at me, and there is one half-second of something passing between us that is very quiet and has no good words for it— something that in another life, in a different room without all the bullets, might have been the beginning of a conversation.

Then Marco screams.

Marco— from across the room— is on his feet now, looking at the guard Rodrigo just shot.

"My cousin!" he shouts.

The words land.

I look at Rodrigo.

Rodrigo looks at me. Now we've killed Marco's *cousin*.

"What kind of fucked-up family business is this?!" I shout.

Something crosses Rodrigo's face that might, in a universe slightly less violent than this one, have been a laugh. The corner of his mouth does a thing. His eyes do a thing. It lasts approximately half a second before he locks it back down.

"It might be good to like, get to the window," Alana says. She's pointing. "Now."

Marco is moving toward us, or trying to in the midst of the shooting— but he is moving, and his face is something I'm going to see in my nightmares. I turn toward the window.

Rodrigo gets there first. The latch gives. He pushes it open and turns back to help me through the window by grabbing my ass and lifting me up. *He is really strong*, I think, but then I remember I'm supposed to be surviving— so I climb over the sill with all the grace of someone who has spent her career in an ergonomic office chair. My shoelace catches the frame. Rodrigo's hand guides my foot free. I land on the other side in a crouch that I would generously call intentional.

Alana comes through behind me without any of this difficulty whatsoever. Her heels touch the ground and she is already moving. Rodrigo follows her, a rogue bullet shattering the window glass as he tumbles out.

The compound grounds open up ahead of us— wide, dark, flat, lit at intervals by lights along the perimeter that make the shadows between them all the more absolute. We run. Rodrigo keeps one hand at my back and Alana runs slightly ahead of us both.

Behind us, through the window, I hear Marco's voice.

It doesn't sound like shouting anymore.

"I'll kill you first, Rodrigo," he shouts. "And then *The Negotiator*. And finally... *La Diabla!* I will take my time! You can run but none of you will live."

I don't look back. I keep my eyes on the dark line of the perimeter ahead, on Alana's pink blazer catching the light, on the ground in front of my feet. Rodrigo's hand stays at the small of my back, and I focus on that—on the warmth of it through my shirt, on the fact that his hand is there.

The perimeter wall rises up ahead of us, and Alana doesn't slow down, so I don't slow down, and somewhere back in that building Marco Ledger is reorganizing his grief into something that has a target.

We have a head start.

We're going to need it.

twenty-three

RODRIGO

AFTER A TENSE DRIVE in Alana's expensive rental car, we're back in the upscale hotel room Billie and Alana have been staying at. A chandelier hangs from the ceiling. Mints wrapped in tinfoil have been left on the pillows. But none of that matters, now, because Alana is racing around the room and throwing everything she can find in her suitcase.

"I figure we have ten minutes, maybe fifteen tops, before Marco's men show up," Alana says cheerfully, shoving her designer shoes in a special compartment of her carry-on. "We'll have to be out of here by then so they don't shoot us all." Alana's tone is chipper— almost like she's happy to have a new adventure on her plate.

"I killed someone," Billie says, lacking even an ounce of Alan's enthusiasm. She's sitting on the end of the plush bed with her head in her hands, looking like she might throw up. She's making no effort to pack. "I mean— I killed someone. A person. Who was alive, and is not now. Because of *me*."

"Billie." I say her name carefully. "You were trying to save my life— it wasn't your fault."

"Technically," Alana says, from across the room, not looking up from the bathroom counter where she's sweeping toiletries into her bag like they're items on a supermarket conveyor belt, "you defended yourself. Big difference, legally speaking!"

"He's dead because of me," Billie whispers, and I can see the genuine remorse in her eyes. I wish I could take it away. I sit down next to her on the bed and put my arm around her shoulders.

"You didn't do it on purpose," I say. "The Twin Ledger is a dangerous organization. Mateo was a bad man who caused thousands of people pain."

"Oh my gosh!" Alana shouts from across the room, holding up her cell phone. "Look, Billie, they've already taken out a hit on you and even given you a nickname! They're calling you *The Negotiator.* It takes most people years to earn an alias. Congratulations!" Alana drops two wrapped soaps into the side pocket of her duffel. Then considers the shower cap. Takes it.

Beside me, Billie groans. She turns to look at me. Her eyes— and I have to be careful here, because I've thought about her eyes constantly since we reunited at the compound— are enormous and brown and full of distress. The kind that comes not from fear, but from someone trying to locate the part of the situation that can still be made right.

"We should call the police," she says.

Silence.

Even Alana stops moving.

Then Alana turns around, one hand on her hip, the other still holding a miniature bottle of mouthwash she has absolutely no intention of putting back. "Oh, sweetie," she says, with the warm, pitying smile she'd use if she were explaining Santa Clause to a five-year-old, "*no.* I mean, can we get over the guilt-fest? Like, Mateo was going to kill both of you the second we walked out of there."

"We should call the police! It's what you do," Billie insists again. "When something happens. You call—"

"The Twin Ledger has three people inside the national police force, two inside Interpol, and at least one judge they keep on retainer for situations exactly like this one." Alana uncaps the mouthwash, sniffs it, recaps it— keeps it. "Calling the police would be like calling Marco directly. Except Marco would at least have the decency to pick up."

I watch Billie absorb this. She does it quietly, which I appreciate. There's no theatrics; just a grounded acceptance as she recalibrates her world.

"Okay," she says finally. "Okay." And then, after a moment: "I'm still going to need to process this later."

"Absolutely," I tell her. "Later is good. Later is *bueno*."

She looks at me, and suddenly I'm aware that we're sitting very close to each other— on a bed. Thoughts of what I'd like to do start to take over my mind, and I'm considering doing them when— a slam from inside the bathroom. Alana emerges with a hotel towel in hand, which she shoves into her suitcase. "Can you believe these are one hundred percent Egyptian cotton?"

I wait for Alana to disappear back into the bathroom before I lean into Billie. She's been looking at me this entire time, as if I might have answers. "I have a plan," I whisper to her, not wanting Alana to hear. "I'll get us out of this, Billie. Don't worry."

Something shifts in her face. Not quite a smile, but the precursor to one— the tectonic movement before the surface breaks. I find I want very badly to be the person who gets to see what's on the other side of it.

There's a loose strand of hair across her cheek. It's been there since we arrived at the hotel room, and some part of my attention has been snagged on it the entire time— a thread caught on a splinter. Without quite deciding to, I reach out and tuck the stray hair behind her ear.

She goes very still.

I do too.

Just then, Alana enters again, and I instinctively move away from Billie.

I want to ask Billie— and the list feels embarrassing in its length— where she grew up, what she does on Sunday mornings, whether she prefers the coast or the mountains, what she was like at twenty-two, what she thinks about when she's trying to fall asleep. I want to take her somewhere that isn't *this*. Somewhere with a tablecloth and a good wine list and enough hours in the evening that we could actually get through the list. I want to ask her questions until I understand exactly who she is.

I don't.

Because Alana is six feet away, and we are currently fugitives, and the timing is— even by my flexible standards — not ideal.

But Billie's big, honest eyes look up at me and they are not closed. They are not guarded. There is something in them that says *yes, I know, I feel it too,* and I tuck that away somewhere careful inside my chest, where it can wait.

"We'll figure it out," I tell her.

"Right," she says quietly. "Figure it out."

"You two are talking to each other without me," Alana says, from the bathroom doorway.

We both turn.

Alana is leaning against the frame, arms folded, watching us with an expression that is both amusement and something more complicated. She's managed to acquire what appears to be a full-size shampoo bottle from somewhere in the last three minutes, and it is tucked under her arm like a clutch at a gala.

"I'm not *jealous*," she says, preemptively, which means she is at least partially jealous. "I'm making an *observation*." She pushes off the doorframe and crosses to the bed, where her bag sits half-zipped. "Also I think it's rude of you to leave me out of strategy discussions when we are actively being hunted by an international crime organization, but that's just me."

Then she stops.

She's still looking at her bag, but I can see it— the change in her. The way she goes quiet has nothing to do with sadness and everything to do with calculation. I've seen this before. It's the face she makes when she's working something out. It is not a face that leads anywhere comfortable.

"Wait a second," She holds up a hand without turning around.

We wait.

"Marco is going to come for *you*," she says slowly, still not turning but pointing at me. "Rodrigo, obviously, and *you*, Billie. My original plan was to ditch you both at the train station. I figured I'd just abandon you and disappear for a while, maybe to Ibiza—"

"Thanks," Billie says, her tone acrid.

"— but it actually makes more sense for us to stick together." She turns the ring on her finger. It's the one she stole from Mateo's corpse; the one she pulled from his cold, dead finger.

"I think you should go to Ibiza," I counter, trying not to shout at her and playing it cool instead. "Leave Billie and me to our own devices."

"Aww," Alana makes a kissy face at me, finally turning around. "Aren't you sweet, always wanting to make sure I'm safe! Nooo... I think we should stick together."

"Why's that?" Billie asks.

Alana smiles at her. "Marco doesn't send people for things that are personal. And you two— "She turns now. "—have made it like, very, very personal. Marco will want to kill you himself. If I know Marco will come to you, I know where Marco will be." She points at both of us. "Which means I know where *the other ring* will be."

The room settles.

Billie looks at me.

"The second ring," Alana says as if to clarify, because we are stupid and don't seem excited enough. "Duh! Together they open The Twin Ledger's vault! Marco will have it on him. He always does— he and Mateo both wear them. It's the whole point and I've already got Mateo's." When Billie just stares at her, speechless, Alana turns to me. "You know what's in those vaults, Rodrigo. You know what we could— "

"No," I say.

"If we—"

"*No*, Alana."

Something in her expression shifts into the pleasant, reasonable mask that means she is about to be completely *un*reasonable. "You and your little— your *Bambi* here—" She waves a hand at Billie, who makes a small, indignant face that I find extremely charming— "my friend, who you seem to be *stealing*— have managed to dismantle years of careful career-building I've done in a single evening. My access is burned. My cover is blown. My relationship with the Ledger is— like," She pauses. "Complicated, now that Mateo is dead, and the person who *killed him* is standing in my hotel room."

"Billie," I say carefully, "defended herself."

"Yes! Absolutely! Still dead, though." Alana holds up both hands. "All I'm saying is that the least you two could do— the *bare minimum*— is help me get both rings so I can be set for life." She looks at me levelly. "You weren't going to give me a wedding ring, Rodrigo. You couldn't even do *that.* The absolute least you can do is help me get this one."

I stare at her.

She stares back.

There is a very long pause.

"I'm not going anywhere with you," I say to her.

The room is quiet for a moment.

Alana looks at me.

"Are you... breaking up with me for real this time?"

"It's always been for real, Alana. I just came back to make sure you didn't drag some other innocent person down with you. I came back— for Billie."

Billie stares at me. That's it. I've admitted out loud why I'm here.

Alana doesn't move. I expect a reaction from her like the first time I broke up with her— knife throwing and a tantrum. Instead, there's a softness that comes across her eyes. An understanding. She clears her throat.

Then, the moment passes and she's back to business— slowly, almost lazily, her hand drifts to her jacket pocket. She doesn't pull anything out. She just rests her fingers there, against the outline of her gun, so I can see it.

"You're welcome to try," she says pleasantly. "Getting rid of me, I mean. If you want. But it's going to be hard."

She tilts her head. "The Twin Ledger has lookouts in this neighborhood. Probably in the lobby right now. You think you're going to walk out of here with your faces and your names and get on a plane home?"

I say nothing. Neither does Billie.

"You need new passports. New identities. I know the man who makes them— the only man worth going to in this part of the world. I know every exit the Ledger watches and every one they don't. I know how they communicate, how they move, how they think." She zips her bag with finality. "I'm not a liability. I'm the only reason you have a chance."

She says it without ego, which is somehow worse. It's just true, and she knows it.

I look at Billie.

Billie has been quiet through this, but she's not the frozen kind of quiet anymore. She's the thinking kind. The watching kind. She looks at Alana. She looks at me. Something moves across her face; a calculation.

"Rodrigo," she says.

"*Billie—*"

"I know." She says it gently. "I know. But Alana knows how all of this works," Billie finishes. "And we don't." She says it simply, not like she's giving in, but like she's reading off a list of facts she's checked twice. "She can get us passports, and in exchange she has a chance to get the other ring." She glances at me, then at herself, then back at me. "I trust her with this," Billie says. She says it quietly, and she says it to me, and she holds my gaze while she does it— those enormous, honest eyes not blinking— and it lands somewhere in the vicinity of my chest with a weight I wasn't prepared for.

She is owed a safe way out. That's what I said. And this is what a safe way out actually requires.

I hate it.

"Fine," I say, looking at Billie again. "Wherever you go, I'll go."

Alana, who has already unzipped her bag again and is now examining the hotel room's complimentary fruit basket, looks up. "Fine what?"

"Fine, you come with us. Fine, you help us get new identities. Fine—" I cross the room in two strides and stand in front of her, and I want to make sure she is listening carefully to what I am about to say. "You help us get clear, you get the other ring, and then we go our separate ways. I am not responsible for you. I am not protecting you. I do not owe you anything. We are done—" I search for the word. "Forever."

Alana stares at me for a moment.

Then she puts a small pear from the fruit basket into her bag.

"Sure," she says.

"I mean it."

"Rodrigo." She zips the bag closed. "I heard you the first time." She swings the duffel up onto her shoulder, adjusts the strap, and looks at both of us with a bright, easy smile. "Now can we please go? In about thirty seconds Marco's men are going to sweep this place."

She walks past us toward the door, pausing to collect her jacket from the back of the desk chair— and, I notice, the notepad from beside the phone, which she apparently also wants.

The door swings shut behind her.

Billie and I stand in the middle of the ruined room, surrounded by the faint evidence of our packing. The room still smells like whatever expensive candle they'd lit at turndown service.

"You okay?" I ask.

Billie considers the question with the seriousness it deserves. "I mean," she says, "I've had better evenings. As a general rule I try to end my nights *before* anyone dies, so this is already statistically unusual for me."

She smiles at me, and my heart melts. "Did you really mean what you said? That you only came back... for me?"

I want to tell her I've been thinking of her since the moment I met her. I want to tell her that she has beautiful eyes, and a kind heart, and a brave soul, and that I see all of this in her and more. But there is no time, so instead, I tuck that piece of hair behind her ear again— the one that's always getting loose— and say, only, "Sí."

For a second, there is only the space between us— one that I close. It's small enough now that I can feel the warmth of her, and the soft brush of her breath against my mouth.

And then...

I lean in and kiss her.

Even though I know I shouldn't do it.

It's the worst idea I've had all week, and I've recently walked into an international arms dealer's compound. But kissing Billie? It needed to be done.

I hope that I've been invited, and— when she presses her whole body against me and wraps her arms around me — I'm sure that I have. *We are in a hotel room,* which is convenient, because I could so easily move us toward the bed, a fact which isn't lost on me. In that moment, my world is Billie, and the idea of her, and the promise of what we could be, together.

We part.

Billie blinks up at me. There's a shout from the hallway: Alana's voice.

"Like, let's go? I'd really like to stock up on some weapons before I try to cut off Marco's finger."

Billie grins, and it turns into a giggle. "She's going to be a lot to deal with."

"That's alright," I say, really meaning it. "Because I will be with you."

Billie picks up her bag and settles it on her shoulder. She looks around the room as if saying goodbye, then back at me. "Let's try not to die, I guess."

I hold the door open.

Billie walks through it. I think about that kiss and I know— even if we *do* die— I can go a happy man.

twenty-four

BILLIE

I SHOULDN'T HAVE LET him kiss me. The memory of his lips on mine lingers as I push my way through Barcelona Sants train station. The sound of people running late echoes through the tiled emporium— shoes clacking, suitcases rolling— but all I can think about, all I've *been thinking about* for hours— is the way it felt to be close to Rodrigo. The moment has stayed with me, an electric jolt of hope underneath a more reasonable, lingering finish of what-the-hell-am-I-doing.

I'm standing near a departure board in the blazer I didn't pay for. Well, technically I *did* pay for it, since it's on my credit card, which Alana stole. I'm trying to look like I belong in a European train station at nine in the morning with an international arms dealer.

I should be worried about the criminal history I'm rapidly building and what it will mean for my future, but instead— *The kiss.* I keep coming back to the kiss. I can't stop thinking about it, which is a problem, because I technically have a boyfriend. *Had* a boyfriend. Have a boyfriend? The tense is unclear because Alana broke up with Tyler on my behalf via text message, which is not how I would have handled it, but which I also haven't tried to correct or even worried about, which says something about me that I'm not ready to examine. *Technically, you're single, Billie,* I think to myself. But the squirming feeling in my stomach confirms what I already know: I feel guilty. I feel like I cheated on Tyler, because I didn't do the breaking up with him myself. This is what I get, for postponing the inevitable. I let one year turn into another and now— I'd like to be free of Tyler, but I'm not. Not really.

Also: Rodrigo was Alana's boyfriend. Recently. As in, days ago. *Am I a bad friend?*

I shake myself out of my musings. Alana kidnapped me and dragged me across an international border. Why do I care if I'm stealing the love of her life? And Tyler's a bad boyfriend who ignores me, lets me do his laundry, and plays video games all day. I shouldn't feel guilty for betraying either one of them. But somehow, I do. Maybe that's the difference between me and Alana.

"You are thinking too much," Rodrigo says, looking over at me with a smile that makes me melt. He's been standing next to me this entire time, letting me think, not saying a word.

"It's the first time since we left the hotel room that I've had a chance to think without Alana yapping in my ear," I say, giggling a little. Something about being around Rodrigo makes me do that. The giggling.

Rodrigo nods somberly, leaning in. "Yes, Billie, I must tell you while Alana isn't here—" he moves closer to me and I can smell his cologne again. Something like the beach and a spice I can't name. "Melissa is here, in Barcelona—"

"No!" I almost shout, covering my mouth. "She's so pregnant!"

"Yes," Rodrigo agrees. "But she came anyway. To find you. She is with Interpol. I sent her to meet my contact there. They are tracking my phone—"

My heart pounds in my chest. "If Alana finds out, we're dead."

"She won't," Rodrigo says gently. "As long as I have my phone they will be able to track us. Melissa is on her way to Interpol right now—"

"Three tickets to Madrid," Alana announces, appearing beside us. We both go quiet immediately. She fans the tickets in front of my face.She's holding my credit card in her other hand, and she slides it back into her own wallet—my card, her wallet. She does it with a seamless ease that says what's mine is actually hers.

"My card," I say.

"Our card," she corrects warmly. "Friendship is about sharing, Billie."

If she's so big on sharing, maybe I should do whatever I want with Rodrigo, I think wryly to myself.

We start walking. Rodrigo is a few steps ahead of us, scanning the station with careful attention. His jaw is doing that thing again— the thing where it exists in a way that is geometrically unfair. I look away.

"The train leaves in twelve minutes," Alana says, motioning toward the platform and skipping ahead of Rodrigo. "Platform seven. Keep up, you two."

I keep up. Rodrigo falls into step beside me, and his arm brushes mine as we walk, and the contact is so brief and so ordinary and so completely devastating that I have to remind myself to breathe.

"You alright?" he asks, low, just for me.

"Fine," I say. "Just processing. A lot of things to process."

He nods. He doesn't push. This is one of the things I've noticed about Rodrigo— he doesn't fill silence with noise. He lets things sit. Tyler would have already changed the subject to something about himself. I think this, and then I feel guilty for thinking it, and then I feel guilty for feeling guilty, and the whole thing becomes a nesting doll of guilt.

On the platform, while we wait for the doors to open, Alana leans over to me with a conspiratorial posture.

"Can I tell you something?" she says.

"Can I stop you?" I ask.

"No." She grins. "I'm actually glad Rodrigo broke up with me."

I look at her. I look at her for a long moment, trying to determine if this is a trap.

"You are?" I say carefully.

"Totally." She flips her hair— a gesture that says she has moved on. "Because here's the thing. Marco has one ring. Mateo had the other. And now that Mateo is— well, no longer with us—" she makes a vague gesture toward the ceiling— "that second ring is somewhere. And if I find it, I don't need to work for the Twin Ledger... or any man. I don't need Marco. I have access to the vault myself. Billions, Billie. Billions in gold and weapons and paintings and God knows what else."

She says this like she's found a really good deal on flights.

"And if Rodrigo and I were still together," she continues, "he'd expect me me to, like, not use it. Or to use it ethically. Or donate to charity or whatever. He's very morally rigid. Very 'let's do the right thing.' Very exhausting. I don't know how some people live like that."

We suffer greatly, I think, considering the moral quandary I've been contemplating for the past few hours.

I glance at Rodrigo, who is standing ten feet away and cannot hear this conversation, and who I know has a good heart. Morally rigid. Sure. If that's what we're calling it. He pushed me behind a table to save me from stray bullets. I'd go with "hero," but to each her own.

"The point is," Alana says, squeezing my arm, "being a little selfish is good. It's healthy. You should try it sometime." She looks at me with real warmth. "You spend your whole life making other people happy. Who's making *you* happy?"

My heart races. Does Alana know about the kiss? Could she possibly be telling me to be happy?

Then, she adds: "You're lucky I dumped Tyler for you. Now you can go find a cute alpaca-farmer somewhere and start a family together."

She pats my arm. Nope. She doesn't know about the kiss.

The doors open. We board.

The train is sleek and modern. Alana leads us to our seats— three in a row, because of course she's orchestrated the seating— and I end up by the window with Rodrigo beside me and Alana on the aisle, already pulling comfort items from her bag like she's getting ready for a spa appointment.

"Three hours to Madrid," Alana says, popping a mint into her mouth. I recognize it as one left on the pillows at our last hotel. "Trains are safer. The Ledger monitors flights and rental cars like crazy, but trains?" She shakes her head. "They think trains are beneath them. Very elitist organization. Works in our favor."

The train begins to move. Barcelona slides past the window— the city pulling away from us like a tide going out. I watch it go and feel relieved.

Rodrigo's knee is close to mine. Not touching. Just—there. The space between us is three inches and contains, I am fairly certain, the entire emotional content of my life. I try to keep my breathing even, as if I sit next to a man this handsome every day.

"Okay," Alana says, once we've cleared the station and the train has found its rhythm. She holds out her hand. "Phones."

"What?" I say.

"Phones. All of them. Now."

Rodrigo looks at her. His expression communicates that he knows where this is going and does not approve.

"The Ledger can track us through our devices," Alana says, with the patience of a kindergarten teacher explaining a concept for the third time. "Cell towers, GPS, all of it. If we keep our phones, they'll know exactly where we are within the hour. Hand them over."

"But you scrubbed mine!" I argue.

"Give it," Alana says.

Rodrigo's jaw tightens. He's holding his phone in his hand like it's the last thread connecting him to the outside world, which, as I just found out— it is.

He looks at me. Something passes between us— an understanding that he's giving up our connection to Melissa. To Interpol. His eyes say he's asking me for permission. I give him the slightest nod. We don't have a choice but to play this Alana's way. Then, he hands his phone over, and pile mine on top of it.

Alana holds both devices up.

"For the record," she says, "I think it's really brave of you guys to go off the grid like this. Very bold. Love the energy. Oprah would approve."

She reaches across Rodrigo, pushes the window glass

open against the rushing wind, and throws both phones out into the Spanish countryside.

I watch them arc and disappear— two small rectangles tumbling against a blur of green and gold— and with them goes my connection to Melissa, to Rodrigo's Interpol contact, to the entire infrastructure of people who might be looking for us.

Alana closes the window and settles back in her seat. She puts an eye mask over her perfect lashes, and sprays an aromatherapy scent— presumably one she stole from our last hotel— over her face, making our seats smell like lavender.

"There," she says, satisfied. "Now we're free."

I look at the landscape streaming past— open and wide and completely indifferent— and think: free is one word for it.

* * *

An hour later, and the train's dining car is a welcome escape. Forks clink against plates. Tourists hold conversations in low, happy tones.

I have been sent here for a grilled cheese. Alana's exact words were: "Get me a grilled cheese, and if they don't have grilled cheese, get me whatever is closest to grilled cheese, and if they don't have anything close to grilled cheese, come back and tell me so I can be upset about it." No one can say Alana isn't an excellent delegator.

I'm standing at the counter, waiting for the man to acknowledge me, when I hear footsteps behind me and know— before I turn, before I see him— that it's Rodrigo. His footsteps have a particular quality: steady, deliberate, and patient, as if everything will happen in its due time.

Tyler's footsteps are shuffly. I hate myself for comparing them.

"I've been sent to tell you she wants tomatoes on her grilled cheese," Rodrigo says, appearing beside me at the counter. I notice, for the first time, that his smile is a little crooked. Yet another charming quality I can add to the list. Why does this man have to be so handsome?

"You care deeply, about the quality of her lunch, I assume?" I say, testing.

"No," Rodrigo shakes his head. "I care about an excuse to come see you." He waves a hand at the man behind the counter, grabbing his attention in mere seconds when I've been waiting for what feels like forever. He orders for both of us. Two coffees, two bocadillos— small sandwiches with jamón— and he does it in Spanish, which is unfair, because hearing him speak Spanish does something to the base of my spine that I cannot be held accountable for. The man behind the counter moves with fractionally more energy than he displayed for me, which I choose not to take personally.

We sit at a small table by the window. The Spanish countryside is streaming past in long, golden panels— dry earth, olive groves, the occasional white farmhouse.

Rodrigo sets the coffee in front of me.

"We have a problem, now that my phone is gone," he sighs, acknowledging the worst of our situation.

"Maybe Melissa can track us some other way—" I say hopefully.

"Perhaps," he agrees. "We will need to try to get a message to her."

"I can't believe she came here for me," I say, shaking my head. Melissa— eight months pregnant, swollen-ankled, cantankerous, wonderful Melissa— is here in Spain. For me. I may not have many friends, but at least I have one good one.

"She brought Steve," Rodrigo adds, clearly trying to assuage my guilt.

"She shouldn't be flying," I say, and my voice comes out smaller than I intend. "She's due in four weeks. What if something happens on the plane? What if the baby comes early because of the stress and—"

"I said this to her," Rodrigo says. "Almost those exact words. She told me if she has the baby here, perhaps it will get dual citizenship." He pauses. "Your friends love you very much. I can see why."

The way he's looking at me knocks the breath right out of my lungs. Thankfully, the sandwiches arrive before I have to formulate a response.

I take a bite, and it's so good that I make a sound I'm not entirely proud of. "Why is all your food here so amazing?"

"Because your food in America is so terrible," Rodrigo jokes. He pauses as if he's trying to think of a way to tell me something. "You are not disappointed, that Tyler did not come?"

Tyler. The name makes a lump form in my throat. *I've basically cheated on him.* The name sits between us on the table like an object neither of us wants to pick up.

Rodrigo's expression shifts— not much, just a small tightening around the eyes that says he's choosing his words with care. "Melissa was trying to reach him. To explain what happened. To get him on a plane as well. She said he was quite upset after the breakup text Alana sent him. I do not know if she convinced him to get on a plane or not."

There it is. The information, landing with its careless, familiar weight.

"Technically," I say, and I hear myself say it, "I'm still with him." I hate myself for saying it outloud. It's like the words pop a magical bubble I wanted so badly to keep.

The sentence hangs in the air between us, and I watch Rodrigo receive it. He nods. His expression doesn't close— it stays open, stays warm— but something in it acknowledges a boundary.

"Of course," he says. "I understand."

A beat. The train sways gently. Outside, a hill covered in scrubby green passes like a slow breath.

"But if he does not come for you, Billie," Rodrigo adds, his tone softer, quieter. "He is an idiot. And he does not deserve you."

I stare into Rodrigo's eyes, feeling lost in them. "Did I cheat on him?" I say, thinking out loud. I never intended to talk about this with Rodrigo, but there's such a gentleness about him— like he'd understand my deepest fears— that it's hard not to confide in him. "I've been with Tyler so long... I can't even imagine what my life would be without him. Have you ever had that happen? It's as if..." I motion out the window at the countryside blurring past us. "... It's as if your life is a train and you're just a passenger on it, and you want to change the destination but you can't?"

Rodrigo nods. "Yes, I know this feeling," he agrees, and I see memories of past mistakes flash across his face. "I accept that I may not be the author of my fate, at least not entirely. But I try not to overthink it," he smiles that crooked smile at me. "Instead, I simply—" he waves a hand in the air. "— decide to know the things I know."

"And what do you know?" I ask him.

There's a long pause as he leans toward me. Then, he

takes my hand across the table. “I know that I do not regret that kiss.”

For a second, I consider lying to him— telling him that I *do* regret it, only because it would make everything simpler — but instead, I tell him the truth:

“I don’t regret it either,” I say.

And there it is— the truth.

Rodrigo lets go of my hand, satisfied. He turns his coffee cup a quarter-inch. “I have a habit,” he says, “of rushing into things. Relationships. Feelings. All my life I have seen a person and thought— yes, this is the one— and jumped, without taking the time to really know them.” He glances up. “It’s how I ended up with Alana. I saw something beautiful and I leaped, and I didn’t ask enough questions. It’s nice that you and Tyler— that you really know each other. That there’s a foundation.”

I think about Tyler and what I know. I know that he leaves wet towels on the bed. I know that he eats cereal at eleven p.m. and leaves the bowl in the sink. I know that he loves me in the way you love a lamp, or a couch, or the exact right temperature of your shower. Present. Functional. And totally uninspiring.

“Sometimes knowing is worse,” I say. “Because then you can’t pretend.” I look at the olive groves outside, the long rows of silver-green trees planted with a patience I’ve never had in my own life. “I spend a lot of time trying to make other people happy. Tyler. My boss. Everyone. Melissa says I should go to therapy.”

Rodrigo smiles— a real one, the kind that crinkles the corners of his eyes and makes him look like someone you'd want to tell your whole life story to over a very long dinner. “Sometimes life itself is therapy, sí? It teaches us something new every day." He tilts his head. "People teach us the most, no?"

I open my mouth to answer and realize I don't have one.

"Perhaps," Rodrigo continues. "You would let me get to really know you, Billie. Perhaps you would let me be your friend, without rushing into things— as it seems you are still— involved."

"I would like that," I agree, secretly relieved, but also... unsure. From what I've seen of Rodrigo, knowing him will only make me want him more. But being a friend to the man isn't cheating on Tyler. I'm allowed to have friends.

"I owe you an apology," he says, and his voice shifts to something more serious. "At the baby shower. I was cold to you. I know how it must have seemed. But I was trying to warn you— about Alana. About what she is. I couldn't say it plainly because she was right there, and I didn't know how to tell a stranger that the woman she just met is—" he gestures vaguely— "what Alana is."

I laugh. It comes out before I can stop it— a real laugh, involuntary and bright. "I thought you didn't like me," I say. "I thought you were this brooding, rude guy who couldn't even smile at a baby shower."

Rodrigo looks at me. His eyes are warm and brown and reflect back at me the entire emotional vocabulary of lovers across the world.

"You were very wrong about that," he says.

His hand moves under the table. His fingers brush against my knee— not grabbing, not holding, just touching — and the contact sends a current through me that starts at my knuckles and ends somewhere behind my sternum, and I don't pull away.

Then, because he's apparently decided I've had enough emotional intensity for one thirty-second interval, he leans back and the corner of his mouth tilts upward.

"Also," he says, "I should point out— Alana has technically broken up with Tyler for you. By text. Which means, technically, you are a single woman sitting in a dining car with a single man on a train through Spain." He raises his coffee cup. "Technically."

I laugh again. Louder this time, the kind of laugh that turns a head two tables over. "How are we supposed to be friends if you continually point out that I'm single?"

"I am a creative person," Rodrigo smirks. "I paint, remember? I'm sure we will find a way." He sets down his cup and his voice lowers. He looks around as if to make sure we're not being overhead. "Billie, I have a family home in the countryside— outside of a small village, quiet, safe. My cousin Benny is there. He's a degenerate," he adds, with familial affection, "but he's loyal, and he knows the area, and the Ledger doesn't know about the house. We must get a message to Melissa. We will tell her to meet us there. Just you and me."

I picture it without meaning to. A stone house in the Spanish countryside. Olive trees. Quiet mornings. Rodrigo painting at an easel while I sit nearby reading a book.

But then I think about Tyler— real Tyler, back in Chicago, who may or may not know I've been kidnapped, who may or may not care— and the guilt returns, thick and complicated. I should have a real conversation with him. A real ending, if it's going to be an ending. Not a text Alana wrote from my stolen phone.

And yet.

I look at Rodrigo, whose eyes are still on me with that steady, unhurried attention that I am not used to receiving from anyone, and I think: *is this real?*

Or is this the adrenaline and the danger and the foreign country and the blazer that makes me feel like someone else?

Am I falling for this man, or am I falling for the version of myself that exists near him— the one who negotiated with arms dealers and jumped out of a moving car and is currently sitting in a Spanish dining car deciding what she wants instead of what everyone else needs?

I don't know. I genuinely don't know. And the not-knowing terrifies me more than the compound did, more than Alana and her drugged drinks and her thrown phones, because the compound had clear stakes and a clear exit, and this— whatever this is— has neither.

But those eyes.

"We'll get to the house in the countryside," I agree.

Rodrigo nods back at me, and that much, at least: is decided.

twenty-five

RODRIGO

BILLIE IS STILL (TECHNICALLY) in a relationship. Billie isn't ready to rush things. I understand this. And I know this is better for me, given that I always jump into matters of the heart without really knowing the person. After our conversation in the dining car, I have spent the last few hours seated next to Billie on the train, telling myself not to touch her, but to be her friend.

It is a difficult assignment.

The way she moves makes it impossible to look away. I want to know everything about her— what music she is listening to on the headphones that cover her ears. What she will think of my family home in the country, if we are lucky enough to make it there without being shot by one of the Twin Ledgers goons.

Billie does not understand the effort she is worth. She does not understand that— although I cannot stop thinking about kissing her, about being with her— there is something about her that makes me care more about her happiness than my own. Even if it's not with me— Billie deserves to be happy.

But then— I simply cannot fathom a man like Tyler could make her happy. Billie deserves a man who would cross oceans for her.

When the train ride ends, it's nighttime, and we immediately step onto the platform, catching the nearest Uber to a shopping district in the heart of Madrid. Alana links arms with Billie and pulls her into a store with club-going attire "Rodrigo!" Alana shouts, waving at me. "Don't you want to pick your clothes?"

"Let Billie choose for me," I say, waving a hand in the air. I don't care what I'm going to wear. I ignore all of it— everything that Alana is doing— because I am focused on scanning the area, looking for a phone or some method to get a message to Melissa safely. I have to let her know where we are without alerting The Twin Ledger to our location. While Alana drags Billie into the store, I stay outside— keeping guard— looking across the square for any sign of a payphone. Nothing.

Minutes later, Billie and Alana emerge in new clothes.

Alana is wearing a neon pink bodysuit— because of course she is— with matching glow-in-the-dark bracelets stacked up both arms like armor. There's glitter on her cheeks. She looks like Barbie at a rave, which I suspect is exactly the aesthetic she was going for.

And then there is Billie.

Billie is wearing a green neon top that's too big for her — it keeps slipping off one shoulder— and someone, probably Alana, has painted glow-in-the-dark streaks across her cheeks like war paint. Her brown hair is pulled back, and the UV light catches the gold flecks in her eyes in a way that makes them look like a new color entirely. She looks like a very small, very serious person who has been asked to attend a costume party she did not agree to.

She is stunning.

She holds out a bag, for me. I open it, exhaling a sigh of relief when I see a simple neon tank top inside. The color is a horrific neon yellow, but other than that— it's fine.

"I wanted to get you a crop top," Alana clucks, "but Billie said you'd like this better."

Thank you, I mouth at Billie as I take off my t-shirt and put on the tank. I swear I see Billie struggling to look away when I remove my shirt, and I can't help but smile. Good. Maybe there is hope for us beyond friendship, after all.

I grab our bags— we're down to my duffell, Billie's small purse, and— after much negotiation— a very large tote bag that belongs to Alana and represents what she refused to part with. We cross the square together, weaving through alleys and cobblestone, finally arriving at a techno club. The bass reaches us before the door does. It comes up through the pavement, through the soles of my boots— and settles somewhere behind my ribs. The building itself is an old industrial thing, all exposed brick and rusted metal, converted into... whatever this is. A sign reads PULSE in letters that throb between ultraviolet and hot pink. There's a line of people wrapped around the corner, most of them dressed like they fell into a vat of highlighter fluid and decided to just go with it.

We fit right in. That was the idea, apparently.

"Okay," Billie says, squinting at the entrance. "So this guy you know who makes passports–"

"Tamor," Alana nods.

"He's– Tamor is in there?" Billie continues.

Alana is already moving toward the door, bypassing the line entirely with the kind of confidence that only someone who has never once listened told no can summon. "He's like, around. Somewhere. He's always around places like this."

"That's— that's your intel?" Billie says. "He's *around*?"

"Billie. Babe. Relax." Alana doesn't look back. "Tamor owns this place. He'll come around... at some point. In the meantime..." She shrugs. With that, she simply walks past the bouncer— a man the width of a refrigerator— and smiles at him. He steps aside. We're in.

The inside of Pulse hits me like a physical thing. The music is enormous— a deep, rolling techno beat that fills every cubic centimeter of the space. The ceiling is high, industrial, strung with strips of LED that pulse in time with the bass. Bodies everywhere. The air smells like sweat and synthetic fog and something vaguely sweet, like someone spilled a cocktail into the smoke machine. Strobe lights carve the crowd into frozen frames— a raised hand here, a turned head there, everyone moving in beautiful, disconnected fragments.

I've worked on construction sites where the jackhammer rattled my teeth. This is louder.

Alana is already gone. I turn to say something to Billie and see her tracking Alana's neon pink form as it cuts through the crowd, moving toward the bar with the precision of a heat-seeking missile. Within thirty seconds, Alana has plucked a drink from the hand of some guy who didn't even see her coming. She takes a sip, makes a face like it's not up to her standards, then keeps it anyway. Then she's dancing. Just like that. Arms up, hips moving, surrounded by strangers who seem thrilled to have her among them.

"She's unbelievable," Billie says, but I can barely hear her over the music. She has to lean close, and her mouth is near my ear. "I thought she had a real contact!"

"What's our next move?" I shout over the music. "We

could try to make it to my family's home. But it would be safer with new identities. New papers, in case we are stopped—"

Billie straightens, and I can see her switching into what I've started thinking of as her Mission Mode. Her jaw sets. Her bambi eyes narrow— as much as they can narrow, which isn't much, because those eyes were engineered by some cosmic artist to be permanently wide and searching. She scans the room.

"I'm going to find Tamor," she says. "Stay close?"

"Always."

We head for the bar and I hide our bags in a corner near the bin for dirty glasses, then follow Billie as she pushes through the crowd toward the nearest security guard— a tall man in all black with an earpiece. Billie taps his arm. He looks down at her like she's a lost child.

"Excuse me," she shouts over the music. "I'm looking for someone named Tamor? He's a— a friend? He should be here?"

The guard stares at her. Then he shakes his head. Not a no, exactly. More of an I-can't-believe-you're-crazy-eough-to-ask.

Billie nods, undeterred. She thanks him— because she is the kind of person who thanks someone for giving her nothing— and moves on to the next one. This guard is shorter, stockier, standing near a roped-off VIP section. Billie repeats her question. He shrugs. Points vaguely at the dance floor, which is like pointing at the ocean and saying *the fish is in there*.

She tries a third. A woman this time, arms crossed, stationed near the back bar. The woman leans down to hear Billie, then straightens and gives her a look that roughly translates to: *you're either a cop or you're crazy, and either way, I can't help you.*

I watch all of this from a few steps behind, close enough to step in if needed but far enough to let her work. And the thing that strikes me— the thing that always strikes me about Billie Harper— is that she doesn't quit. She has the kind of persistence that doesn't announce itself. It's quiet. It's stubborn. It's the most attractive thing I've ever seen. Her long hair is cascading down her back, and she's glowing under these lights, and...

Dios mío. I need to focus.

Billie circles back to me, frustration written across her honest face in a way she probably doesn't realize. She's terrible at hiding her feelings. Her face is an open book— no, it's an open diary, the kind with no lock, left on a park bench for the world to read.

"No one knows who Tamor is," she says. "Or they won't say. I've tried three guards and a bartender and a guy who I think was just a very tall patron."

"Maybe he goes by another name here."

"Maybe he doesn't exist and Alana made him up and we're going to die in a techno nightclub."

I almost laugh. "That's a little dramatic, no?"

"Is it? *Is it* dramatic, Rodrigo? Because two weeks ago I was writing emails in Chicago, and now I'm in a neon tank top in Madrid trying to find an underground fake ID guy in a techno club. I think I've earned dramatic."

She makes me laugh, because she has a point. She has several points.

We find Alana near the center of the dance floor, sandwiched between two men who look like they were carved from marble and then given very expensive haircuts. She's dancing with both of them, her glow bracelets catching the light in arcs and circles. When she sees us approaching, she doesn't stop dancing. She just raises her eyebrows.

"No luck," Billie says, loud enough to cut through the bass. "Nobody knows Tamor."

"Okay, so, like, that's because you're doing it wrong," Alana says, still moving her hips. "You don't *find* Tamor. Tamor finds *you*. He's, like, a vibe-reader. He can tell who needs him. It's honestly one of his better qualities."

"A vibe-reader," Billie repeats.

"Yeah. So, like, just relax. Be in the space. He'll come to us." She spins, catches one of the marble men by the shoulder, and winks at Billie. "Dance, babe. You look like you're at a funeral."

And then she's gone again, absorbed back into the crowd like neon ink into dark water.

Billie turns to me. Her expression is somewhere between *I want to scream* and *she might actually be right and that makes me want to scream more.*

I consider the situation. We're in a nightclub. We can't force a man we've never met to appear. Alana, for all her chaos and stolen cocktails, has spent a lifetime navigating this world. She knows things about its rhythms that we don't. She knows that sometimes you have to stop chasing the thing and let it come to you.

It's not unlike painting, actually. You can't force the right color. You have to let your hand find it.

"Maybe she's not wrong about everything," I say.

Billie looks at me. "You're taking her side?"

"I'm taking the side of— we're here. We can't leave. The music is very loud and I'm wearing a shirt that glows in the dark. We might as well enjoy the absurdity, *no*?"

Something shifts in her face. The tension in her jaw loosens, just a fraction. She looks at the dance floor— this heaving, pulsing organism of bodies and light— and I see her weighing it. The responsible thing against the alive thing.

"Come on," I say, and I hold out my hand. "Dance with me."

She looks at my hand. Then at me. Then at the dance floor. Then back at my hand.

"Fine," she says. "But if we die in here, I'm blaming you."

"*Trato hecho.*" Deal made.

The dance floor swallows us whole.

The first song is pure chaos— fast, pounding, relentless. There is no way to dance to it with any dignity. So we don't try. We jump. We bounce. Billie throws her arms up and the green neon top slips off her shoulder and she doesn't fix it and she's laughing— actually laughing— and the sound of it is completely lost in the music but I can see it in the way her face breaks open, the way her whole body shakes with it.

I haven't seen her laugh like this. Not freely. Not without catching herself halfway through and pulling it back, as if joy is something she's been rationing.

I'm a big man. I'm not built for dance floors. My shoulders take up too much space, my arms are too long, and I have the natural rhythm of someone raised on flamenco but currently trapped in a techno hellscape. But none of that matters, because Billie is grinning at me like I'm the funniest thing she's ever seen, and I would look foolish in every club on this continent if it meant she kept looking at me like that.

We spin. She does some kind of move that I think is supposed to be a robot but looks more like a person experiencing mild electrical shock, and I do it back, and she doubles over laughing, and for a few minutes we are just two people being ridiculous in a room full of strangers, and it is the best I have felt in longer than I can say.

Then the DJ does something.

The transition is subtle at first— a lowering of the tempo, a deepening of the bass, a melody threading through the chaos like a voice in the dark. The strobe lights slow. The UV wash shifts to something warmer, deeper, a purple-blue glow that softens every edge in the room. The song that emerges is still electronic but it's different. It's unhurried. It rolls like water. It breathes.

Around us, the crowd adjusts. Bodies that were jumping are now swaying. Hands that were raised are now finding waists, shoulders, the backs of necks.

Billie stops bouncing. She's standing in front of me, breathing hard from the jumping, her cheeks flushed, those painted glow streaks slightly smeared. The green neon top is still hanging off one shoulder. Her eyes are bright and wide and looking directly into mine.

The music pulls.

I don't decide to step closer. My body just— does it. Like gravity. Like the most natural thing in the world. I step in, and she doesn't step back, and then there's barely any space between us at all.

My hand finds her waist. Not the way it would in a formal dance, not stiff or performative. It settles there like it's been looking for that exact spot her whole life. *My* whole life. Through the thin fabric of her top, I can feel the warmth of her skin, the slight rise and fall of her breathing.

Her hand comes up to my shoulder. Her fingers curl into the fabric of my absurd glowing tank top.

We move.

It's slow. It's nothing— just a sway, really. Two people

shifting their weight in the dark. But the air between us has changed. It's heavier. It hums. Every point where her body touches mine feels like a conversation that words would only ruin.

She looks up at me. Those bambi eyes. *Dios mío*, those eyes. They hold the light from the LEDs and turn it into something softer, something that belongs only to her. The gold flecks catch and scatter. I could paint those eyes for a hundred years and never get them right.

Her lips part, just slightly, like she's going to say something. She doesn't.

I pull her closer. My other hand finds the small of her back, and she leans in, and her forehead is almost touching my jaw, and I can feel her breath on my collarbone, and the music is everywhere— inside the walls, inside my chest, inside whatever small, irrational space in my brain is currently trying to remind me that this is complicated.

It is complicated. I know it's complicated.

She's still figuring things out with Tyler back home. I know this. I know she carries that relationship like a piece of luggage she hasn't decided whether to unpack or throw away. I know she feels guilty about enjoying things when she hasn't yet resolved the thing she's supposed to resolve. I can see it in how she sometimes pulls back mid-laugh, how she checks herself, how she rations her own happiness like it's a finite resource she's afraid of running out.

And I know that I was with Alana. That I have a pattern — *mujeres que me necesitan*— women who need me, who pull me in with their chaos and their beauty and their hunger, and I mistake the intensity of being needed for the warmth of being loved. I project the idea of the woman I want onto them, without getting to know them, truly, as they are. I know I do this. I have done it so many times that it should be tattooed on my forearm as a warning: *Rodrigo Esperanza does not choose well.*

But this— this doesn't feel like a pattern. This feels like something real. Like something I've been waiting for— hoping for— my entire life

Billie shifts, and her cheek brushes my chest, and I feel her exhale, and something in me just— gives way. Like a wall I didn't know I was building, crumbling all at once. Quiet. Without ceremony. Just gone.

I have known this woman for a matter of weeks. We have been chased across countries. We have slept in strange hotels and run from gunfire. I have watched her be kind when kindness made no strategic sense. I have watched her stand up, again and again, after the world told her to sit down.

She doesn't see it. That's the thing that wrecks me. She doesn't see what I see.

She thinks she is ordinary. She thinks she is *The Assistant*. She thinks she is the person who fetches coffee and files paperwork.

She's wrong. She is so spectacularly wrong that I want to take her by the shoulders and shake her until she understands. But you can't shake someone into believing in themselves. I know that. You can only show them, slowly, carefully, by the way you look at them when they're not trying to be anything at all.

The music swells. Billie tips her head back to look at me, and her eyes are enormous and open, and there's a question in them that she doesn't ask. The purple light makes everything feel underwater. Slow. Suspended. The rest of the club has dissolved into background noise. There is only this — her hand on my shoulder, my hand on her back, the space between us that has become no space at all.

I want to tell her.

I know it's too soon. I know the timing is wrong. I know we are standing in a Budapest techno club wearing glow-in-the-dark costumes while an international arms dealer dances somewhere behind. I know that back in her real life there is an apartment and a boyfriend and a version of herself she hasn't quite left behind.

I know all of this.

But my heart— *mi corazón terco*, my stubborn heart— doesn't care about timing. It never has. It cares about what is true, and what is true is that I have never felt this way. Not with Alana. Not with anyone. Not the women who needed me, not the women I thought I could save. This is different. This is not me being needed. This is me being *found*. By someone who doesn't even realize she's been searching.

Her fingers tighten on my shoulder. The music breathes. The lights pulse.

I lean down. My lips are close to her ear— close enough that she'll hear me over the music, over the bass, over everything.

"Billie," I say.

She looks up.

And I know— I know the way I know when a painting is done, when the last brushstroke is exactly right, when there's nothing left to add or take away— I know that what I'm about to say will change everything.

I'm about to tell her that I can't *only* be her friend. I'm about to tell her— that I love her.

twenty-six

BILLIE

THE BASS at Pulse hits somewhere below my ribcage, this deep, tectonic thing that makes my teeth vibrate. The whole club is a blur of dark walls and neon streaks— blues and purples cutting through manufactured fog— and the crowd is a single living organism, all sweat and movement and the kind of anonymity that makes you feel like you could be anyone. Which is sort of the point tonight. We're supposed to be anyone but ourselves. I'm wearing something that glows under the black lights, and so is he, and we look like two radioactive people who wandered in from a different dimension.

But I can't think about any of that because Rodrigo's hand is on the small of my back.

His palm is warm and it sits right there at the base of my spine like it was always meant to be there— like my spine was built for it. A kind of evolution even Darwin wouldn't understand— this is less scientific and more poetry. His other hand finds my waist, and I feel my entire body tilt toward him the way a plant leans toward light, which is embarrassing but also completely involuntary. I've spent thirty-five years on this planet making myself smaller for men. Smaller opinions, smaller appetites, smaller presence. Standing in the back of rooms. Nodding when I should have been talking. But right now, pressed against Rodrigo in a techno club— I don't want to be small.

I have never wanted a man this much.

I want to say it out loud, to tell him, but I'm Billie Harper, so instead I just press my forehead against his collarbone and breathe him in.

The music shifts— something slower, still electronic but with this aching melody threaded through it— and Rodrigo pulls back. Not away. Just enough so he can look at me. The strobe light catches his face in intervals, and each flash is like a photograph I want to keep.

He leans in to whisper something in my ear.

"Billie," he says, and his voice is low enough that I feel it more than hear it. "I—"

My heart does a flutter that seems dangerous and unsound. For a second, I think he might tell me he loves me. Which is impossible, because *we have not known each other long enough*, and because we have promised to be friends and—

I feel his breath against my neck–

And then the world goes black.

Not metaphorically. Actually, literally black— fabric over my face, something rough and heavy that smells like canvas and industrial cleaner and somebody's really bad day.

A bag. Someone has put a bag over my head.

The most romantic moment of my life has been ruined by a fabric bag.

I try to scream, but the sound gets swallowed by the fabric and the bass and the chaos that erupts all at once.

Hands— not Rodrigo's, absolutely not Rodrigo's— grip my arms with the kind of force that suggests these hands have done this before and are very good at it. I'm wrenched backward, away from the warmth of his chest, and the loss of contact is so sudden it feels like a physical wound.

Then, I hear a hitting sound, and suddenly, the bag is off my head. Rodrigo is standing in front of me again, his fist clenched, breathing heavily: "Run, Billie!" he says. It's clear Rodrigo has tackled my assailant to give me time to get away. But then a man behind him pushes him to the floor. They move away from me, getting lost in the crowd— and I run toward him to try to help— but I'm grabbed again, and the bag is back, and I can't see.

"Rodrigo!" I yell into the bag, which is about as useful as yelling into a pillow.

My feet scrape the ground as I'm dragged backward. The music gets louder for a moment— we must be passing a speaker— and then it dims. We're moving away from the dance floor. A door opens. The temperature changes. The air gets cooler and smells like concrete and cigarettes.

I try to catalog what's happening the way a smart person would— direction of travel, number of captors, possible exits— but mostly I'm thinking about the fact that I was two seconds away from hearing the end of that sentence. Two seconds. I've waited my whole life for someone to look at me the way Rodrigo was looking at me, and the universe gave me a single moment before ripping it away.

This is what I get for technically cheating on Tyler. The universe saw Billie Harper on the verge of something beautiful and thought, *absolutely not.*

The hands shove me down into what feels like a chair. The bag stays on. I sit in the dark and try to breathe and think, irrationally, unreasonably— about what Rodrigo was about to tell me. I should be worried about the fact I've probably just been discovered by the Twin Ledger and am about to die... but all I can think about is the feeling of Rodrigo's breath on my neck.

* * *

The light, when the bag comes off, is fluorescent and merciless. I blink against it, my eyes watering, and the room assembles itself in pieces— concrete walls, a metal table shoved against the far side, exposed pipes running along the ceiling. Somewhere far away, the techno music still pulses, but it's muffled now, reduced to a heartbeat behind layers of wall and door. We're in the guts of the club. The part the clientele never sees.

I try to move and discover that I can't. My wrists are zip-tied to the arms of a metal chair, which seems like overkill for someone of my stature, but I suppose professionals are professionals.

Rodrigo is on my left. Also tied to a chair. There's a bruise blooming along his jaw— purple and angry— and his eyes are calm on the surface but there's a wildfire underneath. He catches my gaze and something in his face softens, just fractionally, just enough to communicate: *Are you okay?*

I nod. I am not okay. But I nod.

On my right, Alana sits in her own chair like it's a throne. Her wrists are bound the same as ours, but somehow she's managed to cross her legs, and her posture is the posture of someone waiting for a latte, not someone who's been kidnapped at a nightclub. Her pink outfit still glows faintly under the fluorescent light. Her eyelash extensions are, impossibly, still intact. She looks mildly inconvenienced, the way you'd look if someone told you the restaurant lost your reservation.

"This is *so* rude," she says, to no one in particular.

A door opens behind us, and footsteps approach—measured, deliberate. A man steps into view, circling around to face us, and I get my first look at the person who orchestrated this charming little kidnapping.

He's in his forties, thin in a way that suggests discipline rather than deprivation. His beard is— I want to say *artistic*, but really it's the kind of facial hair that suggests someone who makes eccentric choices and stands by them. There's an intelligence in his eyes that's almost clinical, like he's already done the math on us and is waiting to see if we've arrived at the same answer.

"Alana," he says, and it's more of a confirmation than a greeting.

"Tamor!" Alana smiles brightly. "Love what you've done with the place. Very, like, serial killer chic."

"You came to me for documents, I assume." His tone says this is transactional and boring. "But the situation has changed."

"Changed how?" Rodrigo's voice is steady. Controlled.

Tamor doesn't look at him. He reaches into the inner pocket of his jacket and produces a phone, holding the screen toward us. On it, I can see what looks like a dark web listing— grainy photos, text in multiple languages, and numbers. Big numbers.

"The Twin Ledger has raised the bounties," Tamor says. "On all three of you. Effective as of—" he checks his watch with theatrical precision— "four hours ago."

My stomach drops. Not a gentle descent. A free fall.

"How much?" Alana asks, and there's a flicker of something sharp behind the bubbly facade.

Tamor tilts the phone. "You, Alana— two hundred thousand euros. The man— one hundred fifty thousand." He pauses, and his gaze slides to me. "The very frightened woman. Four hundred thousand."

The room goes very quiet. Even the distant techno seems to hold its breath.

I blink. "I'm sorry— *me?* I'm the highest bounty?"

"You," Tamor confirms.

On my right, Alana's composure cracks. Not in a scared way. In an *offended* way.

"Okay, wait." She sits forward in her chair as much as the zip ties allow. "Four hundred— are you *kidding* me? I'm the one who stole from them! I, like, literally took their ring. I've been in this career field for *years*, and she's—" Alana gestures toward me with her chin, since her hands are otherwise occupied. "No offense, Billie, but you've been doing this for, like, a week."

"None taken?" I manage.

"This is *so* unfair. Like, what do I have to do to get some respect around here? I stole an actual ring from an arms dealer, and the corporate assistant gets double my bounty? This is—" She turns to Tamor. "This is sexism."

"It is economics," Tamor says, unmoved. He nods at me. "Rumor is she killed Mateo. She has destroyed one half of The Twin Ledger. You, Alana... stole some jewelry. Which Marco will certainly get back when he has you in his grasp."

Alana lets out an angry huff, as if she's about to ask to speak to a manager. "Okay, *wow.* Way to diminish my accomplishments, Tamor. And after all our years of friendship! Has anyone ever told you that you need therapy?"

"Regardless," Tamor continues, his voice as flat as the

concrete walls, "I cannot help you. The risk-to-reward ratio no longer favors my involvement. Every forger, fixer, and freelancer between here and Lisbon has seen these postings. Helping you is a suicide note."

The words land like stones. I look at Rodrigo, whose jaw is tight. I look at Alana, who is still visibly processing the bounty disparity. And I realize that no one is going to fix this. Alana is spiraling. Rodrigo is calculating but has no leverage here. And Tamor has already made his decision.

So:

I negotiate.

"Tamor." My voice comes out steadier than I expect. "You're a businessman. So let me talk to you like one."

He raises an eyebrow. It's the most expression I've seen from him.

"You say helping us is a suicide note. But turning us away is worse. Because right now, the three most wanted people in Europe are sitting in *your* back room. If Marco's people track us here— and they *will* track our last known location— what story do you want them to find? That you were the guy who washed his hands and let us walk? Because that's not a story that says *Tamor is untouchable.* That's a story that says *Tamor is afraid.*"

The room is quiet. Even Alana has stopped complaining.

"You're right," Tamor nods. "So I will keep you until Marco's men arrive and he can deal with you. Problem solved."

Alana looks at me as if to say: *great job, help me less.*

"Problem not solved," I continue quickly, "You give us the documents, and we disappear. We become someone *else's* problem immediately. Your exposure is five minutes of work that no one has to know about. But if you keep us and alert Marco, you've just sent a very important message to every assassin around about the quality of your business. About the level or trust and discretion they can expect... from *you*. This is about your *reputation*."

I have no idea where this is coming from. Some deep, hidden room inside my chest that I've never had the key to before. It feels like the negotiation skills I spent years watching other people use at Franklin Luxury Developments, only now the stakes aren't a high-rise in Lincoln Park. They're our lives.

Tamor studies me for a long moment. His expression doesn't change, but something behind his eyes recalibrates. I charge on:

"You see, whether you like it or not, Alana has a reputation for being one of the Twin Ledger's most valuable actors. Sure, they've started the rumor she killed Mateo. But will *everyone* believe that? We've started a little rumor of our own— that the Twin Ledger is picking off their best people to avoid competition. The Twin Ledger is hunting one of their own contractors. And that doesn't inspire trust among assassins. What if the Twin Ledger falls?" I suggest, tracking Tamor's reaction. He's listening. I have his attention. "Marco is the sole survivor. If the Twin Ledger goes down, and you helped them take out their own operative *in the club that you own*, what does that tell everyone else out in the field?" I lean in as much as I can, straining against the ties that keep me secured to the chair. "It says that Tamor plays both sides, and he can't be trusted. It says your club isn't safe. Is that really the message you want to send, when you could just give us the papers and no one would be the wiser?"

There's a heavy silence as Tamor considers what I've told him.

"Five minutes," he says. "Your documents will be ready in five minutes."

I exhale.

"But I will tell you this." He leans forward, and for the first time, his voice carries something heavier than calculation. "I have been in this business for twenty-two years. I have never seen three bounties this large from the Twin Ledger posted simultaneously. Every contract killer, every freelance operative, every desperate amateur with a gun and a debt— they are all looking for you. Right now. Tonight." He straightens. "I will give you your papers. But I do not think you will live long enough to use them."

He turns and walks toward the door. Pauses. Looks back.

"Five minutes," he repeats. "Tell no one." And with that, he disappears.

The silence he leaves behind is enormous. Rodrigo lets out a slow breath beside me. He stares at me, his eyes filled with a warm admiration that makes me want to leap into his arms. "You saved our lives, Billie."

Alana stares at the door, then slowly turns to look at me.

"Okay," she says. "Billie, that was, like, *really* hot."

I almost laugh. Almost. But my hands are shaking too hard.

* * *

When we exit the club, the night air hits my face like a cold glass of water after a fever, and for a moment, I think we might actually be okay.

We're standing on a side street behind Pulse, the three of us blinking in the relative darkness like animals released from a lab. There's some kind of night festival going on, and makeshift booths have been set up in the street. Artists sell their wares, flat tables displaying art and pottery. One of Tamor's men— a broad, silent type— passes a manila folder to Alana, who opens it and flips through the contents like she's received forged identity documents before. Which, of course, she has.

"These are good," she says approvingly, holding one of the passports up to the streetlight. "He even used a great picture of me. I mean every picture of me is great because I'm very photogenic, but still..."

Rodrigo takes his documents and tucks them inside his jacket. I take mine and stare at the photo— it's me, but not me. The photograph is me, but I have a different name and a different country of origin— the United Kingdom— and, presumably, a life that doesn't involve being hunted across a continent. I want to crawl inside this passport and become this other woman. She seems like she has her act together.

"Oh, um, also, like, we left some luggage in the club—" Alana starts to say.

"I put it behind the bar—" Rodrigo adds.

Tamor's man stares at them. Then, adds helpfully, "Tamor says you cannot come back in the club again. As they say in America, get lost, huh?" With that, he disappears into the club, and I think I hear the door locking behind him. *So much for our luggage.*

"Good thing I have my best purse on me," Alana says, hiking her tiny bag over her shoulder.

I stare out at the village square, considering our next move. The street is narrow and cobblestoned, slick from recent rain. To our left, the alley leads back toward the main road, where I can hear the sounds of what seems to be some kind of night festival— music, laughter, the clatter of food vendors. Madrid is in full swing, completely unaware that three glowing criminals are standing in its back alley with a collective bounty that could buy a small island.

"We need to move," Rodrigo says, putting his hand on the small of my back without thinking.

He's right. We need to move. I'm afraid, but I know we're going to be okay. We're free now, we have our documents, and the night is—

A bullet hits the wall three inches from my head.

The sound comes a split second later— a sharp crack that bounces off the stone buildings and multiplies. I don't process it intellectually. My body processes it first, flinching so hard I nearly fall, and then Rodrigo's arm is around me, pulling me down, pulling me sideways into the alley as another shot chips the cobblestone where I was standing.

"I don't even have my best gun!" Alana shouts. "It was in my other bag!" She's already moving, running toward the main street with a purpose that suggests she has a plan or is simply too selfish to die. We run, following her because there's nothing else to do.

The festival swallows us like a wave. One moment we're in a dark alley, and the next we're plunging into a river of people— crowds packed between temporary stalls selling fried dough and mulled wine and knockoff handbags. String lights crisscross overhead. A man on a small stage is playing an accordion with rapid intensity. It should feel safe, all these people, all this warmth and noise and life. But I can feel the danger behind us like heat from a fire you haven't turned around to see yet.

"There!" Rodrigo points— two figures pushing through the crowd from the east, moving with purpose, not browsing.

"And there," I say, because I've spotted another one to the west. A woman in a dark jacket, hand inside her coat, eyes scanning.

"Okay, so, like, there's bounty hunters everywhere," Alana says, and then she produces a handgun from her purse— and she fires twice over the heads of the crowd.

The shots scatter the nearest cluster of festival-goers, screams erupting, people ducking and running, which creates chaos that works both for and against us. The attackers lose their sightlines. But so do we.

"I really thought Marco would show up himself," Alana says, almost pouting as she scans the stampeding crowd. "Like, personally. Is that too much to ask? I stole his ring. The *least* he could do is come try to kill me in person. Sending freelancers is so— ugh. It's like getting broken up with over text. It's like he doesn't think I'm worth it or something—"

"Alana, *focus,*" Rodrigo snaps, and he pulls me behind a vendor's stall— a sturdy wooden structure selling ceramic mugs that we crouch behind as another shot splinters the display above us. Tiny painted Madrid landmarks rain down on our heads.

"Are you hurt?" he asks me, his hands on my shoulders, his eyes doing that full-body scan thing that is both protective and also devastatingly attractive, which is a very confusing combination of feelings to have while someone is actively trying to assassinate you.

"I'm fine," I say, and I mostly am, except for my heart rate, which has left the building entirely.

Another shot. Closer this time. Alana returns fire from behind a pillar. A man crumples somewhere in the crowd, and she doesn't even watch him fall.

We bolt again— through a gap between stalls, down a

narrow lane, into a small plaza where a fountain gurgles peacefully, completely unbothered by our crisis. Rodrigo pulls me into the shadow of an archway, and Alana skids in beside us, barely winded.

"Why do they keep finding us?" Rodrigo hisses.

And that's when I see it.

I look down at myself. At the outfit I'm wearing— the club outfit, the one chosen specifically for Pulse, designed to glow under ultraviolet light. In the dark archway, the fabric on my arms and torso is doing exactly what it was designed to do. It's *glowing*. A soft, unmistakable neon luminescence that turns my silhouette into a beacon. I look at Rodrigo. Same thing— his shirt radiates a pale electric blue. Alana's pink ensemble pulses like a flamingo-shaped nightlight.

We're not hiding in the shadows. We're *illuminating* them. Every time we duck into darkness, we light up like human glow sticks. We might as well be wearing signs that say SHOOT HERE.

"Oh my God," I whisper.

"What?" Rodrigo asks.

"It's the clothes." I gesture at all three of us. "We're glowing. We're literally glowing in the dark. Every time we try to hide, we turn into targets. That's how they keep spotting us."

Rodrigo looks down at himself. Then at me. Then at Alana, who is examining her own luminescent sleeve with a mixture of horror and aesthetic appreciation.

"We have to take them off," I say.

The words leave my mouth before I fully consider their implications. But I'm right. The math is simple— the clothes go, or we go. Permanently.

"But, our bags are back in the club!" Alana says. "And this jumpsuit is panty-free. No lines."

I motion to my own glow-in-the-dark, leather pants, and the highlighter-colored tank top that I'm currently wearing without a bra.

"Same here," I say. "I don't have any underwear because *someone* kidnapped me and didn't bother to pack any so I've been going camo for *days*!"

We both look at Rodrigo. He shrugs. "I do have *mis calzoncillos.* But will depart from them in solidarity if necessary. "

"So should we..." Alana starts to say.

"Do the math, Alana," I answer, rolling my eyes.

Rodrigo looks at me. And slowly, almost imperceptibly, one eyebrow arches.

It's not a *concerned* arch. It's not a *questioning* arch. It's the kind of arch that communicates, in a single muscular movement, that Rodrigo Esperanza thinks taking our clothes off is an excellent idea, and not entirely for strategic reasons. The corner of his mouth twitches. His eyes hold mine with an intensity that has nothing to do with assassins and everything to do with the fact that, apparently, my survival instincts have accidentally proposed that we all get undressed in a Madrid plaza.

A bullet whistles over our heads, and we all duck down at the same time. The bullet slams into the wall behind us, sending ancient stone crumbling into pieces.

"Unless someone has a better idea—" I start.

"No, no," Rodrigo says, already reaching for the hem of his shirt. "*Buena idea.*"

Alana is already unzipping something. "It's actually like, totally fine. A gift to the world, really. This outfit is *so* uncomfortable."

Another bullet ricochets off the fountain behind us, sending a spray of water into the air.

Right. Clothes off. Assassins later. Or— assassins now, clothes off now, everything now, everything all at once, which is apparently just how my life works these days.

I grab the edge of my glowing top and start to pull. And suddenly, I'm naked, running through the marketplace totally in the nude. Tourists point and stare, but thankfully — the square is so crowded I can blend in with the crowd— somewhat.

Rodrigo points across the square to a hotel. "There," he says, and I try not to look at his perfect body. We crouch low among the crowd, making our way to safety. As we move, Rodrigo grabs newspapers from a stand and passes them among our group— an attempt to cover us up.

"Perfect," Alana shouts, and she clutches a newspaper to her chest and takes off across the square, almost at the door to the hotel.

Rodrigo pauses, even in the midst of danger, helping me to arrange the newspapers in a strategic fashion, even tying two together in a sad, uneven knot below my waist. "Thanks," I say, and Rodrigo— as another bullet flies past his head— bursts out laughing. Then his laugh makes me laugh and together we disappear into the crowd, following Alana's form into the night.

twenty-seven

RODRIGO

THERE ARE things a man tells himself when he is standing almost totally-naked in the lobby of a four-star hotel in Madrid, covered in newspaper and what I'm fairly certain is part of a kebab wrapper, trying not to look at the gorgeous woman beside him who is also covered in newspaper. Things like: *you are a gentleman. You are a professional. You have been in worse situations than this.* That last one is a lie. I have never, in thirty-five years of living, been in a worse situation than this.

The hotel is called the Astoria Grand, or something with the word "Grand" in it— I can't read the sign because I'm too busy pressing a crumpled edition of *Madrid a Diario* against my torso to keep from traumatizing the elderly couple exiting through the revolving door. They see us. They see all of us. The woman clutches her husband's arm and quickens her pace in a way that I would find funny if I had any dignity left to laugh with.

I stare at the chandelier. I stare at the marble. I study the veining pattern of the floor tile as if it is the most fascinating geological phenomenon I have encountered in my entire life, because if I look two degrees to my left, I will see Billie Harper, and if I see Billie Harper right now, wrapped in nothing but the international news section I fashioned into a makeshift skirt— *Dios mío*— I will lose the last remaining thread of composure holding me together.

I have already seen too much. Not in the way that sounds. When we were stripping off the glow-in-the-dark clothes in that alley five minutes ago, I caught one single flash of Billie's bare shoulder in the streetlight, and it landed in my chest like a fist. Just her shoulder. The soft slope of it, the freckles scattered there like someone had flicked a paintbrush. I turned away so fast I nearly tripped over a newspaper stand, which is where I found the sports section that is currently preserving what remains of my modesty.

She hasn't looked at me either. I think. I hope. I genuinely cannot tell because I am committed to examining this chandelier for the rest of my natural life.

Alana, meanwhile, walks through the lobby like she owns it. As far as she's concerned, she is a guest. An important one. And the young man behind the front desk, in his pressed uniform and his careful little name tag, is going to treat her like one.

"Hi," she says, leaning one elbow on the counter, her pink-manicured nails— still intact, somehow, after everything— tapping twice on the marble. "I need three rooms. Actually, I need whatever you have. Tonight. I also need clothing purchased and delivered to the rooms by tomorrow morning. Make the clothing sent to my room pink and like, designer. Just bill them to the room. No questions. Oh also, make sure there's no phones in the rooms." She turns and winks at us, clearly communicating that she doesn't want us making any calls. Then, she turns back to the man: "Can you do that?"

The concierge blinks. His eyes travel from Alana to me, to Billie, and back to Alana. He opens his mouth.

"Also," Alana adds, pulling her small crossbody purse around— the only item she managed to keep— and extracting a stack of bills with the casualness of someone pulling out a stick of gum, "this is two thousand euros. That should cover the inconvenience of whatever you're about to say, plus whatever discretion costs in this city. I'm guessing it's less than that, but like, keep the change."

She sets the money on the counter, placing it next to her shiny new passport, courtesy of Tamor. The concierge looks at the money. He looks at Alana. He looks at the newspaper clinging to her décolletage. I can actually see the moment his professional training overrides his survival instincts.

"Madam," he says carefully. "I would be happy to help you. However, we only have two rooms available this evening. One is our premier suite on the seventh floor. The other is a standard single on the fourth."

"Perfect," Alana says.

"The standard room has— it is quite small, I should mention—"

"That's fine." She's already holding her hand out. He places a key card in it. She takes the one for the suite, obviously. "This one's mine."

She turns to face us. Me and Billie, standing there like two people at the world's worst costume party, and Alana's calculating, Barbie-doll eye flick between us with a look I have learned to recognize as cruelty disguised as indifference.

"You two can figure out the other room," she says. "I'm not sharing with my ex-boyfriend *and* my ex-best friend in the same night. I have boundaries." She says the word *boundaries* the way someone might say *vision board*—sincerely and without a trace of irony.

Then she walks to the elevator. The concierge watches her go. I watch her go. Billie watches her go.

There is a small silence. The kind that fills a space when someone like Alana leaves it, like the air rushing back in after a door has been sealed.

"So," Billie says.

I finally look at her. I shouldn't. I do.

She is clutching the newspaper against her chest, her brown hair falling in messy waves against her bare shoulders, and she is looking up at me with those eyes— those enormous, bambi, tell-me-your-secrets eyes— and she's got a piece of newspaper stuck to her collarbone, and she looks mortified and brave and ridiculously, painfully beautiful, and I think, very clearly: *Estoy perdido.*

I'm lost.

"I'll get the key," I say, because it is the only safe sentence in any language.

The concierge hands it over without commentary. He has earned his euros.

Billie and I walk toward the elevator in silence, leaving a small trail of newsprint behind us on the marble floor. Somewhere above us, Alana is already settling into her suite, probably ordering room service. Probably ordering champagne.

The elevator doors open. We step inside. The mirrored walls show us exactly what we look like— two grown adults wrapped in newspapers, standing three inches apart, not touching, not speaking, headed to a room that I am now almost certain contains one bed.

Dios me ayude.

* * *

The room is exactly as small as the concierge promised. One bed, a window with gauze curtains that glow faintly from the streetlights of Madrid below, and approximately four square feet of floor space that I am already mentally claiming as my sleeping territory. There is a bathroom, thank God, and two white robes hanging on the back of the door, and I have never in my life been more grateful for terrycloth.

We take turns changing. That is to say, we take turns going into the bathroom to shed our newspaper armor and put on the robes, and when Billie emerges, hair loose, face washed, wrapped in white cotton that is three sizes too big for her, I have to look at the crooked lampshade and think about construction permits.

"You take the bed," I say. "I'll sleep on the floor."

"Rodrigo."

"It's fine. I've slept on worse. I once slept on a concrete slab in Valencia because my cousin locked me out of his apartment." This is true. My other cousin— Esteban is not a generous man, unlike Benny, who is a degenerate, but a thoughtful one.

"There's like two feet of floor space," she says. "You'd be sleeping under the bed, not on it."

"I'm flexible."

"You're six foot one."

"Six foot two," I correct, which is not the point but feels important to clarify.

She sits on the edge of the bed and looks at me with those eyes. They are enormous, in a way that is incredibly unfair. "I won't be able to sleep," she says, "knowing you're down there. I'll just lie here feeling guilty, which means neither of us will sleep, which means tomorrow we'll both be exhausted and useless, which means Alana wins."

I consider this. The logic is, annoyingly, sound.

"I can be a gentleman," I say, really wishing I didn't have to be.

"Then problem solved," she says. And the way she says it— not teasing, not testing, just certain— does something to the center of my chest that I am not prepared to examine.

So we share the bed.

It is a queen, which is generous for the room, and we lie on our backs with a careful six inches of neutral territory between us, staring at the ceiling like two people who have been placed in a psychological experiment. I can hear her breathing. I can smell the hotel soap on her skin. Outside, a tram rumbles past, and Madrid hums its late-night hum, and I think: *I have been in gunfights that felt less dangerous than this.*

"Can I ask you something?" she says, after a while.

"Sí."

"Why Alana?"

I exhale. It's the question I've been asking myself for months, maybe years, in one form or another.

"Because she was bright," I say. "Dazzling. Like fireworks." I pause. "I have a history of this. Falling for the brightness. The spectacle. Someone walks into a room and everything changes, and I think—*that's it, that's the feeling* — and I give myself to it completely. I build the person in my head before I've seen who they actually are and then I project this person on to them. I fill in the gaps with who I *want* them to be."

The ceiling has a small crack in it, running from the light fixture to the corner. I follow it with my eyes.

"I did it with Alana. I did it before her, with a woman in

Sevilla who turned out to be married. I did it before her, with a woman in Madrid who was kind but we had nothing — nothing real between us. I just wanted it so badly that I invented the connection." I swallow. "I'm good at building things. Structures, houses. But I've been building people, too. And that— that is not something anyone should do."

The silence that follows is not uncomfortable. It's the kind of silence that holds space.

"I know what you mean," Billie says quietly. "Not the building part. The opposite, maybe. I've spent my whole life letting other people build me. Or— not build me. Overlook me. I'm always the one who does the work and never the one who gets the credit. The one who stays late. The one who remembers the details. And people just—" She stops. "They take it for granted. They take *me* for granted. Like I'm furniture. Useful, but not worth noticing."

I turn my head on the pillow. She's looking at the ceiling too, and in the dim light from the window, I can see the gold flecks in her brown eyes, and the freckles on her cheeks, and the small, honest curve of her mouth, and I think that anyone who has ever overlooked this woman must be profoundly, catastrophically blind.

"I can't imagine," I say, "anyone overlooking you. You are impossible to miss."

She turns her head. We are looking at each other now, on the same pillow almost, and the six inches of neutral territory has become four, maybe three.

"You don't really know me," she says. But it's not a deflection. It's an offering. She's giving me the chance to agree, to retreat.

"Perhaps," I muse. "But I *have* run from gunfire with you. I think that makes two people know each other quickly."

"Maybe," Billie offers.

She needs more. She does not believe that I truly see her. So I add: "I know that you are the most honest person I've ever met. You couldn't hide what you feel if your life depended on it— and believe me, lately, it has. I know that you choose what is right in the face of great danger. I know that you are powerful, but that you don't believe it."

She almost laughs. Almost.

"But what if—" She hesitates, and I watch her gather the courage, and it's like watching someone step to the edge of a high place. "What if the way you see me is just you getting swept up again? Projecting onto me instead of seeing me?"

It's a fair question. It's a brave question. It's the kind of question that Alana would never ask, because Alana would never care about the answer.

I take a breath. "No," I say, and I can answer this confidently, because I've wondered the same thing. "And I'll tell you why."

The tram passes again outside. The curtains shift.

"Because you can't be a lie, Billie. You don't know how. Your face— *tu cara*— it tells everything. Every feeling, every thought, it's right there, like a window with no curtain. And that is the opposite of what I've been chasing. I spent years falling for the performance. The dazzle. And then I would build a person underneath it— a person who was kind, and funny, and real, and who actually *cared* about the world beyond herself— and she was never there. She was never the person I invented."

I turn onto my side. She does too. We are close now. Close enough that I could count her freckles if I wanted. I want to.

"But you," I say. "*Tú eres esa persona.* You are that

person. The one I kept imagining. The one I kept looking for inside everyone else. You're not a projection. You're the thing I was always projecting."

Her eyes are shining. Not with tears, exactly, but with something I recognize— the look of someone who has just been told they are worth something, and is trying to decide whether to believe it.

"Rodrigo," she whispers.

I close the distance. Or she does. Or we both do, meeting somewhere in that last inch of space, and when I kiss her, it's not like fireworks. It's not like anything bright or loud or spectacular. It is like finding the room you've been looking for in a house you've been building your whole life. It is like the door was always there, and you just finally turned the handle. It is the easiest thing in the world. The most natural thing.

She kisses me back, and her hand comes up to the side of my face, and her fingers are small and warm, and I pull her closer, and she lets me, and the robe is too big on her anyway— it's been falling off her all night— and when I reach underneath it— a plain white thing, simple, nothing designed to destroy a man and yet here I am, destroyed— she doesn't stop me. She lifts her arms, and I pull the robe off of her, and she is looking at me with those enormous, bambi, tell-me-everything eyes, and I think:

She is not the firework. She is the sky behind it. She is infinite, and she was there the whole time.

I pull her against me. Madrid hums outside the window. The crooked lampshade watches from its post. And whatever happens next— whatever happens next is ours.

twenty-eight

BILLIE

I KNOW I shouldn't do it.

I am in bed with Rodrigo, and I know exactly where this leads, but I don't care.

There's an old version of me— the responsible one who carries her passport everywhere and does laundry on Sundays— who is screaming at me to think this through. But that version of me has never been kissed like this.

His kiss feels familiar, which is strange, because we've only kissed once before— it's not some grand, cinematic observation about electricity, but warmth. The kind that starts at your lips and spreads down through your chest like you've swallowed something golden. His hand is on the side of my face, thumb tracing my jaw like he has all the time in the world— Rodrigo doesn't rush— and I'm not thinking about the fact we're being chased through Europe by assassins. I'm thinking about his mouth. And his hand. And the way his other hand has found the small of my back and is pulling me closer in a way that feels less like a demand and more like a question.

I answer it. I press into him, my fingers sliding up the

back of his neck, into his hair— which is unfairly soft, by the way, for a man who works in construction. This seems like something I should have noticed before now, but in my defense, I've been a little busy running for my life. The responsible part of me tries to narrate my own experience back to me like a nature documentary. *Here we observe the common Billie Harper in her natural habitat: making wildly irresponsible decisions.*

But his mouth moves to my jaw, then my neck, and the nature documentary narrator shuts up.

I have been kissed before. I've had boyfriends and first dates and one memorable New Year's Eve where I kissed a stranger who turned out to be my Uber driver. But none of those kisses felt like this— like being found. Like someone reaching through all the noise and static of who I pretend to be and putting their hand directly on the part of me I keep hidden.

His lips come back to mine. He smiles against my mouth. I feel it— the curve of it— and something in my chest cracks open.

"Billie," he says, and the way he says my name sounds like it belongs to someone more interesting than me. Someone braver. He pulls back, just enough that I can see his face, and his eyes are so serious it almost hurts.

"I know this is complicated," he says.

"The arms dealer situation or the kissing situation?" I manage. My voice comes out rougher than I intended.

He almost laughs. Almost. "The kissing. Though, yes, also the other thing." His thumb is still on my jaw, like he can't quite bring himself to stop touching me. "I know enough about you now, Billie. You will wake up in the morning and you will feel terrible."

"I won't—"

"You will." He says it so gently it doesn't feel like an interruption. It feels like someone handing you a coat when you didn't realize you were cold. "You will feel like this happened because of adrenaline, or because you were scared, or because we are in a situation that is— how do you say— not exactly normal."

"Rodrigo—"

"And I don't want that." His voice drops, quieter now, like he's telling me something he's been carrying around for a while. "I don't want the first time with you to be something you have to explain away tomorrow. I want it to be something you chose. *Completamente.* No regrets. No second thoughts. Perfect."

I stare at him. *That might be the most thoughtful thing a man has ever said to me*— which doesn't say much for the men I've met.

The hotel room is dim, just the pale wash of a streetlamp coming through the curtains, and in this light his face looks like one of those paintings you see in museums that make you stand still for too long. I think about every guy I've ever been with who never once stopped to consider what I might feel afterward. Who never even entertained the possibility that my feelings about something could be more important than getting the something itself.

And here is Rodrigo Esperanza, pulling back in the middle of the best kiss of my life because he's worried about *my* morning-after emotional state.

It hits me: *If I don't sleep with this man— right now— I will regret for the rest of my life.*

Something hot and bright builds behind my eyes. Not quite tears. Something bigger than that.

"I can't imagine regretting this," I tell him.

He searches my face. Those eyes— dark and steady and

so impossibly kind it makes my chest ache— move over me like he's reading something written in a language only he understands.

"You're sure?" he asks.

"I'm sure," I say. And then, because I'm still me, I add: "I think I might regret *not* doing it."

He laughs then. Really laughs. The sound rumbles through his chest and into mine because we're still that close, and it's the best thing I've ever heard.

He kisses me again. Slower this time. More deliberate. Like now that we've both agreed to be here, there's no reason to rush. His hand slides from my jaw to the back of my neck, fingers threading through my hair, and I feel myself go soft in a way I didn't know I was capable of. Like I've been holding myself rigid for years and only just now realized I could stop.

I pull him closer. It feels like we have all the time in the world— and we're going to need it.

We are not running right now. We are not hiding. We are not strategizing or worrying or looking over our shoulders. We are just— this. His mouth on my collarbone. My fingers tracing the lines of his shoulders. The sound of his breathing, and mine, tangled together in the dark.

I stop thinking about tomorrow. I stop thinking about Marco, about the Twin Ledger, about Alana and her pink designer luggage and her casual relationship with international crime. I stop thinking about Tyler, and ethics, and whether or not I deserve my own happiness.

I stop thinking entirely.

And I give myself over to him— to us— to whatever this is. His hands are gentle and certain and everywhere, and I am falling into something I don't have a name for yet, something warm and vast and terrifying in the best possible way, and the last coherent thought I have before I lose myself completely is this:

So this is what it feels like to be chosen.

* * *

The next morning, I wake up to the smell of coffee and the sound of someone quietly arranging silverware, and temporarily I forget that my life has gone completely off the rails. Then I open my eyes and see Rodrigo sitting at the small table by the window, morning light falling across his shoulders, pouring coffee from a silver carafe like we're in a European travel commercial, and I remember everything—the running, the danger, last night.

Especially last night.

"Buenos días," he says, looking up. His smile makes me feel like you've done something right just by existing. "I ordered breakfast. I didn't know what you liked, so I got—well." He gestures at the table, which is covered in plates. Croissants, fruit, eggs, toast, some kind of pastry I don't recognize, and what appears to be an entire wheel of cheese.

"You ordered for a family of six," I say, sitting up and pulling the sheet around me.

"I wanted options."

I grab my robe— which has been unceremoniously dropped on the floor by the bed— and pad over to the table, sitting across from him. He slides a cup of coffee toward me without asking if I want one, which means he already knows me well enough to understand that the answer is always yes.

We eat. And it's— nice. Nicer than it should be, given the circumstances. He tears a croissant in half and hands me the bigger piece without making a thing of it. I watch him spread jam with a kind of careful precision that tells me something about who he is: a man who pays attention to small things. A man who doesn't rush.

"Last night was—" I start.

"Amazing," he finishes. Not cocky. Just honest. He meets my eyes over his coffee cup and holds them there. "*Increíble.*"

I feel heat crawl up my neck. "I was going to say 'unexpected,' but sure, we can go with yours."

He laughs softly, then sets his cup down. The laugh fades. Something shifts in his expression— a tightening around his jaw, a seriousness settling into his features like clouds moving over a field.

"Billie, I want to talk to you about something."

Here it is. The morning-after conversation I was bracing for. Except when he talks, it's not what I expect. *He's going to tell me that last night was fun, but it's over.*

"I've told you about my family home," he says. "In the Italian countryside. A small chalet— it's in the mountains, very quiet. Beautiful village. Cobblestone, flowers. The kind of place where nothing bad has ever happened." He pauses. "I think we should go there."

"I know," I nod, agreeing with him. "It sounds magical."

"You and me. *Without* Alana."

The way he says *without Alana* is deliberate. Like he's been thinking about this for longer than just this morning.

I look at him. The sunlight is catching the edge of his jaw. I'm distracted by how handsome he is, but then I realize what he's trying to tell me:

He wants to abandon Alana and leave her to deal with the Twin Ledger on her own.

"We can be safe there," Rodrigo continues. "Benny is

already there. We can wait things out, contact the right people—"

"But," I stutter. "Alana got us our passports. She did what she said she was going to do and held up her end of the bargain."

Rodrigo sighs, running a hand through his hair. "She is a viper, Billie. I know her better than you do. There is something in this for her. She will feed us to the wolves the first chance she gets."

He leans in, taking my hands in his. "I want to keep you safe," he says gently. "I can't guarantee that as long as Alana is around. Billie— for our own safety— for your own *life*— we need to leave her."

"She's my friend, Rodrigo."

I say it before I fully think it through, which is maybe why it comes out sounding so certain. Because it's true. Somewhere between the running and the hiding and the absurd conversations about vision boards and ammunition, Alana became my friend. A chaotic, morally questionable, possibly sociopathic friend who wears hot pink to crime scenes— but a friend.

She showed me that I'm powerful. And whether she's a good person, or a bad person— I think there's some part of her that actually cares about me. And even if there's not, this adventure has shown me what I'm capable of— and I want to see it through.

"I can't just leave her," I say. "And we can't run from the Twin Ledger forever. Even if I go back to America right now, the Ledger has people everywhere— Alana is Exhibit A. They'll find us if we don't finish this. You know that. Marco isn't going to stop looking." I take a breath. It feels like the kind of breath you take before jumping off something high. "Maybe together— the three of us— we can figure out how to outsmart him. Shut the whole thing down. We can work with your contact at Interpol to finish them once and for all. And Alana can help us."

Rodrigo watches me. Not like he disagrees. More like he's seeing something in me he hasn't seen before and is trying to decide how he feels about it.

"Billie," he says quietly. "I need to get away from that woman."

Something inside me aches. I can feel how much he means it. Only weeks ago, I was jealous that a man like Rodrigo was with Alana and not me. And now: I see the real picture.

"I know," I nod, thinking through our options. "And you will. But if we leave now, the Twin Ledger still has us on their list. I know I'm asking a lot, but—" I sigh. "I need you to trust me. I can feel deep down in my gut that we have to finish this or we'll be running forever. And we need Alana to do it. I've spent my whole life being afraid," I tell him. My voice is steady, which surprises me. "Afraid of speaking up, afraid of asking for things, afraid of— I don't know— taking up space. And I can't do that anymore. I need to see this through."

He's quiet for a long moment. Then he nods, slowly, like he's making a decision of his own.

"Okay," he says. "*Vale.* We see it through. Together."

I smile at him. He smiles back. And something warm and solid settles between us, like the foundation of a house being poured.

But underneath my certainty, there's a thought I don't share. A small, cold thing curled up in the corner of my chest like a cat that doesn't want to be touched. The thought is this: what if Rodrigo doesn't actually love *me*? What if he loves the idea of me? What happens when the danger is over and I'm just Billie again— regular Billie, who can't negotiate a raise and owns too many cardigans?

I don't say any of this. Because last night was amazing. And because the croissant is really, really good. And because sometimes you have to let yourself have the good thing without immediately building a case for why you don't deserve it.

We finish breakfast, get dressed, and take the elevator down to the lobby. The doors open and there she is: Alana. Rodrigo audibly sighs in dismay at her presence.

At least I don't have to worry that he's still attracted to her, I smile to myself.

Alana is sitting in a velvet armchair near the front desk, legs crossed, wearing a hot pink blazer over what a white silk camisole, her hair blown out to perfection, nails freshly done in a shade I can only describe as "crime scene red." She's got oversized sunglasses pushed up on her head and she's reading a magazine— a *fashion* magazine— like she's waiting for a brunch reservation and not hiding from one of Europe's most dangerous criminal networks.

She looks up when she sees us. Her gaze flicks between me and Rodrigo with the precision of a surveillance camera, and a slow, knowing smile spreads across her impossibly beautiful face.

"Good *morning*," she says, in a way that makes it clear she knows exactly what kind of morning it's been. Strangely, she nods... almost as if she approves. "Okay, so, are we doing this? Because I've been, like, packed and ready since six a.m., and this lobby doesn't even have good Wi-Fi."

I look at Rodrigo. He looks at me. We made a deal, and we're keeping it.

"We're doing this," I say.

* * *

We make it to the airport, and my hands sweat during the entire boarding process. Will my new identity pass for a real one? Will I be arrested for using fake credentials? Alana, meanwhile, snacks on chips while we wait for our flight. "Don't worry, Billie," she yawns. "I've done this a hundred times."

I can't believe I'm getting on a plane with this woman again.

Rodrigo puts a comforting arm around my shoulders and whispers in my ear: "There is little border control between Spain and Italy. We will be fine, Billie. *Eres hermosa y valiente.* You are beautiful and brave."

We board the plane without issue, and after a short four-hour flight followed by a very uncomfortable taxi ride, we arrive in Tuscany.

It's stunning. The village where Rodrigo's family owns their home has cobblestone streets and buildings the color of terracotta and rust, and flowers everywhere— spilling from window boxes, climbing stone walls, tucked into corners. The air smells like pine and something herbal I can't name. I catch myself thinking the word quaint, and then charming, and then I just stop trying to think at all.

What I process first is Benny.

He comes barreling out of the front door before we've even parked, arms wide, shouting something in rapid Spanish that I can't follow but that clearly translates to some version of *you're alive and I'm very emotional about it.* He grabs Rodrigo in a bear hug that lifts him slightly off the ground, which is impressive given that Rodrigo is not a small man.

"Primo! *Primo!* I thought you were dead! I told myself—

Benny, this is like the movie, the one with Bruce Willis, when everyone thinks he is dead but he is not dead—"

"Die Hard," Rodrigo says, muffled against his cousin's shoulder.

"Yes! *Die Hard!* You are my Bruce Willis!"

Rodrigo extracts himself with the patient grace of someone who has been bear-hugged by Benny many times before. "Benny, this is Billie."

Benny turns to me. He's rugged, a little weathered, with the kind of face that suggests he's seen traumatic things but decided to find them funny. His eyes are warm and slightly manic, like a golden retriever who's had too much coffee.

"Billie!" He takes my hand and shakes it with both of his. "You are the one my cousin will not shut up about. He says you have eyes like the deer from the Disney movie."

"Benny," Rodrigo says, in a tone that is both a warning and a surrender.

"Bambi," I say. "He means Bambi."

"Yes! *Bambi!*" Benny beams at me like I've just solved world peace. "This man adores people with names like ours, isn't it true? Billie! Benny! We are practically related already." Benny winks at his cousin, then freezes when he sees Alana, standing behind us with yet another bag of chips in her hands. "You brought *El diabla?* No, no, no..."

"Nice to see you too, Benny!" Alana winks at him, then strides into the house. I've got to find the best bed. Be a doll and show me?"

Benny trails after Alana as if it's her house and he's merely the guest. The front door swings shut behind them, and for a moment it's just me and Rodrigo. Rodrigo grabs my arm. Not hard— never hard with him— but with an urgency that snaps me out of my Tuscan reverie.

"Now," he says. "While she's distracted. We need to call Melissa."

Right. Melissa. My *actual* best friend, who is eight months pregnant and probably sitting with Interpol right this second.

We go inside.

The chalet is exactly what Rodrigo described and somehow more than I imagined. It's warm in the way that only old stone houses can be warm— not from heating, but from decades of absorbing sunlight and cooking smells. The ceilings are low and beamed with dark wood. There are paintings on the walls— not expensive ones, I don't think, but beautiful ones, landscapes and abstracts in colors that make me think of wine and earth. Some of them, I realize, are Rodrigo's. I can tell by the brushwork, by the way the colors bleed into each other with a gentleness that reminds me of how he touches me. They feel like him.

I don't say this. I file it away for later, when I'm not in crisis mode.

The kitchen is small and tiled in blue and white, and mounted on the wall next to a wooden shelf of cookbooks is a landline phone. An actual, honest-to-God, corded phone. The kind with a curly wire that you can twist around your finger while you talk, which is exactly what I do when Rodrigo dials the number and hands me the receiver.

It rings twice.

"*Billie*?!"

Melissa's voice hits me like a wave— loud, bright, so full of relief that I feel my throat close up. I can picture her exactly: enormous belly, wild eyes, probably gesturing with both hands even though she's on the phone.

"Mel," I manage. "Hey."

"Oh my *God*. Oh my GOD, Billie. Do you know— do you

have ANY idea— I have been losing my MIND. I'm eight months pregnant and I have been losing my actual mind, Billie, my blood pressure is a health hazard at this point—"

"I know, I'm sorry, I'm so sorry—"

"—and I swear to God if you apologize to me right now I will reach through this phone and strangle you, because you have nothing to be sorry for, you absolute disaster of a human being, I love you so much—"

She's crying. I'm crying. Rodrigo stands next to me, close enough that his shoulder touches mine, and waits.

"Where are you?" I ask, wiping my eyes with the back of my hand.

"I'm with Agent Rakowski," Melissa says, and her voice shifts— still Melissa, still loud, but with an edge of something new. Purpose. "Rodrigo's Interpol contact. She's right here. She's been tracking the Twin Ledger for years, Billie. Years. And she says—" I hear a muffled exchange, like Melissa is turning to someone else in the room. "She says there's a bounty out on you— a *bounty*— and she says this is the closest they've ever been to having enough to bring them down."

My heart does something complicated. Half terror, half hope. The two feelings wrestle in my chest, and hope wins — barely.

"Mel, listen to me." I grip the phone cord tighter. "We want to help. We want to take them down— the whole thing, the Twin Ledger, all of it. And we have Alana with us."

Silence. Then: "Alana. The Barbie assassin."

"She's not an assassin, she's an arms dealer. There's a distinction."

"Billie, babe, that is not the comforting clarification you think it is."

“I know.” I take a breath. “But she knows things, Mel. She knows how the organization works, she knows where the money is, she knows about the rings. And I think— I really believe— that together, we can do this. All of us. We can end it.”

Another pause. Longer this time. I hear Melissa exhale — the kind of exhale that carries the weight of a decision being made.

“Agent Rakowski wants to come to you,” she says. “And I’m coming with her.”

“Mel, you’re eight months—“

“If you finish that sentence, I will name this baby after your worst ex-boyfriend. We’re coming.”

I laugh. It comes out wet and shaky but real. “Okay. Okay, we’re at—“ I look at Rodrigo, who gives me the address, and I relay it.

When Rodrigo reaches over and hangs up the phone, the click of the receiver settling into its cradle sounds final. Definitive. Like a door closing behind us.

We turn around.

Alana is standing in the doorway to the kitchen.

She’s changed clothes already— somehow, in the twelve minutes she’s been inside, she’s found time to put on a different outfit, this one a coral wrap dress that has no business being in a Tuscan countryside chalet. Her arms are crossed. Behind her, Benny hovers, pretending to clean the hallway table.

“So,” Alana says. Her voice is sweet. Dangerously sweet. “Interpol.”

My stomach drops.

“Alana—“

“You called Interpol?!” She uncrosses her arms. Crosses them again. Uncrosses them. “You literally just stood in this adorable kitchen and ratted me out to an international law enforcement agency while I was, like, trying to find a pillow that doesn't smell like mothballs."

"It's not ratting you out," I try. "It's—"

"Telling a federal agent where a person is and what they know? That's ratting."

"Alana, please—"

"I'm not cooperating." She puts her hand up. Her nails are very close to my face. "I'm not talking to Interpol."

Rodrigo steps forward. His voice is calm and measured.

"That's too bad," he says simply. "Because Melissa and Agent Rakowski are coming. Whether *you* like it or not."

Alana's eyes narrow. "Excuse me?"

"Billie and I will not keep running forever, Alana." He says her name like it's a word he's been trying to stop using. "This ends. It ends here. We take down Marco, we take down the Ledger, and we do it the right way. With your help, or without it."

For a moment, Alana is quiet. Genuinely quiet, which might be a first. She looks at Rodrigo, then at me, then at the phone on the wall as if it has personally betrayed her. Behind her, Benny stops dusting the table and stares at all of us.

"I don't want you to run forever," she says finally. Her voice is different now— still her, still Alana, but with the bubbly coating stripped away. She sounds— human. "I just need more time. I need to get the other ring. What's in that vault will fix all my problems."

She turns to me.

"Billie." Her voice goes quiet. "I let you have my boyfriend." She gestures at Rodrigo, who visibly flinches. "I didn't even make it weird. I was, like, super chill about it. Can't you just help me get the ring?"

My breath catches in my throat. She's waiting for my answer.

"Alana, I don't think those two things are—"

But she's already turned away, staring out the kitchen window at the Tuscan hills rolling golden in the afternoon light, her jaw set in a way that looks almost— hurt.

"This totally doesn't fit my vision board at all," she mutters, and I can hear the heartbreak in her voice.

And despite everything— I feel a pang of something that might be guilt. Because Alana is ridiculous. She is a criminal and a manipulator. But somewhere underneath all of that is someone who's running, and has never reached her destination.

I don't know what to do with that yet.

But I'm going to figure it out.

twenty-nine

RODRIGO

BILLIE LOOKS BEAUTIFUL, sitting at a barstool in my family's chalet. Her feet dangle over the edge of the chair, and being near her makes me feel like everything is right with my world.

The air in the chalet is thick with the smell of garlic and olive oil. Benny has made dinner— a paella that he claims is our grandmother's recipe, though I happen to know our grandmother never once made paella; she made tortilla española and she made it badly, and we loved her for it. Benny's paella is, against all probability, very good. He has set the table with mismatched plates from the kitchen's ancient cabinets and lit a candle.

The four of us sit in a square, ready for dinner: Benny and I on one side, Billie and Alana on the other. I try not to glare at Alana with the hatred I feel.

Outside the window, the Spanish countryside is going dark in the slow, unhurried way it does— the hills turning from gold to grey, the olive trees becoming silhouettes, the last of the light collecting along the western horizon.

Agent Rakowski, from Interpol— my contact's contact,

a woman whose voice on the phone communicated confidence— told me she could have people here in just a few hours. Since overhearing our phone call, Alana has thrown multiple temper tantrums about this, but what's done is done. I will keep Billie safe, whatever it takes.

Benny is talking. He is always talking. "You know what this reminds me of?" he says, gesturing with his fork at the table, the candle, the general situation. "Die Hard Two. Not the first one— the second one. The one in the airport. Where they are all waiting, and they know the bad guys are coming, but they eat dinner first because a man must eat." He nods sagely. "Bruce Willis understood this."

"Bruce Willis was not eating dinner in Die Hard Two," I say.

"He was eating something," Benny insists. "I remember this very clearly."

Billie smiles. It is a small smile— careful, tired— but it is there, and I catch it from across the table the way you catch light off water. She is the most beautiful woman I have ever seen. I am aware that this is a thought I keep having, but that it also becomes truer each time.

Alana has been quiet during dinner. This is the detail that should concern me most, and it does. She has eaten her paella without commentary. She has not taken a single photograph. She has not mentioned a single brand name. She is sitting with her hands in her lap.

She looks like someone who has already made a decision and is waiting for the right moment to say it out loud.

"Can I tell you something?" Alana says.

The table goes still. Even Benny stops chewing.

Alana looks at Billie first, and then at me, and then back at Billie.

"You two," she says, "are the closest thing I've had to

real friends." She says it plainly, without the Valley-girl lilt, without the bubbly cadence. "I know that sounds— I know what it sounds like, coming from me. But it's true. Everyone else in my life sees me as a means to an end. Marco. The Ledger. All of it. You pay and you get paid and nobody actually knows you." She presses her lips together. "Billie, you know me. You've seen me at my worst and you're still sitting here, being my friend and eating Benny's terrible paella—"

"It's not terrible," Benny protests quietly.

"—and Rodrigo." She turns to me. Her jaw is set in the way I recognize from the arguments we used to have — not angry, but certain. "I'm over you. I need you to hear that. Not because I never loved you— I did, in my way, which I understand is a complicated way— but because what you and Billie have is..." She pauses, searching for the word. "Real. It's like, annoyingly real. The way you look at her makes me want to throw up, honestly, but in a good way? Like a romantic-comedy throw-up." She waves her hand. "You should be together. You should be happy. Both of you." A beat. Her eyes harden. "Assuming you survive what's about to happen next."

The last sentence lands differently than the rest. It's ominous.

"What do you mean?" Billie asks.

Alana looks at me. Directly at me, and there it is— the thing I sensed underneath her silence all evening. Something hard and resolved.

"Now that Interpol is involved, there's no version of this where I walk away free," she says. "You know that. I know that."

"Alana—" I begin.

"So I had no other choice," she says, and her voice is steady and final. "I called Ivan. From the Twin Ledger."

The name drops into the room like a stone into still water.

Outside— as if the universe has been listening and believes in perfect timing— there is a sound. Two sharp cracks, distant but unmistakable: gunshots. Then silence. Then one more.

Everything happens at once and also very slowly. I am on my feet before I've decided to stand. My hand finds Billie's arm. Benny grabs the cast-iron pan from the stove— the one he used to make the paella— and holds it like a shield, which would be funny if the fear on his face weren't genuine. Billie is rigid beside me, her eyes wide, her body angled toward the door.

"Calm down," Alana says. She hasn't moved from her chair. "They're not here for you."

Through the window, headlights sweep across the gravel path. A jeep— dark, military-grade— pulls to a stop thirty meters from the chalet. The engine idles. Two figures sit in the backseat, visible only as shapes. And standing beside the driver's door, illuminated by the porch light that Benny installed crookedly last summer, is Ivan. I remember him from the compound.

His bald head catches the light like a pale, disapproving moon. He is looking at the chalet with a disappointed expression.

"You called him?" I say. "To double-cross Marco together?"

"Not exactly, although that was my first idea," Alana says, standing now, smoothing her top. "But sadly he's made up with Marco. So I've made a choice. I'm turning myself in. It's the only play that keeps everyone alive." She looks at Billie. "If I go back to Marco myself, I have leverage. I know things he needs. He won't kill me. Probably."

"Probably," Billie repeats.

"High probably," Alana clarifies. "Like, eighty-five percent." She leans in and whispers. "Plus, I have a shot at getting what I want." She winks at Billie, flashing the ring on her finger.

Billie stands. The two women face each other across the table, the candle flickering between them, and something passes between them that I cannot fully read— something that belongs to their friendship, to the strange and terrible and genuine thing they built in a short space of time, the thing that started with a yoga class and a baby shower and ended here, in a stone house in the Spanish countryside, with a jeep idling outside.

"You can't," Billie says. Her voice is quiet and firm.

"I can," Alana says. "And I'm going to." She reaches out and takes Billie's hands. "Listen to me. You are the best friend I've ever had, and I know that's a low bar because my previous best friend was a Serbian weapons manufacturer named Drago, but still. You believed in me when you had absolutely no reason to. You believed in me even when I was literally the worst." She squeezes Billie's hands. "So do something for me. Believe in yourself the way you believed in me. Okay? Because you are— and I say this with love— a designer item on clearance. And someone needs to pay full price for you." She looks at me. "Rodrigo. Pay full price."

"Alana—" Billie's voice breaks.

Alana pulls her into a hug. It is tight and real and lasts exactly long enough. Then she releases Billie, wipes a thumb under her own eye— smearing nothing, because her makeup is flawless, because of course it is— and turns to me.

"Don't screw this up," she says.

She clutches Billie's hand in hers one more time, lingering there. A look of surprise crosses Billie's face, like she's being given a secret message. Then: Alana walks out the front door.

I watch through the window as she crosses the gravel in her heels, her silhouette sharp against the jeep's headlights. Ivan opens the door for her. She gets in without looking back. The door closes. The jeep reverses, turns, and the taillights shrink down the dark road until they are red points, and then nothing.

The chalet is very quiet.

Benny is still holding the paella pan.

Billie stands at the window. The candlelight catches the gold flecks in her eyes, and they are wet, and she is watching the empty road, and I understand— watching her — that she has just lost a friend.

Then, Billie turns, showing me something in her outstretched hand. It's a small, shiny object, a red ruby in the center.

Mateo's ring is sitting in Billie's hand.

"She gave it to me," Billie says. "She gave me the ring."

And now I know, without a doubt, we are in enormous trouble.

* * *

Agent Rakowski sits in the one good chair in the living room, and she holds her coffee the way a soldier holds a weapon: with both hands, at the ready. She is exactly what her voice on the phone suggested: tired, experienced, her dark hair pulled back in a bun so severe it seems to be holding her entire skull together by force of will. Her Interpol uniform is pressed. Her eyes miss nothing.

Melissa is on the couch. She is eight months pregnant and looks it, but— after a tearful reunion with Billie— seems ready to get to business. Steve is beside her, one hand on her knee, the other gripping a glass of water.

When I opened the door for them forty minutes ago, Melissa looked at me for a long moment— taking me in the way a general surveys a battlefield— and then she nodded once. "You're taller than I expected," she said. Then she looked at Billie, who was standing behind me, and something in her face crumpled and rebuilt itself. The two of them embraced in the doorway for a long time, and I stepped aside, because some things are not mine to stand near.

Now the seven of us— Rakowski, Melissa, Steve, Billie, Benny, myself, and Melissa's unborn child, who I am counting because it is clearly already participating in this operation— are arranged in the chalet's living room. Canvases lean against the far wall. My easel stands in the corner like a witness. The paella has been cleared. It is past midnight and the world outside is black and still and full of things we cannot see.

"My recommendation," Rakowski says, setting down her mug, "is that you go home. Both of you." She looks at Billie, then at me. "You've done enough. More than enough. What happens next is institutional— warrants, surveillance, coordination across jurisdictions. It's slow, it's bureaucratic, and it's not something civilians should be anywhere near."

She says this the way doctors tell you to rest: she knows we won't.

Billie leans forward in her chair.

"I'm not going home," she says.

The room adjusts to this information.

"Alana turned herself in to protect us," Billie continues. Her voice is level in a way I have come to recognize as the version of Billie that appears when she's made a decision and the decision has settled into her bones. "I want to help find her, and I want to help bring the Twin Ledger down. It's selfish, too. I won't be able to sleep until I know they're gone. Finished."

Rakowski studies her. "We've been after Marco Ledger for years," she says. "He's careful. Disciplined. He runs the Ledger like a machine— dual authorization on everything, shell companies layered inside shell companies, vault access that requires both rings." She pauses. "His brother Mateo is dead. The missing ring is out there somewhere, and Marco is desperate to find it. You wouldn't happen to know what Alana did with it, would you?"

Billie looks at me and I try my best to avoid letting the truth cross my face. We've agreed to keep Billie's ownership of the ring to ourselves, for now. A pleading look crosses her eyes: she's a terrible liar. I decide to help her out:

"Alana likes to keep her secrets to herself," I offer.

Agent Rakowski nods. "Marco has a personal vendetta," she continues. "Against both of you. And men like Marco don't lose. He will never stop," Rakowski confirms. "Not until he's in custody or dead. You could go home to Chicago or Spain or wherever you want, and he'd find you. Both of you. It might take months, might take years, but the Ledger has long arms."

The room sits with this. Melissa's hand moves to her belly— a reflex, protective, the geometry of a mother already shielding.

"We have intel," Rakowski continues, "that Alana is

being taken to a location in Rome. A casino. On the surface it's a luxury gambling establishment— private, exclusive. But underneath, in the basements, the Ledger has infrastructure. Holding rooms. Communication systems. It's where Marco conducts his most sensitive deals." She sets her jaw. "We believe he'll bring Alana there. If we can get to him at that location, we can take him. But the casino is heavily secured. If Marco gets even a hint that Interpol is nearby, he disappears. We've seen him do it before— he has exit routes planned for every facility he uses. Tunnels, cars, helicopters. The man is meticulous."

She looks at me. Then at Billie. Back at me.

"What we don't have," she says carefully, "is a way to draw him out. Into the open. Where we can make the arrest cleanly." A beat. "But if Marco believed that the two people he most wants to punish were walking into his casino— willingly, vulnerable, to retrieve their friend— he might come out himself. He might want to handle it personally. Men with vendettas often do."

The implication settles over the room like weather.

Billie turns to me. Her eyes— those enormous, golden-brown eyes that I noticed at the baby shower and have not stopped noticing since— are steady and clear and full of something I can only describe as the opposite of fear.

"I want to see this through," she says.

"I'm in," Melissa says immediately, from the couch, with the conviction of a woman who was in before anyone asked.

"I'm—" Steve starts, looks at Melissa, recalibrates. "I'm in too. Obviously. Where she goes, I go. That's the deal."

Benny stands up from the corner where he's been leaning against the wall. "This is exactly like Die Hard

Three," he says, with genuine reverence. "The one with Samuel L. Jackson. They go into the building and they—"

"Benny," I say.

"I'm in," he says simply. "Primo. Always."

Everyone is in. Everyone is brave. Everyone is looking at me with the expectation that I will say yes, because I am the man who stepped between Billie and the guard, because I am the man who fought off an assassin with a rope, because I have been, without choosing it, positioned as the person who walks toward danger when danger presents itself.

But something in me— something that has been building since Barcelona, since the rope, since the gun, since the six months before all of it— something cracks.

"No," I say.

The word lands hard. Billie's face shifts.

"No," I say again, and I stand, because I cannot say this sitting down. "Do you understand what you're asking me? You're asking me to walk back into the world I've spent six months running from. That's Alana's world, not mine." My voice is louder than I intend, and I don't correct it. "I left. I left because that world was killing me— not just the danger, but the person I was becoming inside of it. A man who checks every doorway. A man who doesn't sleep. A man who looks at his cousin's face and calculates whether someone might use him as leverage." I look at Benny. Benny looks at the floor. "I came home to paint. To be quiet. To find out who I am when no one is trying to kill me. To be— a man who can love and be loved."

I turn to Billie. She is watching me with those eyes, and I hate that even in my anger she is the most beautiful thing in this room, and I hate that I cannot separate what I feel for her from what she's asking of me.

"You want me to let you walk into a place where I cannot protect you," I say to Billie. "If something happens to you there and I cannot intervene— I don't know if I can live with that."

The silence that follows is total.

I look at her face. I see the hurt in it— she was trying to be brave and has been told that her bravery is a burden. I see it, and I feel it, and I cannot stay in this room with it.

"I need air," I say.

I walk out the front door into the dark.

The night is cool and smells of sage and dry earth. I walk until the light from the chalet is behind me, and then I stop, and I breathe, and I look at the stars, which are indifferent and do not care what I decide.

Behind me, the door opens again. Footsteps on gravel. Lighter than mine.

Billie doesn't say anything. She just stands there— close enough that I know she's there, far enough that she's giving me the space to decide whether I want her to be.

The countryside stretches out in every direction, dark and vast and patient, and we stand at the edge of it together, and neither of us speaks, and the silence is the most honest thing between us.

BILLIE

THE THING about following someone who doesn't want to be followed is that your footsteps sound twice as loud. Every crunch of gravel beneath my shoes announces itself as a small betrayal, and I'm already cataloguing the ways this conversation is going to go wrong before it even starts. It's a talent, really— anticipating disaster. I've built an entire career on it. Twelve years of fetching coffee and rearranging schedules has taught me people will never be happy, no matter how hard you try. But still: I'm going to try.

"Rodrigo," I say. My voice comes out smaller than I want it to. Classic.

He stops walking. Doesn't turn around. His hands are in his jacket pockets and I watch his back rise and fall with one long breath. The rolling hill of the Tuscan horizon seem to sigh in the distance.

He turns around.

And his face— God. His face does this thing where every emotion he's feeling is right there, just *right there*, like he's never learned to hide a single one. It's the thing I noticed about him first. Rodrigo Esperanza feels things at full volume and it shows.

Right now, what it shows is hurt.

"Tell me something," he says, and his voice is calm, which is worse than yelling. Calm means he's been thinking. "Why are you pushing me back toward her?"

"I'm not— that's not what I'm doing."

"It is, though." He takes a step closer. "You are asking me to go back to everything I have been trying to leave behind."

"That's not—"

"Billie." My name, firm and soft at the same time. Like a door being shut gently but definitely shut. "I have spent— I cannot tell you how long I have spent trying to get away from this. From people like her. From the chaos. And now you want me not just to go back, but to take *you*— this person I've found who is wonderful, and kind— and watch her be in danger— And I am trying— *estoy intentando*— to understand why."

I open my mouth to say something clever. Something that will defuse this the way I defuse everything— with a little self-deprecation, a joke, a shrug that says *don't worry about me, I'm fine, I've always been fine.* But nothing comes out.

"Can we just—" I gesture vaguely at a fallen log near the edge of the clearing, like sitting down will somehow make this easier. Like difficult conversations have ever been improved by seating arrangements. He doesn't move. Okay. We're standing, then.

I try again.

"I know how it looks," I say. "I know it looks like I'm dragging you back into something toxic, and I get why that scares you. I really do. But this isn't about her, Rodrigo. Not really."

"Then what is it about?"

This is the part where I'm supposed to be articulate. Where the version of me that exists in my head— the confident, together, knows-what-she-wants version— steps forward and delivers a speech that makes everything make sense. But that version of me is tired, so I settle for all I've got.

"I mean... I just..." I press my palms against my thighs. Take a breath. "Okay. I'm going to say something, and I need you to let me get through it, because if I stop I'm going to lose my nerve and then I'll just make a joke about it and we'll both pretend this conversation never happened."

Something in his expression shifts. He nods, once. Waiting.

"My whole life," I say, "I have been small."

The word hangs there, and it's such a simple word— *small*— but it holds everything. Every meeting I sat in the back of. Every idea I whispered to someone else so they could say it louder. Every time I drafted the negotiation strategy and then watched my boss take credit while I refilled his water glass. Every time someone asked what I do I said *Oh, I'm just an assistant* with that little laugh, that laugh that says *don't look too closely, there's nothing to see here.*

"I have spent my entire career— my entire *life*— shrinking myself to fit into whatever space other people left for me. I'm the person in the background of the photo. I'm the name in the CC line. I'm— God, I'm the human equivalent of a participation trophy. *Thanks for showing up, Billie. Here's your lanyard.*"

A flicker crosses his face. Almost a smile. Almost. That means he understands. Good.

"And for the first time," I continue, my voice getting steadier in a way that surprises me, "for the *first* time, I have a chance to do something that actually uses what I'm good at. Not fetching coffee. Not scheduling conference calls. Not smiling while someone else takes the bow. This— going back in there, dealing with Alana, using everything I know about negotiation and reading people— this is me standing up. This is me saying I'm not just The Assistant anymore."

I can feel the heat behind my eyes and I blink it back because if I cry right now I'll be furious with myself. Billie Harper does not cry during arguments. Billie Harper cries later, alone, in the shower, like a person with dignity.

"I'm not pushing you toward Alana," I say. "I'm pulling *myself* forward. And I know— I *know*— those two things look the same from where you're standing, but they're not. They're not the same thing. I need to finish this for myself. If I can take down the Twin Ledger, it will change my life in the best possible way. And I— I think all of this is happening because I met you," my voice cracks, and I hate it, but I keep going. "Because you make me—" I pause, trying to find the words. And then: there they are. "You make me feel brave."

The silence that follows is the kind that has texture. It settles between us like something physical, like weather.

Rodrigo's jaw works. For a second I think he's going to walk off and I'll be standing here alone with my big speech and my big feelings and my tiny, hammering heart. But he doesn't walk. He stays.

"Billie, you can do this, yes, of course you can. But the question is— should you?" He sighs, running a hand through his hair. "I believe in you. Of course I believe in you. You are— *Dios mío*— you are the most capable person I have ever met and you don't even know it, which makes it worse. But—"

The *but.* There it is. The word I've been bracing for since I walked out here.

"— I do not understand this."

"So you don't trust me," I say, and my voice is steady. It is absolutely steady. That is the official report.

"That is not what I said."

"It's what you meant."

"No, *corazón.*" He exhales sharply through his nose. Then, he admits it. The thing I've been waiting for him to claim: "I have rushed into every love of my life," Rodrigo throws his hands in the air. "All I wanted was to stay here and paint with you. To spend time in the *truth* of you, not the adventure. Is that so wrong? That I want to know who you really are outside of the gunshots and the danger?"

"You're afraid you're rushing into things again," I say, stung.

He doesn't answer. He stands there in the silence, unable to form the words I need to hear.

There it is. The truth. He's afraid he's rushing into this — into us. This is something broken inside him that has nothing to do with me and everything to do with every woman who came before me, every Alana and pre-Alana and whoever taught him that love and danger feel exactly the same.

And I can't fix it.

I want to close the distance between us. I want to put my hands on his face and say *look at me, really look, I'm right here and I'm real.* But I can't.

Instead, I straighten my spine. I have spent my entire

life putting aside my own adventures to make other people happy. And I can't do it this time.

"You don't have to come," I say. "If you can't trust what this is— if you need more time to figure out whether I'm real or just the next building that's going to fall on you— then stay here. I'll go. I'll handle it."

The words taste like metal in my mouth. Like biting down on a coin. Because I don't want to go alone. I don't want to do *any* of this alone. But I also can't be someone's maybe. I've been a maybe my entire professional life— *maybe we'll promote her, maybe she's ready, maybe next quarter, Billie*— and I am so tired of maybe that I could lie down on this gravel and sleep for a year.

Rodrigo stares at me. Something moves behind his eyes — something that looks like the beginning of a decision being made.

"No," he says.

One word. Simple. Final. It wasn't the answer I expected.

"No?" I ask, surprised.

"I will not let you go alone." He says it like he's angry about it, like the words are being pulled from him against his will. "Whatever I feel— whatever I am afraid of— I will not sit here while you walk into something dangerous without someone watching your back. *Eso no va a pasar.*"

"Because you think I can't handle it?"

"Because I will go where you go," he says, and his voice cracks in a way that makes my eyes sting. "That is not negotiable, so long as you will have me."

"... you will?"

"Yes," he nods.

We stand there. Five feet apart and a thousand miles away from where we were an hour ago, when the chalet was warm and the paintings were catching the light and his hand had been resting near mine on the worktable like it was the most natural thing in the world.

That feels like a very long time ago.

"Okay," I say.

"Okay," he says.

I turn back toward the chalet. The light is still on inside, golden and inviting through the windows. I barely recognize the person I've become— but I know what she needs. I start walking toward the chalet, not expecting Rodrigo to follow me, but he does and somehow— our first fight is not the end.

thirty-one

RODRIGO

I AM STILL angry with Billie Harper when we pull up outside the casino, which is a problem, because anger makes me stupid and I cannot afford to be stupid tonight. Not when I need to protect Billie, and keep us both alive.

The drive from the Tuscan countryside to Rome took four hours. Four hours in the back of an Interpol vehicle with tinted windows and uncomfortable vinyl upholstery. Agent Rakowski drove. Melissa and Steve followed in a second vehicle. Benny sat in the front passenger seat and tried, three separate times, to explain the plot of *Ocean's Eleven* to Agent Rakowski, who responded with a silence so total it should have shut him down, but of course, it did not.

Billie sat beside me in the back, and neither of us spoke.

Four hours is a long time to not speak to someone whose knee is seven inches from yours. Especially when she is gorgeous, and you can think of nothing but the desire to touch her

I kept my eyes on the window and she did the same. The Spanish countryside gave way to coast, and coast gave way to highway, and highway gave way to the outskirts of Rome, and I spent all of it replaying the argument and hating both of us for having it.

Here is what happened in the dark outside the chalet:

Billie wasn't wrong. I *am* afraid of making the same mistakes again. Of rushing into things with someone who is not the person I thought they were. But where she misunderstands me is in the details of the thing. She does not understand that I am so sure I've found the woman I've been seeking, that I'm afraid of losing her: to guns, to danger, and yes, maybe to the world that Alana dragged us both into.

But Billie needs to do this for herself. Fine. So I am here, making sure she does not get hurt, as best I can. I put on a suit that Rakowski procured from somewhere— it fits well enough, dark, narrow-lapeled, the kind of thing a man wears when he expects to be shot at— and now I am standing outside a casino in Rome. Billie is beside me in a dress that takes my breath away, and my degenerate cousin is next to her, adjusting his cufflinks.

Casino Luminara sits at the end of a private road lined with black cars. The building itself is stunning— all glass and pale stone, with a grand entrance flanked by columns. Through the tall windows, I can see chandeliers glittering and the movement of fancy people in formal dress, and it looks, from the outside, like a place someone would aspire to enter.

It is, of course, a place where terrible things happen constantly, just very quietly and several floors below the champagne.

"Can everyone hear me?" Agent Rakowski's voice arrives in my ear, crisp and close. The earpiece is small—

nearly invisible— and she placed it herself before we left the vehicle.

"Loud and clear," I say.

"Copy," Billie says beside me, and her voice is steady.

"I can hear you also!" Benny announces, too loudly. "This is like the movie— what is it called— the one where they have the earpieces and the man says—"

"Benny," Rakowski says. "Less talking."

"Understood," Benny whispers, conspiratorially.

"Here's what we know," Rakowski continues. "Marco arrived two hours ago with a security detail. Alana was seen being escorted through a service entrance on the north side approximately ninety minutes ago. The underground level is accessed through the casino floor— there's a corridor behind the VIP lounge that leads to a service elevator. That elevator goes down. Below, the Ledger maintains holding rooms, communications equipment, and what we believe is a secondary vault." She pauses. "Your job is to get downstairs. Find the corridor. Get eyes on the underground access and report back. Do not engage Marco directly. We want to lure him out of the most secure areas. Do not engage anyone directly. You are guests at a casino. You are gambling. You are having a lovely evening. Understood?"

"Understood," I say.

"We have units positioned at all exits," Rakowski adds. "When we have confirmation of Marco's location inside the facility, we move. Not before. If he gets any indication that law enforcement is present, he will disappear through one of his contingency routes, and we will not get another shot at this."

"So no pressure," Billie says.

"Considerable pressure, actually," Rakowski replies, without humor. "Melissa, are you on the line?"

“I’m here,” Melissa’s voice crackles through. “Steve’s here too. We’re in the van. I can see the front entrance from where we’re parked.”

“Good,” Rakowski says. “Stay in the van.”

“Obviously, I’m staying in the van,” Melissa says. “I’m enormous. I can barely *fit* in the van.”

“You look beautiful, honey,” Steve says, somewhere in the background.

“Focus,” Rakowski says.

I turn to look at Billie, and everything else— the earpiece, the mission, the coal of anger in my chest— recedes for a moment, because she is standing in the light from the casino entrance and she is stunning.

She’s wearing a deep, red dress that’s tight in all the right places, covered in sequins that reflect every fractal of light back at me— but none of them glow the way she does.

Her hair is in loose waves that cascade to one side, soft waves moving without effort. Her shoulders are bare, and the gentle slope of her nose reminds me of the carved statues that circle every piazza in Rome. Let the statues weep— Billie puts them to shame. She is the most beautiful woman in Italy.

Billie Harper— tonight— in this dress— is the most extraordinary thing I have ever seen. If I die tonight— which is likely— I only hope I can leave this world looking at her. As mad as I am, it strikes me:

This is who Billie has been trying to become. This woman, in the red dress. And I tried to convince her to paint with me in the countryside, when she needed this adventure to heal something: to see herself the way I have always seen her.

“Stop staring,” Billie says, without looking at me. But the corner of her mouth moves, just slightly. A smile.

"I'm not staring," I say. "I'm conducting a visual assessment of our operational readiness. I highly doubt you could fit a weapon in that dress."

"You're staring."

"Sí," I admit. "I'm staring."

We approach the entrance. The bouncer is large, and he stands with his arms crossed in front of a velvet rope. He looks at us with complete indifference to our arrival.

Billie steps forward.

I watch it happen. The shift. She straightens a half-inch — I have seen this before, in the compound, the way she assembles herself into the version of Billie that walks into rooms— and her chin comes up, and something in her eyes goes from warm to precise.

"Good evening," she says to the bouncer, and her voice has a quality I can only describe as executive. Calm, unhurried. "We're guests of the Marchetti party." She says this with the confidence of a person who knows there is a Marchetti party because she invented it three seconds ago.

The bouncer looks at her. He looks at me. He looks at Benny, who is standing slightly behind us and attempting to project sophistication, which for Benny involves squinting slightly and holding his hands behind his back.

"Name?" the bouncer says.

"The reservation is under Marchetti," Billie says, and she holds his gaze without blinking, without flinching, with the full, enormous weight of her dark eyes, and she waits. She does not explain further. She does not repeat herself. She simply waits, as if the passage of time will inevitably resolve this in her favor, because it always does.

The bouncer's hand moves to his earpiece. He considers. Then, he moves the rope aside.

"Enjoy your evening," he says.

We walk through.

I'm proud of her. I'm so proud of her that it sits in my throat like something I can't swallow, and I want to tell her, but the casino opens up around us and there is too much to take in.

The interior is what the exterior promised— extravagance. Elegant danger dressed in crystal. High ceilings. Gold fixtures. The sound of glasses and low conversation layered over ambient music. Tables arranged across a vast floor— roulette, blackjack, poker— with dealers in black and patrons in everything else. The light is warm and diffuse, making every face look its best, which is a kindness the architects probably didn't extend to the rooms below.

"Dios mío," Benny breathes, looking around with the wide eyes of a child who has been released into a theme park. "This is exactly like—"

"Don't say it," I warn him.

"*Casino Royale*," he says anyway, reverently referencing the James Bond movie.

And then Benny sees the food.

There is, along the far wall, a spread of elaborate construction. Towers of shellfish. Arrangements of expensive cheese. Tiny, perfect things on tiny, perfect plates. Benny's eyes lock onto this spread the way a heat-seeking missile locks onto its target, and I watch the precise moment when his commitment to our mission is overridden by his commitment to *jamón ibérico.*

"I will scout the area near the food," he says, already moving. "For strategic purposes."

"Benny—"

"Strategic purposes, primo," he repeats, and he is gone, absorbed into the crowd and moving toward the shellfish tower.

Billie and I are alone. Or as alone as two people can be in a room full of strangers, with an Interpol agent in their ears and a criminal overlord somewhere beneath their feet.

She is scanning the room— I can see her doing it, the way her eyes move from table to table, cataloguing exits, looking for the corridor Rakowski described. She is being professional. She is being focused. She is also, I can tell, still angry with me.

It's in her posture. In the careful way she is not looking at me. In the precise distance she's maintaining— close enough to appear together, far enough to communicate that together is, at this moment, a professional arrangement and nothing more.

I take her hand.

She lets me, but her fingers don't close around mine. They stay neutral, neither accepting nor rejecting, the hand equivalent of a polite silence.

I pull her— gently, not commanding, just guiding— toward a column near the edge of the floor, where the crowd is thinner and the music is softer and there is a small pocket of space that belongs, for a moment, only to us.

"Billie," I say.

She looks at me. Her eyes are guarded. Her jaw is set in that way she has— the way that says she has prepared a position and intends to hold it.

I want to say so much to her. I want to tell her how I cannot lose her. But there are no words, so instead:

I kiss her.

It is not the kiss from the hotel corridor— that one was urgent, surprised, a thing that happened because neither of us could stop it. This one is deliberate. An apology. I put my hand on the side of her face and I lean in and I kiss her slowly, because I want her to feel what I cannot seem to say correctly with words. I want her to understand that I am *here*. That I chose this. That I chose her, even though I'm angry, even though I'm afraid, even though every rational part of me said to walk away and I could not, because walking away from Billie Harper is something I am apparently incapable of doing.

For a moment— one suspended, perfect moment— she kisses me back. Her hand comes up to my chest, and her fingers grip the lapel of my jacket, and I feel her lean in, and the casino and the danger and Marco and the Ledger all disappear, and there is only this: her mouth and mine and the devastating warmth of being close to someone who matters.

Then she pulls away.

Not far. Just enough. Her hand stays on my lapel, but her eyes are different now— softer, but also wounded, the way animals look when they've been hurt and are deciding whether to trust again.

"You don't have to do that," she says quietly.

"Do what?"

"Kiss me like that to make me forget that you didn't want to come."

She almost smiles. Almost. But something else comes first— something that has been sitting underneath the anger this whole time, waiting for enough space to surface.

"Rodrigo," she says, and her voice goes to the place where the real things live, the things she usually keeps hidden under humor and self-deprecation and the work of taking care of everyone else. "I need to ask you something, and I need you to be honest."

"Always," I say.

She takes a breath.

"Are you sure about me?" she says. "Because— you said

it yourself. You rush into things. You see something beautiful and you leap— and maybe to you I'm just a passing thing—"

The words hit me with a force I am not prepared for.

I stare at her. I stare at her because I cannot believe— genuinely, with every part of my being, cannot believe— that this woman, this woman standing in front of me in a dress that has rearranged the architecture of my heart, thinks she is a passing thing.

"Billie," I say, and my voice sounds different, even to me. "You are not a passing thing."

She looks at me. Her lips part slightly. The gold in her eyes catches the casino's warm light, and she is— in this moment, in this terrible, beautiful, probably-going-to-kill-us moment— the only real thing in the room.

"I know why you needed to do this," I tell her, nodding. "You have put off all of your adventures for other people. I don't want you to do that for me."

Billie softens. "But I shouldn't have made you come back," she says, shaking her head. "I was thinking about it the entire drive over, and I know you need distance from this life— from Alana— and it's selfish of me to drag you here—"

"*Esta bien, hermosa,*" I tell her. "You are not dragging me back. I am a man, choosing to follow. You are too small to drag me, sadly."

She laughs. Her hand tightens on my lapel. Just slightly. Just enough to tell me: I am forgiven.

Then Rakowski's voice crackles in both our ears simultaneously, breaking the moment. "As touching as this little moment is, I'd recommend you two keeping moving to avoid creating suspicion. The VIP lounge is northeast corner."

Billie releases my lapel. She straightens. She blinks once, resettling herself into the woman who talks her way past bouncers and negotiates with arms dealers.

But before she turns away— before we step back into the crowd and the mission and the terrible, necessary thing we've come here to do— she looks at me. And something in her expression has shifted. Not resolved, not certain, but— open. A door that was closed is now ajar, and behind it is the possibility that she might, eventually, believe me.

"Okay," she says. "Let's go finish this adventure."

I nod. I take her hand again. This time, her fingers close around mine.

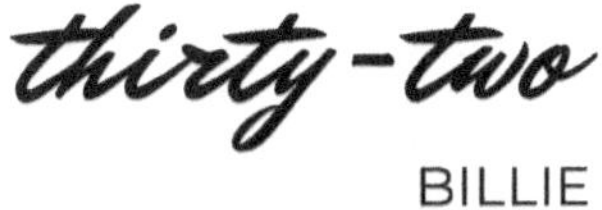

thirty-two

BILLIE

THE CASINO FLOOR stretches out ahead of us— glittering and excessive. Rodrigo's hand is warm in mine, and his fingers have closed around my fingers in a way that communicates something neither of us has said out loud yet, which is fine, because we are in the middle of an international criminal operation and there will be time for declarations later, assuming we survive.

We move through the crowd together— past the roulette tables with their spinning wheels and their tiny, fateful balls, past the blackjack dealers, past a woman in a silver gown who is laughing too loudly. Everyone in this room is beautiful and none of them are thinking about what's underneath the floor.

I am thinking about what's underneath the floor.

But I am also thinking about the man beside me, and the thing he said— the thing that settled something inside my chest like a warm blanket thrown over me in my coldest moment. *You are not a passing thing.* I keep returning to it. The sentence. The way his voice sounded when he said it:

he wasn't performing or trying to win a point, but stating a fact he found so obvious it pained him to discover I didn't already know it.

This is what I have been looking for, I think. Not Rodrigo, in particular— though Rodrigo is doing an excellent job of being what I've been looking for— but *this*. A person who doesn't need me to be smaller so they can feel tall enough. Tyler loved me the way you love a favorite chair: something comfortable, reliable, always in the same place when you need it. Rodrigo looks at me like I'm a person— a whole, interesting person worthy of her own wants and needs.

The difference is staggering. The difference has rearranged things inside me that I thought were permanent fixtures.

"Northeast," I murmur, steering us through the crowd. The VIP lounge should be in this direction— according to Rakowski— and behind it, the corridor. The service elevator. The underground. I scan the room, reading the arrangement of bodies, noting which staff members are real hospitality workers and which are standing a little too still with earpieces that don't match the casino's uniform.

"There," Rodrigo says quietly, his chin tilting fractionally to the right.

I follow his gaze. Past the VIP lounge— which is sectioned off by velvet rope and soft amber light— there is a door. It is not the kind of door that invites attention. It is grey, recessed into the wall, and it would be unremarkable if not for the two men standing in front of it, arms crossed, faces communicating a professional disinterest in conversation. Security. Not casino security— these men are larger, quieter, and dressed in suits that are cut to accommodate shoulder holsters. These guys are Twin Ledger security.

A live band plays on a small stage adjacent to the dance floor, between where we're standing and the grey door. The music is slow and warm— a saxophone doing something romantic. Couples move together in the low light, bodies close.

An idea arrives in my head, and it's stupid, but I still say it out loud:

"Dance with me," I wink at Rodrigo.

Rodrigo looks at me. Then he looks at the guards. Then he looks back at me, and I watch him understand.

"*Con mucho gusto,*" he says, and the way he says it— low, warm, with a curve at the corner of his mouth.

He leads me onto the floor. His hand finds the small of my back. My hand finds his shoulder. We're close, and it feels like coming home.

He pulls me in, and our bodies meet, and the space that was between us collapses to nothing. I can feel his heartbeat through the fabric of his jacket. Or maybe that's my heartbeat. The two have become difficult to distinguish.

"You're good at this," I say, because he is. At the club in Madrid, it was a different kind of dancing. This is more formal.

"My grandmother taught me," Rodrigo says, his mouth near my ear. "She was a terrible cook but an excellent dancer."

"She had her priorities straight," I say.

We turn together, and I let the turn carry us closer to the guards. The saxophone exhales something beautiful. Rodrigo's hand presses gently against my lower back and he gives me a look that tells me I should follow his gaze. I do, and it leads me to a man on the edge of the dance floor:

Then I see the badge dangling from his waistband.

The man is a guard who has shifted his position. He's

watching a woman at a nearby table, distracted. His badge is clipped to his belt on the side nearest to us. The clip is standard— the kind that requires a firm upward pull to release, the kind I have unclipped from my own lanyard a thousand times at work because Mr. Franklin insisted all assistants wear identification at all times, even in the bathroom, which I always thought was excessive but which has now, apparently, been training for this exact moment.

My entire career has been building to this.

I adjust my angle against Rodrigo— just slightly, just a half-turn that brings my right hand down from his shoulder. Our bodies rotate. The guard is eighteen inches away. Twelve. I let my hand drift as we pass him, and the motion looks— I hope— like nothing more than a woman adjusting her dress, and my fingers find the badge, and I pull upward, and the clip releases with a small, decisive sound that the saxophone covers perfectly.

The badge is in my hand. I press it flat against my thigh, against the sequined fabric, invisible.

Rodrigo looks down at me. He felt it— the shift in my movement, the precision of it. His eyes widen fractionally.

"Billie Harper," he whispers. "You're a thief."

"Don't make a thing of it," I whisper back.

We dance for another thirty seconds— enough time to not look suspicious— and then we separate from the floor, moving naturally toward the bar, and finally, toward the grey door.

I hold the badge against the sensor. A small light blinks from red to green. The lock clicks.

Rodrigo opens the door. A corridor stretches beyond it — dim, industrial, the glamour of the casino ending abruptly at the threshold like a sentence cut short. Cold air rises from below.

We step through. The door closes behind us with a sound that is very, very final.

* * *

Rakowski's voice arrives in my ear before we've made it ten steps down the corridor. "Do not engage," she says, with clipped precision. "Report what you see and fall back. We need his location confirmed and we have to wait until he's out in the open. Do not intervene. Do not make contact. Do not—"

I reach up and tap my earpiece twice— the signal, I've decided in this moment, for *I hear you and I'm going to do what I want anyway*— and keep walking.

The corridor descends. The walls shift from painted plaster to raw concrete, and the lighting changes with them. The temperature drops. The air is stale and damp down here.

Rodrigo is beside me, moving quietly, always at my shoulder. We pass a VIP room with leather furniture and a bar cart, empty. A storage room, crates stacked against the walls with markings I can't read.

Then I hear it.

A voice. Low, controlled, and angry. The words are another language— I can't understand them— but the tone is universal. It is the tone of someone demanding something from someone who is not giving it.

We follow the sound down a branching hallway, to a room at the end. The door is heavy— industrial, steel— but it's not fully closed. A gap of perhaps two inches separates the door from its frame, and through that gap, I can see everything.

The room is bare concrete. No windows. A single overhead light, harsh and unforgiving. Pipes run along the ceiling, and from one of those pipes, suspended by her ankles with what appears to be nylon cord— the universe's apparent material of choice for restraining people— hangs Alana.

She is upside down. Her hair cascades toward the floor in a waterfall of blonde. Her pink top has slipped slightly, and her face is flushed— from the position, from the blood rushing to her head, from the general indignity of the situation. Even hanging inverted from a pipe in a basement torture chamber, she looks stunning. This is her gift and also her curse.

Standing in front of her is Marco Ledger.

Well, Alana, I think. *You wanted Marco to come find you in person. Seems like he has.*

Marco is enraged, and it's terrifying. His suit is immaculate. He paces in place, then rolls up his sleeves.

He hits Alana. An open palm, across the cheek, and the sound of it makes my stomach drop. Alana's head snaps to one side.

She recovers. She blinks. She looks at Marco with a calm, appraising expression that says, "That's all you've got."

"I bet this is really good for my circulation," she says, her voice bright and conversational, deliberately wrong for the moment. "Like, who needs botox when you can just hang upside down in a torture chamber?"

Marco does not laugh. Marco does not seem like someone who has ever laughed.

"Where is my brother's ring?" he says, and the edge to his voice tells me this isn't the first time he's asked. He holds up his hand, and on his finger, I see it: his ring. Gold, heavy, ornate. One half of the key to everything.

Then I notice something else. Alana's eyes. They are not looking at Marco's face. They are looking at his hand. At the ring. And in that look is something I recognize:

Desire.

Behind Marco, Ivan stands against the wall like a bald, disapproving monument. Two other guards flank the room.

Rodrigo's hand touches my elbow. I turn. His eyes are dark and serious, and he mouths: *the ring.*

I look at him. He looks at me. And then I do something I would not have done two weeks ago, something the assistant who orders lunch for poodles and books grooming appointments would never have done— I reach into the front of my dress and produce Mateo's ring from where I have kept it hidden, warm against my skin, since the chalet.

Rodrigo watches me produce it. His eyebrows rise. "What else do you keep in there?" he whispers.

"Focus," I whisper back, but I'm smiling.

We press back from the door. Rodrigo leans close, his mouth near my ear.

"We lure him out," he says. "Into the open. The roof. If he sees the ring, he'll follow. He won't be able to stop himself. Rakowski can take him on the roof."

I nod. It's a good plan. It's the only plan.

Rodrigo taps his earpiece. "Benny. Rakowski. Can you hear me?"

"I am here, primo!" Benny's voice explodes through the comm, muffled slightly by what I suspect is a mouthful of shellfish. "The shrimp here is incredible, by the way—"

"Listen to me," Rodrigo says, his voice low and rapid. "Marco is in the basement. We're going to lure him to the roof. Get Rakowski's people positioned up there. Every exit from the rooftop covered."

"Copy," Rakowski's voice cuts through, and I can hear

her already moving, already relaying orders. "Rooftop units repositioning now. You have four minutes."

Rodrigo turns to me. His jaw is set. His eyes are warm and afraid and proud, all at once. "I am a very fast runner," he says. "Construction work is good for the legs."

"Good," I say. "Because you're about to need them."

Rodrigo considers, then pulls me close and kisses me. For a moment, it's just the two of us, his lips on mine, warm and insistent. He grabs my hair with his hand and pulls away, looking deep into my eyes:

"Be safe, Billie," he says.

I look at the ring in my hand. I look at the door. I look at the crack of light spilling through it, and straighten my spine.

"Time to negotiate," I say.

I push the door open.

The room turns toward me. Every face. Every gun. Marco's cold eyes find mine, and I watch them widen— just slightly, just enough to confirm that he was not expecting a woman in a red sequined dress to walk into his torture chamber. Nobody ever is.

I hold up the ring. Mateo's ring. I hold it high, between two fingers, the way Alana held my credit card in the boutique— like it's nothing to me, but everything to *them*.

"Looking for this?" I say, and my voice doesn't shake. My voice is the voice of the woman in the mirror. The one who decides whether the people in the room have earned her presence.

Marco's face transforms. The control fractures. His eyes lock onto the ring with a hunger that makes my skin crawl. He wants me dead— it's written all over his face.

"Billie!" Alana exclaims, like I've just dropped by for tea. "Great dress. A little tight on you in the waist but—"

"The ring," Marco says, holding out his hand.

"You can have it," I say. "If you can catch us."

I toss the ring to Rodrigo. It arcs through the air— small, bright, catching the overhead light— and Rodrigo catches it cleanly, because of course he does, because this man catches everything I throw at him, literally and otherwise. And then he runs.

Rodrigo moves with a speed that surprises even me. He is out the door and into the corridor before Marco's mouth has finished forming the order— *"Uhvatite ih!"*— and then Marco is moving too, and the guards are moving, and the room erupts into the kind of chaos that happens when very angry men with guns decide to chase something.

Two of the guards don't follow. They turn toward me instead— and the air cracks with a gunshot that chips the concrete wall six inches from my head. I drop. My knees hit the floor. My ears ring.

Then I hear a sound I will never forget: the sound of Alana's restraints snapping.

She drops from the pipe, lands on her hands, and rolls — a controlled, athletic, absolutely impossible roll that brings her to her feet in a single fluid motion. She is upright. She is smiling.

"Pilates!" she announces, with the enthusiasm of a woman endorsing a fitness program. "It's really good to have a strong core."

Ivan turns toward her, reaching for his weapon, but Alana is already moving. She bends down, removes her right high-heeled shoe— a stiletto, pink, obviously— and presses something on the heel. There is a sharp, electric crack. The heel, it turns out, contains a taser. Because of course it does.

She drives the electrified heel into Ivan's neck. His body goes rigid. He makes a sound and drops.

Alana looks at me. Her hair is wild. Her cheek is red where Marco hit her. She is, despite everything, radiant.

"Thanks for coming," she says. "That was really, really stupid of you, by the way."

"I know," I say.

"Like, genuinely the dumbest thing anyone has ever done for me, and I once had a man steal a tractor just because I asked him."

"We need to go," I say, because the corridor beyond us is alive with the sound of shouting and running and Rodrigo's footsteps growing distant.

Alana grabs my hand. We run.

The corridor blurs. My heels are wrong for this— everything about my outfit is wrong for this— but I run anyway, because Rodrigo is somewhere ahead of us, and he has the ring, and Marco is behind him, and the rooftop is above, and I have to get to Rodrigo before Marco does.

Alana runs beside me in one shoe. She doesn't seem to notice.

We follow the sound of Rodrigo's footsteps— upward, through a stairwell, the concrete steps spiraling above us— and I think: *I am coming, Rodrigo.* I am coming, and I am not the woman who sat at a desk ordering lunch for a boss who never appreciated her. I am the woman who walked into a torture chamber and held up a ring and said *catch me.* And I will get to this man— this man I think... well, I think I *love* — before anyone has the chance to hurt him.

We make a sharp turn at the end of the hallway, and stop dead in our tracks.

There's a man pointing a gun at Rodrigo, who's standing with his hands in the air. The man's finger is on the trigger. Rodrigo is unarmed— backed into a corner. And I know— without a doubt— that the man I love is about to die, all because I couldn't just stay in the countryside and paint with him. Rodrigo is about to die... and it's all my fault.

And in that moment, I feel like I might be dying, too.

thirty-three

RODRIGO

I AM RUNNING. This is not, I should clarify, the kind of running I do when I am late for something or trying to catch a bus in a city. This is the frantic kind of run a man does when his life depends on it, which mine does. There are three armed men behind me. One of them lets off a shot, and it slams into the concrete corridor, removing a piece of wall where my head was a half-second earlier.

The ring is in my jacket pocket. I can feel it— small, heavy, warm from Billie's body— bouncing against my hip with every stride.

The corridor branches. Left or right. I go left because the stairwell should be this direction— upward, toward the roof, where Rakowski and her teams can retrieve Marco out in the open.

Behind me: boots. Heavier than mine. A shout in Spanish— *stop, or I will make you stop!*

I do not stop. My focus is on luring these men away from Billie.

The corridor narrows. Pipes crowd the ceiling. The light flickers. I round a corner and—

The door is locked.

Not just locked. Sealed. A heavy steel fire door with a magnetic lock, the kind that requires a badge, and I do not have a badge, because the badge is with Billie, who is somewhere behind me, and between us is a collection of armed men who would very much like me to be dead.

I turn.

The first goon rounds the corner. He is large— wider than the corridor seems designed to accommodate— and he is holding his weapon with a two-handed grip. His eyes find me with calm efficiency.

He raises the gun.

I look at the gun. I look at the man. We regard each other in the flickering light, and I have time— in the strange, elastic way— to think about several things at once. I think about my grandmother's house in the countryside and the way the light falls through the kitchen window in the morning. The painting I never finished, the one of the olive grove at dusk. But most of all, I think about Billie's eyes when she said *I don't regret it either*, and the weight of that sentence, and how I will likely never see her again after this moment.

I think: if this is where I die, I would like to have kissed her one more time.

The man's finger moves on the trigger. I see it happen. This is it.

Then: a sound. Electric, sharp, like a wasp the size of a fist. The man's body goes rigid— every muscle contracting at once, his face seizing into an expression of profound and involuntary surprise— and he drops. Straight down. The gun clatters away from him across the concrete and slides until it hits the wall.

Behind where the man stood— in the space he vacated by falling— is Billie. And those eyes.

She is holding a pink high-heeled shoe. The heel is sparking faintly and the man on the ground is twitching. Her hair is slightly wild. Her red dress has a tear near the hem. She is breathing hard, and her enormous brown eyes are wide, and she is the most magnificent thing I have ever seen in my entire life.

Alana stands beside her, one shoe on, one shoe not, looking like she's lent her favorite accessory to a friend and is monitoring its use with proprietary interest.

"Hola," I say, and my voice comes out steadier than it has any right to.

"You tased him," I say, looking at the man on the ground.

"I did," she confirms, and there is something in her face — something new, something wild— that tells me she is as surprised by this as I am. She looks as if she's in shock. "I thought— I thought I might be too late," she says, and her lower lip trembles.

"The shoe," I say, gesturing at the stiletto in her hand.

"My shoe! It has a taser in it," Alana adds helpfully, as if this requires explanation. "I bet you feel dumb for all those times you criticized the money I spend on good footwear."

"I was afraid we were too late—" Billie says, and for the first time, I notice that her eyes are watering. She's flushed, and she throws herself at me, hugging me as if she's never hugged me before. "It would've been my fault—" she says, pressing her body against mine. "I'm sorry, Rodrigo, you were right, we should have just stayed in the countryside and painted—"

"No, no," I murmur, pushing her hair behind her ear. "Where you go I go, *amor*."

I push her hair behind her ear. I want to take her face in my hands and kiss her right here in this terrible corridor over the body of an unconscious man, but there is no time, because from behind them— from the direction they came — footsteps are approaching. Many footsteps. And then a voice, and the voice is worse than the footsteps.

Marco.

He comes around the corner like something inevitable. He is not running— he is walking, which is much more frightening. His suit is still immaculate. His eyes find Billie's back first, because she is closest to him, and his hand reaches for her— reaching for her shoulder, reaching to grab her, to spin her around, to take back what he believes is his.

I see it before she does. The geometry of it— his hand, her shoulder, the distance closing.

I lunge forward and shove her sideways, hard enough that she stumbles into the wall but out of his reach. I square my body toward Marco. My fists come up. Construction work is good for the arms as well as the legs, and I am ready — I am more than ready— to put my hands on this man.

But Alana is faster. She is so fast it surprises me, and I wonder for a moment if she cares about Billie— actually cares about her— the way I do.

She moves with a fluid, devastating precision that says she has been planning this moment. Her hips rotate. Her right leg— the one still wearing a heel— swings in a wide, beautiful, absolutely vicious arc, and the pointed toe of her remaining stiletto connects with Marco's face with a sound like someone dropping a dictionary on a marble floor.

Marco's head snaps back. His body follows, staggering, his arms wheeling. Stars— he is seeing them. I can tell because his eyes go glassy and unfocused and his mouth opens but nothing comes out, which is the first time Marco Ledger has been at a loss for words, possibly in his entire life.

Alana does not waste the moment. She drops to him like a hawk on a field mouse, one hand seizing his right hand, her fingers finding the ring on his finger.

This wasn't about Billie, I think, pushing Billie behind me so we're out of Alana's way. *She wanted the ring.*

She twists it off like a graverobber. Then her other hand is in his jacket pocket, searching, finding, producing— the second ring. Mateo's ring, the one Marco took from her. She holds both rings up, one in each hand, and her smile is incandescent.

"Mine!" she says simply.

Marco's eyes clear. His face twists into something beyond anger. He opens his mouth to scream an order, and from behind him, more boots, more men, more guns converging.

"Run," I say to Billie. It is not a suggestion.

We run. The three of us— Billie in her torn red dress, Alana in one shoe clutching two rings worth more than most nations, and me, bringing up the rear. The stairwell appears— finally, mercifully— and we take it upward, the concrete steps spiraling beneath our feet, the sound of pursuit a thunderclap below us.

We climb. We climb toward the sky, and I can feel it— the air changing, the temperature shifting— and somewhere above us is the roof, and somewhere on that roof is the rest of our lives, assuming we reach it.

* * *

The roof opens above us like a held breath finally released. We burst through the fire door— Billie first, then Alana, then me— and the night air hits my face with a coolness that feels, after the corridors below, like mercy. Rome stretches out in every direction, lit and ancient and full of possibility, indifferent to the fact that three people need its mercy.

The sky above is dark and clear, and I can see stars. The rooftop is flat, bordered by a low concrete border. Ventilation units hum along one edge.

Benny is there.

He is standing by the fire door, holding it open with one hand, and he is visibly, unmistakably... stuffed with food. His jacket pockets bulge. One pocket contains what appears to be an entire lobster tail. The other contains something wrapped in a napkin that could be cheese or could be cake; with Benny, the probability is equal. There is a shrimp tail behind his ear, which I choose to believe is accidental.

“Primo!” he says, his face splitting into a grin. “You made it! I held the door. Like in the movie— you know the one— the one where the guy holds the door and—“

“Benny,” I say. “Not now.”

“Right,” he says, and snaps to attention, or his version of it, which involves standing slightly straighter while still clutching a lobster tail.

Alana moves immediately. She turns to Billie, and something in her posture shifts. She reaches into the waistband of her skirt— where she has been carrying the two rings since she pulled them from Marco’s unconscious fingers— and she holds them out.

Both rings. Gold. Heavy. The two halves of a key to everything the Twin Ledger has built.

“Take them,” Alana says.

Billie stares at her. "Alana—"

"For safekeeping." Alana presses the rings into Billie's hands, folding Billie's fingers over them with a gentleness that seems almost foreign on her. "I trust you. I know you'll always do the right thing.That's why I'm giving them to you and not keeping them. Because if I keep them, I'll do the wrong thing. I know myself." She smiles— small, real, slightly crooked. "You're a better person than me, Billie. You've always been."

Billie looks down at the rings in her hands. She barely glances at them— she is looking at Alana, at the realness of her, at the friend she made in the most improbable circumstances a friendship has ever been built on.

I watch this exchange, and I think: Alana always has a plan.

"Billie, don't—" I start to say, warning her not to take the rings.

But I'm interrupted when the fire door slams open again.

Marco.

He comes through the doorway in a rage. Blood runs from a cut above his eyebrow— Alana's stiletto left its mark— and his jaw is swollen, but he doesn't stop moving.

Behind him: three guards, fanning out, weapons drawn.

Marco has a gun. He raises it, and the muzzle finds Billie with the inevitability of a compass finding north. She's still holding the rings in her hand, shocked and still.

"The rings," he says. His voice is quiet. It cuts through the night air louder than any shout. "Give me the rings. Now."

Billie doesn't move. Her chin is up. Her hands are at her sides. She is standing in the Roman night in her torn red dress, and she does not flinch. Instead... she looks at me, seeking help.

Marco doesn't miss this. His eyes move to me. He studies the space between Billie and me— seeing something there the two of us haven't even admitted to ourselves yet.

"Or I kill your boyfriend," Marco says, and the gun swings to my chest.

Boyfriend. The word lands on me with a weight that is — under the circumstances— inappropriately pleasant. I file this away for later consideration, assuming later exists.

Billie's face changes. The composure cracks— not into fear, but into calculation. I watch her run the math. The rings or my life. The rings or everything.

She looks at Alana, who's watching all of this with a deadpan expression. Then, she turns back to Marco and says, simply: "Catch."

Billie reaches back her hand...

And she throws the rings into the air.

They arc across the rooftop, tumbling through the night sky, catching the ambient light of Rome— two small objects worth more than either of us will ever comprehend — and Marco catches them. Both hands. His fingers close around them with a hunger that is almost physical, and for one fraction of a second, his face shows something like satisfaction.

Then he raises the gun again. Not at me this time.

At Billie.

Because men like Marco do not lose, and they do not forgive, and the rings were never the point. The point was always this: punishment. Revenge, for his brother. For being outsmarted.

I see the gun move. I see where it's aimed. I see Billie

standing there with her enormous eyes and her honest face and her bare shoulders, and something inside me— something deeper than thought— moves.

I leap.

The gun fires. The sound is enormous— it fills the rooftop, fills the sky, fills every space inside my body where silence used to live. The bullet finds my arm. My left arm, just below the shoulder, and the pain is— I will describe it this way— clarifying. It is the kind of pain that removes all ambiguity from the world. There is no confusion about what matters. There is no uncertainty about what I would do again, given the choice. The answer is: this. Exactly this. Every time.

I hit the ground. My shoulder takes the impact, and the concrete roof is cold against my cheek, and the stars above me blur for a moment before sharpening again.

"Noooo!" Alana screams, and for one wild, absurd, deeply Alana moment, I think she is screaming for me— but then she adds: "The rings! He has the rings! Billie, we could have—"

"Rodrigo!" Billie shouts, and then she is beside me, on her knees, and my head is in her lap. Her hands are on my face. Her fingers are warm and shaking and her eyes— those eyes, the ones I first saw at a baby shower in Chicago, the ones with the gold flecks that I have been trying not to drown in since the moment I noticed them— are full of tears.

"Rodrigo," she says, and her voice breaks on my name like a wave against something solid. "Stay with me. Stay right here."

"I'm here," I say. The pain in my arm is a bright, pulsing thing, but her face above me is brighter. "I'm not going anywhere."

"You got shot," she says, as if I might not have noticed.

"Sí," I agree. "In the arm. Not fatal. I have another one."

She laughs— a wet, desperate, beautiful laugh that has tears in it— and presses her forehead to mine.

Then: the sound.

It arrives from everywhere at once— the rhythmic, mechanical thunder of helicopter rotors cutting through the night sky. A searchlight sweeps across the rooftop, turning everything white and stark and sudden. The wind picks up, pressing Billie's hair against her face, making the sequins on her dress scatter light in every direction.

"This is Interpol." Agent Rakowski's voice, amplified through a loudspeaker, fills the rooftop with calm, bureaucratic authority. "Marco Ledger, you are surrounded. Drop your weapon. Get on the ground. Now."

From my position— which is on the ground with my head in the lap of a woman I've taken a bullet for— I watch it happen. Interpol agents pour through every access point. The fire door. The service ladder on the east side. Rappelling lines from the helicopter itself. They move with coordinated precision, weapons drawn, voices calling commands that Marco's guards obey because there is, at last, no other option.

Marco stands in the center of it, the two rings clutched in his fist, and for one long moment he looks like what he is: a man holding everything he's ever wanted and losing it all at the same time. His gun clatters to the concrete. His hands rise. The agents close around him like the sea closing over a stone.

It is over.

Billie's hand is on my chest. Her tears are on my face— hers, not mine, though mine are threatening to arrive as well, which I will deny later. Her thumb traces a line along my jaw, and she is looking at me with an expression that contains everything I have been hoping, quietly, desperately, to see.

"You took a bullet for me," she says.

"I did," I say.

"You jumped in front of a gun."

"Sí."

"For me."

"For you." I reach up— with my good arm, the one that has not been recently perforated— and I touch her face. Her skin is warm. Her freckles are there, scattered across her nose, the most specific and perfect details on the most specific and perfect face. "Billie. Would a man take a bullet for a passing thing?"

She stares at me. The tears come faster, but she is smiling— she is smiling the way people smile when something they were afraid to believe in turns out to be true.

"Only a really dumb one," she whispers.

"True," I agree. "But I am very smart," I pull her closer. The pain in my arm protests, and I do not care. "You are not a passing thing. You have never been a passing thing. You are the thing I've been waiting for. The thing I was afraid to believe existed, because every time before, I was wrong. But I am not wrong about you."

She kisses me. Or I kiss her. Her mouth on mine, gentle and fierce and salt-tasting from tears— is the most important thing that has ever happened to me on a rooftop, or anywhere else.

The helicopter hovers above us, the wind pressing down, and somewhere behind us Benny is shouting something about this being exactly like the end of a movie whose title I cannot hear and do not care about, and Alana is arguing with an Interpol agent about whether her shoes count as weapons and therefore need to be confiscated, and medics are approaching with equipment and concern. The night sky over Rome is vast and clear and full of stars that have been there for millennia and will be there for millennia more, and beneath them, on the concrete roof of a casino, I lie with my head in Billie Harper's lap, and I am shot, and I am bleeding, and I am— without question, without ambiguity, without a single reservation— the happiest man alive.

thirty-four

BILLIE

I CAN'T BELIEVE *I almost lost him.*

The thought arrives not dramatically— not with the cinematic slow-motion replay I'd expect considering I've spent the last several days accidentally living inside an action movie— but quietly, in the pause between one breath and the next, while I sit on a Roman rooftop with a man's blood on the hem of my dress and watch two EMTs argue about gauze.

The rooftop has been a blur. I know, because I've been *inside* the blur for what feels like an hour, but who can be sure? Time has lost its commitment to linear behavior. Things happened: Marco was pulled to his feet, his wrists cuffed behind his back, his face bearing the imprint of Alana's stiletto in a way that will be, I suspect, difficult to explain in his booking photograph. He was escorted toward the fire door by four agents who treated him with a professional detachment he doesn't deserve. The rings were sealed in evidence bags by a woman with latex gloves and a face that communicated she had handled worse, all while Alana cried nearby, shouting something about how she "deserved them" for "catching Marco single-handedly!" The helicopter repositioned, its searchlight sweeping elsewhere, and the rooftop went from a theater of chaos to something quieter: an aftermath. The part of the emergency where the emergency has ended and what remains is the accounting.

Rodrigo is propped against a ventilation unit, his jacket off, his left sleeve cut away by the EMTs to reveal the wound— a through-and-through, they said, which apparently means the bullet entered and exited his arm without lodging itself inside, which is, in the grim calculus of gunshot wounds, the preferable outcome. *He is going to be okay.* They said this— both of them, independently, probably because I kept asking them in rotating turns. *He is going to be okay.* They've promised me this. The bleeding is controlled. The arm is bandaged. He will need a hospital, stitches, probably a sling, definitely rest.

He does not look like a man who is interested in rest.

He is sitting there— bandaged, shirtless under the emergency blanket someone draped over his shoulders, his hair slightly wild, a smear of his own blood still visible on his jaw— and he is smiling. At me. With infuriating, gravity-defying calm.

"You need to stop looking at me like that," I say, sitting beside him. My voice comes out shakier than I intend.

"Like what?" he asks.

"Like you didn't just get shot."

"It's a small hole," he says. "I have had worse from furniture assembly."

"You have not."

"IKEA is very dangerous, Billie."

Benny is orbiting us— a large, food-laden satellite. He has been hovering since the EMTs arrived, his concern for his cousin manifesting as a nonstop monologue about action movie characters who have survived worse injuries. "In Lethal Weapon Two," he is saying, pressing a napkin-wrapped something into Rodrigo's good hand, "Mel Gibson is shot many times. Many, many times. And he is fine. He walks it off. You are tougher than Mel Gibson, primo. You are— eat this, it's prosciutto— you are the Spanish Mel Gibson."

"I don't want prosciutto," Rodrigo says.

"You need the protein," Benny insists. "For the blood. The blood needs protein. I read this somewhere."

"You have never read anything."

"I read it on a menu," Benny clarifies, wounded. He turns to me, seeking an ally. "Billie. Tell him. The blood needs protein."

"The blood probably needs protein," I say, partly because I don't have the energy to argue with Benny, but also because I'm still worried about Rodrigo— and if something has even a small chance at helping him, I'm all for it.

Benny nods, vindicated. He produces, from his other pocket, an entire wheel of brie wrapped in a cocktail napkin. "I also brought cheese," he says.

"What healing properties does cheese have?" Rodrigo asks.

"For morale, obviously primo," Benny says.

Across the rooftop, Melissa is standing with Agent Rakowski, and she is— even from this distance— clearly in command of the conversation. Even at eight months pregnant, Melissa has the energy to oversee an entire crime scene. Her hands are moving. She is making a point. Steve stands beside her, one hand on the small of her back, nodding at whatever she's saying with a supportive expression.

Melissa looks over at me. Our eyes meet across the rooftop. She gives me a look— one look, brief, loaded with years of friendship— and I know what it says. It says: Are you okay? It says: I'm proud of you. It says: We will talk about all of this later, in detail, probably while I eat an entire pizza. I nod back. She nods once. That's enough. That's all we need.

I look at Rodrigo again. At the bandage on his arm and the blood and the blanket and the way his eyes are soft even when the rest of him is hurt, and something inside me— something that has been building since Barcelona, since the boutique, since the baby shower, since long before any of this began— settles.

Not clicks into place. That implies it was a puzzle, that I was assembling something. It's not that. It's more like... something sits down. Something that's been standing for thirty-five years, shifting its weight, waiting to be told it was allowed to rest. It sits down, finally, and I think about what I've learned.

Here is what I know:

I have spent my entire life trying to become the kind of woman who deserves the things she wants. The promotion. The recognition. The proof that I am not just the assistant. But I am changed now. I went into a compound and negotiated with arms dealers, and I walked into a casino in a red dress and talked my way past a bouncer, and I tased a man with a shoe, and I held a billion-dollar ring in my hand and threw it to save the life of someone I love, and all of it— every single insane, terrifying, exhilarating moment of it— was me trying to prove to myself that I was enough.

But I was *always* enough. I was enough before the blazer. I was enough before Spain.

And now, I have a man in my life who really sees me.

I don't need to negotiate with arms dealers to be extraordinary. I don't need to infiltrate casinos. I just need to do the thing that makes me happy, whatever that turns out to be. And right now— in this moment, on this rooftop — what makes me happy sounds remarkably like a stone house in the Spanish countryside, and an easel in the corner, and morning light through the kitchen window, and someone beside me who sees me exactly as I am and finds that sufficient. I look back at Rodrigo— and I know that everything is going to be alright, now.

"Billie!"

Alana materializes beside me the way she always does — as if she has been there the entire time. Her hair is a disaster, by her standards, which means it looks like it belongs in a shampoo commercial by anyone else's. She's holding a glass of bubbling liquid.

"Where did you get champagne?" I ask.

"From the casino," she shrugs, and I wonder at the fact she was able to escape the crime scene to run down stairs for a quick drink.

She takes a sip, then sits down beside me. For a moment, neither of us speaks. We just sit there, two women on a rooftop in Rome, looking out at a city that has seen everything and therefore cannot be shocked by us.

"Can I tell you something?" she says.

I wait.

"I knew," she says, and her voice has that rare quality— the one that surfaces only in the moments when Alana is being completely real. "About you and Rodrigo. I knew from the beginning. From, like, the baby shower. The way he looked at you— I'd never seen him look at anyone like that. Not even me." She pauses. "And the thing is? I wasn't even jealous. I was kind of, like— relieved? Because I'd always known he wasn't mine. Not really. He was always supposed to belong to someone else. And that was obviously you. So I kind of encouraged you two."

I stare at her. "You— you encouraged us to be together?"

"Of course I did." She looks at me like I've said something remarkably obvious. "Why do you think I kept leaving you two alone? The dining car on the train? The chalet? I'm not, like, accidentally bad at chaperoning. I am very *strategically* bad at chaperoning." She smiles. "He's a good guy, Billie. An actually good guy. And you're a good person who deserves a good guy. The math was simple."

"You kidnapped me," I say, because I feel this deserves periodic acknowledgment.

"I did," she agrees. "And it was the best thing that ever happened to you. You're welcome."

I laugh. It comes out wet and full and helpless. I know this is completely messed up, but I'll have to sort it out in therapy on

"I actually really like you, Billie," Alana says, and she says it simply. "You're, like, the first *real* friend I've ever had. Drago doesn't count. Drago was more of a business associate who happened to enjoy brunch and murder."

"I like you too," I say. "You're insane, but I like you."

"Okay, but— and I say this with love— you need therapy." She holds up a manicured finger. "Like, actual therapy. A professional. Someone with a degree. Because you are way, way too much of a pushover, and the fact that it took being kidnapped and dragged across Europe for you to finally start standing up for yourself is, like, clinically significant."

Alana has told me I need therapy, and *she* needs therapy

more than anyone on the planet. I decide not to unpack this irony, right now.

"What about you?" I ask. "What's your plan? Because I assume you have one, and both it's terrible and brilliant."

Her smile widens. The champagne catches the light from a nearby work lamp. "I am living out my vision board," she says, with serene confidence. "I'm going to be on a yacht. In the Mediterranean. With Reginald Ashcroft."

"Reginald Ashcroft," I repeat. "The actor. The one from the show. The one you were definitely lying about knowing?"

"I wasn't *lying*!" she says, aghast, as if I've accused her of being a serial killer, which she kind of is. "He's a friend. A *close* friend, if you catch my drift," she winks, communicating he might be a friend with benefits. "He has a yacht." She takes another sip of champagne. "It's gorgeous. White. Three decks."

"And how exactly do you plan to fund this lifestyle?" I ask. "Because the vault is locked and the rings are in evidence and Interpol is—"

Alana looks at me.

Then she reaches into the waistband of her dress, and produces two rings.

Two rings.

Gold. Heavy. Real.

I stare at them. I stare at her. The rooftop tilts slightly beneath me, or perhaps that's just my understanding of reality rearranging itself, which it does with increasing frequency when Alana is involved.

"Oh, Billie," she says, with the warm, patient tone of a teacher. "You didn't think I'd give you the *real* rings? Those were from the casino gift shop. They were twelve euros each."

"The— the gift shop?"

"Souvenir rings." She holds up the real ones, turning them so they catch the light, and they are— even to my untrained eye— visibly different from the ones I held. Heavier. More intricate. Alive with a weight that has nothing to do with gold and everything to do with what they unlock. "I swapped them. You were too distracted by our impending deaths to notice."

"You— you swapped—"

"I told you... I knew you'd do the right thing," Alana says, and there is genuine tenderness in her voice. "I knew that if it came down to the rings or Rodrigo's life, or even *my* life, you'd give them to Marco. Because that's who you are. You're the person who always does the right thing." She pauses. "And I knew Marco would believe they were real, coming from you. Because you have an honest face. The most honest face I've ever seen. Like a Disney character, but with worse cheekbones." She tucks the rings back into her waistband. "If the swap had come from me, he would have been more skeptical. But from you? Bambi eyes? He didn't question it for a second."

"You used my honesty as a weapon?"

"I prefer 'leveraged your authenticity,'" Alana says. "It sounds better on a résumé."

She stands and brushes off her dress. She looks down at me with an expression that is— beneath the glamour, beneath the performance— the expression of a woman who has found something real and is trying to hold it gently enough not to break it.

"I should go," she says. "Before Interpol realizes those evidence bags contain twelve-euro novelty jewelry and starts asking questions..."

"Alana—"

"Don't." She holds up a hand. "Don't make it sad. Sad is for people who don't have yachts." But her eyes are bright, and her lip does a thing— a small, involuntary thing— that tells me she is feeling this goodbye in a place she doesn't usually let people see.

I stand. I pull her into a hug. She hugs me back— tight, real. And it says everything she can't.

We pull apart.

She turns to the edge of the rooftop, where the fire escape descends along the building's exterior in a zigzag of iron and shadow. She pauses, balanced on the edge, silhouetted against the lights of Rome.

"Tell Rodrigo I said he's welcome!" she calls over her shoulder.

Then she descends. Barefoot, carrying two rings worth more than most countries, climbing down the fire escape of a Roman casino with a fluid ease that suggests she does this all the time. I watch her go— her shape getting smaller against the building's side— and then she's gone. Just like that.

The rooftop feels quieter without her. Everything always feels quieter without her.

I am still standing at the edge, looking at the empty fire escape, when Melissa appears beside me.

"So," She pauses, "Don't be mad at me. But someone is here to see you."

"Who?" I ask, though something in her tone tells me I already know.

"He wouldn't stop calling," Melissa says. "He called me, like, fourteen times. Fourteen."

My stomach tightens.

"Also," Melissa adds, with careful precision, "please

don't get back together with him. I love you. I support all your choices. Except that one."

She steps aside. And there, emerging from between two Interpol officers who look mildly confused by his presence, is:

Tyler.

He looks exactly the same. That's the thing that strikes me first— the absolute sameness of him. The baseball cap. The sneakers. The graphic tee under an unzipped hoodie. He walks over to me, and even though he looks the same, I barely recognize him— maybe it's because I'm different.

"Billie," he says.

He steps closer. His hands are in his pockets.

"I took a really long flight to get here," he says. "Like, really long. There was a layover in Frankfurt. The Frankfurt airport is terrible, by the way— the food court situation is not great." He catches himself. "But that's not the point. The point is— I've been an idiot. A complete idiot. I should have been there for you. I should have noticed you were gone. I should have done— a lot of things. Differently. Better."

He says this with what I can tell is genuine effort. Tyler is not a bad person. He is a person who has floated through life on the current of least resistance, and the current brought him to me, and he stayed because I was comfortable and I stayed because I was afraid of wanting more.

Over Tyler's shoulder, I can see Rodrigo. He is still propped against the ventilation unit, the emergency blanket around his shoulders, Benny beside him with the prosciutto. He is watching me. Not with anxiety, not with jealousy— with trust. The steady, unhurried trust of someone has told me what he feels and is willing to wait for me to choose.

I look back at Tyler.

"Tyler," I say, and my voice is steady. It is the steadiest it has ever been. "We all deserve to be happy."

He blinks. "I know. That's why I came— I want to make you happy, Billie—"

"You can't," I say.

The words come out clean, and maybe a little meaner than I intended. They are not wrapped in apology or softened with qualification.

"I'm breaking up with you," I continue. "We should have done this a long time ago. I don't regret the time we had, but we have to let each other go."

It's me, breaking up with Tyler this time. Not Alana, doing it by text. Not someone else, making the decision for me. Me. Billie Harper. Making the choice. And because of that, I add:

"I hope you find everything you need. I really mean that. Truly."

Tyler stares at me. He looks at the rooftop, the Interpol agents, the helicopter that has repositioned to a landing area nearby.

"Oh," he says. "I did— I came a long way—"

"I'm sorry," I add— because I am Billie Harper and I will probably always add "I'm sorry," but I'm saying it because I mean it, not because I'm afraid. "You're not a bad person, Tyler. You're just not my person."

He nods slowly. He looks at his sneakers. Then he looks up.

"Is it that guy?" he asks, glancing at Rodrigo.

"Yes," I admit. "But it's also me."

He nods again. He puts his hands back in his pockets. He stands there for a moment, on the rooftop, having travelled a very long way to arrive at a conclusion he probably could have reached from his couch. Then he turns to Melissa.

"So," he says. "Do you know if there's a good hotel nearby? The Frankfurt airport had a Marriott, but—"

"I'll help you find something," Melissa says, taking his arm, steering him away with executive prowess. She looks back at me over her shoulder. She mouths: Proud of you. I mouth back: Thank you. She nods. That's enough. That's always been enough with us.

I walk across the rooftop to Rodrigo.

He watches me approach. His eyes— those warm, dark, impossibly steady eyes— follow me the way they have followed me since Barcelona, since the train, since the compound, since every moment in between. He does not ask what happened. He does not need to. He reads it on my face the way he reads everything on my face: clearly, completely, without effort.

I reach him. I kneel down. I take his face in both hands — carefully, mindful of the bandaged arm, the blanket, the general medical situation— and I kiss him.

I kiss him hard. Not the gentle, tentative kiss of the hotel corridor, but one that tells him I'm all in. I pour everything into it— the fear and the relief and the gratitude and the bone-deep want that has been building since I first saw his perfect face at a baby shower in Chicago and thought he was rude. Now, he's the man who took a bullet for me.

He kisses me back. His good arm comes around me, pulling me closer, and the emergency blanket crinkles between us, and Benny says "This is like the end of—" and someone— probably the universe— shushes him.

I pull back just enough to see Rodrigo's face. His eyes are bright. He is smiling— the crooked one, the devastating one, the one that undoes me every single time.

"I've been thinking," I say.

"That's dangerous," he says.

"I'm wondering if it was me or Alana who needed therapy this whole time." I settle against him, careful of his arm. "She's the most selfish person I've ever met. And I'm the biggest pushover. And maybe we were both wrong? Maybe she needed to be a little less selfish, and I needed to be a little more?" I pause. "You won't believe this, but she told me to get therapy."

"Rude," Rodrigo says.

"She also stole the real rings and gave me fakes and I threw twelve-euro souvenir jewelry at an international arms dealer."

Rodrigo processes this. I watch the information travel across his face— surprise, then acceptance. "Of course she did," he says. "Thank God we're leaving with our lives."

"She's going to be on a yacht," I say. "With that actor. The one from the show."

"To each their own," Rodrigo shrugs.

We are quiet for a moment. Rome hums around us, alive and ancient. The stars do their thing. Somewhere below, the casino is being systematically dismantled by law enforcement, and somewhere above, a helicopter is banking toward wherever helicopters go when the crisis is over.

"Billie," Rodrigo says, and his voice has gone to the soft place, the place where the real things live. "I was thinking. Perhaps we can contemplate the question of therapy and selfishness at the country house." He tilts his head. "I could paint. You could read. We could eat terrible food and pretend my grandmother's recipe was good."

I picture it. The stone house with the olive trees. Morning light through the kitchen window. An easel in the corner with a half-finished painting. Coffee on a table in a small garden. Rodrigo, beside me, painting in silence, and me, beside him, being exactly who I am— no blazer, no negotiation, no performance— and finding that it's enough.

"I would like that," I say.

"Sí?" he says.

"Sí," I say, and the word feels like the beginning of something I've been waiting for without knowing I was waiting.

His arm tightens around me. I lean into him. The rooftop holds us— two people who met at a baby shower and ended up here, in the aftermath of everything.

Benny clears his throat. "So," he says, from approximately four feet away, where he has been standing this entire time. "I know this a romantic plan, but you know I will be there too, yes? Because I have more cheese in the car, and also—"

"Benny," Rodrigo says.

"Right," Benny says. "I'll be in the car."

He walks away, eating brie from a napkin, and the night continues, and Rome continues, and somewhere in the Mediterranean a yacht is waiting for a woman who is barefoot and holding two rings and climbing toward whatever comes next, and here— on this rooftop, in this moment— I am not the assistant. I am not the pushover. I am not the woman who puts everyone else first and herself last and wonders why she's tired.

I am Billie Harper. And I am exactly where I'm supposed to be.

thirty-five

RODRIGO

SIX MONTHS LATER.

In the stone studio behind our chalet in Tuscany, Billie Harper is painting a lemon, and it looks like a crime scene. She has been working on this lemon for forty minutes. The lemon— which is sitting on a plate on the windowsill, where the morning light turns it a shade of gold that any painter would be grateful for— has done nothing to deserve what Billie is doing to it on canvas. Her rendition of the fruit is an asymmetrical blob. But she is concentrating with the full intensity of her enormous brown eyes, and a smear of cadmium yellow decorates her left cheekbone like war paint, and she is so beautiful that I would let her murder every lemon in Italy and hang the evidence on our walls.

Six months. We have been here six months. I know this because I have counted them, with quiet gratitude. Every morning I wake up and Billie is beside me— her hair fanned across the pillow, her breathing slow, her body curled toward mine as if even in sleep she is deciding to be near me— and every morning I think: She is still here. Still real. Still not a dream I invented because I wanted it too badly.

My left arm aches when the weather changes. The scar sits just below my shoulder— a puckered, pale line where the bullet entered and a matching one on the other side where it left. Some mornings I catch Billie looking at it. She touches it sometimes, running her thumb along the raised skin, and doesn't say anything, and I don't say anything, because we are both still quietly working out what happened.

"Rodrigo," Billie says, without looking up from her lemon-crime. "Be honest. Does it look like a lemon?"

I lean over to examine her canvas. I tilt my head. I tilt it the other way. I consider the painting from multiple angles, giving it the thoughtful evaluation it deserves. "It looks," I say carefully, "like something that was once a lemon, and has gone through a significant, transformative experience."

"So no."

"It looks like a lemon's feelings?" I offer. "Maybe it's interpretative."

"I want it to look like a lemon's body." She frowns at the canvas with furious concentration, and I am reminded— as I am reminded constantly, daily, in ways large and small— why I love her.

I know her now. Not in the way I knew Alana— the way you know a firework, brightly and briefly— but in the way you know a piece of music you've heard a hundred times and still discover new things in. I know that Billie cannot cook anything except pasta with butter, and that she does not consider this a limitation but a lifestyle. I know that she reads before bed, always fiction, always with her knees pulled up and the book held close to her face as though she is trying to climb inside it. I know that she hums when she brushes her teeth— a different song each morning, unconsciously selected, and I have begun cataloguing them because the selection reveals her mood. I know that she still apologizes too much, and that she is working on this, and that the working-on-it is itself a form of apology that is wildly unnecessary.

I know that she is kind without an agenda. That her kindness is not a strategy but a fact— like her height, or her freckles, or the gold flecks in her eyes that catch the Tuscan light and make me lose sentences mid-thought. I know that she believes in people with a stubbornness that borders on irrational, and that this belief— this *insistence* on seeing the good in others— is both her greatest vulnerability and her greatest strength, and that the line between the two is so thin as to be nonexistent.

I know, in short, that I was right. The thing I felt at the baby shower, the instant recognition that this woman was different— it was not the pattern repeating. It was not me projecting a fantasy onto a stranger because she had beautiful eyes and a face you could trust with your darkest secret. It was instinct, and for once in my impulsive, mistake-prone, leap-before-looking life, my instinct was correct.

Billie is the woman I always wanted. And the wanting has not diminished with knowing. It has deepened.

"We need to review the proposal for the Aleppo site," Billie says, still frowning at her lemon. "The local coordinator sent revisions. I think we can negotiate the materials cost down another twelve percent if we adjust the timeline."

This is the other thing. The project. Our project— the

refugee housing initiative that started as a conversation at this very table three months ago and has since become, through Billie's relentless negotiation skills and my knowledge of construction, something real. Something with blueprints and budgets and partner organizations. Something that uses every part of who we are— her ability to walk into a room and convince people to do things they didn't plan to do, my ability to build things that stand up and keep people safe.

We are going to do good in the world.

This is something we have both decided after seeing the bad.

She negotiates with contractors the way she negotiated with Marco's men in the compound. The contractors find her charming. They also find her terrifying. This is the correct response.

I set down my brush and pick up my phone. The nonprofit account— the one we opened in Rome, the morning after the rooftop, when Billie was in my shirt and I my arm was bandaged and we were deciding what to do next— loads on the screen. I scroll to the balance.

Two hundred and fourteen thousand euros.

I stare at the number. Six months ago, this number was zero. Now we have two hundred and fourteen thousand euros committed to building homes for people who have lost theirs, and the woman responsible for raising most of it is sitting four feet away from me, painting a lemon that looks like it has been through a war.

"Two-fourteen," I say, holding up the phone.

Billie looks up. Her face breaks into that smile. "We'll hit the Phase One target by October," she says.

She is not the assistant anymore. She is the builder. The woman who walks into rooms and makes things happen, not for someone else's empire, but for something that matters.

She reaches for her own phone— hers, a new one, one that has never been thrown from a train— and swipes through it. "Oh! I forgot to show you. Melissa sent the new photos."

She brings the phone to me, and there, on the screen, is a baby. Melissa's baby. A baby girl— round-faced, dark-eyed. In the photo, Melissa is holding her.

The baby was born in Chicago. Four days after they flew home. Melissa called from the delivery room, which we know because she called Billie first and the doctor second, and she said— and I quote, because Billie quotes it regularly— "Billie, my vagina has been through something, and I want you to know this baby is named after you." The baby's middle name is Billie. The first name is something else, something I always forget, because Melissa only ever refers to her as "my baby" or "the tiny dictator" or, on difficult nights, "the reason I will never sleep again."

"She looks like Melissa," I say, studying the photo. "The expression. Very serious. Very much in charge."

Then Billie's phone buzzes. A notification. She looks at the screen, and her face does a thing— a quick succession of emotions.

"What?"

"It's— Alana," she says.

I feel a shiver travel the length of my spine. Not from the cold. From memory. We haven't heard from her since that night, on the rooftop. I have been very happy with this.

"I would be happy," I say, "to never hear from her again."

Billie stares at me as if asking what to do. I sigh, leaning in and looking at the message. It's a video.

"Play it," I nod.

Billie presses play.

The screen fills with Alana's face. She is— of course— wearing something pink and expensive, standing in front of an ocean view.

"Hiii," she says, and her voice fills our studio. "Okay so like I know I've been MIA, but you won't believe what I've been up to." She swipes a hand in front of the camera and takes us back to a video that appears to have been recorded earlier.

The video shows Alana, standing in front of an enormous steel vault door, the kind that belongs in a Bond film or a Central Bank. She turns the camera. The vault door swings open— I hear the mechanism, heavy, precise, the sound of something that does not open often— and beyond it is a room that makes me hold my breath. Gold. Stacks of currency in multiple denominations. Paintings I recognize from auction catalogues. Cases of jewels. The accumulated wealth of the Twin Ledger, the machine that Marco and Mateo built with blood and corruption and the particular human talent for making terrible things profitable.

The video clicks back to the ocean view, which I assume is Alana's most recent location. "So I found the vault," Alana says, smiling. "It was, like, not that hard? Marco's security is honestly embarrassing without him."

She starts walking, and suddenly I realized she's on a yacht. White, gleaming, three decks. The Mediterranean stretches behind her in an endless expanse of blue, and she stretches out, lying on a lounge chair in a bikini as if this is an infomercial.

"Also," she says, adjusting her sunglasses, "I am currently on a yacht in the Mediterranean with Reginald Ashcroft. He's inside because he's, like, super camera shy, which I know sounds fake, but it's true. He's literally right in there. Reggie! Say hi!" She turns the camera toward a cabin door. The door remains closed. No sound emerges. She turns the camera back to herself. "Ugh, he's method-acting or whatever. Actors are so weird."

Billie pauses the video. She looks at me. "Do you think that's true? About Ashcroft?"

"Absolutely not," I say. "Alana is a liar. Reginald Ashcroft is not on that yacht. No one is on that yacht except Alana and whatever stolen goods she has converted into a floating lifestyle."

Billie looks at me with those enormous eyes.

"She *said* she knew him," Billie says.

"She also kidnapped you."

"Fair point." Billie presses play again.

Alana's face reappears, backlit by the Mediterranean sun. "Anyway," she says, "my vision board is, like, fully manifesting right now? Yacht. Check. Mediterranean. Check. Famous British actor. Check. Financial independence through morally flexible means. Big check." She pauses. Her expression shifts— fractionally, but I see it. The bubbly veneer thinning to show something underneath. Something real. "Oh— also. You guys should check the account for that dumb little nonprofit you're doing. The refugee thing. I think there might be something extra in there." She winks. "Love you, Billie. Tell Rodrigo I said he's welcome. Again. As always. Forever."

The video ends. The screen goes black. The studio is quiet except for the sound of birds outside and the particular silence that follows any communication from Alana, which is the silence of people recalibrating their understanding of reality.

Billie looks at me. "Check the account," she says.

“I just did—”

“Check it again.”

I pick up my phone. I open the banking app. I navigate to the nonprofit account— the one that showed two hundred and fourteen thousand euros ten minutes ago.

The balance loads:

Five million euros.

I stare at the screen. The number stares back at me.

“Five million,” I say. My voice sounds strange to my own ears— distant, as though it is coming from a man standing in a different room.

“Five million?” Billie repeats.

“Five million.” I turn the phone toward her. She looks at the screen. Her hand comes up to her mouth. Her eyes— those eyes, the ones that looked at me across a baby shower and a train and a casino and a rooftop and a hundred mornings in this kitchen— go wide and bright and wet.

“We can build everything,” she whispers. “The Aleppo site. The Beirut site. The whole Phase Two—“

“We can build all of it,” I agree, and I am laughing, because what else can you do when your dreams come true? You laugh. You accept that the world is stranger and more generous than you understood, and you laugh.

Billie is laughing too— the bright, involuntary laugh, the one that shows her whole face and crinkles her nose and makes the freckles shift like stars rearranging themselves, and I set down the phone because the number will still be there— her face, her joy, the morning light in our studio— will not come again exactly like this.

“Rodrigo,” she says, still laughing, still looking at me with those eyes, “we can really make the world better.”

“Can I ask you something?” I say.

“Always,” she says.

"If you had a vision board— like Alana— what would you put on it?"

Billie is quiet for a moment. She looks at the studio — at the canvases against the wall, at the light through the windows, at the lemon on the windowsill that has survived its portrait with more dignity than the portrait afforded it. She looks at my easel, at the olive grove taking shape on the canvas, at the brushes in the jar and the paint on the palette and the turpentine smell that has become the smell of home. She looks at me.

"Nothing," she says.

The word lands softly. It has no weight because it carries no wanting. It is the lightest word she has ever spoken.

"Nothing," she says again, and she smiles— not the big smile, not the one that uses her whole face, but the small one, the private one, the one I have learned is reserved for the moments when she is feeling something too large to perform. "Everything I want has already manifested. You're standing right here."

I look at her. She looks at me. The morning light does its work between us— catching the gold in her eyes, the yellow paint on her cheekbone, the small, unrepeatable details of the woman I chose and who chose me back.

I cross the space between us. It is not a large space— the studio is small— but I cross it with intention.

I kiss her.

Her mouth is warm and tastes faintly of the coffee we had this morning— the strong Italian kind, from the moka pot on the stove— and she makes a small sound against my lips, a sound that says she was expecting this and wanted it, and her hands come up to my face, her fingers tracing the line of my jaw the way they do every time, as though she is confirming that I am real.

I am real. I keep wanting to tell her this— I am real, I am here, I am not leaving— but she already knows. She has known for months. The knowing is in the way she touches me: without hesitation, without the careful distance of someone who expects to be disappointed. She touches me like she has decided to believe.

The kiss deepens. Her hands move from my jaw to my neck, pulling me closer, and something in me decides to do a very inappropriate thing.

I sweep my arm across the counter. The painting supplies go— brushes, palette, the shade of yellow that Billie has been using to assassinate her lemon— all of it clattering to the stone floor in a cascade of color and noise that would be dramatic if either of us were paying attention, which we are not. We are paying attention only to each other.

I lift her onto the counter. She is small— her frame fitting against mine like an answer to a question I did not know I was asking— and she wraps her legs around me and pulls me closer and I think: this. This is what I was building toward. Not the country house. Not the paintings. Not the nonprofit or the money or the adventure or the rooftop. This. Billie's hands on my neck. Her breath against my mouth. Her body warm and real and present, in a room full of art and morning light.

I kiss down her neck. Slowly. With the specific, unhurried attention of someone who has learned— through a lifetime of rushing— that the best things are the ones you take your time with. I feel her pulse under my lips, rapid and alive, and her fingers thread through my hair, and she says my name— "Rodrigo"— in a voice that makes the word sound like something sacred, which, coming from her, it is.

Her collarbone. The hollow of her throat. The slope of her chest, where her skin is warm and faintly freckled, the freckles scattered like a private constellation visible only from this distance. I map them with my mouth because I can, because she lets me, because in this life we have built together there is time for this— time to be slow, time to be thorough.

She is laughing again. Softly. Everything blends together; her fingers in my hair, her laughter in the air, the morning light on the stone walls of a studio in Tuscany.

I think: I have never been so happy. Rodrigo Esperanza, in this room, with this woman, at this moment: happiest he has ever been.

I kiss down her stomach. Her breath catches.

And I think about something I've carried for a long time — the idea that I am broken in some fundamental way. That the pattern— the rushing, the falling, the choosing wrong— was evidence of a flaw in my design.

But here is what I have learned, in six months: the difference between seeing someone as crazy or sane— the difference is just finding the person who fits. The one whose chaos complements your calm. Whose doubt meets your certainty. Whose enormous, golden-brown eyes look at you and see not the man you're afraid of being, but the man you've always hoped you were.

Billie fits with me. She fits the way music fits silence. The way light fits a room.

Every day in the future is ours.

Billie pulls me back up to her. Her forehead presses against mine. Our breathing mingles in the small, sacred space between our faces.

"I love you," she says.

"*Te quiero,*" I tell her. "*Más que todo.*" More than everything.

On the floor, the paint spreads in slow rivers of color— yellow and blue and red running together across the stone, mixing into something new. The lemon painting lies among the wreckage, face-up, and it is— I will admit this now— a terrible painting.

Billie Harper smiles at me. She has paint on her cheekbone and coffee on her breath and the morning sun in her hair, and she is— exactly as she is, without revision— the most extraordinary thing I have ever seen.

And I am exactly where I am supposed to be, no vision board required.

I'll end this story the way I began, with one small alteration:

My name is Rodrigo, and my girlfriend— is perfect.

thirty-six

ALANA

ON THE DECK of a yacht in a glistening harbor off the Mediterranean coast, I'm being held hostage by Shakespeare.

Not, like, the actual William Shakespeare— he's dead, which is honestly probably the only thing that could make him tolerable at this point— but by an actor who *believes* he is the spiritual reincarnation of William Shakespeare, or at least the closest living approximation, which is somehow worse.

Reginald Ashcroft is sitting in the lounge chair beside mine, wearing a white linen shirt unbuttoned to a degree that suggests either confidence or a fundamental misunderstanding of buttons, and he is reciting something. He has been reciting something for forty-five minutes. I know this because my attendant— a lovely woman named something... I don't know, I can't remember... is currently holding my sunglasses above my face, hovering them there so that the bridge doesn't leave marks on my nose. This is a service I require. Sunglass marks are violence against the face, and I will not tolerate violence against my face unless

I'm the one committing it, which has happened, but that's a different story.

"Shall I compare thee to a summer's day?" Reginald declares, and the question is clearly rhetorical because he does not pause for my input before continuing. "Thou art more lovely and more temperate—"

"Reggie," I say, without moving, without opening my eyes, without disrupting the sunglasses hovering above my face. "Who are you comparing to a summer's day?"

"You, darling," he says, in that voice— that rich, plummy, deeply British voice that sounds like it was raised on private schools. "I am comparing you to a summer's day, because you are—"

"I know what the poem is about," I say. "I've seen the movie."

"There isn't a movie of Sonnet Eighteen."

"There should be. They could cast you." I say this because it will distract him, and it does— his face does the thing where he's pretending to be humble but is actually already mentally accepting the award— and for a brief, merciful moment, the Shakespeare stops.

The yacht— *my* yacht, technically, or at least the yacht I am currently occupying by virtue of having befriended the man who owns it and then having gently, lovingly, suggested that he let me stay on it indefinitely— is anchored in a harbor somewhere off the coast of southern Italy. I'm not totally sure which harbor. They all look the same from this angle: blue water, white buildings stacked up the hillside like sugar cubes, little boats going back and forth. The sun is golden and the light on the water is so pretty it almost makes me mad, because beauty shouldn't be this easy. It should require effort. A filter, at minimum.

I'm wearing a pink bikini— Valentino, custom— and

my nails are fresh, and my hair is behaving, and I have a drink in my hand. The garnish is a tiny paper umbrella. I like the umbrella. It makes me feel like the drink is on vacation, too.

So here I am. On a yacht. In the Mediterranean. Totally rinch since I robbed The Twin Ledger's vault. Sitting with a famous British actor who is real and knows me, which I told Billie approximately one million times and which she never believed.

I sent her a video three days ago. One where I showed her the vault and the yacht and tried to get Reggie to say hi and he didn't because he was "in character," which— okay, I get it, you're an artist, but also we're on a boat, and the character you should be playing is "person who says hello when asked." Billie sent me a heart emoji as an answer and said "Thank you for the donation," because I donated to her new non-profit and Billie is always polite.

Billie and Rodrigo are happy. I can tell. Not the kind of happy where you post about it constantly and use hashtags. The kind where you post a blurry photo of a lemon painting on your Instagram and don't even bother with a caption because you're too busy being alive to curate it. That kind.

And now, I want my own version of that happiness.

Which brings me to the vision board.

It's propped against the railing on the upper deck, right next to the champagne bucket. I made it this morning. I make all my vision boards in the morning because that's when the manifesting energy is strongest. It's a big board— poster-sized, with a white border— and I've covered it in images cut from magazines the crew brought me from shore. Pictures of sunsets. Pictures of couples holding hands on beaches. A picture of a golden retriever, because

I've always wanted a golden retriever but my lifestyle has historically been incompatible with pet ownership due to the running from authorities and the international travel.

But the centerpiece of the vision board— the big image, the one in the middle, surrounded by hearts I drew with a pink marker— is a picture I cut from a bridal magazine. Two people. Looking at each other. Just looking, with that expression that says: I see you. All of you. And I'm staying.

That's what Billie and Rodrigo have. I saw it on the rooftop in Rome, when he was bleeding and she was crying and they were looking at each other like the rest of the world had been politely asked to leave. I saw it, and I thought: *oh. That's the thing. That's the thing I've been replacing with yachts and vault codes and vision boards full of material goals.* That's the thing that no amount of stolen money or designer bikinis or Mediterranean sunlight can substitute for.

True love.

I know. I know. It sounds, like, so basic. Alana, international woman of mystery and occasional felony, wants true love? It's embarrassing. It's pedestrian.

But I want it.

My old operating principle was simple: everyone is out for themselves, so you should be out for yourself harder and faster and with better accessories. This is a principle that served me well for years. It got me the vault combination. But now, I want to find real love. The kind that makes you selfless, or at least... makes someone selfless towards *you.*

"Rough winds do shake the darling buds of May!" Reginald announces, having apparently resumed his recitation at some point during my internal reflection, which is rude, because I was having a moment. He has stood up from his lounge chair. He has moved to the railing, where the yacht meets the open air and the Mediterranean stretches out. He is standing there, one hand on the railing, one hand raised to the sky, silhouetted against the sun.

"And summer's lease hath all too short a date!" he continues, his voice rising with a conviction that says believes the harbor needed this. "Sometime too hot the eye of heaven shines—"

I look at him. I *really* look at him. Reginald Ashcroft. Famous. Handsome. Rich. Owner of this yacht. Star of that show I used to watch— the one where he plays a brooding detective who solves murders while being emotionally unavailable, which, in retrospect, should have been a red flag about his personality.

I thought I wanted this. I thought: yacht plus famous actor plus Mediterranean equals happiness. It was on my *old* vision board.

The one from before. Before I met Billie, and saw what she had with Rodrigo, and thought: I want that with someone.

I've been on this yacht for two weeks, and here is what I've learned about Reginald Ashcroft: he talks about himself in the third person. He refers to his own face as "the instrument." He once made the chef remake a salad because the lettuce wasn't "crunchy to fulfillment." He recites Shakespeare at every possible opportunity and several impossible ones. He asked me yesterday if I thought his left profile or his right profile was "more Hamlet," and when I said neither, he didn't speak to me for three hours, which was actually the best three hours I've had on this boat.

He doesn't *see* me. He sees an audience.

And that's the thing, isn't it? That's the difference between what Reginald offers and what I actually want.

So. Step two of the new vision board: find true love. Step one of the new vision board: get rid of Reginald Ashcroft.

I stand up from my lounge chair. My attendant, sensing the shift, withdraws the hovering sunglasses. I take the sunglasses from her, put them on— marks be damned, this moment requires eyewear— and walk across the deck toward Reginald.

He is still at the railing. He is still reciting. He has moved on from Sonnet Eighteen to something I don't recognize.

"Once more unto the breach, dear friends!" he proclaims to the harbor. A seagull passes overhead, unimpressed. "Once more, or close the wall up with our—"

"Reggie," I say, arriving beside him.

He pauses. He turns to me. "Yes, darling?"

"This has been really fun," I say. I mean it. Parts of it were fun. The champagne was excellent. The harbor is pretty. The yacht is nice. "But I've been thinking about my vision board, and you're not on it."

His face does something complicated— a journey from confusion to offense that plays out across his features with dramatic clarity.

"I beg your—"

"It's not you," I say, which is a lie— it is *entirely* him, it is so uniquely him that if you looked up "it's you" in the dictionary there would be a picture of Reginald Ashcroft reciting Shakespeare to a seagull. "It's me. I'm on a journey. A love journey. And the journey doesn't include—" I gesture at him, at the unbuttoned shirt, at the hand still raised toward the sky in a gesture that has forgotten it's no longer performing. "This."

"Alana," he says, drawing himself up to his full height. "I am Reginald Ashcroft. I am a three-time BAFTA nominee.

I have been called the finest classical actor of my generation by no fewer than—"

I put both hands on his chest and push.

It's not, like, a hard push. It's a firm push. A decisive push. Just a little extra "oomph" if you will.

Reginald Ashcroft— three-time BAFTA nominee, Shakespearean enthusiast— goes over the railing with the poetic grace of someone whose body has been trained to fall dramatically. His arms pinwheel. His linen shirt billows. His mouth opens in an O of profound and theatrical surprise, and I think, for one brief moment, that he looks like a painting.

He hits the Mediterranean with a splash that is, honestly, better than anything he did on his show.

I lean over the railing. He surfaces— sputtering, his hair plastered to his forehead— and he looks up at me with an expression that combines outrage and bewilderment. It's quite striking— I can see, now, why he won the BAFTA.

"So sorry!" I call down to him, and I wave— a real wave, friendly, the kind you give to someone you've had a nice time with but won't be seeing again. "It's not gonna work out!"

"I— you— this is— I am Reginald Ashcroft!" he sputters, treading water.

"You're gonna be fine!" I shout. "The harbor's right there! Swim toward the sugar-cube buildings!"

I turn away from the railing. The Mediterranean sun is warm on my face, and the breeze is doing nice things to my hair, and somewhere below me a famous actor is learning to swim with humility, which is probably good for him, honestly. Character development.

I walk across the deck to the crew member standing near the bridge stairs— a man with a white uniform and a face that suggests he has seen unusual things on this yacht before and has made peace with the pattern.

"Can you tell the Captain something for me?" I say.

"Of course, ma'am."

"Pull the anchor up. I'm thinking it's time to try Ibiza." He looks at me like he's not sure he should listen to me, so I walk over to my purse and pull out a few thousand euros. "Maybe this will help?"

He nods. He turns and walks toward the bridge, and within seconds I hear the anchor chain beginning its heavy, mechanical ascent, and the yacht hums beneath my feet with the vibration of engines waking up.

I've commandeered a yacht. I'm basically a pirate. Fun!

I walk back to my vision board. I pick up the pink marker. In the space beneath the picture of the couple— the one in the middle, the one surrounded by hearts— I write, in my best handwriting:

Find true love.

I cap the marker. I look at the board. The sun catches the magazine cutouts and the glitter glue and the hearts, and it looks, from this angle, like the most important document I've ever created.

The yacht begins to move. The harbor slides backward. Reginald's voice carries across the water. He's either shouting for help or still reciting Shakespeare— it's hard to tell over the sound of the engine roaring. His voice fades as we pull away, and then it's gone, and there is only the water, the possibility, and me.

I settle back into my lounge chair. My attendant reappears with the sunglasses, hovering them into position with wordless precision. I close my eyes. The yacht points itself toward the horizon, toward Ibiza, toward whatever comes next.

I think about Billie, in her stone house in Tuscany, being loved by a man who took a bullet for her. I think about how she told me to get therapy. I *should* probably get therapy. I should also probably stop pushing people off boats.

“Hey— whatever your name is?” I ask the attendant. “Look up remote therapists, would you? Get me three names by like, later tonight.”

“Of course,” the woman nods.

I’ll see a therapist. But growth is a process, and I am— as of today, as of this yacht, as of this vision board— *in* the process.

Somewhere ahead of me: Ibiza. A dance floor. A person I haven’t met yet. Someone who can handle the show.

I smile. The sun is warm. The sea is endless. The future is a thing I am sailing toward with both rings in a safe I’ll never open again, millions of Euros richer, one British actor shorter, and— for the first time in my life— genuinely, stupidly, embarrassingly hopeful. My true love is out there. I just know it.

Oh, and I look incredible, by the way.

Just in case anyone was wondering.

letter from the author

Dear Reader,

Thank you for dedicating your time to the **Chaos & Chemistry Romantic-Comedy Series**! Look for Book Two, "He Needs Boundaries," which will follow Alana as she searches for love (and danger!)

To stay in touch, scan the QR code below and join my mailing list. You'll get updates on new releases, free give-aways, behind-the-scenes news, and more— all just for members of my author club.

You can also sign up at: **www.valeriebrandy.com**

I also write cozy mysteries and mystery novels under the name **Valerie Brandy**, so if you're ever in the mood for a puzzling case, a quirky cast, or a mystery to solve, I hope you'll check out those books too.

More to come,

– V. Brandy (aka Valerie Brandy)

www.ingramcontent.com/pod-product-compliance
Lightning Source LLC
Chambersburg PA
CBHW032143050726
47591CB00001B/70

* 9 7 8 1 9 6 4 1 6 1 9 8 3 *